Fathers of Men by E. W. Hornung

Ernest William Hornung was born in Middlesbrough, England on 7th June 1866, the third son and youngest of eight children.

Although spending most of his life in England and France he spent two years in Australia from 1884 and that experience was to colour and influence much of his written works.

His most famous character A. J. Raffles, 'the gentleman thief', was published first in Cassell's Magazine during 1898 and was to make him famous across the world as the new century dawned.

Hornung also wrote several stage plays and was a gifted poet.

Spending time with the troops in WWI he published Notes of a Camp-Follower on the Western Front during 1919, a detailed account of his time there. This was especially close to his heart as his son, and only child, was killed at the Second Battle of Ypres on 6th July 1915.

Ernest William Hornung died in Saint-Jean-de-Luz, in the south of France on 22nd March 1921.

Index of Contents

Chapter I - Behind the Scenes
Chapter II - Change and Chance
Chapter III - Very Raw Material
Chapter IV - Settling In
Chapter V - Nicknames
Chapter VI - Boy to Boy
Chapter VII - Reassurance
Chapter VIII - Likes and Dislikes
Chapter IX - Coram Populo
Chapter X - Elegiacs
Chapter XI - A Merry Christmas
Chapter XII - The New Year
Chapter XIII - The Haunted House
Chapter XIV - "Summer-Term"
Chapter XV - Sprawson's Masterpiecs
Chapter XVI - Similia Similibus
Chapter XVII - The Fun of the Fair
Chapter XVIII - Dark Horses
Chapter XIX - Fame and Fortune
Chapter XX - The Eve of Office
Chapter XXI - Out of Form
Chapter XXII - The Old Boys' Match
Chapter XXIII - Interlude in a Study
Chapter XXIV - The Second Morning's Play
Chapter XXV - Interlude in the Wood

Chapter XXVI - Close of Play
Chapter XXVII - The Extreme Penalty
Chapter XXVIII - "Like Lucifer"
Chapter XXIX - Chips and Jan
Chapter XXX - His Last Fling
Chapter XXXI - Vale
E. W. Hornung – A Short Biography
E. W. Hornung – A Concise Bibliography

CHAPTER I

BEHIND THE SCENES

The two new boys in Heriot's house had been suitably entertained at his table, and afterwards in his study with bound volumes of Punch. Incidentally they had been encouraged to talk, with the result that one boy had talked too much, while the other shut a stubborn mouth tighter than before. The babbler displayed an exuberant knowledge of contemporary cricket, a more conscious sense of humour, and other little qualities which told their tale. He opened the door for Miss Heriot after dinner, and even thanked her for the evening when it came to an end. His companion, on the other hand, after brooding over Leech and Tenniel with a sombre eye, beat a boorish retreat without a word.

Heriot saw the pair to the boys' part of the house. He was filling his pipe when he returned to the medley of books, papers, photographic appliances, foxes' masks, alpen-stocks and venerable oak, that made his study a little room in which it was difficult to sit down and impossible to lounge. His sister, perched upon a coffin-stool, was busy mounting photographs at a worm-eaten bureau.

"How I hate our rule that a man mayn't smoke before a boy!" exclaimed Heriot, emitting a grateful cloud. "And how I wish we didn't have the new boys on our hands a whole day before the rest!"

"I should have thought there was a good deal to be said for that," remarked his sister, intent upon her task.

"You mean from the boys' point of view?"

"Exactly. It must be such a plunge for them as it is, poor things."

"It's the greatest plunge in life," Heriot vehemently agreed. "But here we don't let them make it; we think it kinder to put them in an empty bath, and then turn on the cold tap—after first warming them at our own fireside! It's always a relief to me when these evenings are over. The boys are never themselves, and I don't think I'm much better than the boys. We begin by getting a false impression of each other."

Heriot picked his way among his old oak things as he spoke; but at every turn he had a narrow eye upon his sister. He was a lanky man, many years her senior; his beard had grown grey, and his shoulders round, in his profession. A restless energy marked all his movements, and was traceable in the very obstacles to his present perambulations; they were the spoils of the inveterate wanderer from the beaten track, who wanders with open hand and eye. Spectacles in steel rims twinkled at each alert turn of the grizzled head; and the look through the spectacles, always quick and keen, was kindly rather than kind, and just rather than compassionate.

"I liked Carpenter," said Miss Heriot, as she dried a dripping print between sheets of blotting-paper.

"I like all boys until I have reason to dislike them."

"Carpenter had something to say for himself."

"There's far more character in Rutter."

"He never opened his mouth."

"It's his mouth I go by, as much as anything."

Miss Heriot coated the back of the print with starch, and laid it dexterously in its place. A sheet of foolscap and her handkerchief—an almost unfeminine handkerchief—did the rest. And still she said no more.

"You didn't think much of Rutter, Milly?"

"I thought he had a bad accent and—"

"Go on."

"Well—to be frank—worse manners!"

"Milly, you are right, and I'm not sure that I oughtn't to be frank with you. Let the next print wait a minute. I like you to see something of the fellows in my house; it's only right that you should know something about them first. I've a great mind to tell you what I don't intend another soul in the place to know."

Heriot had planted himself in British attitude, heels to the fender.

Miss Heriot turned round on her stool. She was as like her brother as a woman still young can be like a rather elderly man; her hair was fair, and she had not come to spectacles; but her eyes were as keen and kindly as his own, her whole countenance as sensible and shrewd.

"You can trust me, Bob," she said.

"I know I can," he answered, pipe in hand. "That's why I'm going to tell you what neither boy nor man shall learn through me. What type of lad does this poor Rutter suggest to your mind?"

There was a pause.

"I hardly like to say."

"But I want to know."

"Well—then—I'm sure I couldn't tell you why—but he struck me as more like a lad from the stables than anything else."

"What on earth makes you think that?" Heriot spoke quite sharply in his plain displeasure and surprise.

"I said I couldn't tell you, Bob. I suppose it was a general association of ideas. He had his hat on, for one thing, when I saw him first; and it was far too large for him, and crammed down almost to those dreadful ears! I never saw any boy outside a stable-yard wear his hat like that. Then your hunting was the one thing that seemed to interest him in the least. And I certainly thought he called a horse a 'hoss'!"

"So he put you in mind of a stable-boy, did he?"

"Well, not exactly at the time, but he really does the more I think about him."

"That's very clever of you, Milly—because it's just what he is."

Heriot's open windows were flush with the street, and passing footfalls sounded loud in his room; but at the moment there were none; and a clock ticked officiously on the chimneypiece while the man with his back to it met his sister's eyes.

"Of course you don't mean it literally?"

"Literally."

"I thought his grandfather was a country parson?"

"A rural dean, my dear; but the boy's father was a coachman, and the boy himself was brought up in the stables until six months ago."

"The father's dead, then?"

"He died in the spring. His wife has been dead fourteen years. It's a very old story. She ran away with the groom."

"But her people have taken an interest in the boy?"

"Never set eyes on him till his father died."

"Then how can he know enough to come here?"

Heriot smiled as he pulled at his pipe. He had the air of a man who has told the worst. His sister had taken it as he hoped she would; her face and voice betokened just that kind of interest in the case which he already felt strongly. It was a sympathetic interest, but that was all. There was nothing sentimental about either of the Heriots; they could discuss most things frankly on their merits; the school itself was no exception to the rule. It was wife and child to Robert Heriot—the school of his manhood—the vineyard in which he had laboured lovingly for thirty years. But still he could smile as he smoked his pipe.

"Our standard is within the reach of most," he said; "there are those who would tell you it's the scorn of the scholastic world. We don't go in for making scholars. We go in for making men. Give us the raw material of a man, and we won't reject it because it doesn't know the Greek alphabet—no, not even if it was fifteen on its last birthday! That's our system, and I support it through thick and thin; but it lays us open to worse types than escaped stable-boys."

"This boy doesn't look fifteen."

"Nor is he—quite—much less the type I had in mind. He has a head on his shoulders, and something in it too. It appears that the vicar where he came from took an interest in the lad, and got him on as far as Cæsar and Euclid for pure love."

"That speaks well for the lad," put in Miss Heriot, impartially.

"I must say that it appealed to me. Then he's had a tutor for the last six months; and neither tutor nor vicar has a serious word to say against his character. The tutor, moreover, is a friend of Arthur Drysdale's, who was captain of this house when I took it over, and the best I ever had. That's what brought them to me. The boy should take quite a good place. I should be very glad to have him in my own form, to see what they've taught him between them. I confess I'm interested in him; his mother was a lady; but you may almost say he never saw her in his life. Yet it's the mother who counts in the being of a boy. Has the gentle blood been hopelessly poisoned by the stink of the stables, or is it going to triumph and run clean and sweet? It's a big question, Milly, and it's not the only one involved."

Heriot had propounded it with waving pipe that required another match when he was done; through the mountain tan upon his face, and in the eager eyes behind the glasses, shone the zeal of the expert to whom boys are dearer than men or women. The man is rare; rarer still the woman who can even understand him; but here in this little room of books and antique lumber, you had the pair.

"I'm glad you told me," said Miss Heriot, at length. "I fear I should have been prejudiced if you had not."

"My one excuse for telling you," was the grave rejoinder. "No one else shall ever know through me; not even Mr. Thrale, unless some special reason should arise. The boy shall have every chance. He doesn't even know I know myself, and I don't want him ever to suspect. It's quite a problem, for I must keep an eye on him more than on most; yet I daren't be down on him, and I daren't stand up for him; he must sink or swim for himself."

"I'm afraid he'll have a bad time," said Miss Heriot, picking a print from the water and blotting it as before. Her brother had seated himself at another bureau to write his letters.

"I don't mind betting Carpenter has a worse," he rejoined without looking up.

"But he's so enthusiastic about everything?"

"That's a quality we appreciate; boys don't, unless there's prowess behind it. Carpenter talks cricket like a Lillywhite, but he doesn't look a cricketer. Rutter doesn't talk about it, but his tutor says he's a bit of a bowler. Carpenter beams because he's got to his public school at last. He has illusions to lose. Rutter knows nothing about us, and probably cares less; he's here under protest, you can see it in his face, and the chances are all in favour of his being pleasantly disappointed."

Heriot's quill was squeaking as he spoke, for he was a man with the faculty of doing and even thinking of more than one thing at a time; but though his sister continued mounting photographs in her album with extreme care, her mind was full of the two young boys who had come that night to live under their roof for good or ill. She wondered whether her brother was right in his ready estimate of their respective characters. She knew him for the expert that he was; these were not the first boys that she had heard him sum up as confidently on as brief an acquaintance; and though her knowledge had its obvious limitations, she had never known him wrong. He had a wonderfully fair mind. And yet the boy of action, in whom it was possible to stimulate thought, would always be nearer his heart than the thoughtful boy who might need goading into physical activity. She could not help feeling that he was prepared to take an unsympathetic view of the boy who had struck her as having more in him than most small boys; it was no less plain that his romantic history and previous disadvantages had already rendered the other newcomer an object of sympathetic interest in the house-master's eyes. The material was new as well as raw, and so doubly welcome to the workman's hand. Yet the workman's sister, who had so much of his own force and fairness in her nature, felt that she could never like a sulky lout, however cruel the circumstances which had combined to make him one.

She felt a good deal more before the last print was in her album; in the first place that she would see really very little of these two boys until in years to come they rose to the Sixth Form table over which she presided in hall. Now and then they might have headaches and be sent in to keep quiet and look at the Punches; but she would never be at all in touch with them until they were big boys at the top of the house; and then they would be shy and exceedingly correct, of few words but not too few, and none too much enthusiasm, like all the other big boys. And that thought drew a sigh.

"What's the matter?" came in an instant from the other bureau, where the quill had ceased to squeak.

"I was thinking that, after all, these two boys have more individuality than most who come to us."

"One of them has."

"Both, I think; and I was wondering how much will be left to either when we run them out of the mould in five years' time!"

Heriot came to his feet like an exasperated advocate.

"I know where you get that from!" he cried with a kind of jovial asperity. "You've been reading some of these trashy articles that every wiseacre who never was at a public school thinks he can write about them now! That's one of their stock charges against us, that we melt the boys down and run them all out of the same mould like bullets. We destroy individuality; we do nothing but reduplicate a type that thinks the same thoughts and speaks the same speech, and upholds the same virtues and condones the same vices. As if real character were a soluble thing! As if it altered in its essence from the nursery to the cemetery! As if we could boil away a strong will or an artistic temperament, a mean soul or a saintly spirit, even in the crucible of a public school!"

His breezy confidence was almost overwhelming; but it did not overwhelm his hearer, or sweep her with him to his conclusion. She had her own point of view; more, she had her own coigne of observation. Not every boy who had passed through the house in her time was the better for having been there. She had seen the weak go under—into depths she could not plumb—and the selfish ride serenely on the crest of the wave. She had seen an unpleasant urchin grow into a more and more displeasing youth, and inferiority go forth doubly inferior for the misleading stamp—that precious stamp—which one and all acquired. She loved the life as she saw it, perforce so superficially; it was a life that appealed peculiarly to Miss Heriot, who happened to have her own collegiate experience, an excellent degree of her own, and her own ideas on education. But from the boys in her brother's house she held necessarily aloof; and in her detachment a clear and independent mind lay inevitably open to questionings, misgivings, intuitions, for which there was little time in his laborious days.

"But you admit it is a crucible," she argued. "And what's a crucible but a melting-pot?"

"A melting-pot for characteristics, but not for character!" he cried. "Take the two boys upstairs: in four or five years one will have more to say for himself, I hope, and the other will leave more unsaid; but the self that each expresses will be the same self, even though we have turned a first-rate groom into a second-rate gentleman. 'The Child,' remember, and not the school, 'is father of the Man.'"

"Then the school's his mother!" declared Miss Heriot without a moment's hesitation.

Heriot gave the sudden happy laugh which his house was never sorry to hear, and his form found the more infectious for its comparative rarity.

"Does she deny it, Milly? Doesn't she rub it into every one of them in Latin that even they can understand? Let's only hope they'll be fathers of better men for the help of this particular alma mater!"

The house-master knocked out his pipe into a wooden Kaffir bowl, the gift of some exiled Old Boy, and went off to bid the two new boys good-night.

CHAPTER II

CHANGE AND CHANCE

Rutter had been put in the small dormitory at the very top of the house. Instead of two long rows of cubicles as in the other dormitories, in one of which he had left Carpenter on the way upstairs, here under the roof was a square chamber with a dormer window in the sloping side and a cubicle in each of its four corners. Cubicle was not the school word for them, according to the matron who came up with the boys, but "partition," or "tish" for short. They were about five feet high, contained a bed and a chair apiece, and were merely curtained at the foot. But the dormitory door opened into the one allotted to Rutter; it was large enough to hold a double wash-stand for himself and his next-door neighbour; and perhaps he was not the first occupant whom it had put in mind of a loose-box among stalls.

He noted everything with an eye singularly sardonic for fourteen, and as singularly alive to detail. The common dressing-table was in the dormer window. The boy had a grim look at himself in the glass. It was not a particularly pleasant face, with its sombre expression and stubborn mouth, but it looked brown and hard, and acute enough in its dogged way. It almost smiled at itself for the fraction of a second, but whether in resignation or defiance, or with a pinch of involuntary pride in his new state of life, it would have been difficult even for the boy to say. Certainly it was with a thrill that he read his own name over his partition, and then the other boys' names over theirs. Bingley was the fellow next him. Joyce and Crabtree were the other two. What would they be like? What sort of faces would they bring back to the glass in the dormer window?

Rutter was not conscious of an imagination, but somehow he pictured Joyce large and lethargic, Crabtree a humorist, and Bingley a bully of the Flashman type. He had just been reading Tom Brown by advice. He wondered would the humorist be man enough to join him in standing up to the brutes, and whether pillow-fights were still the fashion; he did not believe they were, because Master Evan had never mentioned them; but then Master Evan had only been at a preparatory school last spring, and he might have found it quite otherwise at Winchester. The new boy undressed with an absent mind. He was wondering what it would have been like if he had been sent to Winchester himself, and there encountered Master Evan on equal terms. He had never done so much wondering in his life; he found a school list in the dormitory, and took it to bed with him, and lay there doing more.

So there was an Upper Sixth and a Lower Sixth, and then a form called the Remove; and in the Remove, by the way, was friend Joyce of the corner opposite. Then came the Fifths—three of them—with Crabtree top of the Lower Fifth. Clever fellow, then, Crabtree! The bully Bingley was no doubt notoriously low in the school. The Middle Remove came next, and through each column of strange names the boy read religiously, with a fascination he could not have explained, here and there conjuring an incongruous figure from some name he knew. He had got down to the Middle Fourth when suddenly his breath was taken as by a blow.

Heriot came in to find a face paler than it had looked downstairs, but a good brown arm and hand lying out over the coverlet, and a Midsummer List tightly clutched. The muscles of the arm were unusually developed for so young a boy. Heriot saw them relax under his gaze as he stood over the bed.

"Got hold of a school list, have you?"

"Yessir," said Rutter with a slurring alacrity that certainly did not savour of the schoolroom. Heriot turned away before he could wince; but unluckily his eyes fell on the floor, strewn with the litter of the new boy's clothes.

"I like the way you fold your clothes!" he laughed.

"I beg your pardon, sir, but where am I to put them?"

It was refreshingly polite; but, again, the begging-pardon opening was not the politeness of a schoolboy.

"On this chair," said Heriot, suiting the action to the word. The boy would have leapt out of bed to do it himself. His shyness not only prevented him, but rendered him incapable of protest or acknowledgement; and the next moment he had something to be shy about. Mr. Heriot was holding up a broad and dirty belt, and without thinking he had cried, "What's this?"

Rutter could not answer for shame. And Heriot had time to think.

"I can sympathise," he said with a chuckle; "in the holidays I often wear one myself. But we mustn't betray each other, Rutter, or we shall never hear the last of it! I'll give you an order for a pair of braces in the morning."

"I have them, sir, thanks."

"That's right." Heriot was still handling the belt as though he really longed to buckle it about himself. Suddenly he noticed the initials, "J. R."

"I thought your name was Ian, Rutter?"

"So it is, sir; but they used to call me Jan."

Heriot waited for a sigh, but the mouth that appealed to him was characteristically compressed. He sat a few moments on the foot of the bed. "Well, good-night, and a fair start to you, Jan! The matron will put out the gas at ten."

The lad mumbled something; the man looked back to nod, and saw him lying as he had found him, still clutching the list, only with his face as deep a colour as his arm.

"Have you come across any names you know?"

"One."

"Who's that?"

"He won't know me."

They were the sullen answers that had made a bad impression downstairs; but they were strangely uttered, and Rutter no longer lay still.

"He must have a name," said Heriot, coming back into the room.

No answer.

"I'm sorry you're ashamed of your friend," said Heriot, laughing.

"He's not my friend, and—"

"I think that's very likely," put in Heriot, as the boy shut his lips once more. "What's in a name? The chances are that it's only a namesake after all."

He turned away without a sign of annoyance or of further interest in the matter. But another mumble from the bed intercepted him at the door.

"Name of Devereux," he made out.

"Devereux, eh?"

"Do you know him, sir?"

"I should think I do!"

"He'll not be in this house?"

Rutter was holding his breath.

"No, but he got my prize last term."

"Do you know his other name?"

It was a tremulous mumble now.

"I'm afraid I don't. Wait a bit! His initials are either E. P. or P. E. He only came last term."

"He only would. But I thought he was going to Winchester!"

"That's the fellow; he got a scholarship and came here instead, at the last moment."

The new boy in the top dormitory made no remark when the matron put out the gas. He was lying on his back with his eyes wide open, and his lips compressed out of sight, just as Heriot had left him. It was almost a comfort to him to know the worst for certain; and now that he did know it, beyond all possibility of doubt, he was beginning to wonder whether it need necessarily be the worst after all. It might easily prove the best. He had always liked Master Evan; that was as much as this boy would admit even in his heart. The fact would have borne a warmer recognition. Best or worst, however, he knew it as well as though Evan Devereux had already come back with the rest of the school, and either cut him dead or grasped his hand. The one thing not to be suspected for an instant was that the lean oldish man, with the kind word and the abrupt manner, could possibly know the secret of a new boy's heart, and have entered already into his hopes and fears.

It was very quiet in the top dormitory. Rutter wondered what it would be like when all the boys came back. Carpenter's dormitory was downstairs, but they were all within earshot of each other. He wondered what it would have been like if Master Evan had been in that house, in that little dormitory, in the partition next his own. Master Evan! Yet he had never thought of him as anything else, much less addressed him by any other name. What if it slipped out at school! It easily might; indeed, far more easily and naturally than "Devereux." That would sound very like profanity, in his ears, and on his lips.

The new boy grinned involuntarily in the dark. It was all too absurd. He had enjoyed ample opportunity of picking up the phraseology of the class to which he had been lately elevated: "too absurd" would certainly have been their expression for the situation in which he found himself. He tried to see it from that point of view. He was not without a wry humour of his own. He must take care not to magnify a matter which nobody else might think twice about. A public school was a little world, in which two boys in different houses, even two of an age, might seldom or never meet; days might elapse before Evan as much as recognised him in the throng. But then he might refuse to have anything to do with him. But then—but then—he might tell the whole school why!

"He was our coachman's son at home!"

The coachman's son heard the incredible statement as though it had been shouted in his ear. He felt a thousand eyes on his devoted face. He knew that he lay blushing in the dark. It took all his will to calm him by degrees.

"If he does," he decided, "I'm off. That's all."

But why should he? Why should a young gentleman betray a poor boy's secret? Rutter was the stable-boy again in spirit; he might have been back in his trucklebed in the coachman's cottage at Mr. Devereux's. The transition of standpoint at any rate was complete. He had always liked Master Evan; they had been very good friends all their lives. Incidents of the friendship came back in shoals. Evan had been the youngest of a large family, and that after a gap; in one sense he had been literally the only child. Often he had needed a boy to play with him, and not seldom Jan Rutter had been scrubbed and brushed and oiled to the scalp in order to fill the proud position of that boy. He must have known how to behave himself as a little kid, though he remembered as he grew older that the admonition with which he was always dispatched from the stables used to make it more difficult; there were so many things to "think on" not to do, and somehow it was harder not to do them when you had always to keep "thinking on." Still, he distinctly remembered hearing complimentary remarks passed upon him by the ladies and gentlemen, together with whispered explanations of his manners. It was as easy to supply as to understand those explanations now; but it was sad to feel that the manners had long ago been lost.

And, boy as he was, and dimly as may be, he did feel this: that in the beginning there had been very little to choose between Evan and himself, but that afterwards the gulf had been at one time very wide. He could recall with shame a phase in which Master Evan had been forbidden, and not without reason, to have anything to do with Jan Rutter. There was even a cruel thrashing which he had received for language learnt from the executioner's own lips; and it was characteristic of Jan that he had never quite forgiven his father for that, though he was dead, and had been a kind father on the whole. Later, the boy about the stables had acquired more sense; the eccentric vicar had taken him in hand, and spoken up for him; and nothing was said if he bowled to Master Evan after his tea, or played a makeshift kind of racquets with him in the stable-yard, so long as he kept his tongue and his harness clean. So the gulf had narrowed again of late years; but it had never again been shallow.

It was spanned, however, by quite a network of mutual offices. In the beginning Evan used to take all his broken toys to Jan, who was a fine hand at rigging ships and soldering headless horsemen. Jan's reward was the reversion of anything broken beyond repair, or otherwise without further value to its original owner. Jan was also an adept at roasting chestnuts and potatoes on the potting-shed fire, a daring manipulator of molten lead, a comic artist with a piece of putty, and the pioneer of smoking in the loft. Those were the days when Evan was suddenly forbidden the back premises, and Jan set definitely to work in the stables when he was not at the village school. Years elapsed before the cricket stage that drew the children together again as biggish boys; in the interim Jan had imbibed wisdom of more kinds than one. On discovering himself to be a rude natural left-hand bowler, who could spoil the afternoon at any moment by the premature dismissal of his opponent, he was sagacious enough to lose the art at times in the most sudden and mysterious manner, and only to recover it by fits and starts when Evan had made all the runs he wanted. And as Jan had but little idea of batting, there was seldom any bad blood over the game. But in all their relations Jan took care of that, for he had developed a real devotion to Evan, who could be perfectly delightful to one companion at a time, when everything was going well.

And then things had happened so thick and fast that it was difficult to recall them in their chronological order; but the salient points were that Rutter the elder, that fine figure on a box, with his bushy whiskers and his bold black eyes, had suddenly succumbed to pneumonia after a bout of night-work in the month of February, and that the son of an ironmaster's coachman by a northern town awoke to find himself the grandson of an East Anglian clergyman whose ancient name he had never heard before, but who sent for the lad in hot haste, to make a gentleman of him if it was not too late.

The change from the raw red outworks of an excessively modern and utilitarian town, to the most venerable of English rectories, in a countryside which has scarcely altered since the Conquest, was not appreciated as it might have been by Jan Rutter. He had nothing against the fussy architecture and the highly artificial garden of his late environment; on the contrary, he heartily preferred those familiar immaturities to the general air of complacent antiquity which pervaded his new home. That was the novelty to Jan, and there was a prejudice against it in his veins. It was the very atmosphere which had driven his mother before him to desperation. Her blood in him rebelled again; nor did he feel the effect the less because he was too young to trace the cause. He only knew that he had been happier in a saddle-room that still smelt of varnish than he was ever likely to be under mellow tiles and mediæval trees. The tutor and the strenuous training for a public school came to some extent as a relief; but the queer lad took quite a pride in showing no pride at all in his altered conditions and prospects. The new school and the new home were all one to him. He had not been consulted about either. He recognised an authority which he was powerless to resist, but there the recognition ended. There could be no question of gratitude for offices performed out of a cold sense of duty, by beings of his own blood who never so much as mentioned his father's death, or even breathed his mother's name. There was a tincture of their own pride even in him.

He had heard of public schools from Evan, and even envied that gilded child his coming time at one; but, when his own time came so unexpectedly, Jan had hardened his heart, and faced the inevitable as callously as any criminal. And then at its hardest his heart had melted within him: an arbitrary and unkind fate held out the hope of amends by restoring to his ken the one creature he really wished to see again. It was true that Jan had heard nothing of Evan since the end of the Christmas holidays; but then the boys had never exchanged a written word in their lives. And the more he thought of it, the less Jan feared the worst that might accrue from their meeting on the morrow or the day after. Not that he counted on the best: not that his young blood had warmed incontinently to the prospect which had chilled it hitherto. Master Evan as an equal was still an inconceivable figure; and the whole prospect remained grey and grim; but at least there was a glint of excitement in it now, a vision of depths and heights.

So the night passed, his first at a public school. The only sounds were those that marked its passage: the muffled ticking of his one treasure, the little watch under his pillow, and the harsh chimes of an outside clock which happened to have struck ten as he opened the Midsummer List. It had since struck eleven; he even heard it strike twelve. But life was more exciting, when he fell asleep soon after midnight, than Jan Rutter had dreamt of finding it when he went to bed.

CHAPTER III

VERY RAW MATERIAL

It was all but a summer morning when Jan got back into the trousers without pockets and the black jacket and tie ordained by the school authorities. Peculiarly oppressive to Jan was the rule about trouser pockets; those in his jacket were so full in consequence that there was barely room for his incriminating belt, which he rolled up as small as it would go, and made into a parcel to be hidden away in his study when he had one. This was his last act before leaving the dormitory and marching downstairs at an hour when most of the household were presumably still in bed and asleep; but Jan was naturally an early riser, and he had none of the scruples of conventionality on the score of an essentially harmless act. He was curious to see something of his new surroundings, and there was nothing like seeing for oneself.

At the foot of the lead-lined stairs, worn bright as silver at the edges, there was a short tiled passage with a green baize door at one end and what was evidently the boys' hall at the other. The baize door communicated with the master's side of the house, for the new boys had come through it on their way up to dormitory. The hall was a good size, with one very long table under the windows and two shorter ones on either side of the fireplace. On the walls hung portraits of the great composers, which Jan afterwards found to be house prizes in part-singing competitions discontinued before his time; at the moment, however, he took no kind of interest in them, and but very little in the two challenge cups under the clock. What did attract him was the line of open windows, looking like solid blocks of sunlight and fresh air. On the sill of one a figure in print was busy with her wash-leather, and she accosted Jan cheerily.

"You are down early, sir!"

"I always am," remarked Jan, looking for a door into the open air.

"You're not like most of the gentlemen, then," the maid returned, in her cheerful Cockney voice. "They leaves it to the last moment, and then they 'as to fly. You should 'ear 'em come down them stairs!"

"Is there no way out?" inquired Jan.

"You mean into the quad?"

"That's the quad, is it? Then I do."

"Well, there's the door, just outside this door; but Morgan, 'e keeps the key o' that, and I don't think 'e's come yet."

"Then I'm going through that window," announced the new boy, calmly; and carried out his intention without a moment's hesitation.

Had his object been to run away on his very first morning, before his house-master was astir, as the maid seemed to fear by the way she leant out of her window to watch him, the next step would have taxed all Jan's resources.

Heriot's quad was a gravel plot very distinctively enclosed, on the left by the walls of buildings otherwise unconnected with the house, on the right by the boys' studies. At the further extremity were twin gables over gothic arches which left the two interiors underneath open at one end to all the elements; never in his life had Jan beheld such structures; but he had picked up enough from his tutor to guess that they were fives-courts, and he went up to have a look into them. To the right of the fives-courts was an alley ending at a formidable spiked gate which was yet the only obvious way of escape, had Jan been minded to make his. But nothing was further from his thoughts; indeed, there was a certain dull gleam in his eyes, and a sallow flush upon his face, which had not been there the previous evening. At all events he looked wider awake.

The studies interested him most. There was a double row of little lattice windows, piercing a very wall of ivy, like port-holes in a vessel's side. Not only were the little windows deep-set in ivy, but each had its little window-box, and in some of these still drooped the withered remnant of a brave display. Jan was not interested in flowers, or for that matter in anything that made for the mere beauty of life; but he peered with interest into one or two of the ground-floor studies. There was little to be seen beyond his own reflection broken to bits in the diamond panes. Between him and the windows was a border of shrubs, behind iron palings bent by the bodies and feet of generations, and painted green like the garden seats under the alien walls opposite. On the whole, and in the misty sunlight of the fine September morning, Jan liked Heriot's quad.

"You're up early, sir!"

It was not the maid this time, but a bearded man-servant whom the boy had seen the previous night. Jan made the same reply as before, and no sort of secret of the way in which he had got out into the quad. He added that he should like to have a look at the studies; and Morgan, with a stare and a smile quite lost on Jan, showed him round.

They were absurdly, deliciously, inconceivably tiny, the studies at Heriot's; each was considerably smaller than a dormitory "tish," and the saddle-room of Jan's old days would have made three or four of them. But they were undeniably cosy and attractive, as compact as a captain's cabin, as private as friar's cell, and far more comfortable than either. Or so they might well have seemed to the normal boy about to possess a study of his own, with a table and two chairs, a square of carpet as big as a bath-sheet, a book-shelf and pictures, and photographs and ornaments to taste, fretwork and plush to heart's content, a flower-box for the summer term, hot-water pipes for the other two, and above all a door of his own to shut at will against the world! But Jan Rutter had not the instincts of a normal schoolboy, nor the temperament favourable to their rapid growth. He had been brought up too uncomfortably to know the value of comfort, and too much in the open air to appreciate the merits of indoor sanctuary. Artistic impulse he had none; and the rudimentary signs of that form of grace, to be seen in nearly all the studies he was shown, left him thoroughly unimpressed.

"Is it true," he asked, "that every boy in the school has one of these holes?"

"Quite true," replied Morgan, staring. "You didn't say 'holes,' sir?"

"I did," declared Jan, enjoying his accidental hit.

"You'd better not let Mr. Heriot hear you, sir, or any of the gentlemen either!"

"I don't care who hears me," retorted Jan, boastfully; but it must not be forgotten that he had come to school against his will, and that this was his first opportunity of airing a not unnatural antagonism.

"You wait till you've got one of your own," said the well-meaning man, "with a nice new carpet and table-cloth, and your own family portraits and sportin' picters!"

"At any rate I should know a horse from a cow," returned Jan, examining something in the nature of a sporting print, "and not hang up rot like that!"

"You let Mr. Shockley hear you!" cried Morgan, with a laugh. "You'll catch it!"

"I've no doubt I shall do that," said Jan, grimly. He followed Morgan into an empty study, and asked if it was likely to be his.

"Not unless you take a pretty high place in the school. It's only the top dozen in the house that get these front studies upstairs. You can make up your mind to one at the back, and be glad if it's not downstairs, where everybody can see in and throw in stones."

Jan felt he had not made a friend of Morgan; and yet in his heart he was more favourably impressed with what he had seen than his peculiar temperament permitted him to show. Little as their adventitious attractions might appeal to him, there was something attractive to Jan about this system of separate studies. It appealed, and not without design, to that spirit of independence which happened to be one of his stronger points. Moreover he could conceive a very happy intimacy between two real friends in one of these little dens; and altogether he brought a brighter face to the breakfast-table than he had shown for an instant overnight. Heriot glanced at it with an interested twinkle, as though he had been at the explorer's elbow all the morning; but whatever he might have known, he betrayed his knowledge neither by word nor sign.

After breakfast the two boys sallied forth with orders signed by Heriot for a school cap apiece; and saw the long old-fashioned country street for the first time in broad daylight. It gave the impression of a street with nothing behind it on either side, the chance remnant of a vanished town. Nothing could have been more solid than the fronts of the drab stone houses, and nothing more startling than the glimpses of vivid meadowland like a black-cloth close behind. The caps were procured from the cricket professional, a maker of history whose fame provided Carpenter with a congenial topic on the way, but sat sadly on the failing giant who was there to serve them in the little shop. The caps were black but not comely, as Carpenter more than once remarked; they were a cross between a cricket-cap and that of a naval officer, with the school badge in red above the peak. Jan chose the biggest he could find, and crammed it over his skull as though he was going out to exercise a horse.

The day was fully occupied with the rather exhaustive examination designed to put the right boy in the right form. There were no fewer than three papers in the morning alone. There was, however, a short break between each, which Carpenter was inclined to spend in boring Rutter with appreciative comments upon the striking mural decorations of the great schoolroom in which the examination was held. There were forty-two new boys, some of them hulking fellows of fifteen or more, some quite small boys in Eton jackets; and the chances are that none among them was more impressed than Carpenter by the reproductions of classical statuary hung upon the walls of Pompeian red, or by the frieze of ancient and modern authors which a great mind had planned and a cunning hand had made; but it is certain that none thought less of them than Jan Rutter. To pacify his companion he did have a look at the frieze, but it was exactly the same look as he had cast into the studies before breakfast. The two had more in common when they compared notes on the various papers.

"I didn't mind the Latin grammar and history," said Jan. "I've had my nose in my grammar for the last six months, and you only had to answer half the history questions."

Jan's spirits seemed quite high.

"But what about the unseen?" asked Carpenter.

"I happened to have done the hardest bit before," said Jan, chuckling consumedly; "and not so long since, either!"

Carpenter looked at him.

"Then it wasn't unseen at all?"

"Not to me."

"You didn't think of saying so on your paper?"

"Not I! It's their look-out, not mine," chuckled Jan.

The other made no comment. It was the long break in the middle of the day, and the pair were on their way back to Heriot's for dinner.

"I wish they'd set us some verses," said Carpenter. "They'd be my best chance."

"Then you're a fool if you take it," put in a good-humoured lout who had joined them in the street.

"But it's the only thing I can do at all decently," explained the ingenuous Carpenter. "I'm a backward sort of ass at most things, but I rather like Latin verses."

"Well, you're another sort of ass if you do your best in any of these piffling papers."

"I see! You mean to make sure of a nice easy form?"

"Rather!"

"There's no fagging over the Upper Fourth, let me tell you, even for us."

"Perhaps not, but there's more kinds of fagging than one, you take my word for it; and I prefer to do mine out of school," said the big new boy, significantly, as their ways parted.

Carpenter wanted to discuss his meaning, but Jan took no interest in it, and was evidently not to be led into any discussion against his will. He had in fact a gift of silence remarkable in a boy and not a little irritating to a companion. Yet he broke it again to the extent of asking Heriot at table, and that à propos of nothing, when the other boys would "start to arrive."

"The tap will be turned on any minute now," said Heriot, with a look at his sister. "In some houses I expect it's running already."

"Which house is Devereux in?" asked Rutter, always direct when he spoke at all.

"Let me think. I know—the Lodge—the house opposite the chapel with the study doors opening into the quad."

Carpenter's silence was the companion feature of this meal.

The boys had time for a short walk afterwards, and more than a hint to take one. But they only went together because they were thrown together; these two had obviously as little else in common as boys could have; and yet, there was something else, and neither dreamt what a bond it was to be.

"Do you know Devereux?" Carpenter began before they were out of their quad.

"Why? Do you know him?"

Jan was not unduly taken aback; he was prepared for anything with regard to Devereux, including the next question long before it came.

"We were at the same preparatory school, and great pals there," replied Carpenter, wistfully. "I suppose you know him at home?"

"I used to, but only in a sort of way," said Jan, warily. "I don't suppose we shall see anything of each other here; he mayn't even recognise me, to start with."

"Or me, for that matter!" cried Carpenter, with less reserve. "He's never written to me since we left, though I wrote to him twice last term, and once in the holidays to ask him something."

It was on the tip of Jan's tongue to defend the absent Evan with injudicious warmth; but he remembered what he had just said, and held his tongue as he always could. Carpenter, on the other hand, apparently regretting his little show of pique, changed the subject with ingenuous haste and chattered more freely than ever about the various school buildings that they passed upon their way. There was a house at the end of the street with no fewer than three tiers of ivy-covered study windows; but it had no quad. There were other houses tucked more out of sight; but Carpenter knew about them, and which hero of the Cambridge eleven had been at this, that, or the other. His interest in his school was of the romantic and imaginative order; it contrasted very favourably with Jan's indifference, which grew the more perversely pronounced as his companion waxed enthusiastic. It appeared that Carpenter was following a number of youths from his part of the world, who had been through the school before him, and from whom he had acquired a smattering of its lore. The best houses of all, he had heard, were not in the town at all, but on the hill a quarter of a mile away. The pair went to inspect, and found regular mansions standing back in their own grounds, their studies and fives-courts hidden from the road; for the new boys trespassed far enough to see for themselves; and Rutter at once expressed a laconic preference for the hill houses, whereat Carpenter stood up as readily for the town.

"There's no end of rivalry between the two," he explained, as they trotted down into the valley, pressed for time. "I wouldn't be in a hill house for any money, or in any house but ours if I had my choice of all the lot."

"And I wouldn't be here at all," retorted Jan, depriving his companion of what breath he had as they hurried up the hill towards the town. By turning to the left, however, in the wake of other new boys in a like hurry, they found themselves approaching the chapel and the great schoolroom by a shorter route. It led through a large square quad with study doors opening upon it down two sides, and nothing over these studies but their own roof.

"There's plenty of time," said Jan, with rather a furtive look at a little gold lady's watch that he pulled out in his fist. "I wonder if this is the Lodge?"

"No—it's the next—opposite the chapel. This is the School House. Do come on!"

The School House and the Lodge were like none of the other houses. Instead of standing by themselves in the town or on the hill, each formed a part of the distinctive group of which the chapel and the great schoolroom were the salient features. Their quadrangles not only adjoined, but there was no line of demarcation to show where one began or the other ended. In both the study doors opened straight into the fresh air; but in neither was a boy to be seen as Carpenter and Rutter caught up the flying remnant of the forty-two.

"Let's go back by the Lodge," said Jan, when at last they were let out for good. But now the scene was changing. Groups of two and three were dotted about in animated conversation, some still in their journey hats, others in old school caps with faded badges, but none who took the smallest notice of the new boys with the new badges, which they had still to learn to crease correctly over the peak.

And now it was that Rutter horrified his companion by accosting with apparent coolness a big fellow just emerged from one of the Lodge studies.

"Do you mind telling us if a boy they call Devereux has got back yet?" asked Jan, with more of his own idioms than he had often managed to utter in one breath.

"I haven't seen him," the big fellow answered civilly enough. But his stare followed the retreating couple, one of whom had caught the other by the arm.

"I shouldn't talk about 'a boy,' if I were you," Carpenter was saying as nicely as he could.

But Rutter was quite aware of his other solecisms, though not of this one, and was already too furious with himself to brook a gratuitous rebuke.

"Oh! isn't it the fashion? Then I'll bet you wouldn't!" he cried, as he shook off the first arm which had ever been thrust through his by a gentleman's son.

A ball like a big white bullet was making staccato music in Heriot's outer fives-court; two school caps were bobbing above the back wall; and a great thick-lipped lad of sixteen or seventeen, who was hanging about the door leading to the studies, promptly asked the new boys their names.

"What's your gov'nor?" he added, addressing Carpenter first.

"A merchant."

"A rag-merchant, I should think! And yours?"

Jan was not embarrassed by the question; he was best prepared at all his most vulnerable points. But his natural bluntness had so recently caused him such annoyance with himself, that he replied as politely as he possibly could:

"My father happens to be dead."

"Oh, he does, does he?" cried the other with a scowl. "Well, if you happen to think it funny to talk about 'happening' to me, you may jolly soon happen to wish you were dead yourself!"

The tap had indeed been turned on, and the water was certainly rather cold; the more fortunate for Rutter that his skin was thick enough to respond with a glow rather than a shiver.

CHAPTER IV

SETTLING IN

Jan's impressions were not the less vivid for his determination not to be impressed at all; for no attitude of mind is harder to sustain than one of deliberate indifference, which is not real indifference at all, but at best a precarious pose. Jan was really indifferent to a large extent, but not wholly, and the leaven of sensibility rendered him acutely alive to each successive phase of his experience; on the other hand, the fact that he was not too easily hurt was of immense value in keeping his wits about him, and his whole garrison of senses at attention. Sensitive he was, and that to the last degree, on a certain point; but it was a point no longer likely to arise that night. And meanwhile there was quite enough to occupy his mind.

There was the long-drawn arrival of the house, unit by unit, in bowler hats which changed as if by magic into old school caps, and even in "loud" ties duly discarded for solemn black. Then there was tea, with any amount of good cheer in hall, every fellow bringing in some delicacy of his own, and newcomers arriving in the middle to be noisily saluted by their friends. Nobody now took the slightest notice of Jan, who drifted into a humble place at the long table, which was still far from full, and fell to work upon the plain bread and butter provided, until some fellow pushed a raised pie across the table to him without a word. The matron dispensed tea from a gigantic urn, and when anybody wanted another cup he simply rattled it in his saucer. Jan could have made even more primitive use of his saucer, for the tea was hot if not potent. But fortunately there were some things it was not necessary for Carpenter to tell him, for that guide and counsellor was not in hall; he had gone out to tea with another new boy and his people, who knew something about him at home.

Jan was allowed to spend the evening in an empty study which he might or might not be able to take over next day, according to the place assigned to him in the school; meanwhile the bare boards, table, Windsor chair, and book-shelf, with an ironically cold hot-water pipe, and the nails with which the last occupant had studded the walls, looked dismal enough in the light of a solitary candle supplied by Morgan. The narrow passage resounded with shouts of laughter and boyish badinage from the other studies; either the captain of the house had not come back, or he was not the man to play the martinet on the first night of the term; and Jan, left as severely alone as even he could have wished, rose with alacrity when one in passing pounded on his door and shouted that it was time for prayers. He was in fact not sorry to mingle with his kind again in the lighted hall, where the fellows were already standing in their places at table, armed with hymn-books but chatting merrily, while one of the small fry stood sentinel in the flagged passage leading to the green baize door. Jan had scarcely found a place when in flew this outpost with a sepulchral "hush!" In the ensuing silence came Miss Heriot followed by her brother, who began by giving out the hymn which she played on the piano under the shelf with the cups, and which the house sang heartily enough.

It was one of the many disadvantages of Jan's strange boyhood that he had been brought up practically without religion. Mention has been made of an eccentric clergyman who was the first to take an interest in Jan's intellectual welfare; unhappily, his eccentricities had been of such a character as almost to stultify his spiritual pretensions; and in his new home the boy had encountered another type of clerical example which had been but little better in its effect upon his mind. Prayer had never been to him the natural practice which it is to young English schoolboys of all shades of character and condition. So he paid very little attention to the prayers read by Heriot, at this first time of hearing; but even so the manly unaffected voice, and a few odd phrases on which it dwelt in gentler tones, were not altogether lost upon Jan. Nevertheless, when he went up to dormitory, after biscuits (which he heard called "dog-rocks") and milk, and another dreary half-hour in the empty study, the last thing he feared or thought about was the kind of difficulty which had beset little Arthur in a certain chapter of Tom Brown which had not appealed to Jan. And all this may be why he was so much impressed by what happened in the little dormitory at the top of the house, when he and his three companions were undressing for bed.

Joyce, the captain of the dormitory, who proved to be a rather delicate youth with a most indelicate vocabulary, suddenly ceased firing, as it were, and commanded silence for "bricks."

"Know what 'bricks' are?" asked Bingley, who occupied the "tish" adjoining Jan's, and turned out to be a boy of his own age, instead of the formidable figure of his imagination.

"It's your prayers," said Joyce, with such an epithet that Jan could not possibly believe him.

"You are a brute, Joyce!" cried Crabtree, poking a clever red head through his curtains.

"Nevertheless, my boy," rejoined Joyce, imitating a master through his nose, "I know what bricks are, and I say them."

"Obvious corruption of prex," began Crabtree, in didactic fashion, when Joyce cut him short with a genial malediction, and silence reigned for the best part of a minute.

Jan went on his knees with the others, though he had not done so the night before, and his lips moved through the Lord's Prayer; but in his heart he was marvelling at the language of the nice tall fellow in the far corner. It was the kind of language he had often heard in the stables, but it was the last kind that he had expected to hear in a public school; and somehow it shocked him, for the first time in his life. But on the whole he was thankful to find himself in such pleasant company in dormitory, and it came to him to express his thankfulness while he was on his knees.

Nothing occurred, as they lay talking in the dark, to modify the new boy's feeling on this point; nor had he subsequent occasion to revise a triple opinion which might well have proved premature in one case or the other. It revealed on the contrary an unusually sound instinct for character. Joyce's only foible was his fondness for free language. He had a redeeming sense of humour, and it was in treatment rather than in choice of subject that he erred. Crabtree was irreproachable in conversation, and a kindly creature in his cooler moods; but he suffered from the curse of intellect, was precociously didactic and dogmatic, and had a temperament as fiery as his hair. Bingley was a lively, irresponsible, curly-headed dog, who enjoyed life in an insignificant position both in and out of school. The other two had nicknames which were not for the lips of new boys; but Jan called Bingley "Toby" after the first night.

Prayers were in houses on the first morning of the term, and nothing else happened before or after breakfast until the whole school assembled in the big schoolroom at ten o'clock to hear the new school order. Jan pulled his cap over his eyes as he found himself wedged in a crowd from all the houses, converging at the base of the worn stone spiral stair up and down which he had trotted at his ease between the papers of the previous day. Now he was slowly hoisted in the press, the breath crushed from his body, his toes only occasionally encountering a solid step, a helpless atom in a monster's maw. At the top of the stone stairs, however, and through the studded oak door, there was room for all; but here it was necessary to uncover face and head; and yet none that he knew of old was revealed to Jan's close though furtive scrutiny.

Carpenter, who had come with him, and squeezed into the next seat, watched the watcher in his turn, and then whispered:

"He's not come back yet."

"Who's not?"

"Evan Devereux. I asked a fellow in his house."

"What made you think of him now?"

"Oh, nothing. I only thought you might be looking to see if he was here."

"Well, perhaps I was," said Jan, with grumpy candour. "But I'm sure I don't care where he is."

"No more do I, goodness knows!" said Carpenter.

And between three and four hundred chattered on all sides with subdued but ceaseless animation; the præpostors keeping order more or less, but themselves chatting to each other as became the first morning of the term. Then suddenly there fell an impressive silence. The oak door opened with a terrible click of the latch, like the cocking of a huge revolver, and in trooped all the masters, cap in hand and gown on shoulders, led by a little old man with a kindly, solemn, and imperious air. And Jan felt that this could only be Mr. Thrale, the Head Master, but Carpenter whispered:

"That's Jerry!"

"Who?"

"Old Thrale, of course, but everybody calls him Jerry."

And Jan liked everybody's impudence as Mr. Thrale took his place behind a simple desk on the dais, and read out the new list, form by form, as impressively as Holy Writ.

The first names that Jan recognised were those of Loder, the captain of his house, and Cave major, its most distinguished representative on tented field; they were in the Upper and Lower Sixth respectively. Joyce was still in the Remove, as captain of the form, but Crabtree had gained a double remove from the Lower to the Upper Fifth. Next in Jan's ken came Shockley—the fellow who had threatened to make him wish he was dead—and then most thrillingly—long before either expected it—Carpenter's name and his own in quick succession.

"What form will it be?" whispered Jan into the other's ear.

"Middle Remove," purred Carpenter. "And we don't have to fag after all!"

Devereux was the next and the last name that Jan remembered hearing: it was actually in the form below his!

The new boys had already learnt that it was customary for the masters to take their forms in hall in their own houses; they now discovered that Mr. Haigh, the master of the Middle Remove, had just succeeded to the most remote of all the hill houses—the one house in fact on the further slope of the hill. Thither his new form accordingly repaired, and on the good ten minutes' walk Carpenter and Rutter had their heads violently knocked together by Shockley, for having the cheek to get so high and to escape fagging their first term.

"But you needn't think you have," he added, ominously. "If you young swots come flying into forms it takes the rest of us two years to get to—by the sweat of our blessed brows—by the Lord Harry you shall have all the swot you want! You'll do the construe for Buggins and me and Eyre major every morning of your miserable lives!"

Buggins (who rejoiced in a real name of less distinction, and a strong metropolitan accent) was climbing the hill arm-in-arm with Eyre major (better known as Jane), his echo and his shadow in one distended skin. Buggins embroidered Shockley's threats, and Eyre major contributed a faithful laugh. But Jan heard them all unmoved, and thought the less of Carpenter when his thinner skin changed colour.

Mr. Haigh gave his new form a genial welcome, vastly reassuring those who knew least about him by laughing uproariously at points too subtle for their comprehension. He was a muscular man with a high colour and a very clever head. His hair was turning an effective grey about the temples, his body bulging after the manner of bodies no longer really young and energetic. Energy he had, however, of a spasmodic and intemperate order, though he only showed it on this occasion by savagely pouncing on a rather small boy who happened to be also in his house. Up to that moment Carpenter and Rutter were ready to congratulate themselves and each other upon their first form-master; but, though he left them considerably alone for a day or two, they were never sure of Mr. Haigh again.

This morning he merely foreshadowed his scheme of the term's work, and gave out a list of the new books required; but some of these were enough to strike terror to the heart of Jan, and others made Carpenter look solemn. Ancient Greek Geography was not an enticing subject to one who had scarcely beheld even a modern map until the last six months; and to anybody as imperfectly grounded as Carpenter declared himself to be, it was an inhuman jump from somebody's Stories in Attic Greek to Thucydides and his Peloponnesian War.

"I suppose it's because I did extra well at something else," said Carpenter with unconscious irony on their way down the hill. "What a fool I was not to take that fat chap's advice! Why, I've never even done a page of Xenophon, and I'm not sure that I could say the Greek alphabet to save my life!"

"I only hope," rejoined Jan, "that they haven't gone and judged me by that unseen!"

But their work began lightly enough, and that first day the furnishing of their studies was food for much more anxious thought, with Carpenter at any rate. As for Jan, he really was indifferent to his surroundings, but the excitable enthusiasm of his companion made him feign even greater indifference than he felt. He was to retain the back upstairs study in which he had spent the previous evening, and Carpenter had the one next it; after dinner Heriot signed orders for carpet, curtains, candles and candlesticks, a table-cloth and a folding arm-chair apiece, as well as for stationery and a quantity of books; and Carpenter led the way to the upholsterer's at a happy trot. He was an age finding curtains, carpet and table-cloth, of a sufficiently harmonious shade of red; and no doubt Jan made all the more point of leaving the choice of his chattels entirely to the tradesman.

"Send me what you think," he said. "It's all one to me."

Carpenter rallied him in all seriousness on their way back to the house.

"I can't understand it, Rutter, when you have an absolute voice in everything."

"I hadn't a voice in coming here," replied Rutter, so darkly as to close the topic.

"I suppose I go to the other extreme," resumed Carpenter, with a reflective frankness which seemed a characteristic. "I shall have more chairs than I've room for if I don't take care. I've bought one already from Shockley."

"Good-night!" cried Jan. "Whatever made you do that?"

"Oh, he would have me into his study to have a look at it; and there were a whole lot of them there—that fellow Buggins, and Jane Eyre, and the one they call Cranky—and they all swore it was as cheap as dirt. There are some beasts here!" added Carpenter below his breath.

"How much was it?"

"Seven-and-six; and I didn't really want it a bit; and one of the legs was broken all the time!"

"And," added Jan, for his only comment, "the gang of them are in our form and all!"

They met most of the house trooping out of the quad, with bats and pads, but not in flannels. They were going to have a house-game on the Middle Ground, as the September day was warmer than many of the moribund summer, and there was no more school until five o'clock. Nor did it require the menaces of Shockley to induce the new pair to turn round and accompany the rest; but their first game of cricket was not a happy experience for either boy. Cave major, who was in the Eleven, was better employed among his peers on the Upper. Loder, who was no cricketer, picked up with a certain Shears major, who was not much of one. Nobody took the game in the least seriously except a bowler off whom the unlucky Carpenter managed to miss two catches. The two new men were chosen last on either side.

They failed to make a run between them, and of course had no opportunity of showing whether they could bowl. Both were depressed when it was all over.

"It served me right for dropping those catches," said Carpenter, however, with the stoicism of a true cricketer at heart.

"I only wish it was last term instead of this!" muttered Jan.

There was another thing that disappointed both boys. The Lodge happened to be playing a similar game on an adjacent pitch. But Devereux was not among the players, and Carpenter heard somebody say that he was not coming back till half-term. Jan's heart jumped when he heard it in his turn: by half-term he would have settled down, by half-term many things might have happened. Yet the deferred meeting was still fraught in his mind with opposite possibilities, that swung to either extreme on the pendulum of his mood; and on the whole he would have been glad to get it over. At one moment this half-term's grace was a keen relief to him; at another, a keener disappointment.

CHAPTER V

NICKNAMES

The ready invention and general felicity of the public-school nickname are points upon which few public-school men are likely to disagree. If it cannot be contended that either Carpenter or Rutter afforded a supreme example, at least each was nicknamed before he had been three days in the school, and in each case the nickname was too good an accidental fit to be easily repudiated or forgotten. Thus, although almost every Carpenter has been "Chips" in his day, there was something about a big head thrust forward upon rather round shoulders, and a tendency to dawdle when not excited, that did recall the most dilatory of domestic workmen. Chips Carpenter, however, albeit unduly sensitive in some things, had the wit to accept his immediate sobriquet as a compliment. And in the end it was not otherwise with Rutter; but in his case there were circumstances which made his nickname a secret bitterness, despite the valuable stamp it set upon his character in the public eye.

It happened that on the Saturday afternoon, directly after dinner, the majority of the house were hanging about the quad when there entered an incongruous figure from the outer world. This was a peculiarly debased reprobate, a local character of pothouse notoriety, whose chief haunt was the courtyard of the Mitre, and whom the boys in the quad saluted familiarly as "Mulberry." And that here was yet another instance of the appropriate nickname, a glance was enough to show, for never did richer hue or bigger nose deface the human countenance.

The trespasser was only slightly but quite humorously drunk, and the fellows in the quad formed a not unappreciative audience of the type of entertainment to be expected from a being in that precise condition. Mulberry, however, was not an ordinary stable sot; it was obvious that he had seen better days. He had ragged tags of Latin on the tip of a somewhat treacherous tongue: he inquired quite tenderly after the binominal theororum, but ascribed an unpleasant expression correctly enough to a lapsus linguae.

"I say, Mulberry, you are a swell!"

"We give you full marks for that, Mulberry!"

"My dear young friends," quoth Mulberry, "I knew Latin before any of you young devils knew the light."

"Draw it mild, Mulberry!"

"I wish you'd give us a construe before second school!"

Jan remembered all his days the stray strange picture of the debauched intruder in the middle of the sunlit quad, with the figures of young and wholesome life standing aloof from him in good-natured contempt, and more fresh faces at the ivy-mantled study windows. Jan happened to be standing nearest Mulberry, and to catch a bloodshot eye as it flickered over his audience in a comprehensive wink.

"You bet I wasn't always a groom," said Mulberry; "an' if I had ha' been, there are worse places than the stables, ain't there, young fellow?"

Jan looked as though he only wished the ground would open and engulf him; and the look did not belie his momentary feeling. But he had a spirit more easily angered than abased, and the brown flush which swept him from collar to cap was not one of unmixed embarrassment.

"How should I know?" he cried in a voice shrill with indignation.

"He seems to know more about it than he'll say," observed Mulberry, and with another wink he fastened his red eyes on Jan, who had his cap pulled over his eyes as usual, and arms akimbo for the want of trousers pockets. "Just the cut of a jock!" added Mulberry, in quite a complimentary murmur.

"You're an ugly blackguard," shouted Jan, "and I wonder anybody can stand and listen to you!"

It was at this point that Heriot appeared very suddenly upon the scene, took the intruder by either shoulder, and had him out of the quad in about a second; in another Heriot rejoined the group in the sun, with a pale face and flashing spectacles.

"You're quite right," he said sharply to Jan. "I wonder, too—at every one of you—at every one!"

And he turned on his heel and was gone, leaving them stinging with his scorn; and Jan would have given a finger from his hand to have gone as well without more words; but he found himself hemmed in by clenched fists and furious faces, his back to the green iron palings under the study windows.

"You saw Heriot coming!"

"You said that to suck up to him!"

"The beastly cheek, for a beastly new man!"

"But we saw through it, and so did he!"

"Trust old Heriot! You don't find that sort o' thing pay with him."

"I never saw him," said Jan steadily, despite a thumping heart, "so you can say what you like."

And he took a heavy buffet from Shockley without wincing.

"And why should you lose your wool with poor old Mulberry?" that worthy demanded with a fine show of charity. "One would think there was something in what he said."

"You fairly stink of the racing-stables," said Buggins. "You know you do, you brute!"

And Eyre major led a laugh.

"Racing-stables!" echoed Shockley. "There's more of the stable-boy about him than the jock."

Jan folded his arms and listened stoically.

"Ostler's lad," said one satirist.

"Nineteenth groom," from another.

"The tiger!" piped a smaller boy than Jan. "The tiger that sits behind the dog-cart—see how he folds his arms!"

And the imp folded his at the most untimely moment; for this was more than Jan was going to stand. Submission to superior force was a law of nature which his common sense recognised and his self-control enabled him to keep; but to take from a boy inches shorter than himself what had to be taken from one as many inches taller, just because they were all against him, was further than his forbearance would go. His flat left hand flew out as the smaller boy folded his arms, and it fell with a resounding smack upon the side of an undefended head.

Within the fewest possible moments Jan had been pinned against the palings by the bigger fellows, his arm twisted, his person violently kicked, his own ears soundly boxed and filled with abuse. This was partly because he fought and kicked as long as he had a free leg or arm. But through it all the satisfaction of that one resounding smack survived, and kept the infuriated Jan just sane enough to stop short of tooth and nail when finally overwhelmed.

"Tiger's the word," panted Shockley, when they were about done with him. "But if you try playing the tiger here, ever again, you son of a gun, you'll be killed by inches, as sure as you're blubbing now! So you'd better creep into your lair, you young tiger, and lie down and die like a mangy dog!"

It had taken some minutes to produce the tears, but the tears did not quench the fierce animosity of the eyes that shed them, and they were dry before Jan gained his study and slammed the door. And there you may picture him in the chair at the table, on the still bare boards: hot, dishevelled, aching and ashamed, yet rejoicing in his misery at the one shrewd left-hand smack he had somehow administered upon an impudent though defenceless head.

He could hear it for his consolation all the afternoon!

The studies emptied; it was another belated summer's day, and there was a game worth watching on the Upper. Soon there was no sound to be heard but those from the street, which came through the upper part of the ground-glass window, the only part of the back study windows that was made to open; but Jan sat staring at the wall before his eyes, as though the fresh air was nothing to him, as though he had not been brought up in his shirtsleeves in and out of the open air in all weathers.... And so he was still sitting when a hesitating step came along the passage, paused in the next study, and then, but not for a minute or two, at Jan's door.

"What do you want?" he demanded rudely, when he had responded to a half-hearted knock by admitting Chips Carpenter. Now, Chips had witnessed just the bitter end of the scene in the quad, but Jan did not know he had been there at all.

"Oh, I don't exactly want anything. I can clear out if you'd rather, Rutter."

"All right. I'd rather."

"Only I thought I'd tell you it's call-over on the Upper in half-an-hour."

"I'm not going to call-over."

"What?"

"Damn call-over."

Carpenter winced: he did not like swearing, and he did like Rutter well enough to wince when he swore. But the spirit of the oath promptly blotted the letter from his mind. Carpenter was a law-abiding boy who had been a few terms at a good preparatory school; he could scarcely believe his ears, much less a word of Rutter's idle boast. Rutter certainly looked as though he meant it, with his closed lid of a mouth, and his sullen brooding eyes. But his mad intention was obviously not to be carried out.

"My dear man," said Carpenter, "it's one of the first rules of the school. Have you read them? You'd get into a frightful row!"

"The bigger the better."

"You might even get bunked," continued Chips, who was acquiring the school terminology as fast as he could, "for cutting call-over on purpose."

"Let them bunk me! Do you think I care? I never wanted to come here. I'd as soon've gone to prison. It can't be worse. At any rate they let you alone—they got to. But here ... let them bunk me! It's the very thing I want. I loathe this hole, and everything about it. I don't care whether you say it's one of the best schools going, or what you say!"

"I say it's the best. I know I wouldn't swop it for any other—or let a little bullying put me against it. And I have been bullied, if you want to know!"

"Perhaps you're proud of that?"

"I hate it, Rutter! I hate lots of things more than you think. You're in that little dormitory. You're well off. But I didn't come here expecting to find it all skittles. And I wouldn't be anywhere else if it was twenty times worse than it is!"

Rutter looked at the ungainly boy with the round shoulders and the hanging head; for the moment he was improved out of knowledge, his flat chest swelling, his big head thrown back, a proud flush upon his face. There was a touch of consciousness in the pride, but it was none the less real for that, and Jan could only marvel at it. He could not understand this pride of school; but he could see it, and envy it in his heart, even while a fresh sneer formed upon his lips. He wished he was not such an opposite extreme to Carpenter: he could not know that the other's attitude was possibly unique, that few at all events came to school with such ready-made enthusiasm for their school, if fewer still brought his own antagonism.

But, after all, Carpenter did not understand, and never would.

"You weren't in the quad just now," said Jan, grimly.

Chips looked the picture of guilt.

"I was. At the end. And I feel such a brute!"

"You? Why?" Jan was frowning at him. "You weren't one of them?"

"Of course I wasn't! But—I might have stood by you—and I didn't do a thing!"

The wish to show some spirit in his turn, the envious admiration for a quality of which he daily felt the want, both part and parcel of one young nature, like the romantic outlook upon school life, were equally foreign and incomprehensible to the other. Jan could only see Carpenter floundering to the rescue, with his big head and his little wrists; and the vision made him laugh, though not unkindly.

"You would have been a fool," he said.

"I wish I had been!"

"Then you must be as big a one as I was."

"But you weren't, Rutter! That's just it. You don't know!"

"I know I was fool enough to lose my wool, as they call it."

"You mean man enough! I believe the chaps respect a chap who lets out without thinking twice about it," said Carpenter, treading on a truth unawares. "I should always be frightened of being laughed at all the more," he added, with one of his inward glances and the sigh it fetched. "But you've done better than you think. The fellows at the bottom of the house won't hustle you. I heard Petrie telling them he'd never had his head smacked so hard in his life!"

Jan broke into smiles.

"I did catch him a warm 'un," he said. "I wish you'd been there."

"I only wish it had been one of the big brutes," said Chips, conceiving a Goliath in his thirst for the ideal.

"I don't," said Jan. "He was trading on them being there, and by gum he was right! But they didn't prevent me from catching him a warm 'un!"

And in his satisfaction the epithet almost rhymed with harm.

Nevertheless, Jan looked another and a brighter being as he stood up and asked Carpenter what his collar was like.

Carpenter had to tell him it was not fit to be seen.

Jan wondered where he could find the matron to give him a clean one.

"Her room's at the top of the house near your dormitory. I daresay she'd be there."

"I suppose I'd better go and see. Come on!"

"Shall we go down to the Upper together?" Chips asked as they reached the quad.

"I don't mind."

"Then I'll wait, if you won't be long."

And the boy in the quad thought the other had quite forgotten his mad idea of cutting call-over—which was not far from the truth—and that he had not meant it for a moment—which was as far from the truth as it could be. But even Carpenter hardly realised that it was he who had put Rutter on better terms with himself, and in saner humour altogether, by the least conscious and least intentional of all his arguments.

Jan meanwhile was being informed upstairs that he was not supposed to go to his dormitory in daytime, but that since he was there he had better have a comfortable wash as well as a clean collar. So he came down looking perhaps smarter and better set-up than at any moment since his arrival. And at the foot of the stairs the hall door stood open, showing a boy or two within looking over the new illustrated papers; and one of the boys was young Petrie.

Jan stood a moment at the door. Either his imagination flattered him, or young Petrie's right ear was still rather red. But he was a good type of small boy, clear-skinned, bright-eyed, well-groomed. And even as Jan watched him he cast down the Graphic, stretched himself, glanced at the clock, and smiled quite pleasantly as they stood face to face upon the threshold.

"I'm sorry," said Jan, not as though he were unduly sorry, but yet without a moment's thought.

"That's all right, Tiger!" replied young Petrie, brightly. "But I wouldn't lose my wool again, if I were you. It don't pay, Tiger, you take my tip."

CHAPTER VI

BOY TO BOY

The match on the Upper, although an impromptu fixture on the strength of an Indian summer's day, was exciting no small interest in the school. It was between the champion house at cricket and the best side that could be got together from all the other houses; and the interesting point was the pronounced unpopularity of the champions (one of the hill houses), due to the insufferable complacency with which they were said to have received the last of many honours. The whole house was accused of having "an awful roll on," and it was the fervent hope of the rest of the school that their delegates would do something to diminish this offensive characteristic. Boys were lying round the ground on rugs, and expressing their feelings after almost every ball, when Chips and Jan crept shyly upon the scene. But within five minutes a bell had tinkled on top of the pavilion; the game had been stopped because it was not a real match after all; and three or four hundred boys, most of them with rugs over their arms, huddled together in the vicinity of the heavy roller.

It so happened that Heriot was call-over master of the day. He stood against the roller in a weather-beaten straw hat, rapping out the names in his abrupt, unmistakable tones, with a lightning glance at almost every atom that said "Here, sir!" and detached itself from the mass. The mass was deflating rapidly, and Jan was moistening his lips before opening them for the first time in public, when a reddish head, whose shoulders were wedged not far in front of him, suddenly caught Jan's eye.

"Shockley."

"Here, sir."

"Nunn minor."

"Here, sir."

"Carpenter."

"Here, sir."

"Rutter."

No answer. Heriot looking up with pencil poised.

"Rutter?"

"Here, sir!"

And out slips Jan in dire confusion, to join Carpenter on the outskirts of the throng; to be cursed under Shockley's breath; and just to miss the stare of the boy with reddish hair, who has turned a jovial face on hearing the name for the second time.

"I say, Carpenter!"

"Yes?"

"Did you see who that was in front of us?"

"You bet! And they said he wasn't coming back till half-term! I'm going to wait for him."

"Then don't say anything about me—see? He never saw me, so don't say anything about me."

And off went Jan to watch the match, more excited than when he had lost self-control in the quad; the difference was that he did not lose it for a moment now. He heard the name of Devereux called over in its turn. He knew that Carpenter had joined Devereux a moment later. He wondered whether Devereux had seen him also—seen him from the first and pretended not to see him—or only this minute while talking to Chips? Was he questioning Chips, or telling him everything in a torrent?

Jan felt them looking at him, felt their glances like fire upon his neck and ears, as one told and the other listened. But he did not turn round. He swore in his heart that no power should induce him to turn round. And he kept his vow for minutes and minutes that seemed like hours and hours.

It was just as well, for he would have seen with his eyes exactly what he saw in his mind, and that was not all there was to see. There was something else that Jan must have seen—and might have seen through—had his will failed him during the two minutes after call-over. That was the celerity with which Heriot swooped down upon Devereux and Carpenter; laid his hand upon the shoulder of the boy who had won his last term's prize; stood chatting energetically with the pair, chatting almost sharply, and then left them in his abrupt way with a nod and a smile.

But Jan stood square as a battalion under fire, watching a game in which he did not follow a single ball; and as he stood his mind changed, though not his will. He wanted to speak to Evan Devereux now. At least he wanted Evan to come and speak to him; in a few minutes, he was longing for that. But no Evan came. And when at length he did turn round, there was no Evan to come, and no Chips Carpenter either.

The game was in its last and most exciting stage when Jan took himself off the ground; feeling ran high upon the rugs, and expressed itself more shrilly and even oftener than before; and such a storm of cheering chanced to follow Jan into the narrow country street, that two boys quite a long way ahead looked back with one accord. They did not see Jan. They were on the sunny side; he was in the shade. But he found himself following Devereux and Carpenter perforce, because their way was his. He slackened his pace; they stopped at the market-place, and separated obviously against Carpenter's will. Carpenter pursued his way to Heriot's. Devereux turned to the left across the market-place, into the shadow of the old grey church with the dominant spire, with the blue-faced clock that struck in the night, and so to the school buildings and his own quad by the short cut from the hill. And Jan dogged him all the way, lagging behind when his unconscious leader stopped to greet a friend, or to look at a game of fives in the School House court, and in the end seeing Devereux safely into his study before he followed and gave a knock.

Evan had scarcely shut his door before it was open again, but in that moment he had cast his cap, and he stood bareheaded against the dark background of his tiny den, in a frame of cropped ivy. It was an effective change, and an effective setting, in his case. His hair was not red, but it was a pale auburn, and peculiarly fine in quality. In a flash Jan remembered it in long curls, and somebody saying, "What a pity he's not a girl!" And with this striking hair there had always been the peculiarly delicate and transparent skin which is part of the type; there had nearly always been laughing eyes, and a merry mouth; and here they all were in his study doorway, with hardly any difference that Jan could see, though he had dreaded all the difference in the world. And yet, the smile was not quite the old smile, and a flush came first; and Evan looked past Jan into the quad, before inviting him in; and even then he did not shake hands, as he had often done on getting home for the holidays, when Jan's hand was not fit to shake.

But he laughed quite merrily when the door was shut. And Jan, remembering that ready laugh of old, and how little had always served to ring a hearty peal, saw nothing forced or hurtful in it now, but joined in himself with a shamefaced chuckle.

"It is funny, isn't it?" he mumbled. "Me being here!"

"I know!" said Evan, with laughing eyes fixed none the less curiously on Jan.

"When did you get back?" inquired Jan, speedily embarrassed by the comic side.

"Only just this afternoon. I went and had mumps at home."

"That was a bad job," said Jan, solemnly. "It must have spoilt your holidays."

"It did, rather."

"You wouldn't expect to find me here, I suppose?"

"Never thought of it till I heard your name called over and saw it was you. I hear you're in Bob's house?"

"In Mr. Heriot's," affirmed Jan, respectfully.

"We don't 'mister' 'em behind their backs," said Evan, in tears of laughter. "It's awfully funny," he explained, "but I'm awfully glad to see you."

"Thanks," said Jan. "But it's not such fun for me, you know."

"I should have thought you'd like it awfully," remarked Evan, still looking the new Jan merrily up and down.

"After the stables, I suppose you mean?"

Evan was more than serious in a moment.

"I wasn't thinking of them," he declared, with an indignant flush.

"But I was!" cried Jan. "And I'd give something to be back in them, if you want to know!"

"You won't feel like that long," said Evan, reassuringly.

"Won't I!"

"Why should you?"

"I never wanted to come here, for one thing."

"You'll like it well enough, now you are here."

"I hate it!"

"Only to begin with; lots of chaps do at first."

"I always shall. I never wanted to come here; it wasn't my doing, I can tell you."

Evan stared, but did not laugh; he was now studiously kind in look and word, and yet there was something about both that strangely angered Jan. Look and word, in fact, were alike instinctively measured, and the kindness perfunctory if not exactly condescending. There was, to be sure, no conscious reminder, on Evan's part, of past inequality; and yet there was just as little to show that in their new life Evan was prepared to treat Jan as an equal; nay, on their former footing he had been far more friendly. If his present manner augured anything, he was to be neither the friend nor the foe of Jan's extreme hopes and fears. And the unforeseen mien was not the less confusing and exasperating because Jan was confused and exasperated without at the time quite knowing why.

"You needn't think it was because you were here," he added suddenly, aggressively—"because I thought you were at Winchester."

"I didn't flatter myself," retorted Evan. "But, as a matter of fact, I should be there if I hadn't got a scholarship here."

"So I suppose," said Jan.

"And yet I'm in the form below you!"

Evan was once more openly amused at this, and perhaps not so secretly annoyed as he imagined.

"I know," said Jan. "That wasn't my fault, either. I doubt they've placed me far too high."

"But how did you manage to get half so high?" asked Evan, with a further ingenuous display of what was in his mind.

"Well, there was the vicar, to begin with."

"That old sinner!" said Evan.

"I used to go to him three nights a week."

"Now I remember."

"Then you heard what happened when my father died?"

"Yes."

"It would be a surprise to you, Master Evan?"

It had been on the tip of his tongue more than once, but until now he had found no difficulty in keeping it there. Yet directly they got back to the old days, out it slipped without a moment's warning.

"You'd better not call me that again," said Evan, dryly.

"I won't."

"Unless you want the whole school to know!"

"You see, my mother's friends—"

"I know. I've heard all about it. I always had heard—about your mother."

Jan had only heard that pitiful romance from his father's dying lips; it was then the boy had promised to obey her family in all things, and his coming here was the first thing of all. He said as much in his own words, which were bald and broken, though by awkwardness rather than emotion. Then Evan asked, as it were in his stride, if Jan's mother's people had a "nice place," and other questions which might have betrayed to a more sophisticated observer a wish to ascertain whether they really were gentlefolk as alleged. Jan answered that it was "a nice enough place"; but he pointed to a photograph in an Oxford frame—the photograph of a large house reflected in a little artificial lake—a house with a slate roof and an ornamental tower, and no tree higher than the first-floor windows.

"That's a nicer place," said Jan, with a sigh.

"I daresay," Evan acquiesced, with cold complacency.

"There's nothing like that in Norfolk," continued Jan, with perfect truth. "Do you remember the first time you took me up to the tower?"

"I can't say I do."

"What! not when we climbed out on the roof?"

"I've climbed out on the roof so often."

"And there's our cottage chimney; and just through that gate we used to play 'snob'!"

Evan did not answer. He had looked at his watch, and was taking down some books. The hint was not to be ignored.

"Well, I only came to say it wasn't my fault," said Jan. "I never knew they were going to send me to the same school as you, or they'd have had a job to get me to come."

"Why?" asked Evan, more stiffly than he had spoken yet. "I shan't interfere with you."

"I'm sure you won't!" cried Jan, with the bitterness which had been steadily gathering in his heart.

"Then what's the matter with you? Do you think I'm going to tell the whole school all about you?"

Jan felt that he was somehow being put in the wrong; and assisted in the process by suddenly becoming his most sullen self.

"I don't know," he answered, hanging his head.

"You don't know! Do you think I'd think of such a thing?"

"I think a good many would."

"You think I would?"

"I don't say that."

"But you think it?"

Evan pressed him hotly.

"I don't think anything; and I don't care what anybody thinks of me, or what anybody knows!" cried Jan, not lying, but speaking as he had suddenly begun to feel.

"Then I don't know why on earth you came to me," said Evan scornfully.

"No more do I," muttered Jan; and out he went into the quad, and crossed it with a flaming face. But at the further side he turned. Evan's door was still open, as Jan had left it, but Evan had not come out.

Jan found him standing in the same attitude, with the book he had taken down, still unopened in his hand, and a troubled frown upon his face.

"What's the matter now?" asked Evan.

"I'm sorry—Devereux!"

"So am I."

"I might have known you wouldn't tell a soul."

"I think you might."

"And of course I don't want a soul to know. I thought I didn't care a minute ago. But I do care, more than enough."

"Well, no one shall hear from me. I give you my word about that."

"Thank you!"

Jan was holding out his hand.

"Oh, that's all right."

"Won't you shake hands?"

"Oh, with pleasure, if you like."

But the grip was all on one side.

CHAPTER VII

REASSURANCE

Jan went back to his house in a dull glow of injury and anger. But he was angriest with himself, for the gratuitous and unwonted warmth with which he had grasped an unresponsive hand. And the sense of injury abated with a little honest reflection upon its cause. After all, with such a different relationship so fresh in his mind, the Master Evan of the other day could hardly have said more than he had said this afternoon; in any case he could not have promised more. Jan remembered his worst fears; they at least would never be realised now. And yet, in youth, to escape the worst is but to start sighing for the best. Evan might be loyal enough. But would he ever be a friend? Almost in his stride Jan answered his own question with complete candour in the negative; and having faced his own conclusion, thanked his stars that Evan and he were in different houses and different forms.

Shockley was lounging against the palings outside the door leading to the studies; the spot appeared to be his favourite haunt. It was an excellent place for joining a crony or kicking a small boy as he passed. Jan was already preparing his heart for submission to superior force, and his person for any violence, when Shockley greeted him with quite a genial smile.

"Lot o' parcels for you, Tiger," said he. "I'll give you a hand with 'em, if you like."

"Thank you very much," mumbled Jan, quite in a flutter. "But where will they be?"

"Where will they be?" the other murmured under his breath. "I'll show you, Tiger."

Jan could not help suspecting that Carpenter might be right after all. He had actually done himself good by his display of spirit in the quad! Young Petrie had been civil to him within an hour, and here was Shockley doing the friendly thing before the afternoon was out. He had evidently misjudged Shockley; he tried to make up for it by thanking him nearly all the way to the hall, which was full of fellows who shouted an embarrassing greeting as the pair passed the windows. They did not go into the hall, however, but stopped at the slate table at the foot of the dormitory stairs. It was covered with parcels of all sizes, on several of which Rutter read his name.

"Tolly-sticks—don't drop 'em," said Shockley, handing one of the parcels. "This feels like your table-cloth; that must be tollies; and all the rest are books. I'll help you carry them over."

"I can manage, thanks," said Jan, uncomfortably. But Shockley would not hear of his "managing," and led the way back past the windows, an ironical shout following them into the quad.

"You should have had the lot yesterday," continued Shockley in the most fatherly fashion. "I should complain to Heriot, if I were you."

Jan's study had also been visited in his absence. A folding chair, tied up with string, stood against the wall, with billows of bright green creton bulging through string and woodwork; an absurd bit of Brussels carpet covered every inch of the tiny floor; and it also was an aggressive green, though of another and a still more startling shade.

"Curtains not come yet," observed Shockley. "I suppose they're to be green too?"

"I don't know," replied Rutter. "I left it to them."

"I rather like your greens," said Shockley, opening the long soft parcel. "Why, you've gone and got a red table-cloth!"

"It's their doing, not mine," observed Jan, phlegmatically.

"I wonder you don't take more interest in your study," said Shockley. "Most chaps take a pride in theirs. Red and green! It'll spoil the whole thing; they don't go, Tiger."

Jan made some show of shaking off his indifference in the face of this kindly interest in his surroundings.

"They might change it, Shockley."

"I wouldn't trust 'em," said that authority, shaking and scratching a bullet head by turns. "They're not too obliging, the tradesmen here—too much bloated monopoly. If you take my advice you'll let well alone."

"Then I will," said Jan, eagerly. "Thanks, awfully, Shockley!"

"Not that it is well," resumed Shockley, as though the matter worried him. "A green table-cloth's the thing for you, Tiger, and a green table-cloth you must have if we can work it."

"It's very good of you to bother," said Jan, devoutly wishing he would not.

Shockley only shook his head.

"I've got one myself, you see," he explained in a reflective voice, as he examined the red cloth critically. "It's a better thing than this—better taste—and green—but I'd rather do a swop with you than see you spoil your study, Tiger."

"Very well," said Jan, doubtfully.

Shockley promptly tucked the new table-cloth under his arm. "Let's see your tolly-sticks!" said he, briskly.

"Tolly-sticks?"

"Candle-sticks, you fool!"

Jan unpacked them, noting as he did so that the fatherly tone had been dropped.

"I suppose you wouldn't like a real old valuable pair instead of these meagre things?"

"No, thanks, Shockley."

"Well, anyhow you must have a picture or two."

"Why must I?" asked Jan. He had suddenly remembered Carpenter's story of the seven-and-sixpenny chair.

"Because I've got the very pair for you, and going cheap."

"I see," said Jan, in his dryest Yorkshire voice.

"Oh, I don't care whether you've a study or a sty!" cried Shockley, and away he went glaring, but with the new cloth under his arm. In a minute he was back with the green one rolled into a ball, which he flung in Jan's face. "There you are, you fool, and I'm glad you like your own colour!" he jeered as he slammed the door behind him.

Neither had Jan much mercy on himself, when he had fitted two candles into the two new china sticks, and lit them with a wax match from the shilling box included in his supplies. Shockley's table-cloth might once have been green, but long service had reduced it to a more dubious hue; it was spotted with ink and candle-grease, and in one place cut through with a knife. To Jan, indeed, one table-cloth was like another; he was only annoyed to think he had been swindled as badly as Carpenter, by the same impudent impostor, and with Carpenter's experience to put him on his guard. But even in his annoyance the incident appealed to that prematurely grim sense of the ironic which served Jan Rutter for the fun and nonsense of the ordinary boy; and on the whole he thought it wiser to avoid another row by saying no more about it.

But he was not suffered to keep his resolution to the letter: at tea Buggins and Eyre major were obviously whispering about Jan before Buggins asked him across the table how he liked his new table-cloth.

"I suppose you mean Shockley's old one?" retorted Jan at once. "It'll do all right; but it's a good bargain for Shockley."

"A bargain's a bargain," remarked Buggins with his mouth full.

"And a Jew's a Jew!" said Jan.

The nice pair glared at him, and glanced at Shockley, who was two places higher up than Jan, but deep in ingratiating conversation with a good-looking fellow on his far side.

"God help you when the Shocker hears that!" muttered Buggins under his breath.

"You'll be murdered before you've been here a week, you brute!" added Eyre major with a titter.

"I may be," said Jan, "but not by you—you prize pig!"

And, much as he was still to endure from the trio in his form and house, this was the last Jan heard directly of the matter. Whether his reckless words ever reached the ears of Shockley, or whether the truth was in them, Jan never knew. As a good hater, however, he always felt that apart from thick lips, heavy nostrils, pale eyes and straight light hair, his arch-enemy combined all the most objectionable characteristics of Jew and Gentile.

So this stormy Saturday came to a comparatively calm close, and Jan was left to wrestle in peace with a Latin prose set by Mr. Haigh at second school. On other nights everybody went back to his form-master after tea, for a bout of preparation falsely called "private work"; but on Saturdays some kind of composition was set throughout the school, was laboriously evolved in the solitude of the study, and signed by the house-master after prayers that night or on the Sunday morning. Unfortunately, composition was Jan's weak point. By the dim light of the dictionary, with the frail support of a Latin grammar, he could grope his way through a page of Cæsar or of Virgil without inevitably plunging to perdition; but the ability to cast English back into Latin implies a point of scholarship which Jan had not reached by all the forced marches of the past few months. He grappled with his prose until head and hand perspired in the warm September evening. He hunted up noun after noun in his new English-Latin, and had a shot at case after case. And when at length his fair copy was food for Haigh's blue pencil, and Jan leant back to survey his own two candles and his own four walls, he was conscious, in the first place, that he had been taken out of himself, and in the second that a study to oneself was a mitigating circumstance in school life.

Not that he disliked his dormitory either; there, nothing was said to him about the row in the quad, of which in fact he had heard very little since it occurred. He was embarrassed, however, by a command from Joyce to tell a story after the gas was out; stories were not at all in Jan's line; and the situation was only relieved by Bingley's sporting offer to stand proxy in the discharge of what appeared to be a traditional debt on the part of all new boys entering that house. Bingley, permitted to officiate as a stop-gap only, launched with much gusto and more minutiæ into a really able account of a revolting murder committed in the holidays. Murders proved to be Bingley's strong point; his face would glow over the less savoury portions of the papers in hall; and that night his voice was still vibrating with unctuous horror when Jan got off to sleep.

The school Sunday in his time was not desecrated by a stroke of work; breakfast of course was later, and Heriot himself deliberately late for prayers, which were held in the houses as on the first day of the term, instead of in the big school-room. Chapel seemed to monopolise morning and afternoon. Yet there was time for a long walk after either chapel, and abundant time for letter-writing after dinner. Not that Jan availed himself of the opportunity; he had already posted a brief despatch to the rectory, and nowhere else was there a soul who could possibly care to hear from him. He spent the latter end of the morning in a solitary stroll along a very straight country road, and the hour after dinner over a yellow-back borrowed from Chips.

Morning chapel had been quite a revelation to Jan. He had been forced to go to church in Norfolk; he went to chapel in the stoical spirit born of chastening experience. Yet there was something in the very ringing of the bells that might have prepared him for brighter things; they were like joy-bells in their almost merry measure. The service proved bright beyond belief. The chapel itself was both bright and beautiful. It was full of sunlight and fresh air, it lacked the heavy hues and the solemn twilight which Jan associated with a place of worship. The responses came with a hearty and unanimous ring. The psalms were the quickest thing in church music that Jan had ever heard; they went with such a swing that he found himself trying to sing for the first time in his life. His place in chapel had not yet been allotted to him, and he stood making his happily inaudible effort between two tail-coated veterans with stentorian lungs. Crowning merit of the morning service, there was no sermon; but in the afternoon the little man with the imperious air grew into a giant in his marble pulpit, and impressed Jan so powerfully that he wondered again how the fellows could call him Jerry, until he looked round and saw some of them nodding in their chairs. Then he found that he had lost the thread himself, that he could not pick it up again, that everything escaped him except a transfigured face and a voice both stern and tender. But these were flag and bugle to the soldier concealed about most young boys, and Jan for one came out of chapel at quick march.

The golden autumn day was still almost at its best, but Jan had no stomach for another lonely walk. A really lonely walk would have been different; but to go off by oneself, and to meet hundreds in sociable twos and threes, with linked arms and wagging tongues, was to cut too desolate a figure before the world. Carpenter apparently had found a friend; at least Jan saw him obviously waiting for one after chapel; yet hardly had he settled to his novel, than a listless step was followed by the banging of the study door next his own.

"I thought you'd gone for a walk," said Jan, when he had gained admission by pounding on Carpenter's door.

"Did you! You thought wrong, then."

Carpenter smiled as though to temper an ungraciousness worthier of Jan, but the effort was hardly a success. He was reclining in a chair with a leg-rest, under the window opposite the door. He had already put up a number of pictures and brackets, and photograph frames in the plush of that period. Everything was very neat and nice, and there was a notable absence of inharmonious or obtrusive shades.

"How on earth did you open the door from over there?" asked Jan.

"Lazy-pull," said Carpenter, showing off a cord running round three little walls and ending in a tassel at his elbow. "You can buy 'em all ready at Blunt's."

"You have got fettled up," remarked Jan, "and no mistake!"

Carpenter opened his eyes at the uncouth participle.

"I want to have a good study," he said. "I've one or two pictures to put up yet, and I've a good mind to do them now."

"You wouldn't like to come for a walk instead?"

The suggestion was very shyly made, and as candidly considered by Chips Carpenter.

"Shall I?" he asked himself aloud.

"You might as well," said Jan without pressing it.

"I'm not sure that I mightn't."

And off they went, but not with linked arms, or even very close together; for Chips still seemed annoyed at something or other, and for once not in a mood to talk about it or anything else. It was very unlike him; and a small boy is not unlike himself very long. They took the road under the study windows, left the last of the little town behind them, dipped into a wooded hollow, and followed a couple far ahead over a stile and along a right-of-way through the fields; and in the fields, bathed in a mellow mist, and as yet but thinly dusted with the gold of autumn, Carpenter found his tongue. He expatiated on this new-found freedom, this intoxicating licence to roam where one would within bounds of time alone, a peculiar boon to the boy from a private school, and one that Jan appreciated as highly as his companion. It was not the only thing they agreed about that first Sunday afternoon. Jan was in a much less pugnacious mood than usual, and Carpenter less ponderously impressed with every phase of their new life. They exchanged some prejudices, and compared a good many notes, as they strolled from stile to stile. Haigh came in for some sharp criticism from his two new boys; the uncertainty of his temper was already apparent to them; but Heriot, as yet a marked contrast in that respect, hardly figured in the conversation at all. A stray remark, however, elicited the fact that Carpenter, who had disappeared in the morning directly after prayers, had actually been to breakfast with Heriot on the first Sunday of his first term.

Jan was not jealous; from his primitive point of view the master was the natural enemy of the boy; and he was not at the time surprised when Carpenter dismissed the incident as briefly as though he were rather ashamed of it. He would have thought no more of the matter but for a chance encounter as they crossed their last stile and came back into the main road.

Swinging down the middle of the road came a trio arm-in-arm, full of noisy talk, and so hilarious that both boys recognised Evan Devereux by his laugh before they saw his face. Evan, on his side, must have been almost as quick to recognise Carpenter, who was first across the stile, for he at once broke away from his companions.

"I'm awfully sorry!" he cried. "I quite forgot I'd promised these fellows when I promised you."

"It doesn't matter a bit," said Carpenter, in a rather unconvincing voice.

"You didn't go waiting about for me, did you?"

"Not long," replied Carpenter, dryly.

"Well, I really am awfully sorry; but, you see, I'd promised these men at the end of last term, and I quite forgot about it this morning at Heriot's."

"I see."

"I won't do it again, I swear."

"You won't get the chance!" muttered Carpenter, as Devereux ran after his companions. He looked at his watch, and turned to Jan. "There's plenty of time, Rutter. Which way shall we go?"

Jan came out of the shadow of the hedge; he had remained instinctively in the background, and had no reason to think that Evan had seen him. Certainly their eyes had never met. And yet there had been something in Evan's manner, something pointed in his fixed way of looking at Carpenter and not beyond him, something that might have left a doubt in Jan's mind if a greater doubt had not already possessed it.

"Which way shall we turn?" Carpenter repeated as Jan stood looking at him strangely.

"Neither way, just yet a bit," said Jan, darkly. "I want to ask you something first."

"Right you are."

"There are not so many here that you could say it for, so far as I can see," continued Jan, the inscrutable: "but from what I've seen of you, Carpenter, I don't believe you'd tell me a lie."

"I'd try not to," said the other, smiling, yet no easier than Jan in his general manner.

"That's good enough for me," said Jan. "So what did Devereux mean just now by talking about 'this morning at Heriot's'?"

"Oh, he had breakfast with Heriot, too; didn't I tell you?"

"No; you didn't."

"Well, I never supposed it would interest you."

"Although I told you I knew something about him at home!"

The two were facing each other, eye to eye. Those of Jan were filled with a furious suspicion.

"I wonder you didn't speak to him just now," remarked Carpenter, looking at his nails.

"He never saw me; besides, I'd gone and said all I'd got to say to him yesterday in his study."

"I see."

"Didn't Devereux tell you I'd been to see him?"

"Oh, I think he said he'd seen you, but that was all."

"At breakfast this morning?"

"Yes."

"Did Heriot ask him anything about me?"

"No."

"Has he told you anything about me at home, Chips?"

"Hardly anything."

"How much?"

"Only that he hardly knew you; that was all," declared Carpenter, looking Jan in the face once more. "And I must say I don't see what you're driving at, Rutter!"

"You'd better go and ask Devereux," said Jan, unworthily; but, as luck would have it, he could not have diverted his companion's thoughts more speedily if he had tried.

"Devereux? I don't go near him!" he cried. "He promised to wait for me after chapel, and he cut me for those fellows we saw him with just now."

"Although you were friends at the same private school?"

"If you call that friendship! He never wrote to me all last term, though I wrote twice to him!"

"I suppose that would be why Heriot asked you both to breakfast," said Jan, very thoughtfully, as they began walking back together. "I mean, you both coming from the same school."

"What? Oh, yes, of course it was."

Jan threw one narrow look over his shoulder.

"Of course it was!" he agreed, and walked on nodding to himself.

"But he didn't know Evan Devereux, or he'd have known that an old friend was nothing to him!"

"I wouldn't be too sure," said Jan with gentle warmth. "I wouldn't be too sure, if I were you."

CHAPTER VIII

LIKES AND DISLIKES

By the beginning of October there was a bite in the air, and either fives or football every afternoon; and before the middle of the month Jan began now and then to feel there might be worse places than a public school. He had learnt his way about. He could put a name to all his house and form. He was no longer strange; and on the whole he might have disliked things more than he did. There was much that he did dislike, instinctively and individually; but there was a good deal that he could not help enjoying, over and above the football and the fives. There was the complete freedom out of school, the complete privacy of the separate study, above all the amazing absence of anything in the way of espionage by the masters. These were all surprises to Jan; but they were counterbalanced by some others, such as the despotic powers of the præpostors, which only revived the spirit of sensitive antagonism in which he had come to school. The præpostors wore straw hats, had fags, and wielded hunting-crops to keep the line at football matches. This was a thing that made Jan's blood boil; he marvelled that no one else seemed to take it as an indignity, or to resent the authority of these præpostors as he did. Then there were boys like Shockley whom he could cheerfully have attended on the scaffold. And there was one man he very soon detested more than any boy.

That man was Mr. Haigh, the master of the Middle Remove; and Jan's view of him was perhaps no fairer than his treatment of Jan. Haigh, when not passing more or less unworthy pleasantries, and laughing a great deal at very little indeed, was a serious and even passionate scholar. He had all the gifts of his profession except coolness and a right judgment of boys. His enthusiasm was splendid. The willing dullard caught fire in his form. The gifted idler was obliged to work for Haigh. He had hammered knowledge into all sorts and conditions of boys; but here was one who would get up and wring the sense out of a page of Virgil, and then calmly ask Haigh to believe him incapable of parsing a passage or of scanning a line of that page! Of course Haigh believed no such thing, and of course Jan would vouchsafe no explanation of his inconceivable deficiencies. Pressed for one, indeed, or on any other point arising from his outrageously unequal equipment, Jan invariably sulked, and Haigh invariably lost his temper and called Jan elaborate names. The more offensive they were, the better care Jan took to earn them. Sulky he was inclined to be by nature; sulkier he made himself when he found that it exasperated Haigh more than the original offence.

Loder, the captain of his house, was another object of Jan's dislike. Loder was not only a præpostor, who lashed your legs in public with a hunting-crop, but he was generally accounted a bit of a prig and a weakling into the bargain, and Jan thought he deserved his reputation. Loder had a great notion of keeping order in the house, but his actual tactics were to pounce upon friendless wretches like Chips or Jan, and not to interfere with stalwarts of the Shockley gang, or even with popular small boys like young Petrie. Nor was it necessary for Jan to be caught out of his study after lock-up, or throwing stones in the quad, in order to incur the noisy displeasure of the captain of the house. Loder heard of the daily trouble with Haigh; it was all over the house, thanks to Shockley & Co., whose lurid tales had the unforeseen effect of provoking a certain admiration for "the new man who didn't mind riling old Haigh." Indifference on such a point implied the courage of the matador—to all who had been gored aforetime in the Middle Remove—save and except the serious Loder. Passing Jan's door one day, this exemplary præpostor looked in to tell him he was disgracing the house, and stayed to inquire what on earth he meant by having such a filthy study. The epithet was inexact; but certainly the study was ankle-deep in books and papers, with bare walls still bristling with the last tenant's nails; and it was not improved by a haunting smell of sulphur and tallow, due to the recent firing of the shilling box of wax matches.

"It says nothing about untidy studies in the School Rules," said Jan, tilting his chair back from his table, and glowering at his interrupted imposition.

"Don't you give me any cheek!" cried Loder, looking dangerous for him.

"But it does say," continued Jan, quoting a characteristic canon with grim deliberation, "that 'a boy's study is his castle,' Loder!"

Jan had to pick himself up, and then his chair, with an ear that tingled no more than Jan deserved. But this was not one of the events that rankled in his mind. He had made a swaggering præpostor look the fool he was; no smack on the head could rob him of the recollection.

With such a temper it is no wonder that Jan remained practically friendless. Yet he might have made friends among the smaller fry below him in the house; and there was one unathletic boy of almost his own age, but really high up in the school, whose advances were summarily repulsed because they appeared to Jan to betray some curiosity about his people and his home. It was only human that the lad should be far too suspicious on all such points; the pity was that this often made him more forbidding and hostile in his manner than he was at heart. But in all his aversions and suspicions there was no longer a hard or a distrustful thought of Evan Devereux, though Jan and he had not spoken since that first Saturday, and though they often met upon the hill or in the street without exchanging look or nod.

Otherwise his likes were not so strong as his dislikes, or at any rate not so ready; and yet in his heart even Jan soon found himself admiring a number of fellows to whom he never dreamt of speaking before they spoke to him. Head and chief of these was Cave major, who was already in the Eleven, and who got his football colours after the first match. How the whole house clapped him in hall that night at tea! The only notice he had ever taken of Jan was to relieve him of Carpenter's yellow-back novel, which the great man read and passed on to another member of the Fifteen in another house. To the owner of the book that honour was sufficient solace; but neither new boy had ever encountered quite so heroic a figure as the great Charles Cave. Then there was Sprawson—Mother Sprawson, to Cave and Loder— reputed a tremendous runner, but seen to be several things besides. Sprawson amused Jan immensely by carrying an empty spirit-flask in his pocket, and sometimes behaving as though he had just emptied it; he was rather a bully, but more of a humorist, who would administer a whole box of pills prescribed for himself to some unfortunate urchin in no need of them; and yet when he drew Jan in the house fives, and was consequently knocked out in the first round, nobody could have taken a defeat or treated a partner better. Then there were Stratten and Jellicoe. Stratten seemed a very perfect gentleman, and Jellicoe a distinct though fiery one; they were always about arm-in-arm together, or playing fives on the inner court; and Jan enjoyed watching them when he could not get a game himself on the outer. At closer range he developed a more intimate appreciation of Joyce, with his bad language and his good heart, and of Bingley and his joyous interest in violent crime.

As for old Bob Heriot, he completely upset all Jan's ideas about schoolmasters. He was never in the least angry, yet even Cave major looked less dashing in his presence, and the likes of Shockley ludicrously small. Not that his house saw too much of Heriot. He was not the kind of master who is continually in and out of his own quad. His sway was felt rather than enforced. But he had a brisk and cheery word with the flower of the house most nights after prayers, and somehow Jan and others of his size generally lingered in the background to hear what he had to say; he never embarrassed them by taking too much notice of them before their betters, and seldom chilled them by taking none at all. The Shockley fraternity, however, had not a good word to say for poor Mr. Heriot. And that was not the least of his merits in Jan's eyes.

On Sunday evenings between tea and prayers it was Heriot's practice to make a round of the studies, staying for a few minutes' chat in each; and on the second Sunday of the term he gave Jan rather more than his time allowance. But he seemed to notice neither the stark ugliness of the uncovered walls, nor the heavy fall of waste paper; and though he did speak of Jan's difficulties in form, he treated them also in a very different manner from that employed by the captain of his house. The truth was that Haigh had said a good deal about the matter to Heriot, and Heriot very little to Haigh, whose tongue was as intemperate out of school as it was in form. But to Jan he spoke plainly on this second Sunday evening of the term.

"It's obvious that you were placed a form too high. Such mistakes will occur; there's no way of avoiding them altogether; the question is, shall we try to rectify this one? It's rather late in the day, but I've known it done; the Head Master might allow it again. It would rest with him, so you had better not speak of it for the present. I mean, of course, that he might allow you to come down to Mr. Walrond's form, or even into mine."

At which Jan displayed some momentary excitement, and then sat stolidly embarrassed.

"It would be a desperate remedy, Rutter; it would mean your being a fag, after first escaping fagging altogether; in fact, it would be starting all over again. I don't say it wouldn't make your work easier for you during the whole time you're here. But I shall quite understand it if you prefer the evils that you know."

"It isn't the fagging. It isn't that I shouldn't like being in your form, sir," Jan blurted out. "But I don't want to run away from Mr. Haigh!" he mumbled through his teeth.

"Well, you'd only have to fight another day, if you did," said Heriot, with a laugh. And so the matter went no further; and not another boy or master in the school ever knew that it had gone so far.

But the being of whom Jan saw most, and the only one to whom he spoke his odd mind freely, was the other new man, Carpenter, now Chips to all the house. And Chips was another oddity in his way; but it was not Jan's way at any single point. Chips had always been intended for a public school. But in some respects he was far less fit for one than Jan. To be at this school was to realise the dream of his life; but it was not the dream that it had been before it came true, and the dreamer took this extraordinary circumstance to heart, though he had the character to keep it to himself. Jan was the last person to whom he would have admitted it; he still stood up for the school in all their talks, and gloried in being where he was; but it was none the less obvious that he was not so happy as he tried to appear.

Chips's troubles, to be sure, were not in form; they were almost entirely out of school, just where Jan got on best. Chips's skin was thinner; the least taunt hurt his feelings, and he hid them less successfully than Jan could hide his. He was altogether more squeamish; lying and low talk were equally abhorrent to him; he would not smile, and had the courage to confess his repugnance under pressure, but not the force of personality to render a protest other than ineffectual. Such things ran like water from off Jan's broader back; he was not particularly attracted or repelled.

One bad half-hour that the pair spent together almost daily was that between breakfast and second school. It was the recognised custom for fellows in the same house and form to prepare their construe together; this took Carpenter and Rutter most mornings into Shockley's study, where Buggins and Eyre major completed the symposium. On a Virgil morning there would be interludes in which poor Chips felt himself a worm for sitting still; even when Thucydides claimed closer attention there was a lot of parenthetical swearing. But Chips—whose Greek was his weak point—endured it all as long as the work itself was fairly done.

One morning, however, as Jan was about to join the rest, Chips burst in upon him, out of breath, and stood with his back to Jan's bare wall.

"They've gone and got a crib!" he gasped.

"What of?"

"Thicksides."

"And a jolly good job!" said Jan.

Chips looked as though he distrusted his ears.

"You don't mean to say you'll use it, Tiger?"

"Why not?"

"It's so—at least I mean it seems to me—so jolly unfair!"

Chips had stronger epithets on the tip of his tongue; but that of "pi" had been freely applied to himself; and it rankled in spite of all his principles.

"Not so unfair as sending you to a hole like this against your will," retorted Jan, "and putting you two forms too high when you get here."

"That's another thing," said Chips, for once without standing up for the "hole," perhaps because he knew that Jan had called it one for his benefit.

"No; it's all the same thing. Is that beast Haigh fair to me?"

"I don't say he is—"

"Then I'm blowed if I see why I should be fair to him."

"I wasn't thinking of Haigh," said Chips. "I was thinking of the rest of the form who don't use a crib, Tiger."

"That's their look-out," said the Tiger, opening his door with the little red volume of Thucydides in his other hand.

"Then you're going to Shockley's study just the same?"

"Rather! Aren't you?"

"I've been. I came out again."

"Because of the crib?"

"Yes."

"Did you tell them so, Chips?"

"I had to; and—and of course they heaved me out, Tiger! And I'll never do another line with the brutes!"

He turned away; he was quite husky. Jan watched him with a shrug and a groan, hesitated, and then slammed his door.

"Aren't you going, Tiger?" cried Chips, face about at the sound. "Don't mind me, you know! I can sweat it out by myself."

"Well you're not going to," growled Jan, flinging the little red book upon the table. "I'd rather work with an old ass like you, Chips, than a great brute like Shockley!"

So that alliance was cemented, and Chips at any rate was Jan's friend for life. But Jan was slower to reciprocate so strong a feeling; his nature was much less demonstrative and emotional; moreover, the term he had applied to Carpenter was by no means one of mere endearment. There was in fact a good deal about Chips that appealed to Jan as little as to the other small boys in the house. He was indubitably "pi"; he thought too much of his study; he took in all kinds of magazines, and went in for the competitions, being mad about many things including cricket, but no earthly good at fives, and not allowed to play football. He had some bronchial affection that prevented him from running, and often kept him out of first school. "Sloper" and "sham" were neither of them quite the name for him; but both became unpleasantly familiar in the ears of Carpenter during the first half of his first term; and there was just enough excuse for them to keep such a lusty specimen as Jan rather out of sympathy with a fellow who neither got up in the morning nor played games like everybody else.

Nevertheless, they could hardly have seen more of each other than they did. They went up and down the hill together, for Chips was always at Jan's elbow after school, and never sooner than when Jan had made a special fool of himself in form. Chips was as little to be deterred by the gibes of the rest on the way back, as by the sullen silence in which the Tiger treated his loyalty and their scorn. If Rutter had recovered tone enough to play fives after twelve, Carpenter was certain to be seen looking over the back wall; and as sure as Jan went up to football in the afternoon, Chips went with him in his top-coat, and followed the game wistfully at a distance. Down they would come together when the game was over, as twilight settled on the long stone street, and tired players shod in mud tramped heavily along either pavement. Now was Chips's chance for the daily papers before the roaring fire in hall, while Jan changed with the rest in the lavatory; and as long as either had a tizzy there was just time for cocoa and buns at the nearest confectioner's before third school.

The nearest confectioner's was not the fashionable school resort, but it was quite good enough for the rank and file of the lower forms. The cocoa was coarse and thick, and the buns not always fresh; but the boys had dined at half-past one; tea in hall was not till half-past six; and even then there was only bread-and-butter to eat unless a fellow had his own supplies. Jan had not been provided with a hamper at the beginning of the term, or with very many shillings by way of pocket-money; he would have starved rather than write for either, for it was seldom enough that he received so much as a letter from his new home. But it did strike him as a strange thing that a public-school boy should habitually go hungrier to bed than a coachman's son at work about his father's stables.

Milk and "dog-rocks" were indeed provided last thing at night and first thing in the morning; but if you chose to get up late there was hardly time for a mouthful as you sped out of the quad and along the street to prayers, buttoning your waistcoat as you ran. This was not often Jan's case, but it was on the morning after the match between his house and another in the first round of the Under Sixteen. Heriot's had won an exciting game, and Jan was conscious of having done his share in the bully. He was distinctly muscular for his age, and had grown perceptibly in even these few weeks at school. His sleep was haunted by an intoxicating roar of "Reds!" (his side's colour for the nonce) and stinging counter cries of "Whites!" Once at least he had actually heard his own nickname shouted in approval by some big fellow of his house; and he heard it all again as he dressed and dashed out, on a particularly empty stomach, into a dark and misty morning, with the last bell flagging as if it must stop with every stroke; he heard it above his own palpitations all through prayers; on his knees he was down in another bully, smelling the muddy ball, thirsting to feel it at his feet again.

It chanced to be a mathematical morning, and Jan felt thankful as he went his way after prayers; for he was not in Haigh's mathematical, but in the Spook's; and the Spook was a peculiarly innocuous master, who had a class-room in his quarters in the town, but not a house.

"The Thirteenth Proposition of the First Book of Euclid," sighed the Spook, exactly as though he were giving out a text in Chapel. "Many of you seem to have found so much difficulty over this that I propose to run over it again, if you will kindly hold your tongues. Hold your tongue, Kingdon! Another word from you, Pedley, and you'll have whipping in front of you—or rather behind you!"

The little joke was a stock felicity of the Spook's, and it was received in the usual fashion. At first there was a little titter, but nothing more until the Spook himself was seen to wear a sickly smile; thereupon the titter grew into a roar, and the roar rose into a bellow, and the bellow into one prolonged and insolent guffaw which the cadaverous but smiling Spook seemed to enjoy as much as the smallest boy in his mathematical. Jan alone did not join in the derisive chorus; to him it sounded almost as though it were in another room; and the figure of the Spook, standing before his blackboard, holding up a piece of chalk for silence, had become a strangely nebulous and wavering figure.

"'The angles that one straight line makes with another straight line,'" began the Spook at last, in a voice that Jan could hardly hear, "'are together equal ... together equal ... together equal ...'"

Jan wondered how many more times he was to hear those two words; his head swam with them; the Spook had paused, and was staring at him with fixed eyes and open mouth; and yet the words went on ringing in the swimming head, fainter and fainter, and further and further away, as Jan fell headlong into the unfathomable pit of insensibility.

He came to earth and life on a dilapidated couch in the Spook's study, where the Spook himself was in the act of laying him down, and of muttering in sepulchral tones, "A little faint, I fear!"

Jan had never fainted before, and in his heart he was rather proud of the achievement; but he was thankful that he had chosen the one first school of the week that was given over to mathematics. He would have been very sorry to have come to himself in the arms of Haigh. The Spook was a man who had obviously mistaken his vocation; but it was least obvious when mere kindness and goodness were required of him. Jan was detained in his study half the morning, and regaled with tea and toast and things to read. Heriot also looked in before second school, but was rather brusque and unsympathetic (after the Spook) until Jan ventured to say he hoped he would be allowed to play football that afternoon, as he had never felt better in his life. Heriot said that was a question for the doctor, who would be in to see Jan during the forenoon.

The doctor came, and Jan could not remember the last time a doctor had been to see him. This one sat over him with a long face, felt his pulse, peered into his eyes, looked as wise as an owl at the other end of his stethoscope, and then began asking questions in a way that put Jan very much on his guard.

"So you've been playing football for your house?"

"Yessir—Under Sixteen."

"I suppose you played football before you came here?"

"No, sir," said Jan, beginning to feel uncomfortable.

"Weren't you allowed?"

This question came quickly, but Jan took his time over it as coolly as he could. Obviously the doctor little dreamt that this was his first school. On no account must he suspect it now. And it was true, as it happened, that his father had once and for all forbidden Jan to play football with Master Evan, because he played so roughly.

"No, sir."

"You were not allowed?"

"No, sir."

"Do you know why?"

"No, sir."

"Well, I think I do," said the doctor, rising. "And you mustn't play here, either, at any rate for the present."

Jan shot upright on the sofa.

"Your heart isn't strong enough," said the doctor.

"My heart's all right!" cried Jan, indignantly.

"Perhaps you'll allow me to be the best judge of that," returned the doctor. "You may go back to your house, and I shall send a line to Mr. Heriot. There's no reason why you should lie up; this is Saturday, you'll be quite fit for school on Monday; but no football, mind, until I give you leave."

Jan tried to speak, but he had tied his own tongue. He could not explain to the doctor, he could not explain to Heriot. He did not know why he had fainted for the first time in his life that morning; he only knew that it was not his heart, that he had never felt better than after yesterday's match. And now he was to be deprived of the one thing he liked at school, the one thing he was by way of getting good at, his one chance of showing what was in him to those who seemed to think there was nothing at all! And another Under Sixteen house-match would be played next week, perhaps against Haigh, who had also won their tie. And all he would be able to do would be to stand by yelling "Reds!" and having his shins lashed by some beastly præpostor, and hearing himself bracketed with Chips as a "sham" and a "sloper"—and knowing it was true!

That was the worst of it. His heart was all right. It was all a complete misunderstanding and mistake. It was a mistake that Jan knew he could have set right by going to Heriot and explaining why he had never played football before, and why it was barely true to say that he had not been allowed.

But Jan was not going to anybody to say anything of the kind.

CHAPTER IX

CORAM POPULO

On the notice-board in the colonnade there was a sudden announcement which no new boy could understand. It was to the effect that Professor Abinger would pay his annual visit on the Monday and Tuesday of the following week. Neither Carpenter nor Rutter had ever heard his name before, and, on the way up the hill to second school, they inquired of Rawlinson, the small fellow in his own house whom Haigh had begun reviling on the first morning of the term.

"Who's Abinger?" repeated Rawlinson. "You wait and see! You'll love him, Tiger, as much as I do!"

"Why shall I?" asked Jan, who liked Rawlinson, and only envied him his callous gaiety under oppression.

"Because he'll get us off two days of old Haigh," said Rawlinson, capering as though the two days would never end.

"Don't hustle!"

"I'm not hustling. I take my oath I'm not. Grand old boy, Abinger, besides being just about the biggest bug alive on elocution!"

"Who says so?"

"Jerry, for one! Anyhow he comes down twice a year, and takes up two whole days, barring first school and private work; that's why Abinger's a man to love."

"But what does he do? Give us readings all the time?" asked Chips, one of whose weaknesses was the inane question.

"Give us readings? I like that!" cried Rawlinson, shouting with laughter. "It's the other way about, my good ass!"

"Do we have to read to him?"

"Every mother's son of us, before the whole school, and all the masters and the masters' wives!"

Chips went on asking questions, and Jan was only silent because he took a greater interest in the answers than he cared to show. The ordeal foreshadowed by Rawlinson was indeed rather alarming to a new boy with an accent which had already exposed him to some contumely. Yet his ear, sharpened by continual travesties of his speech, informed Jan that he was by no means the only boy in the school whose vowels were of eccentric breadth. It was a point on which he was not unduly sensitive, but, in his heart, only too willing to improve. He was, however, more on his guard against the outlandish word and the rustic idiom, which still cropped up in his conversation, but could not possibly affect his reading aloud. The result of the last reflection was that Jan subdued his fears, and rejoiced with Rawlinson at the prospect of a break in the term's work.

Their joy was enhanced by the obvious exasperation of Haigh, who scarcely concealed from his form his own opinion of Professor Abinger and the impending function. Many were his covert sneers, and loud his angry laughter, as he hit upon something for the Middle Remove to declaim piecemeal between them. The chosen passage was taken almost at random from one of Hans Andersen's Fairy Tales, which for some reason formed a standard work throughout the school, and which drew from Haigh the next thing to a personal repudiation of the volume in his hands. It was at least plain that means and end shared his cordial disapproval, but outward loyalty clipped the spoken word, and the form were not surprised when he finished with a more satisfying fling at Jan.

"Some of you fellows in Mr. Heriot's house," said Haigh, "may perhaps find time to rehearse Rutter in the few words that are likely to fall to his tender mercies. Otherwise we may trust him to disgrace us before everybody."

Indignant glances were cast at Jan's hangdog head by those who wished to stand well with Haigh; one within reach dealt him a dexterous kick upon the shins; and Jan took it all with leaden front, for that was his only means of getting the least bit even with his adult tormentor. Nevertheless, on the Sunday evening, when one could sit in another's study after lock-up by special leave, and Jan and Chips had availed themselves of the privilege, Hans Andersen was the author that each had open before him, as the pair munched their way through a bag of biscuits bought with their Saturday allowance.

They were not disappointed in the elderly gentleman who opened his campaign next morning. He had an admirable platform presence, and a fine histrionic face in a cascade of silvery hair. Nor had he made many of his opening observations—in a voice like a silver bell—before the youngest of his new hearers perceived that Professor Abinger was really as distinguished as he looked. He was evidently the companion of even more distinguished men. He spoke of the statesmen and the judges whom he had specially coached for the triumphs of their political and forensic careers. He mentioned a certain Cabinet Minister as a particularly painstaking pupil in his younger days. He laid the scene of a recent personal experience in a ducal mansion, and that led him into an indiscreet confession involving an even more illustrious name. Professor Abinger seemed quite embarrassed by his inadvertence; and the Head Master, who had taken a side seat on his own platform, might have been seen frowning at his watch, which he closed with a very loud snap. But the two new boys in the Middle Remove saw how difficult it must be for a member of such exalted circles to avoid all mention of his most intimate acquaintance.

And when Rawlinson looked at them and laughed, they nodded their complete agreement with his estimate of the eminent professor.

"When I look about me in this schoolroom," concluded Mr. Abinger somewhat hastily, as he beamed upon the serried ranks before him, "and when I see the future generals and admirals, bishops and statesmen, lawyers and physicians of high standing—men of mark in every sphere—even Peers of the Realm itself—who hear me now, whom I myself am about to hear in my turn—when I dip into your futures far as human eye can see—then I realise afresh the very wide responsibility—the—the imperial importance—of these visits to this school!"

There might have been applause; a certain amount of sly merriment there was; but Mr. Thrale prevented the one, and cut the other mighty short, by sternly summoning the Upper Fourth.

There was a scraping and shambling of feet in the rows behind the Middle Remove, and up to the platform trooped the pioneer force. Jan could only think of the narrowness of his escape—he had heard that the forms were called up in any order—and he was wondering whether there was so much to fear after all, from such a perfect gentleman and jolly old boy, when Evan Devereux passed quite close to him with the other pioneers. And Evan's ears were red to the tip—Evan who looked neat and dapper enough to stand up before the world—Evan who was a gentleman if there was one in the school!

The Upper Fourth huddled together on the platform, each boy with a fat blue volume of Hans Christian Andersen open at the fatal place. Then, at a sign from the Head Master, the captain of the form took a step forward, threw out his chest like a man, and plunged into the middle of one of the tales with a couple of sentences that made the rafters ring. The professor stood smiling his approval at the intrepid youth's side, and Mr. Thrale nodded his head as he called for the second boy in form's order. The successful performer sidled to the end of an empty bench immediately below the platform, and sat down against the wall. His place was taken by one bent on following his good example, but in too great a hurry to get it over. "'A myrtle stood in a pot in the window,'" he had begun in a breath, when the Head Master exclaimed "Three o'clock!" in portentous tones, and the second performer melted from the platform like a wraith.

"That's the worst he does to you," whispered Carpenter, who had been making his usual inquiries. "It only means coming in at three for another shot with the other failures."

Meanwhile the professor was pointing out the second boy's mistake. He laid it down as the first of first principles that a distinct pause must separate the subject of any sentence from its predicate; he added that he had preached that doctrine in that place for so many years that he had hoped it was unnecessary to begin preaching it again; but perhaps he had never had the advantage of meeting his young friend before? His young friend had to rise in his place of premature retirement, next but one to the wall, and confess with burning cheeks that such was not the case. And when the point had been duly laboured, proceedings were resumed by a lad who cleared the obstacle with an audaciously protracted pause after the word "myrtle."

It was an obstacle at which many fell throughout the morning, the three o'clock sentence being promptly pronounced upon each; but there were other interludes more entertaining to the audience and more trying to the temporary entertainer. There were several stammerers who were made to beat time and to release a syllable at each beat; and there was more than one timid child to be paternally conducted by the professor to the very far end of the huge room, and made to call out, "Can you hear my voice?" until the Head Master at his end signified that he could. ("No, I can't!" he replied very sternly on one occasion.) There were even a few mirthful seconds supplied by Devereux, of all fellows, over something which Jan quite failed to follow, but which made him almost as hot and miserable as Evan had turned upon the platform.

Devereux, however, had looked rather nervous all the time; as he waited his turn at Abinger's elbow he seemed uncomfortably conscious of himself, and he stepped into the breach at last as though the cares of the school were on his insignificant shoulders. Jan felt for him so keenly as to hold his breath. Evan had to utter an extravagant statement about a bottle, but his reading was no worse than nervous until he came to the word "exhilarated." He said "exhilyarated." The professor invited him to say it again, and with the request his paternal smile broadened into a grin of less oppressive benevolence. It was a very slight change of expression, which had occurred more than once before, but on this occasion it filled Jan with a sudden revulsion of feeling towards Professor Abinger. Then Evan said "ex-hill-yarated," making a mountain of the hill, and a stern voice cried "Three o'clock!" The unlucky culprit looked utterly wretched and crestfallen, and yet so attractive in his trouble that the professor himself was seen to intercede on his behalf. But a still sterner voice reiterated "Three o'clock!"

That was all, and it was so quickly over that Devereux was himself again before the Upper Fourth returned in a body to their place. Indeed, he came back smiling, and with a jaunty walk, as some criminals foot it from the dock. But Jan could not catch his eye, though his own were soft with a sympathy which he longed to show, but only succeeded in betraying to Carpenter.

"I might have known you were hustling," Jan said to Rawlinson, as they got out nearly an hour later than from ordinary second school. "I say, though, I do bar that old brute—don't you?"

"What! When he's coached a Cabinet Minister, and been staying as usual with the same old dukes and dukesses?"

"If he ever did," said Jan, his whole mind poisoned by the treatment meted out to Evan. "It's easy enough for him to stand up there scoring off chaps. I'd like to score off him!"

"Well, you wouldn't be the first. He was properly scored off once, by a chap called Bewicke in the Upper Sixth. Come my way," said Rawlinson, "and I'll tell you. Bewicke had heard that opening speech about the Cabinet Minister, and all the rest of it, so often that he knew the whole thing by heart, and used to settle down to sleep as soon as old Abinger got a start. So one time Jerry catches him safe in the arms of Morpheus, and says, 'Bewicke, be good enough to get up and repeat to the school the substance of Professor Abinger's last remarks.' So Bewicke gets up, blinking, not having heard a blooming word, and begins: 'The other day, when I had the privilege of being an honoured guest of his Grace the Duke of —' 'Three o'clock!' says Jerry, and they say Bewicke was jolly near bunked. It was before my time, worse luck! I wish I'd heard it, don't you? I say, we were lucky to escape this morning, weren't we? But I'm not sure I don't wish we'd got it over, myself."

Four of the lower forms had been polished off between ten and twelve-thirty, and three more followed in the hour-and-a-half of third school; but the Middle Remove was not one of the three. There remained only second school on the second day—a half-holiday—and Carpenter had heard that much of the morning would be devoted to a Sixth Form Competition for the Abinger Medal. He had also learnt for a fact that all the forms were not always called upon, and Jan agreed that in that case they were beginning to stand an excellent chance of being missed out. However, no sooner were the proceedings resumed on a pink and frosty morning, than the bolt fell for the Middle Remove.

The big schoolroom looked abnormally big as Jan took a shy peep down from the platform. It seemed to contain four thousand boys instead of four hundred. It felt as cold as an empty church. The Head Master's fingers looked blue with a joiner's pencil poised between them over a school list; and as he sat with bent head and raised ear his breath was just visible against his sombre gown. But Professor Abinger in black spats and mittens was brisker and crisper and more incisive than on the previous day; his paternal smile broke more abruptly into the grin of impaired benevolence; his flowing mane looked merely hoary, and his silvery voice had rather the staccato ring of steel.

He might almost have heard Haigh's opinion of him, he was so hard upon that form. The passage which Haigh had chosen was from a story called "The Mermaid," and the very first reader had to say "colossal mussel shells"—perhaps a better test of sobriety than of elocution—but Abinger would have it repeated until a drunken man could have done it better and the whole school was in a roar. Jan set his teeth at the back of the little knot upon the platform: he knew what he would do rather than make them laugh like that. But no one else made them laugh like that, though Buggins was asked whether he had been born within sound of Bow Bells, and created some amusement by the rich intonation of his denial. Gradually the little knot melted, and the bench below the platform filled up. Jan began reading over and over to himself the sentences that seemed certain to fall to him, as he was still doing when Carpenter left his side and lurched into the centre of the platform.

Now, poor Chips happened to have had a bad night with his tiresome malady, but on his speech it had the effect of a much more common disorder.

"The bleached bodes of bed," he began, valiantly, and was still making a conscientious pause after the subject of the sentence when a hand fell on his shoulder and the wretched Chips was looking Professor Abinger in the face.

"Have you got a cold?" inquired the professor, with his most sympathetic smile.

"Yes, sir," said Carpenter, too shy to explain the permanent character of the cold by giving it its proper name.

"Then stand aside, and blow your nose," said the professor, grinning like a fatherly fiend, "while the next boy reads."

Jan was the next boy, and the last; and he strode forward too indignant on his friend's account to think of himself, and cut straight into the laugh at Carpenter's expense. Nothing, in fact, could have given Jan such a moral fillip at the last moment. He cried out his bit aggressively at the top of his voice, but forgot none of the rules laid down, and even felt he had come through with flying colours. He saw no smile upon the sea of faces upturned from the body of the schoolroom. Not a syllable fell from the Head Master on his right. Yet he was not given his dismissal, and was consequently about to begin another sentence when Professor Abinger took the book from Jan's hand.

"I think you must hear yourself as others hear you," said he. "Have the goodness to listen to me." And he read: "'The bleached bawnes of men who had perished at sea and soonk belaw peeped forth from the arms of soome, w'ile oothers clootched roodders and sea chests or the skeleeton of some land aneemal; and most horreeble of all, a little mermaird whom they had caught and sooffercairted.' There!" cried the professor, holding up his hand to quell the shouts of laughter. "What do you think of that?"

Jan stood dumfounded by his shame and rage, a graceless and forbidding figure enough, with untidy hair and a wreck of a tie, and one lace trailing: a figure made to look even meaner than it was by the spruce old handsome man at his side.

"What dost tha' think o' yon?" pursued the professor, dropping into dialect with ready humour.

"It's not what I said," muttered Jan, so low that his questioner alone could hear.

"Not what you said, eh? We'll take you through it. How do you pronounce 'bones'?"

No answer, but a firmer cast to the jaw of Jan, a less abject droop of the shoulders, a good inch more in actual stature.

"B, o, n, e, s!" crooned the professor, shewing all his teeth.

But Jan had turned into a human mule. And the silence in the great room had suddenly grown profound.

"Well, we'll try something else," said the professor, consulting the text somewhat unsteadily, and speaking in a rather thin voice. "Let us hear you say the word 'sunk.' S, u, n, k—sunk. Now, if you please, no more folly. You are wasting all our time."

Jan had forgotten that; the reminder caused him a spasm of satisfaction. Otherwise he was by this time as entirely aware of his folly as anybody else present; but it was too late to point it out to him; it was too late to think of it now; his head was burning, his temples throbbed, his tongue clave. He could not have spoken now if he had tried. But it would have taken a better man than Abinger to make him try. And the better man sat by without a word, pale, stern, and troubled with a complex indignation.

"I can do nothing with this boy," said Abinger, turning to him with just a tremor in his thin high tones. "I must leave him to you, Mr. Thrale."

"Twelve o'clock!" cried the other with ominous emphasis; and as he stabbed the school list with his joiner's pencil, the Middle Remove rose and returned down the gangway to their accustomed place.

Jan went with them as one walking in his sleep. And Carpenter followed Jan with a tragic face and tears very near the surface. But as one sees furthest before rain, so Chips saw a good deal as he walked back blinking for his life. And one of the things he happened to see was Evan Devereux and the fellow next him doubled up in fits of laughter.

The Head Master usually sat in judgment on the culprits of the day without vacating his oaken throne in the Upper Sixth class-room until the first of them knelt down for his deserts. But the Abinger visitation upset everything; and on this occasion, when the campaign ended with the award of a medal to the præpostor who had done least violence to a leading article in the day's Times, Mr. Thrale remained on his platform in conversation with Professor Abinger while the school filed out form by form. Meanwhile three delinquents besides Jan awaited his arrival on the scene of trial and execution, while a number of the smaller fry pressed their noses to the diamond panes of the windows overlooking the school yard; and the public gallery in a criminal court could not have been better patronised for a notorious case than were these windows to-day.

One of the other malefactors had brought a slip of paper which he showed to Jan; on it was set forth a crime of a type which Mr. Thrale was at that time taking Draconic measures to stamp out of the school. "Hornton says πεποιηκασι is a Dative Plural.... I think he deserves a good flogging," the committing master had written, and signed the warrant with his initials. Jan had just reached that hieroglyph when in sailed their judge and executioner in his cap and gown.

The boy who deserved the good flogging advanced and delivered his certificate of demerit. Mr. Thrale examined the damning document, and when he came to the pious opinion at the end, exclaimed with simple fervour, "So do I!" With that he opened his desk and took out his cane, and the boy who deserved it knelt down with stolid alacrity. The venerable executioner then gathered half his gown into his left hand, and held it away at arm's length to give free play to his right. And there followed eight such slashing cuts as fetched the dust from a taut pair of trousers, and sent their wearer waddling stiffly from the room.

"Wasn't padded," whispered one of those left to Jan, who put an obvious question with a look, which was duly answered with a wink.

Meanwhile a sturdy youth in round spectacles was being severely interrogated, and replying promptly and earnestly, without lowering his glasses from the awful aspect of the flogging judge.

"You may go," said Mr. Thrale at length. "Your honesty has saved you. Trevor next. I've heard about you, Trevor; kneel down, shirker!"

And the wily Trevor not only knelt with futile reluctance, but writhed impotently during his castigation, though the eight strokes made half the noise of the other eight; and once up he went his way serenely with another wink at Jan.

Now by these days Jan had discovered that out of his pulpit Mr. Thrale was sufficiently short and sharp of speech, rough and ready of humour, with a trick of talking down to fellows in their own jargon as well as over their heads in parables. "Sit down, Rutter, and next time you won't sit down so comfortably!" he had rapped out at Jan when the Middle Remove went to construe to the Head Master early in the term. And it was next time now.

Jan was left alone in the presence, and that instant became ashamed to find he was already trembling. He had not trembled on the platform before the whole school; his blood had been frozen then, now it was bubbling in his veins. He was being looked at. That was all. He was receiving such a look as he had never met before, a look from wide blue eyes with hidden fires in them, and dilated nostrils underneath, and under them a mouth that looked as though it would never, never open.

It did at last.

"Rebel!" said a voice of unutterable scorn. "Do you know what they do with rebels, Rutter?"

"No, sir."

It never occurred to Jan not to answer now.

"Shoot them! You deserve to be shot!"

Jan felt he did. The parable was not over his diminished head; it might have been carefully concocted from uncanny knowledge of his inmost soul. All the potential soldier in him—the reserve whom this General alone called out—was shamed and humbled to the dust.

"You are not only a rebel," the awful voice went on, "but a sulky rebel. Some rebels are good men gone wrong; there's some stuff in them; but a sulky rebel is neither man nor devil, but carrion food for powder."

Jan agreed with all his contrite heart; he had never seen himself in his true colours before, had never known how vile it was to sulk; but now he saw, and now he knew, and the firing-party could not have come too quick.

The flogging judge had resumed his carved oak seat of judgment behind the desk. Jan had not seen him do it—he had seen nothing but those pregnant eyes and lips—but there he was, and in the act of putting his homely weapon back in the desk. Jan could have groaned. He longed to expiate his crime.

"Thrashing is too good for you," the voice resumed. "Have you any good reason to give me for keeping a sulky rebel in a standing army? Any reason for not drumming him out?"

Drumming him out! Expelling him! Sending him back to the Norfolk rectory, and thence very likely straight back to the nearest stables! More light rushed over Jan. He had seen his enormity; now he saw his life, what it had been, what it was, what it might be again.

"Oh, sir," he cried, "I know I speak all wrong—I know I speak all wrong! You see—you see—"

But he broke down before he could explain, and the more piteously because now he felt he never could explain, and this hard old man would never, never understand. That is the tragic mistake of boys—to feel they can never be understood by men!

Yet already the hard old man was on his feet again, and with one gesture he had cleared the throng from the diamond-paned windows, and laid tender hand upon Jan's heaving shoulder.

"I do see," he said, gently. "But so must you, Rutter—but so must you!"

CHAPTER X

ELEGIACS

Jan was prepared never to hear the last of his outrageous conduct in the big schoolroom; that was all he knew about his kind. It cost him one of the efforts of his school life to show his face again in Heriot's quad; and the quad was full of fellows, as he knew it would be; but only one accosted him, and that was

Sprawson, whose open hand flew up in a terrifying manner, to fall in a hearty slap on Jan's back. "Well done, Tiger!" says Sprawson before half the house. "That's the biggest score off Abinger there's been since old Bewicke's time." And Jan rushed up to his study with a fresh lump in his throat, though he had come in vowing that the whole house together should not make him blub.

That night at tea Jane Eyre of all people (who was splendidly supplied with all sorts of eatables from home) pushed a glorious game pie across the table to Jan; and altogether there was for a few hours rather more sympathy in the air than was good for one who after all had made public display of a thoroughly unworthy propensity. It is true that Jan had gone short of sympathy all his life, and that a wave of even misplaced sympathy may be beneficial to a nature suffering from this particular privation. But a clever gentleman was waiting to counteract all that, and to undo at his leisure what Mr. Thrale had done in about two minutes.

No sooner had the form re-assembled in his hall next day than Haigh made them a set sarcastic speech on the subject of Jan's enormity. He might have seen at a glance that even outwardly the boy was already chastened; that his jacket and his hair were better brushed than they had been all the term, his boots properly laced, his tie neatly tied; that in a word there were more signs of self-respect. Haigh, however, preferred to look at his favourites at the top of the form, and merely to jerk the thumb of contempt towards his aversion at the bottom. He reminded them of his prophecy that Rutter would disgrace them all before the school, and the triumph of the true prophet seemed at least as great as his indignation at what had actually happened. Even he, however, had not foreseen the quality of the disgrace, or anticipated a fit of sulks in public. Yet for his own part he was not sorry that the headmaster, and Mr. Heriot and all the other masters and boys in the school, should have had an opportunity of seeing for themselves what they in that room had to put up with almost every day of the term. And the harangue concluded with a plain hint to the form to take the law into its own hands, and "knock the nonsense out of that sulky bumpkin, who has made us the laughing-stock of the place."

To all of which Jan listened without a trace of his old resentment, and then stood up in his place.

"I'm very sorry, sir," said he. "I apologise to you and the form."

Haigh looked unable to believe his eyes and ears. But he was not the man to revise judgment of a boy once labelled Poison in his mind. He could no longer fail to note the sudden improvement in Jan's looks and manner; all he could do was to put the worst construction upon it that occurred to him at the moment.

"I shall entertain your apology when you look less pleased with yourself," he sneered. "Sit down."

But Jan's good resolutions were not to be eradicated any more easily than the rooted hostility of Haigh, who certainly surpassed himself in his treatment of the boy's persistent efforts at amendment. Jan, though no scholar, and never likely to make one now, could be sharp enough in a general way when he chose. But he never had chosen under Mr. Haigh. It was no use attending to a brute who "hotted" you just the same whether you attended or not. And yet that little old man in the Upper Sixth class-room, with a single stern analogy, had made it somehow seem some use to do one's best without sulking, even without looking for fair play, let alone reward. And, feeling a regular new broom at heart, Jan was still determined to sweep clean in spite of Haigh.

It chanced to be a Virgil morning, and of course the new broom began by saying his "rep" as he had never said it before. Perhaps he deserved what he got for that.

"I thought you were one of those boys, Rutter," said Haigh, "who affect a constitutional difficulty in learning repetition? I only wish I'd sent you up to Mr. Thrale six weeks ago!"

Yet Jan maintained his interest throughout the fresh passage which the form proceeded to construe, and being put on duly in the hardest place, got through again without discredit. It was easy, however, for a member of the Middle Remove to take an interest in his Virgil, for that poet can have had few more enthusiastic interpreters than Mr. Haigh, who indeed might have been the best master in the school if he had been less of a bullying boy himself. His method in a Virgil hour, at any rate, was beyond reproach. If his form knew the lesson, there was no embroidery of picturesque detail or of curious information which it was too much trouble for him to tack on for their benefit. The Æneid they were doing was the one about the boat-race; and what Mr. Haigh (who had adorned both flood and field at Cambridge) did not know about aquatics ancient and modern was obviously not worth knowing. He could handle a trireme on the blackboard as though he had rowed in one in the Mays, and accompany the proceeding with a running report worthy of a sporting journalist. But let there be one skeleton at the feast of reason, one Jan who could not or would not understand, and the whole hour might go in an unseemly duel between intemperate intellect and stubborn imbecility. Otherwise a gloating and sonorous Haigh would wind up the morning with Conington's translation of the lesson; and this was one of those gratifying occasions; in fact, Jan was attending as he had never before attended, when one couplet caught his fancy to the exclusion of all that followed.

"These bring success their zeal to fan;
They can because they think they can."

"Perhaps I can," said Jan to himself, "if I think I can. I will think I can, and then we'll see."

Haigh had shut the book and was putting a question to the favoured few at the top of the form. "Conington has one fine phrase here," he said. "I wonder if any of you noticed it? Possunt quia posse videntur; did you notice how he renders that?"

The favoured few had not noticed. They looked seriously concerned about it. The body of the form took its discomfiture more philosophically, having less to lose. No one seemed to connect the phrase with its English equivalent, and Mr. Haigh was manifestly displeased. "Possunt quia posse videntur!" he repeated ironically as he reached the dregs; and at the very last moment Jan's fingers flew out with a Sunday-school snap.

"Well?" said Haigh on the last note of irony.

"'They can because they think they can'!" cried Jan, and went from the bottom to the top of the form at one flight, amid a volley of venomous glances, but with one broad grin from Carpenter.

"I certainly do wish I'd sent you up six weeks ago!" said Haigh. "I shall be having a decent copy of verses from you next!"

Yet Jan, though quick as a stone to sink back into the mud, made a gallant effort even at his verses; but that was his last. They were much better than any attempt of his hitherto; but it was clear to everybody that Haigh did not believe they were Jan's own. Rutter was asked who had helped him. Rutter replied that he had done his verses himself without help. No help whatever? No help whatever. Haigh laughed to himself, but said nothing. Jan said something to himself, but did not laugh. And now at last he might never have been through those two minutes in the Upper Sixth class-room.

November was a month of the past; another week would finish off the term's work, leaving ten clear and strenuous days for the Exams. Haigh could only set one more copy of Latin verses, and Carpenter was as sorry on his own account as he was thankful for Jan's sake. Carpenter had acquired an undeniable knack of making hexameters and pentameters that continually construed and invariably scanned; it was the one thing he could do better than anybody in the form, and it had brought him latterly into considerable favour with a master whose ardour for the Muse betrayed a catholicity of intellect in signal contrast to his view of boys. It was not only the Greeks and Latins whose august measures appealed to Haigh; never a copy of elegiacs set he, but it was a gem already in its native English, and his voice must throb with its music even as he dictated it to his form. All this was another slight mistake in judgment: the man made a personal grievance of atrocities inevitably committed upon his favourite poets, and the boys conceived a not unreasonable prejudice against some of the noblest lyrics in the language. Carpenter was probably the only member of the form who not only revelled in the original lines, but rather enjoyed hunting up the Latin words, and found a positive satisfaction in fitting them into their proper places as dactyls and spondees.

"That's the finest thing he's set us yet," said Chips, when Haigh had given them Cory's "Heraclitus" for the last copy of the term.

"It'll be plucky fine when I've done with it," Jan rejoined grimly.

"I should start on it early, if I were you," said Chips, "like you did last week."

"And then get told you've had 'em done for you? Thanks awfully; you don't catch me at that game again. Between tea and prayers on Saturday night's good enough for me—if I'm not too done after the paper-chase."

"You're not going to the paper-chase, Tiger?"

"I am if I'm not stopped."

"When you're not even allowed to play football?"

"That's exactly why."

The paper-chase always took place on the last Saturday but one, and was quite one of the events of the winter term. All the morning, after second school, fags had been employed in tearing up scent in the library; and soon after dinner the road under Heriot's study windows began to resound with the tramp of boys on their way in twos and threes to see the start from Burston Beeches. A spell of hard weather had broken in sunshine and clear skies; the afternoon was brilliantly fine; and by half-past two the scene in the paddock under the noble beeches, with the grey tower of Burston church rising behind the leafless branches, was worthy of the day. Practically all the school was there, and quite a quarter of it in flannels and jerseys red or white, trimmed or starred with the colour of some fifteen. Off go the two hares—gigantic gentlemen with their football colours thick upon them. Hounds and mere boys in plain clothes crowd to the gate to see the last of them and their bulging bags of scent. The twelve minutes' law allowed them seems much more like half-an-hour; but at last time is up, the gates are opened, and the motley pack pours through with plenty of plain clothes after them for the first few fields. In about a mile comes the first check; it is the first of many, for snow is still lying under the trees and hedges, and in the distance it always looks like a handful of waste-paper. The younger hounds take a minute off, leaving their betters to pick up the scent again, and their laboured breath is so like tobacco smoke that you fancy that young master in knickerbockers is there to see that it is not. Off again to the first water-jump—which everybody fords—and so over miles of open upland, flecked with scent and snow—through hedges into ditches—a pack of mudlarks now, and but a remnant of the pack that started. Now the scent takes great zigzags, and lies in niggardly handfuls that tell their tale. Now it is thick again, and here are the two fags who met the hares with the fresh bags, and those gigantic gentlemen are actually only five minutes ahead, for here is the high road back past the Upper, and if it wasn't for the red sun in your eyes there should be a view of them from the top of one of those hills.

On the top of the last hill, by the white palings of the Upper Ground, there is a group of boys and masters, and several of the masters' wives as well, to see the finish; and it is going to be one of the best finishes they ever have seen. Here come the gigantic gentlemen, red as Indians with the sun upon their faces, and one of them plunging headlong in a plain distress. They rush down that hill, and are half-way up this one, the wet mud shining all over them like copper, when the first handful of hounds start up against the sky behind them.

"Surely that's rather a small boy to be in the first dozen," says Miss Heriot, pointing out a puppy in an untrimmed jersey, who is running gamely by himself between the first and second batches of hounds.

"In no fifteen, either," says Heriot, noticing the jersey rather than the boy, who is still a slip of muddy white on the opposite hill.

The hares are already home. They have been received with somewhat perfunctory applause, the real excitement being reserved for the race between the leading hounds, now in a cluster at the foot of the last hill; but half-way up the race is over, and Sprawson is increasing his lead with every stride.

"Well run, my house!" says Heriot, with laconic satisfaction.

"The house isn't done with yet, sir," pants Sprawson, turning his back to the sun. "There's young Rutter been running like an old hound all the way; here he is, in the first ten!"

And there indeed was the rather small boy in the plain jersey whom neither Heriot nor his sister had recognised as Jan; but then he looked another being in his muddy flannels; slimmer and trimmer, and somehow more in his element than in the coat and collar of workaday life; and the flush upon his face is not merely the result of exercise and a scarlet sky, it is a flush of perfect health and momentary happiness as well.

In fact it has been the one afternoon of all the term which Jan may care to recall in later life; and how it will stand out among the weary walks with poor Carpenter and the hours of bitterness under Haigh! But the afternoon is not over yet. Sprawson is first back at the house; his good-natured tongue has been wagging before Jan gets there, and Jan hears a pleasant thing or two as he jogs through the quad to change in the lavatory. But why has he not been playing football all these weeks? It might have made just the difference to the Under-Sixteen team; they might have beaten Haigh's in the second round, instead of just losing as they had done to his mortification before Jan's eyes. What did he mean by pretending to have a heart, and then running like this? It must be jolly well inquired into.

"Then you'd better inquire of old Hill," says Jan, naming the doctor as disrespectfully as he dares to the captain of the house. "It was he said I had one, Loder, not me!"

And Loder looks as if he would like to smack Jan's head again, but is restrained by the presence of Sprawson and Cave major, both of whom have more influence in the house than he. The great Charles Cave has not been in the paper-chase; he will win the Hundred and the Hurdles next term, but he is too slender a young Apollo to shine across country, and is not the man to go in for the few things at which he happens not to excel. He does not address Jan personally, but deigns to mention him in a remark to Sprawson.

"Useful man for us next term, Mother," says Cave, "if he's under fifteen."

"When's your birthday, Tiger?" splutters Sprawson from the showerbath.

"End of this month," says Jan.

"Confound your eyes!" cries Mother Sprawson, "then you won't be under fifteen for the sports, and I'll give you a jolly good licking!"

But what Sprawson really does give Jan is cocoa and biscuits at Maltby's in the market-place: a most unconventional attention from a man of his standing to a new boy: who knows enough by this time to feel painfully out of place in the fashionable shop, and devoutly to wish himself with Carpenter at one of their humble haunts. But even this incident is a memory to treasure, and not to be spoilt by the fact that Shockley waylays and kicks him in the quad for "putting on a roll," and that Heriot himself has Jan into his study after lock-up, for the first time since the term began, and first gives him a severe wigging for having run in the paper-chase at all, but sends him off with a parting compliment on having run so well.

"He said he'd only been forbidden to play football," so Bob Heriot reported to his sister. "Of course I had to jump on him for that; but I own I'm thankful I didn't find out in time to stop his little game. It's just what was wanted to lift him an inch out of the ruck. It augurs the sportsman I believe he'll turn out in spite of us."

"But what about his heart?"

"He hasn't a heart, never had one, and after this can never be accused of such a thing again."

"I wonder you didn't go to Dr. Hill about it long ago, Bob."

"I did go to him. But Hill said he wouldn't take the responsibility of letting the unfortunate boy play football without inquiring into his past history. That was the last proceeding to encourage, and so my hands are tied. They always are where poor Rutter is concerned. It was the same thing with Haigh over his Latin verses. He wanted me to write to the boy's preparatory schoolmaster! I haven't interceded with him since. Rutter's the one boy in my house I can't stick up for. He must sink or swim for himself, and I think he's going to swim; if he were in any other form I should be sure. But I simply daren't hold out the helping hand that one would to others."

Miss Heriot gave an understanding nod.

"I've often heard you say you can't treat two boys alike. Now I see what you mean."

"But I can't treat Rutter as I ever treated any boy before. I've got to keep my treatment to myself. I mustn't make him conscious, if I know it; that applies to them all, of course, but it would make this boy suspicious in a minute. He puts me on my mettle, I can tell you! I'm not sure that he isn't putting the whole public-school system on its trial!"

"That one boy, Bob?"

"They all do, of course. They're all our judges in the end. But this one is such a nut to crack, and yet there's such a kernel somewhere! I stake my place on that. The boy has more character even than I thought."

"Although he sulks?"

"That's often a sign. It means at the least courage of one's mood. But what you and I know, and have not got to forget, is that his whole point of view is probably different from that of any fellow who ever went through the school."

"As a straw plucked from the stables?" laughed Miss Heriot under her breath.

"Hush, Milly, for heaven's sake! No. I was thinking of the absolute adventure the whole thing must be to him, and has been from the very first morning when he got up early to look about for himself like a castaway exploring the coast!"

"Well, I only hope he's found the natives reasonably friendly!"

The sudden friendliness of the natives was of course Jan's greatest joy, as for once he revelled in the peace and quiet of the untidiest study in the house. He was more tired than he had ever been in his life before, but also happier than he had ever dreamt of being this term. The hot-water pipes threw a modicum of grateful warmth upon his aching legs, outstretched on the leg-rest of the folding-chair. The curtains were closely drawn, the candles burning at his elbow. On his knees lay a Gradus ad Parnassum, open, upon an open English-Latin; and propped against the candle-sticks was the exercise book in which he had taken down the beautiful English version of "Heraclitus." It is to be feared that the beauty was lost upon Jan, who was much too weary to make a very resolute attack upon a position which he was not equipped to capture, or to lead another forlorn hope in which the least degree of success would be deemed a suspicious circumstance. But he did make certain idle demonstrations with a pencil upon a bit of foolscap. And ten minutes before prayers he pulled himself sufficiently together to write his eight lines out in ink.

"Let's have a look," said Carpenter, as they waited for the Heriots in hall; and a look was quite enough. "I say, Tiger, you can't show this up! You'll be licked as sure as eggs are eggs," whispered Chips.

"I don't care."

"You would care. You simply shan't get this signed to-night. I'll touch it up after prayers, and let you have it in time to make a clean copy before ten, and Heriot'll sign it after prayers in the morning."

And he put that copy in his pocket as the sentinel in the passage flew in with his sepulchral "Hush!"

By gulping down his milk and taking his dog-rock with him to his study, Carpenter was able to devote a good half-hour to Jan's verses and still give Jan ten minutes to copy out the revised version; the ten minutes was ample, but the half-hour was all too short. The very first line began with a false quantity, and ended with a grammatical blunder. Carpenter rectified the false quantity by a simple transposition, and made so bold as to substitute perisse for moriri at the end of the hexameter. The second half of the pentameter was hopeless: Chips fell back on his own, merely changing causa doloris to fletus acerbus, and plumed himself on his facility. But in the second couplet every other foot was a flogging matter if Jan got sent up.

"I wept, as I remembered, how often you and I
Had tired the sun with talking and sent him down the sky."

Chips loved the lines well enough to blush for his own respectable attempt at a Latin rendering; but his blood ran cold at Jan's—

"Flevi quum memini nostro quam sæpe loquendo
Defessum Phœbum fecimus ire domum."
He flung himself on the monstrosity, but had to leave it at—

"Cum lacrymis memini nostro quam sæpe loquendo
Hesperias Phœbus fessus adisset aquas."

Chips did not plume himself on this; but at any rate nostro loquendo was Jan's own gem, and just bad enough to distract attention from the suspicious superiority of the rest without invoking the direst consequences. This was a subtle calculation on the part of Carpenter. He was quite conscious of the subtlety, and by no means as ashamed of it as such a desperately honest person should have been. He justified the means by the end, which was to save Jan a certain flogging; and the stage after justification was something very like a guilty relish in a first offence. There was an artistic satisfaction in doing the thing as deftly as Chips was doing it. The third couplet might almost have passed muster as Jan had left it; a touch or two and it was safe. But the last hexameter would never do, and Chips replaced it with a plagiarism of his own corresponding line which might have sufficed if he himself had not come curiously to grief over the last hexameter.

"Excellent, as usual, Carpenter," said Haigh in the fulness of time. "I could have given you full marks but for an odd mistake of yours towards the end. You seem to have misread the original penultimate line: 'Still are thy pleasant voices, thy nightingales, awake;' what part of speech do you take that 'still' to be?"

"Adjective, sir," said Chips, beginning to wonder whether it was one.

"Exactly!" cried Haigh, with the guffaw of his lighter moments. "So you get Muta silet vox ista placens, tua carmina vivunt—'Thy pleasant voices are still; on the other hand, however, thy nightingales are awake'—eh?"

"Yes, sir," said Chips, more doubtfully than before.

"Have you a comma after the word 'nightingales' in the English line as you took it down?"

"No, sir."

"That accounts for it! Ha, ha, ha! But it may be my fault." Nothing could exceed the geniality of Haigh towards a boy with Carpenter's little gift. He was going through the week's verses on the chimneypiece in his hall, but now he turned his back to the blazing fire. "Will those who have a comma after 'nightingales' be good enough to hold up their hands?" A forest of hands flew up. "I'm afraid it's your mistake, Carpenter," resumed Haigh, with a final guffaw. "Well, I couldn't have pitched upon a finer object-lesson in the importance of punctuation, if I had tried; but when you come to look at it again, Carpenter, you'll find that even without the comma your reading was more ingenious than plausible." He turned back to the chimneypiece and the pile of verses. The incident seemed closed, when suddenly Haigh was seen frowning thoughtfully into the fire. "Surely there was some other fellow did the same thing!" he exclaimed, and began glancing through the pile. "Ah! Rutter, of course! Jucundæ voces tacitæ sunt, carmina vivunt!"

His voice was completely changed as it rasped out the abhorred surname; it changed again before the end of Jan's hexameter.

"Were you helped in this, Rutter?"

"Yes, sir."

"Did you help him, Carpenter?"

"Yes, sir."

There was not an instant's hesitation before either answer. Yet the very readiness of the culprits to confess their crime was an evident aggravation in the eyes of Haigh, who flew into a passion on the spot.

"And you own up to it without a blush between you! And you, Rutter, expect me to believe that the same thing didn't happen last week, when you denied it!"

"It did not happen last week, sir," said Jan; but all save the first three words were drowned by Haigh.

"Silence!" he roared. "I don't believe a word you say. But I begin to think you're not such a fool as you pretend to be, Rutter; you saw you were found out at last, so you might as well make a clean breast of it! That doesn't minimise the effect of cheating, or the impudence of the offence in a brace of beggarly new boys. Perhaps you are not aware how dishonesty is treated in this school? I would send you both up to Mr. Thrale at twelve o'clock, but we don't consider that a flogging meets this kind of case. It's rather one in which the whole must suffer for the corruption of a part. I shall consider the question of a detention for the entire form, and we'll see if they can't knock some rudimentary sense of honour into you!"

The two delinquents trembled in their shoes; they knew what they were in for now. Had they entertained a single doubt about the matter, a glance at the black looks encompassing them would have prepared them for the worst. But Chips had not the heart to lift his eyes, and so a slip of paper was thoughtfully passed down to him by Shockley. "I'll murder you for this," it said; and the storm burst upon the hapless couple the moment they were out in Haigh's quad after second school.

"What the deuce do you both mean by owning up?"

"I wasn't going to tell a lie about it," said Jan, doggedly.

"No more was I!" squealed Chips, as Shockley twisted his arm to breaking point behind his back.

"Oh, yes, you're so plucky pious, aren't you? Couldn't do Thicksides with other people; too highly moral and plucky superior for that; but not above doing the Tiger's verses, and getting the whole form kept in!"

"It isn't for getting your verses done," cried another big fellow, frankly, as he tried but failed to get a free kick at Rutter: "it's for being such infernal young fools as to own up!"

So much for the sense of honour to be knocked into the fraudulent pair by the rest of the form! It was a revelation to Carpenter and Rutter. They knew that Shockley and Buggins rarely did a line of any sort of composition for themselves, and more than once they had heard the pair indignantly repudiate the slightest suggestion against their good faith on the part of Haigh. But these poor specimens in their own house and form were the only fellows whose code of honour they had been hitherto able to probe. And it did surprise them to find some of the nicest fellows in the form entirely at one with their particular enemies in condemning the honesty which had got them all into trouble.

Was it a good system that could bring this about? The two boys did not ask themselves that question; nor did it occur to them to carry their grievance to Mr. Heriot, whose expert opinion would have been as interesting as his almost certain action in the matter. But in the bitterness of their hearts they did feel that an injustice had been done; and one of them at any rate was very sorry that he had told the truth. He would know what to say another time. Yet how human the fury of the form, threatened with punishment for an offence for which only two of their number were responsible, and subtly suborned by the master to do his dirty work by venting their natural anger on the luckless pair! Could any trick be shabbier in a master? Could any scheme be more demoralising for boys? The effect on them was easily seen. They were to inculcate a higher sense of schoolboy honour. And the first thing they did was to curse and kick you for not piling dishonour on dishonour's head!

Chips and Jan did not see the fiendish humour of the situation, any more than they looked beyond their immediate oppressors for first principles and causes. But whatever may be said for the punishment of many for the act of one or two, as the only thing to do in certain cases, it would still be hard to justify the course pursued by Mr. Haigh, who held his threat over the whole form until the two boys' lives had been made a sufficient misery to them, and then only withdrew it in consideration of a special holiday task, to be learnt by heart at home and said to him without a mistake (on pain of further penalties) when they came back after Christmas.

CHAPTER XI

A MERRY CHRISTMAS

Christmas weather set in before the holidays. Old Boys came trooping down from Oxford and Cambridge, and stood in front of their old hall fires in astonishing ties and wondrous waistcoats, patronising the Loder of the house, familiar only with the Charles Cave. But when they went in a body to inspect the Upper, it was seen at once that the Old Boys' Match could not take place for the ground was still thickly powdered with snow, and a swept patch proved as hard and slippery as the slide in Heriot's quad. This slide was a duly authorised institution, industriously swept and garnished by the small fry of the house under the personal supervision of old Mother Sprawson, who sent more than one of them down it barefoot, as a heroic remedy for chilblains rashly urged in excuse for absence. Indeed it was exceptionally cold, even for a nineteenth-century December. The fire in the hall was twice its usual size; the study pipes became too hot to touch, yet remained a mockery until you had your tollies going as well and every chink stopped up. Sprawson himself was understood to be relying more than ever on his surreptitious flask; but as he never betrayed the ordinary symptoms of indulgence, except before a select and appreciative audience, and could sham sober with complete success whenever necessary, these entertainments were more droll than thrilling. It was Sprawson, however, who lit up the slide with tollies after lock-up on the last night, and kept the fun fast and furious until the school bell rang sharply through the frost, and the quad opened to dispatch its quota of glowing faces to prize-giving in the big schoolroom.

The break-up concert had been given there the night before; but the final function was more exciting, with the Head Master beaming behind a barricade of emblazoned volumes, the new school list in his hand. It was fascinating to learn the new order form by form, and quite stirring to hear and abet the thunders of applause as the prize-winners went steaming up for their books and came back with them almost at a run. Crabtree was the only one whom Jan clapped heartily; he was top of his form as usual, as was Devereux lower down the school, but Jan was not going to be seen applauding Evan unduly. Chips could not keep still when it came to the Middle Remove, and even Jan sat up with a tight mouth then. On their places depended their chance of a remove out of the clutches of old Haigh. And Jan was higher than he expected to be, but Chips was higher still, with the Shocker and Jane Eyre just above him, and Buggins the lowest of the group.

"I wish to blazes old Haigh would hop it in the holidays, Tiger," said Buggins, and actually thrust his arm through Jan's on their way back through the snow. "You and I may have another term of the greaser if he don't."

Jan said little, but it was not because he was particularly surprised at the sudden friendliness of an inveterate foe. Everybody was friendly on the last day. Jane Eyre was profuse in his hospitality at tea. Shockley himself had borrowed a bit of string that he would certainly have seized a week ago; as for Chips, he had already presented Jan with a German-silver pencil-case out of his journey money. And what made these signs so remarkable was that Jan himself had never been more glum than during the last days of the term, when all the rest were packing or looking up trains, and talking about their people and all they were going to do at home, and making Jan realise that he had no home and no people to call his own.

That was not perhaps a very fair or a grateful way of putting it, even to himself; but Jan had some excuse for the bitterness of his heart. He had not received above three letters from the rectory in all these thirteen weeks; the poverty of his correspondence had in fact become notorious, because he soon ceased looking for a letter, and when there was one for him it lay on the window-sill until some fellow told him it was there. This circumstance had provided the chivalrous Shockley with yet another taunt. Then that occasional letter never by any chance enclosed a post-office order, or heralded a hamper on its way by rail; and Jan had brought so little with him in the first instance, in the way either of eatables or of pocket-money, that a time had come when he flatly refused Chips's potted-meat because he saw no chance of ever having anything to offer him in return. These of course had been among the minor troubles of the term; but they were the very ones a fellow's people might have foreseen and remedied, if they had really been his people, or cared for a moment to do the thing properly while they were about it. But all they had done was to write three times to remind him of their charity in doing the thing at all, and to impress upon him what a chance in life he was getting all through them! That again was only Jan's view of their letters, and was perhaps as ungrateful and unfair as his whole instinctive feeling towards his mother's family; but it was strong enough to make him more than ever the pariah at heart when he came down from dormitory on the last morning, in his unaccustomed bowler (but not the "loud tie" of all the bigger fellows), and partook of the meat breakfast provided in the gaslit hall; and so out into the chilling twilight, to squeeze into some omnibus because he had failed to take Chips's advice and order a trap in the middle of the term.

Jan's journey was all across country, and long before the end he had shaken off the last of his schoolfellows travelling in the same direction. It happened that he knew very few of that contingent even by name, and yet he was sorry when they had all been left behind; they were the last links with a place where he now realised that he felt more at home than he was ever likely to feel in the holidays. Eventually he reached a bleak rural station, where there was nothing to meet him, and walked up to the rectory, leaving casual instructions about his luggage.

It was not a pleasant walk; there had evidently been more snow in Norfolk than at school, and it had started to thaw while Jan was in the train. The snow stuck to his boots, and the cold was far more penetrating than it had seemed during the frost. The rectory, however, was the nearest point of the thatched and straggling hamlet of which it was also the manor house. It stood in its own park, a mile and more from the vast flint church in which a handful of people were lost at its two perfunctory services a week. The rector was in fact more squire than parson, though he wore a white tie as often as not, and conducted a forbidding form of family prayer every week-day of his life. He chanced to be the first person whom Jan saw in the grounds, on the sweep of the drive between house and lawn. On the lawn itself a lady and a number of children were busy making a snow-man; and the old gentleman, watching with amusement from the swept gravel, cut for the moment a sympathetic figure enough. Jan had to pass so close that he felt bound to go up and report his return; but no one seemed to see him, which made it awkward. He had been for some moments almost at the rector's elbow, too shy to announce himself in words, when the lady came smiling across the snow.

"Surely this is Jan, papa?" she said, whereupon the rector turned round and exclaimed: "Why, my good fellow, when did you turn up?"

Jan succeeded in explaining that he had just walked up from the station; then there was another awkward interval, in which his grandfather took open stock of him, with quite a different face from that which had beamed upon the children in the snow. The lady made amends with a readier and heartier hand, and a kind smile into the bargain.

"I'm your Aunt Alice," she announced, "and these little people are all your cousins. We've come for Christmas, so you'll have plenty of time to get to know each other."

Clearly there was no time then; the children were already clamouring for their mother's return to the work in hand, and she rejoined them with a meek alacrity that told its tale. Jan did not know whether to go or stay, until the rector relieved him by observing, "If you want anything to eat they'll look after you indoors;" and Jan accepted his dismissal thankfully, though he felt its cold abruptness none the less. But the old man had been curt and chilling to him from the first moment of their first meeting, and throughout these holidays it was to remain evident that he took no sort of interest in the schooling which it was his arbitrary whim to provide. Nor would Jan have minded this for a moment—for it was nothing new—if he had not caught such a very different old fellow smiling on the other grandchildren in the snow.

His grandmother went to the opposite extreme; she took only too much notice of the lad, for it was notice of a most embarrassing kind. Her duty towards Jan, as she conceived it, was to supplement the Public School in turning him out as much of a gentleman as was possible at this advanced stage of his development. Mrs. Ambrose began the holidays by searching through her spectacles for the first term's crop of visible improvements. Very few were brought to light by this method; but a number of inveterate blemishes were found to have survived, and each formed a subject of summary stricture as it reappeared. Mrs. Ambrose was one of those formidable old ladies whom no exigencies of time or place can restrain from saying exactly what they think. Jan could not come into a room, but her spectacles dogged his footsteps, and he was always liable to be turned back on the threshold "to wipe them properly"; if he had changed his boots, his fingers and nails came in for scrutiny instead, or it might be his collar or his hair. He seldom sat at table without hearing that he had used the wrong fork, or that knives were not made to enter mouths, even with cheese upon their point. As in the case of his reception by the rector, the lad would have been much less resentful if the other grandchildren had not been present, and their equally glaring misdemeanours consistently overlooked; he did not realise that the old lady's sight was failing, and that she deliberately had him next her "for his own good."

He disliked the other grandchildren none the less, but chiefly because his Aunt Alice was the one member of the party whom he really did like, and they would never let him have a word with her. They were the most whining, selfish, exacting little wretches; and their father spent most of his time shooting with another uncle, a soldier son of the house, and left the whole onus of correction to dear uncomplaining Aunt Alice. But now and then Jan got her to himself; and her gentle influence might have sweetened all the holidays if her eldest had not celebrated the New Year by nearly putting out Jan's eye with a snowball containing a lump of gravel. Now, Jan was externally good-tempered and long-suffering with his small cousins, but on this occasion he told the offender exactly what he thought of him, in schoolboy terms.

"I don't care what you think," retorted the child, who was quite old enough to be at a preparatory school but had refused to go to one. "Who are you to call a thing 'caddish'? You're only a stable-boy—I heard Daddy say so!"

Jan promptly committed the unpardonable sin of "bullying" by smacking the head of "a boy not half your size." It was no use his repeating in his own defence what the small boy had said to him. "And so you are!" cried his poor Aunt Alice, mixing hysterical tears with her first-born's passionate flood. And coming from those gentle lips, the words cut Jan to the heart, for he could not see that the poor soul was not a reasonable being where her children were concerned; he only saw that it was no use his trying to justify his conduct for a moment. Everybody was against him. His grandfather threatened him with a horse-whipping; his grandmother said it was "high time school began again"; and Jan broke his sullen silence to echo the sentiment rudely enough. He had to spend the rest of that day in his own room, and to support a further period of ostracism until the military uncle's return from a country-house visit. The military uncle, being no admirer of his younger nephews and nieces, took a seditious view of the heinous offence reported to him by the ladies, and backed it by tipping the offender a furtive half-sovereign at the earliest opportunity.

"I'm afraid you've been having a pretty poor time of it," said Captain Ambrose; "but take my advice and don't treat little swabs spoiling for school as though you'd actually got 'em there. They'll get there in time, thank the Lord, and I wouldn't be in their little breeches then! Found something good to read?"

"I'm not reading," said Jan, displaying the book which had occupied him in his disgrace. "I'm learning 'The Burial-March of Dundee.'"

"That sounds cheerful," remarked the captain. "So they give you saying-lessons for holiday tasks at your school?"

"I can't say what they do," replied Jan. "There's no holiday task these holidays; this is something special."

And he explained what without much hesitation, and likewise why and wherefore under friendly pressure from the gallant captain, whose sympathetic attitude was making another boy of Jan, but whose views were more treasonable than ever on the matter of the vindictive punishment meted out by Haigh.

"But I never heard of such a thing in my life!" cried he. "A master spoil a boy's holidays for something he's done at school? It's perfectly monstrous, if not illegal, and if I were you I wouldn't learn a line of it."

"I doubt I've learnt very near every line already," responded Jan, shamefacedly. "And there's a hundred and eighty-eight altogether."

"A hundred and eighty-eight lines in the Christmas holidays! I should like to have seen any of our old Eton beaks come a game like that!"

"He said he'd tell Jerry if either of us makes a single mistake when we get back."

"Let him! Thrale's an O.E. himself, and one of the very best; let your man go to him if he likes, and see if he comes away without a flea in his ear. Anyhow you shan't hang about the house to learn another line while I'm here; out you come with me, and try a blow at a bird!"

So after all Jan had a few congenial days, in which he slew his first pheasant and conceived a secret devotion to his Uncle Dick, who occasionally missed a difficult shot, but never a single opportunity of encouraging a young beginner. Now encouragement in any direction was what Jan needed even more than open sympathy and affection; and a natural quickness of hand and eye enabled him to repay the pains which were bestowed upon him. Captain Ambrose told his mother they would make something of the boy yet, if they did not worry him too much about trifles, and he only wished his own leave could last all the holidays. But he had to go about the middle of January, a few days after Aunt Alice and her party, and Jan had a whole dreary week to himself after that. It is to be feared that he spent much of the time in solitary prowling with a pipe and tobacco bought out of Uncle Dick's tip. Of course he had learnt to smoke in his stable days, and, unlike most boys, he genuinely enjoyed the practice; at any rate a pipe passed the time, albeit less nobly than a gun; but he was not allowed to shoot alone, and his grandfather never took him out, or showed the slightest interest in his daily existence under the rectory roof. His grandmother, however, continued to equalise matters with such unwearied fault-finding, and so many calls to order in the course of every day, that the end of the holidays found Jan longing for the privacy of his unsightly little study at school, and for a life in which at all events there were no old ladies and no little children.

He was therefore anything but overjoyed when a telegraph-boy tramped up through the heavy snow of what should have been the eve of his return to school, with a telegram to say that the line was blocked and it was no use his starting till the day after to-morrow. Some four hundred of these telegrams had been hurriedly dispatched from the school to the four quarters of Great Britain; and one may suppose that the other three hundred and ninety-nine had been received with acclamation as surprise packets of rapture and reprieve. But Jan took his news, not indeed without a smile, but with a very strange one for a boy of fifteen on the verge of that second term which is notorious for all the hard features of a first, without its redeeming novelty and excitement.

CHAPTER XII

THE NEW YEAR

Shockley, Eyre and Carpenter found themselves duly promoted to the Lower Fifth. Rutter and Buggins had failed to get their remove, the line being actually drawn at Jan, who therefore was left official captain of the Middle Remove. His dismay was greater than he would own to himself, but Chips was articulate enough for two on the subject of their separation in school hours. Jan, however, was less depressed about that than at the prospect of spending most of his time in the same class as Evan Devereux. It was bad enough to be "hotted" by Haigh, but how much worse before Master Evan! Jan felt that he was safe to make a bigger fool of himself than ever, and he spent the first morning in an angry glow, feeling the other's eyes upon him, and wondering what reports would go home about him now, but apparently forgetting what was hanging over Chips and himself at the hands of Haigh.

Chips, however, had not forgotten, but had written to Jan about the matter in the holidays, without receiving any reply, and had taxed him to little better purpose the moment they met. It was impossible to tell, from a certain dry, somewhat droll, and uncouthly secretive demeanour, in part product of his Yorkshire blood, which made Jan very irritating when he chose to put it on, whether he was actually word-perfect in "The Burial-March of Dundee" or not. This was Chips's sole anxiety, since he himself had left nothing to chance, when he attended Haigh after second school on the first day, and found Jan awaiting him with impassive face.

"Now, you boys!" exclaimed Haigh, when the three of them had his hall to themselves. "Begin, Carpenter."

"'Sound the fife, and cry the slogan—'" began Chips, more fluently than most people read, and proceeded without a hitch for sixteen unfaltering lines.

"Rutter!" interrupted Haigh.

But Jan made no response.

"Come, come, Rutter," said Haigh, with an unforeseen touch of compassionate encouragement, as though the holidays had softened him and last term's hatchet cried for burial with Dundee. "'Lo! we bring with us the hero'"—and in the old snarl after a pause: "'Lo! we bring the conquering Græme?'"

But even this prompting drew never a word from Jan.

"Give him another lead, Carpenter;" and this time Chips continued, more nervously, but not less accurately, down to the end of the first long stanza:

"Bade us strike for King and Country,
Bade us win the field, or fall!"

"Now then, Rutter: 'On the heights of Killiecrankie'—come on, my good boy!"

The anxious submissiveness of the really good boy, with the subtle flattery conveyed by implicit obedience to an overbearing demand, had so far mollified the master that Jan was evidently to have every chance. But he did not avail himself of the clemency extended by so much as opening his mouth.

"Have you learnt your task, or have you not, Rutter?"

And no answer even to that!

"Sulky brute!" cried Haigh, with pardonable passion. "I suppose you don't remember what was to happen if either of you failed to discharge the penalty of your dishonesty last term? But you remember, Carpenter?"

"Yes, sir."

"Carpenter, you may go; you've taken your punishment in the proper spirit, and I shall not mention your name if I can help it. You, Rutter, will hear more about the matter from Mr. Thrale to-morrow."

"Thank you, sir," said Jan, breaking silence at last, and without palpable impertinence, but rather with devout sincerity. Mr. Haigh, however, took his aversion by the shoulders and ran him out of the hall in Chips's wake.

Chips was miserable about the whole affair. He made up his mind either to immediate expulsion for his friend, or such public degradation as would bring the extreme penalty about by hardening an already obdurate and perverse heart. The worst of it was that Jan did not treat Chips as a friend in the matter, would not talk about it on the hill or in his study, or explain himself any more than he had done to Mr. Haigh. The one consoling feature of the case was that only the two boys knew anything at all about its latest development; and Chips was not the person to discuss with others that which Jan declined to discuss with him.

Next day, however, in his new form, which happened to be taken by the master who had the Lodge, there was no more absent mind than Carpenter's as second school drew to an end. It was after second school that the day's delinquents were flogged by the Head Master before the eyes of all and sundry who liked to peer through the diamond panes of his class-room windows. Chips had to pass close by on his way out of school; but there were no spectators looking on outside, no old gentleman playing judge or executioner within. In response to an anxious question Chips was informed, by a youth who addressed him as "my good man," that even old Thrale didn't start flogging on the second day of a term. Instead of being relieved by the information, he only felt more depressed, having heard that really serious cases were not taken in this public way at all, but privately in the Head Master's sanctum. Chips went back to his house full of dire forebodings, and shut himself in his study after looking vainly into Jan's; and there he was still sitting when Jan's unmistakable slipshod step brought him to his open door.

"Tiger!" he called under his breath; and there was a world of interrogation and anxiety in his voice.

"What's up now?" inquired Jan, coming in with a sort of rough swagger foreign to his habit, though Chips had observed it once or twice in the course of their confidential relations.

"That's what I want to know," said he. "What has happened? What's going to happen? When have you got to say it by?"

"I've said it."

Chips might have been knocked down with a fledgling's feather.

"You've said your Aytoun's Lay to Haigh?"

"Without a mistake," said Jan. "I've just finished saying it."

"But when on earth did you learn it, man?"

"In the holidays."

And Jan grinned uncouth superiority to the other's stupefaction.

"Then why the blazes couldn't you say it yesterday?"

"Because I wasn't going to! He'd no right to set us a holiday task of his own like that; he'd a right to do what he liked to us here, but not in the holidays, and he knew it jolly well. I wanted to see if he'd go to Jerry. I thought he durs'n't, but he did, and you bet the old man sent him away with a flea in his ear! He never got on to me all second school, and he looked another chap when he told me that Mr. Thrale said I was to be kept in till I'd learnt what I'd got to learn. It was the least he could say, if you ask me," remarked Jan, with a complacent grin, "and Haigh didn't seem any too pleased about it. So then I said I thought I could say it without being kept in, just to make him sit up a bit, and by gum it did!"

"But he heard you, Tiger?"

"He couldn't refuse, and I got through without a blooming error."

"But didn't he ask you what it all meant?"

"No fear! He'd too much sense; but he knows right enough. Instead of him sending me up to the old man, it was me that sent him, and got him the wigging he deserved, you bet!"

By this time Chips was in a fever of enthusiastic excitement, and the conclusion of the matter reduced him to a mood too demonstrative for Jan's outward liking, however much it might cheer his secret heart.

"Tiger!" was all Chips could cry, as he wrung the Tiger's paw perforce. "O, Tiger, Tiger, you'll be the hero of the house when this gets known!"

"Don't be daft," replied Jan in his own vernacular—under no restraint in Chips's company. "It's nobody's business but yours and mine. It won't do me any good if it gets all over the place."

"It won't do you any harm!" said Chips eagerly.

"It won't do me any good," persisted Jan. "Haigh knows; that's good enough for me, and you bet it's good enough for Haigh!"

And Chips respected his friend the more because there was no bid for his respect in Jan's attitude, and he seemed so unconscious of the opportunity for notoriety, or rather of its advantages as they presented themselves to the more sophisticated boy.

"But who put you up to it?" inquired Chips, already vexed with his own docility in the whole matter of the Aytoun's Lay; it would be some comfort to find that the Tiger had not thought of such a counterstroke himself. And the Tiger was perfectly candid on the point, setting forth his military uncle's views with much simplicity, and thereafter singing the captain's praises in a fashion worthy of the enthusiastic Chips himself.

"What's his initials?" exclaimed that inquirer when the surname had slipped out.

"R. N., I believe," replied the Tiger. "I know they call him Dick."

"R. N. it is!" cried Chips, and stood up before a little row of green and red volumes in his shelves. "He's the cricketer—must be—did he never tell you so?"

"We never talked about cricket," said Jan, with unfeigned indifference. "But he used to wear cricketing ties, now you remind me. One was green and black, and another was half the colours of the rainbow."

"That's the I. Z.," cried Chips, "and here we have the very man as large as life!" And he read out from the green Lillywhite of a bygone day: "'Capt. R. N. Ambrose (Eton), M.C.C. and I. Zingari. With a little more first-class cricket would have been one of the best bats in England; a rapid scorer with great hitting powers.' I should think he was! Why, he made a century in the Eton and Harrow; it's still mentioned when the match comes round. And I've got to tell you about your own uncle!"

"It only shows what he is, not to have told me himself," said Jan, for once infected with the other's enthusiasm. "I knew he was a captain in the Rifle Brigade, and a jolly fine chap, but that was all."

"Well, now you should write and tell him how you took his advice."

"I'll wait and see how it comes off first," returned Jan, with native shrewdness. "I've had my bit of fun, but old Haigh has the term before him to get on to me more than ever."

Yet on the whole Jan had a far better term in school than he expected. If, as he felt, he was deservedly deeper than ever in the master's disesteem, at least the fact was less patent and its expression less blatant than heretofore. Haigh betrayed his old animosity from time to time, but he no longer gave it free rein. He gave up loading Jan with the elaborate abuse of a trenchant tongue, and unnecessarily exposing his ignorance to the form. He started systematically ignoring him instead, treating him as a person who seldom existed, and was not to be taken seriously when he did, all of which suited the boy very well without hurting him in the least. He would have been genuinely unmoved by a more convincing display of contempt on the part of Mr. Haigh; on the other hand, he often caught that gentleman's eye upon him, and there was something in its wary glance that gave the Tiger quite a tigerish satisfaction. He did not flatter himself that the man was frightened of him, though such was in a sense the case; but he did chuckle over the thought that Haigh would be as glad to be shot of him as he of Haigh.

He had a double chuckle when, by using the brains which God had given him, and thinking for himself against all the canons of schoolboy research, he would occasionally go to the top of the class at a bound, as in the scarcely typical case of possunt quia posse videntur. On these occasions it was not only Haigh's face that was worth watching as he gave the devil his due; the flushed cheeks of Master Evan, who was quick to acquire but slower to apply, who nevertheless was nearly always top, and hated being displaced, were another sight for sore eyes. And Jan was sore to the soul about Evan Devereux, now that they worked together but seldom spoke, nor ever once went up or down the hill in each other's company, though that was just when Evan was at his best and noisiest with a gang of his own cronies.

Jan was in fact unreasonably jealous and bitter at heart about Evan, and yet grateful to him too for holding his tongue as he evidently was doing; better never speak to a chap than speak about him, and one day at least the silence was more golden than speech. Haigh was late, and Buggins, who was rather too friendly with Jan now that they were the only two of their house in the form, had described the old Tiger as his "stable companion." Evan happened to be listening. He saw Rutter look at him. His eyes dropped at once, and Rutter in turn saw the ready flush come to his cheeks. That was enough for simple Jan; everything was forgiven in the heart that so many things conspired to harden. Evan was as sensitive about his secret as he was himself!

One thing, however, was doing Jan a lot of good about this time; that was his own running in the Mile. It was very trying for him to find himself accounted a bit of a runner, and yet just too old for the Under Fifteen events; but he never dreamt of entering for any of the open ones until Sprawson gave out in the quad that he had put that young Tiger down for the Mile and Steeplechase. Jan happened to be crossing the quad at the time; he could not but stop and stare, whereupon Sprawson promised him a tremendous licking if he dared to scratch or run below the form he had shown in last term's paper-chase.

"Little boys who can run, and don't want to run, must be made to run," said Sprawson, with the ferocious geniality for which he was famed and feared.

"But it's All Ages," protested Jan aghast. "I shan't have the ghost of a chance, Sprawson."

"We'll see about that, my pippin! It's a poor entry, and some who've entered won't start, with all this eye-rot about." The pretty reference was to a mild ophthalmic affection always prevalent in the school this term. "Don't you get it yourself unless you want something worse, and don't let me catch you making a beast of yourself with cake and jam every day of your life. Both are forbidden till further orders, and ever after if you don't get through a heat! You've got to go into training, Tiger, and come out for runs with me."

And Jan said he didn't mind doing that, and Sprawson said that he didn't care whether he minded or not, but said it so merrily that Jan didn't mind that either. And away the two of them would trot in flannels down the Burston road, and then across country over much the same ground as Chips and Jan had covered on their first Sunday walk, and would get back glowing in time for a shower before school or dinner as the case might be. But Jan had to endure a good deal of "hustle" about it when Sprawson was not there, and offers of jam from everybody within reach (except Chips) at breakfast and tea, until Sprawson came over from the Sixth Form table and genially undertook to crucify the next man who tried to nobble his young colt. Sprawson would boast of the good example he himself had set by pawning his precious flask until the Finals. He was certainly first favourite for both the Mile and the Steeplechase, in one or other of which he seemed to have run second or third for years. As these two events for obscure reasons obtained more marks than any others, and as the great Charles Cave was expected to render a characteristic account of himself in the Hundred and the Hurdles, there was a strong chance of adding the Athletic Cup to the others on the green baize shelf in Heriot's hall. It might have been a certainty if only Jan had been a few weeks younger than he was. As it was he felt a fool when he turned out to run off his first heat in the Mile; his only comfort was that it would be his first and last; but he finished third in spite of his forebodings, and won some applause for the pluck that triumphed over tender years and an ungainly style.

Chips was jubilant, and Joyce vied with Buggins in impious congratulations. The Shocker volunteered venomous advice about not putting on a "roll" which only existed in his own nice mind. Heriot said a good word for the performance in front of the fire after prayers. And Sprawson took the credit with unctuous humour, but had allowed his man jam that night at tea. "Now, you fellows who were so keen on giving him some before; now's your chance!" said Sprawson. And Chips's greengage proved the winning brand, though Jane Eyre's fleshpot was undoubtedly a better offer which it went hard to decline with embarrassed acknowledgments. Neither Sprawson nor anybody else, however, expected his young colt to get a place in the second round. But by this time the field was fairly decimated by "eye-rot," and again Jan ran third; and third for the third time in the Semi-final; so that Sprawson's young 'un of fifteen and a bit actually found himself in for the Final with that worthy and four other young men with bass voices and budding moustachios.

Not that Jan looked so much younger than the rest when they stripped and toed the line together. He was beginning to shoot up, and his muscles were prematurely developed by his old life in the stable-yard; indeed, his arms had still a faintly weather-beaten hue, from long years of rolled-up sleeves, in comparison with the others. Again his was the only jersey without the trimming or the star of one or other of the football fifteens. And his ears looked rather more prominent than usual, and much redder in a strong west wind.

The quartette from other houses were Dodds (who fell on Diamond Hill), Greenhill (already running an exalted career in black gaiters), Sproule and Imeson (on whom a milder light has shone less fitfully). Poor Dodds (as you may read in that year's volume of the Magazine) "directly after the start began to make the pace, showing good promise if he had been able to keep it up. By the end of the first round he had got a good long way ahead. Imeson, however, stuck pretty near him, and the rest followed with an interval of some yards. Dodds, Imeson, and Sproule was the order maintained for the first three rounds. Towards the end of the second round, however, Dodds began to show signs of distress, and he was observed to begin to limp, owing to an old strain in his leg getting worse again with the exertion. Then Imeson, and Sproule, closely followed by Sprawson, began to gain fast on him." (Observe how long before the born miler creeps into prominence and print!) "At this point the race began to get very exciting, intense interest being manifested when, about the middle of the fourth round, Sproule and Imeson, who had gradually been lessening the distance between themselves and Dodds, now passed him; Sprawson too was coming up by degrees, and had evidently been reserving his pace for the end, having passed Dodds, he made up the ground between himself and Sproule, and passing him before the last corner, got abreast of Imeson. Both of them had a splendid spurt left, especially Sprawson, who had gained a great deal in the last half round, and now passed Imeson, breaking the tape four or five yards ahead of him. Sproule was a good third, closely followed by Rutter, who had run very pluckily and had a gallant wind."

Italics are surely excused by the extreme youth of him whom they would celebrate after all these years. They do not appear in the original account; let us requite the past writer where we can. He is not known to have followed the literary calling, but his early fondness for a "round," in preference to the usual "lap," suggests a quartogenarian whom the mere scribe would not willingly offend.

There are some things that he leaves out perforce. There is no mention of Jan's unlovely, dogged, flat-footed style, of which Sprawson himself could not cure his young 'un, while the extreme brilliance of his ears at the finish was naturally immune from comment. Posterity has not been vouchsafed a picture of the yelling, chaffing horde of schoolboys; but posterity can see the same light-hearted crowd to-morrow, only in collars not invented in those days, and straw hats in place of the little black caps with the red creased badges. The very lists are twice their ancient size, and the young knights no longer enter them in cricket-trousers tucked into their socks as in simpler times. It may be that preliminary heats do not spread over as many weeks as they did, that it was necessary to make the most of them in the days before boxing and hockey. But it is good to think that one custom is still kept up, at all events in the house that once was Heriot's. When a boy has got his colours for cricket or football, or gained marks for his house in athletics, that night at tea the captain of the house says "Well played," or "Well run, So-and-So!" And over sixty sounding palms clap that hero loud and long.

On the night of the Mile it was old Mother Sprawson, who looked round to the long table in the middle of the uproar in his honour, and himself shouted something that very few could hear. But Chips always swore that it was "Well run, Tiger!" And although there were no marks for fourth place, it is certain that for the moment the row redoubled.

CHAPTER XIII

THE HAUNTED HOUSE

Next day was a Saint's Day, which you had to yourself in the good old times from chapel in the early forenoon till private work after tea. Jan had just come out of chapel, and was blinking in the bright spring sunlight, when of a sudden his blood throbbed more than the Mile had made it. Evan Devereux had broken away from some boon companions, and was gaily smiling in Jan's path.

"I say, I do congratulate you on yesterday! Everybody's talking about it. I meant to speak to you before. That's the worst of being in different houses; we never see anything of each other, even now we're in the same form."

The boy is an artless animal; here were two, and the second simpleton outshining the first in beams of pure good-will.

"That can't be helped," said Jan, with intentionally reassuring cordiality, so that Master Evan should not think he was, or possibly could have been, offended for a single instant.

"Still, I don't see why we shouldn't help it for once," responded Evan, looking the other rather frankly up and down. "There's nothing on this morning, except the final of the School Fives, is there? Why shouldn't we go for a stroll together?"

Darkness descended upon beaming Jan like funeral pall on festal board. "I—I—I'd promised another chap," he almost groaned, with equal loyalty and reluctance.

"What other chap?"

Was it contempt in Evan's tone, or merely disappointment?

"Carpenter in our house."

"Chips Carpenter! I know him well; we were at the same old school before this. I never see enough of him either. Let's all go together."

But Jan was not through his difficulty yet. "We were going to the haunted house," he explained in a lower key. "It's an old arrangement."

"The haunted house!" exclaimed Evan in a half-tone between approval and disapproval. "I never heard of one here."

"It's a couple of miles away. They only say it's haunted. We thought we'd have a look and see."

"But is it in bounds?" inquired Evan, with some anxiety.

"I should hope so," replied Jan, unscrupulously. "But here's Chips; you ask him."

Devereux, however, despite his law-abiding instincts, was not the one to draw back when two were for going on. He was an excitable boy with a fund of high spirits, but not an infinity; they ran out sometimes when least expected. This morning, however, he was at his best, and incomparably better company than either of his companions. Jan was shy and awkward, though his soul sang with pride and pleasure. But Chips the articulate, Chips the loquacious, Chips the irrepressible in congenial company, had least of all to say, except in the bitterness of his own heart against the boy who had usurped his place.

"He's hardly spoken to either of us," Chips was saying to himself, "since the very beginning of our first term; and I should like to have seen him now, if the Tiger hadn't finished fourth in the Mile!"

The worst of the enthusiastic temperament is that it lends itself to cynicism almost as readily, and vice versa as in Jan's case now. Jan also had felt often very bitter about Evan, if not exactly against him, yet here he was basking in the boy's first tardy and almost mercenary smile. But Jan's case was peculiar, as we know; and everything nice had come together, filling his empty cup to overflowing. He might despise public-school traditions as much as he pretended for Chips's benefit, but he was too honest to affect indifference to his little succès d'estime of the day before. He knew it was not little for his age. He would have confessed it some consolation for being at school against his will—but it was not against his will that he was walking with Master Evan on equal terms this fine spring morning. He had always seen that the making or the marring of his school life lay in Evan's power. It had not been marred as it might have been by a cruel or a thoughtless tongue; it might still be made by kind words and even an occasional show of equality by one whom Jan never treated as an equal in his thoughts. He was nervous as they trod the hilly roads, but he was intensely happy. Spring was in the bold blue sky, and in the hedgerows faintly sprayed with green—less faintly if you looked at them aslant—and in Jan's heart too. Spring birds were singing, and Evan bubbling like a brook with laughter and talk of home and the holidays that Jan knew all about; yet never a word to let poor Chips into the secret of their old relations, or even to set him wondering. Any indiscretion of that sort was by way of falling from Jan himself.

"Do you ever see the Miss Christies now?" he had inadvertently inquired.

"The Christies!" Evan exclaimed, emphatically, and not without a sidelong glance at Carpenter. "Oh, yes, the girls skated on our pond all last holidays. Phyllis can do the outside edge backwards."

"She would," said Jan. "I doubt you're too big for Fanny now?"

Fanny had been Evan's pony, on which he had ridden a great deal with his friends the Christies; hence the somewhat dangerous association of ideas. He said he now rode one of the horses, when he rode at all. His tone closed that side of the subject.

"Do you remember how you used to hoist a flag, the first day of the holidays, to let the young—to let the girls know you'd got back?"

Evan turned to Carpenter with a forced laugh. "All these early recollections must be pretty boring for you," said he. "But this chap and I used to know each other at home."

"I wish we did now," said Jan. "There's nobody to speak to down in Norfolk."

"Except R. N. Ambrose," put in Chips, dryly. "I suppose you know that's his uncle?"

Devereux did not know it, and the information was opportune in every way. It reminded him that Mrs. Rutter had been a lady, and it reminded Jan himself that all his people had not sprung from the stables. It made him distinctly less liable to say "the Miss Christies" or "Master Evan." Above all it introduced the general topic of cricket, in which Chips and his statistics got a chance at last, so that in argument alone a mile went like the wind. Chips could have gained full marks in any paper set on the row of green and red booklets in his shelves. He was a staunch upholder of Middlesex cricket, but Jan and Evan were Yorkshire to the marrow, and one of them at least was glad to be heart and soul with the other in the discussion that followed. It was not a little heated as between Carpenter and Devereux and it lasted the trio until they tramped almost into the straggling and deserted street of the village famous for its haunted house.

"I suppose it's at the other end of the village. We shan't see it yet a bit."

Jan spoke with the bated breath and sparkling eye of the born adventurer; and Chips whispered volubly of ghosts in general; but Evan Devereux became silent for the first time. He was the smallest of the three boys, but much the most attractive, with his clean-cut features, his auburn hair, and that clear, radiant, tell-tale skin which even now was saying something that he found difficult to put into so many words.

"Aren't haunted houses rather rot?"

Such was his first attempt.

"Rather not!" cried Chips, the Tiger concurring on appeal.

"Still, it strikes me we're bound to be seen, and it seems rather a rotten sort of row to get into."

Carpenter was amused at the ostensible superiority of this view. It was hardly consistent with a further access of colour for which Chips was waiting before it came. He knew Devereux of old at their private school, and that what he hated above all else was getting into a row of any description. Jan might have known it, too, by the pains he took to reduce the adverse chances to decimals. Nobody was about, to see them; nobody who did would dream of reporting chaps; but for that matter, now there were three of them, one could keep watch while the other two explored. The house was no better than an empty ruin, if all Jan had heard was true, but they must have a look for themselves now that they were there. It was one of the two things worth doing at that school, let alone the games, and you had to go in for them, whether you liked them or not.

"What's the other thing?" asked Evan, with a bit of a sneer, as became one who had been longer in the school and apparently learnt less.

"Molton Tunnel."

"Yes, I have heard of that. Some fellows are fool enough to walk through it, aren't they?"

"Some who happen to have the pluck," said Chips, taking the answer on himself. "There aren't too many."

"Are you one?" inquired sarcastic Evan.

"No; but he is," returned Chips, with a jerk of the head towards Jan. "I turned tail at the last."

"Don't you believe him," says Jan, grinning. "I wouldn't take him with me; he's too blind, is Chips. Wait till he starts specs; then I'll take you both if you like. There's nothing in it. You can see one end or the other half your time; it's only a short bit where you can't see either, and then you can feel your way. But by gum it makes you mucky!"

"It'd make you muckier if you met a train," Evan suggested, with a sly stress on Jan's epithet.

"But I didn't, you see."

"You jolly nearly did," Chips would have it. "The express came through the minute after he did, Devereux."

"Not the minute, nor yet the five minutes," protested Jan. "But here we are at the end of the village, and if that isn't the haunted house I'll eat my cap!"

It stood behind a row of tall iron palings, which stand there still, but the deadly little flat-faced villa was pulled down years ago, and no other habitation occupies its site. The garden was a little wilderness even as the three boys first saw it through the iron palings. But a million twigs with emerald tips quivered with joy in the breezy sunshine. It was no day for ghosts. The house, however, in less inspiriting circumstances, might well have lent itself to evil tradition. Its windows were foul and broken, and some of them still flaunted the draggled remnants of old futile announcements of a sale by auction. Its paint was bleached all over, and bloated in hideous spots; mould and discoloration held foul revel from roof-tree to doorstep; the whole fabric cried for destruction, as the dead for burial.

"I doubt they won't have got much of a bid," said Jan, pointing out the placards. "Yet it must have been a tidy little place in its day."

He had forced the sunken gate through the weedy path, and was first within the disreputable precincts. Evan was peering up and down the empty road, and Chips was watching Evan with interest.

"I shouldn't come in," said Chips, "if I were you, Devereux."

"Why not?" demanded Evan, with instantaneous heat.

"Well, it is really out of bounds, I suppose, and some master might be there before us, having a look round, and then we should be done!"

Before an adequate retort could be concocted, Jan told Chips to go to blazes, and Evan showed his indignation by being second through the garden gate, which Carpenter shoved ajar behind them. Jan was already leading the way to the back of the house. Instinctively the boys stole gently over the weeds, though there was but a dead wall on the other side of the main road, and only open fields beyond the matted ruin of a back garden.

The back windows had escaped the stones of the village urchins, but the glass half of a door into the garden was badly smashed. Jan put in his hand to turn the key, but the door was open all the time. Inside, the boys spoke as softly as they had trodden without, and when Carpenter gave an honest shudder, Devereux followed suit with a wry giggle. It was all as depressing as it could be: mouldy papers peeling off the walls, rotting boards that threatened to let a leg clean through, and a more than musty atmosphere that made the hardy leader pull faces in the hall.

"I should like to open a window or two," said Jan, entering a room better lighted and still better aired by broken panes.

"I should start my pipe, if I were you," suggested Chips, with the perfectly genuine motive implied. But it was a pity he did not think twice before making the suggestion then.

Not that it was the first time he had thought of Jan's pipe that morning. He had been rather distressed when Jan showed it to him after the holidays, for Chips had been brought up to view juvenile smoking with some contempt; but he preferred to tolerate the smoker than to alienate the friend, and earlier in the term he had looked on at many a surreptitious rite. Jan certainly smoked as though he enjoyed it; but Sprawson had shown expert acumen when he threatened his young 'un with "hot bodkins if I catch you smoking while we're training!" And Jan had played the sportsman on the point. But to-day he was to have indulged once more, and in the haunted house of all places. Carpenter had kept an eye on the pocket bulging with Jan's pipe and pouch, wondering if Evan's presence would retard or prevent their appearance, feeling altogether rather cynical in the matter. But he had never meant to let the cat out like this, and he turned shamefacedly from Jan's angry look to Evan's immediate air of superiority.

"You don't mean to say you smoke, Rutter?"

"I always did, you know," said Jan, with uncouth grin and scarlet ears.

"I know." Evan glanced at Chips. "But I didn't think you'd have done it here."

"I don't see any more harm in it here than at home."

"Except that it's a rotten kind of row to get into. I smoke at home myself," said Evan, loftily.

"All rows are rotten, aren't they?" remarked Carpenter, with apparent innocence. But Devereux was not deceived; these two were like steel and flint to-day; and more than sparks might have flown between them if Jan had not created a diversion by creeping back into the hall.

"I'm going upstairs before I do anything else," he announced. "There's something I don't much like."

"What is it?"

"I want to see."

Jan's brows were knit; the other two followed him with instant palpitations, but close together, for all their bickering. The stairs and landing were in better case than the lower floor next the earth; the stairs were sound enough to creak alarmingly as the boys ascended them in single file. And at that all three stood still, as though they expected an upper door to open and a terrible challenge to echo through the empty house. But Jan's was the first voice heard, as he picked up a newspaper which had been left hanging on the landing banisters.

"Some sporting card's been here before us," said Jan. "Here's the Sportsman of last Saturday week."

A landing window with a border of red and blue glass, in peculiarly atrocious shades, splashed the boys with vivid colour as they stood abreast; but no light came from the upper rooms, all the doors being shut. Jan opened one of them, but soon left his followers behind in another room sweetened by a shattered pain. Their differences forgotten in the excitement of the adventure, these two were chatting confidentially enough when a dreadful cry brought them headlong to the door.

It was Jan's voice again; they could see nothing of him, but a large mouse came scuttling through an open door at the end of the landing, and almost over their toes. Carpenter skipped to one side, but Devereux dashed his cap at the little creature with a shout of nervous mirth.

"Don't laugh, you chaps!" said Jan, lurching into the doorway at the landing's end. They could not see his face; the strongest light was in the room behind him, but they saw him swaying upon its threshold.

"I can't help it," said Evan, hysterically. "Frightened by a mouse—you of all people!"

Jan turned back into the room without a word, but they saw his fist close upon the handle of the door, and he seemed to be leaning on it for support as the other two came up. "Oh, I say, we must smash a window here!" Evan had cried, with the same strained merriment, when Chips, bringing up the rear, saw the other spring from Jan's side back into the passage. Chips pushed past him, and hugged Jan's arm.

It was not another empty room; there was a tall fixed cupboard between fireplace and window, its door standing as wide open as the one where the two boys clung together; and in the cupboard hung a suit of bursting corduroys, with a blackened face looking out of it, and hobnail boots just clear of the floor.

"Dead?" whispered Chips through chattering teeth.

"Dead for days," Jan muttered back. "And he's come in here and hung himself in the haunted house!"

Crashing noises came from the stairs; it was Evan in full flight, jumping many at a time. Chips was after him on the instant, and Jan after Chips when he had closed the chamber of death behind him.

The horrified boys did not go by the gate as they had come, but smashed the rotten fence at the end of the awful garden in the frenzy of their flight across country. It was as though they had done the hideous deed themselves; over the fields they fled pell-mell, up-hill and down-dale, through emerald-dusted hedge and brimming ditch, as in a panic of blood-guiltiness. Spring still smiled on them sunnily, breezily. Spring birds welcomed them back with uninterrupted song. The boys had neither eyes nor ears, but only bursting hearts and breaking limbs, until a well-known steeple pricked the sky, and they flung themselves down in a hollow between a ploughed field, rich as chocolate, and a meadow alive with ewes and lambs.

Chips was speechless, because he was not supposed to run; but Evan, a notoriously dapper little dandy, seldom to be seen dishevelled out of flannels, was the one who looked least like himself. He lay on his stomach in the fretted shadow of a stunted oak. But Jan sat himself on the timber rails between bleating lambs and chocolate furrows, and made the same remarks more than once.

"It's a bad job," said Jan at intervals.

"But are you sure about it?" Evan sat up to ask eventually. "Are you positive it was a man, and that the man was dead?"

"I can swear to it," said Jan.

"So can I," wheezed Chips, who was badly broken-winded. "And that's what we shall have to do, worse luck!"

"Why?" from Evan.

"How can we help it?"

"Nobody saw us go in or come out."

"Then do you mean to leave a dead man hanging till his head comes off?"

Chips had a graphic gift which was apt to lead him a bit too far. Devereux, looking worried, and speaking snappily, promptly told him not to be a beast.

"I didn't mean to be, but I should think myself one if I slunk out of a thing like this without a word to anybody."

"I don't see what business it is of ours."

"The man may have a wife and kids. They must be half-mad to know what's become of him."

"We can't help that. Besides—"

Evan stopped. Jan was not putting in his word at all, but stolidly listening from his perch.

"Besides what, Devereux?"

"Oh, nothing."

"Of course we shall get into a row," Chips admitted, cruelly; "but I shouldn't call it a very rotten one, myself. It would be far rottener to try to avoid one now, and it might get us into a far worse row."

Evan snorted an incoherent disclaimer, to the general effect that the consequences were of course the very last consideration with him, at all events so far as his own skin went. He was quite ready to stand the racket, though he had been against the beastly haunted house from the first, and it was rather hard luck on him. But what he seemed to feel still more strongly was the hard luck on all their people, if the three of them had to give evidence at an inquest, and the whole thing got into the papers.

Chips felt that he would rather enjoy that part, but he did not say so, and Jan still preserved a Delphic silence.

"Besides," added Devereux, returning rather suddenly to his original ground, "I'm blowed if I myself could swear I'd ever seen the body."

"You wouldn't," remarked Jan, sympathetically. "You didn't have a good enough look."

"Yet you saw enough to make you bolt," said that offensive Chips, and opened all the dampers of Evan's natural heat.

"It wasn't what I saw, my good fool!" he cried angrily. "You know as well as I do what it was like up there. That's the only reason I cleared out."

"Well, there you are!" said Jan, grinning aloft on his rail.

"Then you agree with Carpenter, do you, that it's our duty to go in and report the whole thing, and get a licking for our pains?"

Carpenter laughed satirically at the "licking," but refrained from speech. He knew of old that Evan's horror of the rod was on a par with the ordinary citizen's horror of gaol. And he could not help wanting Jan to know it—but Jan did.

Once, in the very oldest days, when the pretty boy and the stable brat were playing together for almost the first time, the boy had broken a window and begged the brat to father the crime. Jan would not have told Chips for worlds; indeed, he was very sorry to have recalled so dim an incident out of the dead past; but there it was, unbidden, and here was the same inveterate abhorrence, not so much of actual punishment, but of being put in an unfavourable light in the eyes of others. That was a distinctive trait of Evan's, peculiar only in its intensity. Both his old companions were equally reminded of it now. But Jan's was the hard position! To have got in touch with Evan at last, to admire him as he always had and would, and yet to have that admiration promptly tempered by this gratuitous exhibition of a radical fault! Though he put it to himself in simpler fashion, this was Jan's chief trouble, and it would have been bad enough just then without the necessity that he foresaw of choosing between Chips and Evan.

"I don't know about duty," he temporised, "but I don't believe we should be licked."

"Of course we shouldn't!" cried Chips. "But it wouldn't kill us if we were."

"You agree with him?" persisted Evan, in a threatening voice of which the meaning was not lost on Jan. It meant out-of-touch again in no time, and for good!

"I don't know," sighed Jan. "I suppose we ought to say what we've seen; and it'll pay us, too, if it's going to get out anyhow; but I do think it's hard on you—Devereux. We dragged you into it. You never wanted to come in; you said so over and over." Jan gloomed and glowered, then brightened in a flash. "Look here! I vote us two tell Heriot what we've seen, Chips! Most likely he won't ask if we were by ourselves; he's sure to think we were. If he does ask, we can say there was another chap, but we'd rather not mention his name, because he was dead against the whole thing, and never saw all we did!"

Jan had unfolded his bright idea directly to Carpenter, whose opinion he awaited with evident anxiety. He resented being placed like this between the old friend and the new, and having to side with one or the other, especially when he himself could not see that it mattered so very much which course they took. They could not bring the dead man back to life. On the whole he supposed that Chips was right; but Jan would have held his tongue with Evan against any other fellow in the school. It was the new friend, however, who had been the true friend these two terms, and it was not in Jan's body to go against him now, though he would have given a bit of it to feel otherwise.

"If that's good enough for Devereux," said Chips, dryly, "it's good enough for me. But I'm blowed if I could sleep till that poor chap's cut down!"

Devereux now became far from sure that it was good enough for him; in fact he declared nearly all the way back that he would own up with the others, that they must stand or fall together, even if he himself was more sinned against than sinning. That was not indeed the expression he used, but the schoolboy paraphrase was pretty close, and his companions did not take it up. Chips, having gained his point, was content to look volumes of unspoken criticism, while Jan felt heartily sick of the whole discussion. He was prepared to do or to suffer what was necessary or inevitable, but for his part he had talked enough about it in advance.

Evan, however, would not drop the subject until they found the familiar street looking cynically sleepy and serene, the same and yet subtly altered to those young eyes seared with a horror to be fully realised only by degrees. It began to come home to them now, in the region of other black caps with red badges, and faces that met theirs curiously, as though they showed what they had seen. Their experience was indeed settling over them like a blight, and two of the trio had forgotten all about the consequences when the third blushed up and hesitated at Heriot's corner.

"Of course," he stammered, "if you found, after all, that you really were able to keep my name out of it, I should be awfully thankful to you both, because I never should have put my nose into the beastly place alone. But if it's going to get you fellows into any hotter water I'll come forward like a shot."

"Noble fellow!" murmured Carpenter as the pair turned into their quad.

"You shut up!" Jan muttered back. "I've a jolly good mind not to open my own mouth either!"

But he did, and in the event there was no call upon Evan's nobility. Heriot knew that the two boys who came to him after dinner were always about together, and he was too much disturbed by what they told him to ask if they had been alone as usual. He took that for granted, in the communications which he lost no time in making both to the police and to the Head Master, who took it for granted in his turn when the pair came to his study in the School House. He was very stern with them, but not unkind. They had broken bounds, and richly deserved the flogging he would have given them if their terrible experience were not a punishment in itself; it was indeed a very severe one to Carpenter, who was by this time utterly unstrung; but Rutter, who certainly looked unmoved, was reminded that this was the second time he had escaped his deserts for a serious offence, and he was grimly warned against a third. If they wished to signify their appreciation of his clemency, the old man added, they would both hold their tongues about the whole affair.

And the two boys entered into a compact to that effect between themselves, though not without considerable reluctance on the part of poor Chips, who felt that he was locking up the conversational capital of a school lifetime. Yet within a week the adventure was being talked about, and that despite the fact that the Chief Constable of the county, an old friend of Heriot's, had prevailed upon the County Coroner to dispense with the actual evidence of either boy.

Jan asked Chips if he had told anybody, only to meet with an indignant denial.

"I've never said a word, my good Tiger!"

"Well, I haven't, that's a sure thing."

"Then it must be Devereux."

"I thought you'd say that," said Jan, but kept his ears open in form, and actually overheard Evan boasting of the adventure before Haigh came in. Moreover, as he was not questioned about it himself, Jan was forced to the conclusion that Evan was acting on the principle of one good turn deserving another, and leaving out every name but his own.

"Well?" asked Chips when next they met.

"Well, I'm afraid you're right; and I don't know what to think of it," said poor Jan, hiding his feelings as best he could.

"I won't say what I think," returned Chips.

And he never did.

CHAPTER XIV

"SUMMER-TERM"

"O Summer-Term, sweet to the Cricketer, whose very existence is bliss;
O Summer-Term, sweet to the Editor, who needs write but two numbers of this—"

"But he doesn't write them," objected Jan, "any more than the captain of a side makes all the runs."

"Oh! I know it should be 'edit,' but that doesn't scan," explained Chips, and continued:

"O Summer-Term, sweet to the sportsman, who makes a good book on the Oaks—"
"Why the Oaks?" interrupted Jan again. "Why not the Derby, while you are about it?"

Chips told him he would see, confound him!

"O Summer-Term, sweet to the Jester, who's plenty of food for his jokes!"
"I see; but not enough rhymes for them, eh?"

"That's about it, I suppose."

Chips was laughing, though Jan was just a little too sardonic for him, as had often been the case of late. The scene was the poet's study, and the time after lock-up on a Sunday evening, when the friends always sat together until prayers. The tardy shades of early June were intensified by the opaque window overlooking the road and only opening at the top. Chips had his candles burning, and the minute den that he kept so spick and span, with its plush frames brushed, and its little pictures seldom out of the horizontal, looked quite fascinating in the two dim lights. The poet, looking the part in pince-nez started in the Easter holidays, was seated at his table; the critic lounged in the folding chair with the leg-rest up and a bag of biscuits in his lap.

The evolution of the Poet Chips was no novelty to Jan, who had been watching the phenomenon ever since Chips had received a Handsome Book as second prize for his "The school-bell tolls the knell of parting play," in a parody competition in Every Boy's Magazine. That secret triumph had occurred in their first term, and Chips had promptly forwarded a companion effort ("In her ear he whispers thickly") to the School "Mag.," in which it was publicly declined with something more than thanks. "C.—Your composition shows talent, but tends to vulgarity, especially towards the end. Choose a more lofty subject, and try again!" C. did both without delay, in a shipwreck lay ("The sea was raging with boisterous roar") which impressed Jan deeply, but only elicited "C.—Very sorry to discourage you, but—" in the February number. Discouraged poor C. had certainly been, but not more than was now the case under the grim sallies of his own familiar friend.

It was really too bad of Jan, whose Easter holidays had been redeemed by a week of bliss at the Carpenters' nice house near London. The two boys had done exactly what they liked—kept all hours—seen a play or two, besides producing one themselves ("Alone in the Pirates' Lair") in a toy theatre which showed the child in old Chips alongside the precocious poetaster. But even Jan had printed programmes and shifted scenes with a zest unworthy of the heavier criticism.

"Go it, Chips!" cried the critic through half a biscuit. "It's first-class; let's have some more."

But Chips only went it for another couplet:—

"When 'tis joy on one's rug to be basking, and watching a match on the Upper,
When the works of J. Lillywhite, junior, rank higher than those of one Tupper—"

"Who's he when he's at home?" inquired the relentless Jan.

"Oh, dash it all, you want to know too much! You're as bad as the old man; last time our form showed up verses to him I'd got Olympus, meaning sky. 'Who's your friend Olympus?' says Jerry, with a jab of his joiner's pencil. And now you say the same about poor old Tupper!"

"I didn't; but who is your friend Tupper?"

"He's no friend of mine," explained candid Chips, "but I'd a good rhyme ready for him, so he came in handy, like my old pal Olympus at the end of a hexameter. I expect he's some old penny-a-liner. 'Tupper and Tennyson, Daniel Defoe,' as the song says."

Chips might or might not have been able to say what song he meant. His mind was full of the assorted smatterings of an omnivorous but desultory reader, and he never had time to tidy it like his study. He sat pinching the soft rim of one of the candles into a chalice that overflowed and soused his fingers in hot grease. He was not going to read any more aloud, because he knew what rot it all was; but there Jan warmly contradicted him, until he was allowed to listen to the rest like a better friend.

Yet just then Jan was not at his best as friend or companion; and it did rather try his temper to have to listen to fulsome numbers on a sore subject.

"An ode to the balmiest season endowed us by Nature's decree,
A wild panegyric in praise of the jolliest term of the three!"

So Chips chose to characterise his doggerel and its theme; but as he rarely made a run at cricket, and was always upset about it, Jan could not think why. He only knew it was not "the jolliest term of the three" for him, but quite the unluckiest so far, despite the fact that he was free at last from the clutches of Mr. Haigh. It was out of school that the bad luck of his first term had repeated itself in aggravated form; his cricket had been knocked on the head even quicker than his football.

Cricket in a public school is a heavy sorrow to the average neophyte; if he goes with a reputation, he will get his chance; unknown talent has to wait for it, mere ardour is simply swamped. Jan had not only no reputation, but no private school where he could say that he had played the game. He did not know he was a cricketer, nor was he at that time any such thing; but he was a natural left-hand bowler. He began the term talking about "notches" instead of runs, "scouting" instead of fielding, and a "full" ball when he meant a fast one. Once he even said "cuddy-handed" for "left-handed," in speaking of his own bowling to Chips. Luckily they were alone at the time. Chips was shocked to find his friend so unversed in the very alphabet of cricket, and began coaching him out of Lillywhite without delay. Yet the first three balls which Jan delivered, at their first net, did an informal hat-trick at the expense of the theoretical exponent of the game.

Chips, having had his stumps disturbed a great many times on that occasion, went about talking more generously than wisely of the Tiger's prowess with the ball; for he was already accounted a bit of a windbag about the game, and his personal ineptitude soon found him out. Chips had put his name down for the Lower Ground, and Jan his for the adjoining Middle, owing to his decidedly superior stature. But there were plenty of lusty louts on the Middle, and Jan had to go some days without a game; when he got one he was not put on to bowl; and May was well advanced before he found himself taking wickets in the second Middle game.

It was Shockley of all people who had tossed the ball to him, with a characteristic reference to poor Chips's vicarious bragging. "That young lubber Carpenter says you can bowl a bit; if you can't I'll give the ruddy little liar the biggest licking he's ever had in his life!" It was significant that Jan himself was not threatened with violence; but perhaps it was the Shocker's subtlety that devised the surest means of putting the new bowler on his mettle. The fact remains that Jan shambled up to the wicket, gave an ungainly twiddle of the left arm, and delivered a ball that removed the leg bail after pitching outside the off stump.

The defeated batsman proceeded to make a less creditable stand than the one the Tiger had broken up. "I'm not going," said he, without stirring from the crease.

"You jolly well are!" thundered Shockley, who was first captain of the game. "The umpire didn't give it a no-ball, did he?"

"No, and he didn't give me guard, either. New guard for a left-hand bowler, if you don't mind, Shockley; you should have said he was one."

"I'm blowed if I knew," replied the Shocker, truly enough, and turned from the other big fellow to the luckless bowler. "Why the blue blazes didn't you tell us, Rutter?"

"I never thought of it, Shockley."

Curses descended on Jan's head; but the batsman would have to go. The batsman stuck to his crease. The umpires, as usual the two next men in, had a singular point to settle; one gave it "out" with indecent promptitude, and so off with his coat; the other umpire, a younger boy in the batsman's house, was not so sure.

Jan offered a rash solution of the difficulty.

"Suppose I bowl him out again?" he suggested with the dryest brand of startling insolence.

"I don't know your beastly name," cried the batsman, "but you'll know more about me when the game's over."

"Quite right," said Shockley; "it'll do the young lubber all the good in the world." And partly because the batsman was an even bigger fellow than himself, partly out of open spite against Jan, the Shocker allowed the game to proceed.

The batsman took fresh guard, and Jan his shambling run. This time the ball seemed well off the wicket, and the batsman took a vindictive slash, only to find his off stump mown down.

"You put me off, you devil!" he cried, shaking his bat at Jan; but this time he did retire, to vow a vengeance which in the event he was man enough not to take. For the formidable Tiger had secured the remaining wickets at a nominal cost.

In any other game, on any one of the three grounds, such a performance would have led to the player's immediate promotion to the game above; but Shockley managed to keep Jan down, and on his own side, over the next half-holiday, when another untoward event marked the progress of the second Middle game.

It was a rainy day, hardly fit for cricket, but sawdust was a refinement then unknown on the Middle, and Jan would not have understood its uses if it had been there. He had never bowled with a wet ball before, and he lost his length so completely that Shockley abused him like a pickpocket, and took him off after a couple of expensive overs. But nobody else could do any better, and Jan had just resumed when a half-volley was returned between himself and mid-off. Jan shot out his left hand, but the wet ball passed clean through his fingers, which he shook with pain while a single was being run. He was about to bowl again before he observed blood pouring over his flannels, from his bowling hand. It was split so badly that he could see between the knuckles of the second and third fingers.

He went dripping to the doctor who had falsely convicted him of a heart. That practitioner was out, and the dripping ceased before he came in; so he washed nothing, but strapped the two fingers together in their drying blood, and in the next three weeks they grew almost into one. The greater part of that time Jan carried his arm in a sling, and the days were full of ironies not incorporated by Chips in his gushing pæan. House matches began, and in the Under Sixteen Heriot's were promptly defeated by a side which must have perished before a decent bowler; in the All Ages, in spite of Charles Cave and the runs he could not help making in house matches, they only survived one round; and Chips would have it that even there Jan would just have made the difference. It is right to add that the rest of the house did not realise their loss, though Shockley might have made them if he had chosen. Then the Elevens came out, and Jan was not even in the Fifth Middle, then the lowest on the ground; Chips just scraped into the Fourth Lower, the lowest Eleven of all, and one for which (to his grief) no cap was given.

Founder's Day came with the Old Boys' Match, and a galaxy of gay and brilliant young men, from whom a very good side was chosen to do battle against the school; and Founder's Day was a whole holiday, when you were free to take your rug to the Upper directly after chapel. Jan took his ball as well, because his arm was out of a sling, though he was still forbidden to play in a game. That did not prevent him from bowling to one of the long line of cricketers who stuck single stumps down the length of the white palings that bounded the ground on one side. Volunteer batteries bombarded each, but Jan's batsman eventually requested the other volunteers to wait while the left-hander gave him a little practice. And after that (but not before the single stump had been laid low once) the Old Boy asked Jan his name, and why he was not bowling for the school; it is true that he was laughing as he spoke, and a knot of listeners laughed louder, which sent Jan off to his rug in some little dudgeon.

There Chips soon joined him with a startling statement to the effect that Jan's fortune was as good as made. "I suppose you know who it was you were bowling to?" he inquired in self-defence against the Tiger's claws.

"No, I don't, and I don't care either."

"It's only A. G. Swallow!"

"I never heard of him."

"He was captain here before we were born, and only about the best all-round man we ever turned out! He's played for the Gentlemen again and again."

"What's that to me?"

"It may be everything! He went straight up to Dudley Relton and told him all about you. I'll swear he did. I saw him imitate your action—no mistaking it—and I saw Relton look this way."

Jan did not affect any further indifference; but he refused to accept a sanguine interpretation of the alleged interview. Dudley Relton was a new master that term, but as an Oxford cricketer his fame was scarcely past its height. He had led that University at Lord's the very year before; and here he was in the van of a new movement, as perhaps the earliest pioneer of the so-called "cricket master" to whom the school professional now plays second fiddle. The innovation was characteristic of Mr. Thrale, and not out of harmony with a general feeling that no mere player could replace the giant who had completed his mortal innings since Chips and Jan obtained their first school caps of him. It remained to be seen, however, whether Dudley Relton was the right man in an anomalous place. It was said that he was disposed to interfere with the composition of the Eleven, that a strong captain would have put him in his place, that the great Charles Cave had done so on his own account, and that Dudley Relton had still to justify his existence as a professed discoverer of buried talent. Of such material Chips constructed a certain castle in the air, and put in Jan as tenant for the term of his school life; and was so full of his unselfish dream that the July Mag., actually containing the "wild panegyric in praise of the jolliest term of the three," came out, as it were, behind the poet's back; and he had the rare experience of hearing himself quoted before he saw himself in print.

It was after second school, and Chips had gone into hall to see the cricket in the papers. He found a group of fellows skimming the new Magazine, just out that minute, and chuckling indulgently over some item or other in its contents.

"That's not bad about 'basking on the rugs on the Upper,'" remarked Crabtree, critically; and Chips felt his heart between his teeth.

"The whole thing isn't bad," affirmed no other than Charles Cave, and that made Chips feel as though a royal palm had rested on his head; but there was just an element of doubt about the matter, owing to Crabtree's slight misquotation, which was more than literary flesh and blood could stand.

"You might let me see!" gasped Chips, at Crabtree's elbow.

"Why should I?" demanded that worthy, with all the outraged dignity of his very decided seniority.

Chips knew too well that he had taken a liberty which the actual circumstances alone could excuse; but nobody else was listening yet, so he whispered in Crabtree's ear, "Because I wrote it!"

"You what?" cried Crabtree, irritably.

"I wrote that thing."

"What thing?"

Everybody was listening now.

"That thing you're reading about 'Summer-Term,'" said Chips shamefacedly.

"What a lie!" cried half the fellows in the hall.

"It isn't. I swear I did."

Charles Cave was too great a man either to pass any comment on the situation, or to withdraw the one he had already made on the verses themselves. But Crabtree was nodding his great red head with intimidating violence.

"Oh! so you wrote the thing, did you?"

"I did, I swear!"

"Then it's the greatest rot I ever read in my life," said Crabtree, "and the most infernal piece of cheek for a kid of your standing!"

Chips never forgave himself for not having held his tongue; but there was something bracing both about this rough sally and the laugh it raised. The laughter at any rate was not ill-natured, and Chips received a good many compliments mingled with the chaff to which his precocious flight exposed him. He was always sorry that he had not held his tongue and enjoyed the sweets of anonymity a little longer. But nothing could rob him of that great moment in which Cave major praised "the whole thing" in the highest schoolboy terms, which were not afterwards retracted.

CHAPTER XV

SPRAWSON'S MASTERPIECE

Sprawson was among those who congratulated the author of the "wild panegyric," though his praise was tempered with corporal punishment for the use of the word "eulogic" in the same opening stanza. Sprawson declared it was not a word at all, but the base coinage of the poetaster's brain, and when Chips showed him the epithet in a dictionary he got another cuff for defending the indefensible. A man of unsuspected parts was Sprawson; but there was no venom in his hearty violence. It was Sprawson who told Jan he had heard he was a bit of a bowler, and promised him a game on the Upper before the term was out and a licking if he got less than five wickets. Sprawson himself was no cricketer, but as Athletic Champion he had been made captain of the second game on the Upper Ground.

He was a youth who took few things as seriously as his own events in the sports. He loved to pose as a prematurely hard liver, and perhaps he was one; the famous flask had been known to smell of spirits. He came into sharp contact at times with Heriot, who, however, had early diagnosed him as a rather theatrical villain, and treated him accordingly as a clown. Even Sprawson, even in the summer term, with Satan continually on his idle hands, got no change out of Mr. Heriot; but with a man like the unfortunate Spook he was a terrible handful. The Spook took the Upper Fifth, in which Sprawson had lain comfortably fallow for several terms: relays of moderate workers, who had found and left him there, compared notes upon his insolent audacity in what was known indeed as "Sprawson's form." How he would daily affix the page of Horace or of Sophocles by drawing-pin to the boys' side of the Spook's tall desk, and read off his "rep" under the master's nose; how methodically he devoured the Sportsman behind a zariba of dictionaries, every morning of his life in second school, and how the cover of his Bible was profaned as the cloak of fiction not to be found in the school library; these were but a few of the practices and exploits of Sprawson that were common talk not only in the school but among the younger masters. And yet when the Heriots lost an aged father in July, and hurried across England to the funeral, who but the gallant Spook should volunteer to look after the house in their absence!

The staff were divided as to whether it was an act of heroic hardihood or of supreme insensibility on the volunteer's part; they were perhaps most surprised at Heriot, who knew the Spook as well as they did, but had been in no mood to resist his dashing importunity. It was not the house that they distrusted as a whole. Heriot was a great house-master, though on principle disinclined to pick and choose as sedulously as some of them; he conceived it his whole duty to make the best of the material that came his way unsought; but he had not made much of Sprawson, and it was with Sprawson that the solicitous staff were reckoning on their colleague's account.

It did not say much for their knowledge of boys, as the Spook himself told them in common-room next day. Apparently the house was behaving like a nonconformist chapel. Cave major was indeed stated to have tried his haughty and condescending airs on the great proconsul, but without success according to proconsular report.

"I introduced a pestiferous insect into the young fellow's auricle," boasted the Spook; "our good Heriot will find his stature reduced by a peg or two, if I mistake not. As for the rest of the house, I can only say I have been treated as a gentleman by gentlemen—quorum pars maxima my friend Sprawson. His is a much misjudged character. I begin to fear that I myself have done him less than justice in form. I have been harsh with him—too harsh—poor Sprawson! And now he heaps coals of fire on my head; it has touched me deeply—deeply touched me—I assure you. He has quite constituted himself my champion in the house; amusing, isn't it? As if I needed one. But I haven't the heart to say him nay. A new boy, with a misguided sense of postprandial humour, brings me an order to sign for a ton of candles; only a ton, to go on with, I suppose. I just say, 'Make it out for a truck!' But what does Sprawson? I send the young gentleman about his business; back he comes, sobbing his little heart out in apologies for which I never stipulated. I had reckoned without my Sprawson! Sprawson, I fear, had spared neither rod nor child; the little man was in a pitiable state until I promised to tell Sprawson I had forgiven him. Sprawson, a thorn in my form, who must be sat upon, but the white rose of chivalry in his house!"

That was not the only instance. There had been some tittering at prayers. Sprawson had picked up the offenders like kittens, and gently hurled them into outer darkness; and now the house could not have been better behaved if it had accompanied poor Heriot on his sad errand. It was all quite true. Sprawson was ruling the house with a rod of iron. The order for the ton of candles was the instigation of some minor humorist, who caught it hotter than the tearful apologist. The giggling at prayers was a real annoyance to Sprawson. He meant the house to behave itself in Heriot's absence; he was going to keep order, whatever Loder did. This to Loder's face, after prayers, with half the house listening, and Charles Cave, standing by with his air of supercilious detachment, but without raising voice or finger in defence of his brother præpostor.

The house went to bed like mice. Joyce in his partition used blood-curdling language about Sprawson, and Crabtree's criticism was not the less damaging for being fit for publication in the Times. They were alike, however, in employing a subdued tone, while Bingley and Jan exchanged lasting impressions in a whisper. Chips was still in another dormitory, where he was not encouraged to air his highly-coloured views; but the conversion of Sprawson in the hour of need was to him more like a page out of Bret Harte than any incident within his brief experience.

The house had seldom been sooner asleep. In the little dormitory Crabtree was the first to return no answer to Joyce, who told the other two to shut up as well, and was himself soon indulging in virtuous snores. There was no more talking in the neighbouring dormitory either, and none in the one downstairs so far as Jan could hear before he also sank into the heavy sleep of active youth.

It took a tremendous shaking to wake him up. It was not morning; it was the middle of the night. Yet there were mutterings and splutterings in the other partitions, and an unceremonious hand had Jan by the shoulder.

"Get up, will you? It's a case of burglars! All the chaps are getting up to go for them; but you can hide between the sheets if you like it better."

And Crabtree retreated to his corner as Jan swung his feet to the ground. He was still quite dazed; he asked whether anybody had told Heriot.

"Heriot's away, you fool!" Joyce reminded him in a stage whisper.

"That's why they've come," explained Bingley, in suppressed excitement. "They've seen his governor's death in the papers. I'll bet you it's a London gang."

Bingley was more than ever the precocious expert in matters criminal. He had seen a man condemned in the Easter holidays. But this was the night of Bingley's life.

Sounds of breakage came from Joyce's 'tish. "I'm not going down unarmed," said he. "Who wants a rung of my towel rail?" Crabtree and Bingley were supplied in the darkness. "None left for you, Rutter; take a boot to heave at their heads."

"I'll take my jug," said Jan, emptying it into his basin; "it'll do more damage."

"Come on, you chaps!" urged Crabtree. "He'll have got the Spook by this time."

Instinctively Jan guessed that the pronoun stood for old Mother Sprawson, and he was right. It was that born leader of boys and men who had alarmed the dormitories before going through into the private part to summon the Spook from his slumbers; but where the thieves were now, what damage they had done, or who had discovered their presence in the house, Jan had no idea as he accompanied the others down the leaden stairs. Here there was more light, or at any rate less darkness, for a fine moon streamed through skylight and staircase window, and spectre forms were drifting downward through its pallid rays. It was still the day of the obsolete nightshirt, and that ghostly garment was at its best or worst upon a moonlight night. Some boys had tucked theirs into their trousers; a few had totally eclipsed themselves in jackets or dressing-gowns as well; but the majority came as they had risen from their beds, white and whispering, tittering a little, but not too convincingly at first, and for the most part as ignorant of what had happened as Jan himself.

At the foot of the stairs, on the moonlit threshold of the open door into the quad, two portentous figures dammed the descending stream of unpresentable attire: one was the Spook, his master's gown (and little else that could be seen) covering his meagre anatomy, but in his hand a Kaffir battle-axe which usually hung over Heriot's stairs. His companion was the redoubtable Sprawson, a pioneer in striped pyjamahs, armed for his part with a carving-knife of prodigious length which was daily used in hall.

"My good boys!" expostulated the Spook. "My good boys! I wish you'd go back to your beds and leave the intruder to me!"

"We couldn't do that, sir," said one or two. "We'll stand by you, sir, never fear!"

"My brave lads! I wish you wouldn't, I do really. He'll have short shrift from me, I promise you. Short shrift—"

"Silence!" hissed Sprawson, as a titter spread on the stairs. "I'll murder the fellow who laughs again!" and his carving-knife filled with moonlight from haft to point. "It's no laughing matter. They've been at Mr. Heriot's silver; the dining-room's ransacked. I heard them come through this way; that made me look out. One at least is hiding in the studies."

"I'll hide him!" said the Spook, readily.

"Silence!" commanded Sprawson, with another flourish of his dreadful blade. "If you will make jokes, sir, we shall never have a chance; are we to take the whole house with us, or are we not?"

"I don't like leaving them behind, Sprawson, to the tender mercies of any miscreants whose ambush we may have overlooked. Are the whole house there?" inquired the Spook.

"Yes, sir! Yes, sir!" from a dozen tongues, and another terrifying "Silence!" from Sprawson.

"Shall I call over, sir?" suggested Loder, emerging from obscurity to raise a laugh from the rank and file. Sprawson was too quick for him with crushing snub; he was surprised at the captain of the house: what next? So the laugh that came was at Loder's expense, but it again was promptly quelled by the inimitable Sprawson.

"If we waste any more time here, sir, they'll have the bars off the back study-windows and get clean away. I believe all the house are here. I should let them come, sir, if I were you; there's safety in numbers, after all."

"Then I lead the way," said the Spook, diving under the raised carving-knife. "No, Sprawson, not even to you, my gallant fellow; second to none, if you'll permit me, Sprawson, on this occasion. Follow me, my lads, follow me!"

And follow him they did on bare tip-toe, over the cold flags of the alley alongside the hall, and so out into the untrammelled moonlight of the quad. Sure enough, the nearer door to the studies was seen to be ajar. But as the Spook approached it boldly, Sprawson plucked him by the gown.

"The fives-courts, sir! I thought I saw something moving behind the back-wall!"

All eyes flew to the fives-courts at the opposite end of the quad; the back-wall, their unorthodox peculiarity as Eton courts, would have sheltered a band of robbers until the last moment, when their pursuers peeping over might be shot down comfortably at arm's length. No better bulwark against carving-knives and battle-axes, no finer mask for a whole battery of small-arms; and yet the valiant Spook was for advancing single-footed, under that treacherous moon, upon this impregnable position. Sprawson would not hear of it; together, said Sprawson, or not at all, even if he got expelled for lifting his hand against a master. The master shook it melodramatically instead, and with a somewhat painful gait the pair started off across the stretch of moonlit gravel. Jan was the next to follow, with his jug; but all the small dormitory, being more or less armed, were to the fore in an advance which became all but universal before the leaders reached the rampart. Cave major alone had the wit to stay behind, a majestic rearguard with his hands in his dressing-gown pockets, and something suspiciously like a cigarette between his lips.

The courts were discovered empty at a glance; yet Sprawson seized Jan's jug, and dashed it to fragments against the buttress in the outer court while the Spook was busy peering into the inner.

"I thought I saw something move behind the pepper-box," explained Sprawson. "Very sorry, sir! I'll buy a new one. I'm ashamed of showing such bad nerve."

"Bad nerve! You're a hero, Sprawson. I'll pay for it myself," the Spook was saying, kindly enough, when a piercing "Yoicks!" rang out from the deserted end of the quad.

Charles Cave was holding his cigarette behind his back, and waving airily to the study windows with the other hand.

"It's all right, sir; you needn't hurry; only I thought you might like to know there was a light up there this minute!"

The stampede back across the gravel was in signal contrast to the stealthy and circumspect advance; and many a late laggard found himself swept off his feet in the van; but Sprawson outstripped all with a rush that spilt the small fry right and left, and he was first up the study stairs. But the Spook panted after him, and once more insisted on taking the actual lead.

The procession which he headed down the long study passage was no longer the somewhat faltering force which had deployed in the moonlit quad; it was as though confidence had come with protracted immunity, and high spirits had come of confidence; in any case, Sprawson had to lay about him more than once to stop a giggle or a merry scuffle in the dark. He appealed to Loder to keep better order (Cave major was finishing his cigarette quietly in the quad), and Loder promptly smacked the unoffending head of Chips. Merriment, moreover, was unpreventable under the Spook's leadership in the study passage; for into each of the little dark dens would he peer after pounding on the door with the blunt end of the Kaffir battle-axe, and his cry was always, "Come out, fellow!" or "You'd better come out, my man!" or "It's fourteen years for this, you know; only fourteen years' hard labour!" and once— "You think I can see you, but I can't!"—a signal instance of absence of mind in the presence of danger.

There were other diversions to which the Spook did not contribute, as when Sprawson screamed "Got him!" from the depths of some study, and emerged dragging young Petrie after him by the hair of his innocent head; but the dramatic effect of this interlude was immediately discounted by a clumsy imitation on the part of Shockley, of whom wonderfully little had been seen or heard during the earlier proceedings. Sprawson made short work of him now.

"You fool, do you want to spoil the whole thing?" whispered Sprawson, fiercely, in Jan's hearing; and those few words spoilt the whole thing for Jan. He retired into his own study, and sat down in the dark, wiping his forehead on his sleeve, and chuckling and shaking his head by turns, as amusement mingled in his mind with a certain vexatious disappointment.

Meanwhile a climax was deducible in or about the big studies up the two or three steps at the inner end of the passage. General clamour drowned the individual voice; but the devil's own tattoo with the battle-axe proclaimed a door fastened on the inside according to the best burgling traditions as expounded by Bingley in dormitory. Jan was not going to see the fun; he was not out of bed for fun; but he could not resist a grin when the belaboured door gave way audibly, and the crash was succeeded by a louder outcry than ever from the bloodthirsty pack. It was a chorus of disgust and discomfiture, shouted down eventually by Sprawson, and at length followed by some muffled remarks from the Spook and subdued cheers from his audience. Then master and boys trooped back along the passage, and all but Chips Carpenter passed Jan's open door without looking in.

"Tiger! is that you?"

"It's me, Chips. I'd had enough."

"But you missed the best of all! The thief or thieves had got out through Sprawson's study—locked the door—fixed a rope to his table leg, and heaved it back through the open window after they'd got down into the street!"

"Does anybody know what they took away with them?"

"Nothing, it's hoped, because Sprawson disturbed them at their work."

"Oh, he did, did he? And it was Sprawson's study they got out by?"

"Yes. That was a bit of a coincidence, wasn't it?"

"Just a bit! But I think all the more of Sprawson."

"So does all the house," said Chips, eagerly. "The old Spook's let the lot of us off first school to-morrow, or rather to-day, and he and Sprawson are looking for the key of the beer-barrel to serve out some all round! So I advise you to look sharp."

But Jan elected to enlighten his friend about something on the way; and the now lighted hall presented an animated scene when at length they passed the windows. Flushed faces emerging from the various degrees of dishabille were congregated by force of habit about the fireplace. Sprawson and Cave major ("bracketed supreme," as Chips afterwards remarked) were the salient and central pair; Loder and others, such as Shockley, were plying them with questions, only to receive subtle smiles and pregnant shakes of the head; on the outer skirts were the nobodies, and the less than nobodies, whispering together in excited knots, or pressing forward for a crumb of first-hand information.

"And I never saw it!" muttered Chips outside the door. "But old Bob Heriot will, the very moment he hears. And what on earth do you think he'll do?"

"Score off the whole house," Jan suggested, "to make sure of one or two!"

"And make a laughing-stock of the wretched Spook into the bargain? No fear! Bob's not another Haigh. He'll do something cleverer than that, or he won't do anything at all."

CHAPTER XVI

SIMILIA SIMILIBUS

Chips was right and Jan was wrong, but there was just one moment when it looked the other way about.

Heriot did nothing at all—until the next Saint's Day. That, however, was almost immediately after his return, while he still looked sadder than when he went away, and years older than his age. The chief event of the day was the annual match between the Sixth Form and the School. Heriot had not been near the ground, though he had no dearer haunt, and yet by dinner-time he seemed suddenly himself again. Stratten and Jellicoe, whose places in hall that term were on either side of him at the long table, afterwards declared that they had never known the old boy in better form. Stratten and Jellicoe were cricketers of high promise, and Heriot chatted with them as usual about their cricket and the game in general. When Miss Heriot had left the hall, however, her brother did not resume his seat preparatory to signing orders for his house, as his practice was, but remained standing at the head of the long table, and ordered the door to be shut. There was a certain dry twinkle behind his glasses; but his beard and moustache were one, and the beard jutted out abnormally.

"If I've been slow to allude to your strange adventures of two or three nights ago," said Heriot, "I need hardly tell you it has only been because my mind has been full of other things. I'm very sorry not to have been with you in what certainly appears to have been the most exciting hour the house has known since I took it over. I have evidently missed a great deal; but I congratulate you all on the conspicuous gallantry said to have been displayed by every one of you, at a moment's notice, in the middle of the night. I've heard of two-o'clock-in-the-morning courage, but I never heard of such a wholesale example of it. I'm sure I should be very proud of a whole house whom I can trust to play the man like this behind my back!"

There was even some little feeling in the tone employed by Heriot. Jan could not understand it; he had never looked upon the man as a fool; but this deep appreciation of an utter hoax was worthy of the Spook himself. Fellows moved uneasily in their places, where they stood uncomfortably enough between table and form; one or two played with what they had left of their bread. Sprawson, to be sure, looked hotly indifferent, but his truculent eye might have been seen running down the lines of faces, as if in search of some smiling head to smack afterwards as a relief. Both Sprawson and Charles Cave were in flannels, the popular Champion having found a place in the match which had begun that morning. But even the great cricketer looked less pleased with himself than usual. And the only smile to be seen by Sprawson had lightened the countenance of old Bob Heriot himself.

"Where all seem to have distinguished themselves," he continued, "it may seem invidious to single out individuals. But I am advised to couple with my congratulations the honoured names of Cave major and Sprawson. I was afraid you were going to cheer"—the honoured names had been received in dead silence—"but I like these things to be taken as a matter of course, and I'm sure neither Cave nor yet Sprawson would wish to pose as popular heroes. I have an important message for them both, however, from a very important quarter. My friend Major Mangles, the Chief Constable of the county, wishes to have an interview with Cave and Sprawson, with a view to the early apprehension of the would-be thieves."

Living people are not often quite so silent as the boys at that moment in Heriot's hall. Major the Hon. Henry Mangles was known to the whole school by sight and reputation as the most dashing figure of a military man in all those parts. Sometimes he played in a match against the Eleven, and seldom survived many balls without lifting at least one out of the ground. Sometimes he was to be seen and heard in Heriot's inner court, and then the entire house would congregate to catch his picturesque remarks. He inhabited a moated grange some four miles from the school, broke a fresh bone in his body every hunting season, and often gave Bob Heriot a mount.

"When does he wish to see us, sir?" inquired Cave major, with becoming coolness.

"This afternoon."

"Here in the town?"

"No—at his place."

"I'm sorry, sir," said Cave, firmly—"but that's impossible."

"Any other time, sir," suggested Sprawson, civilly. "To-day we're both playing in the Sixth Form match."

"Et tu, Sprawson?" cried Heriot, merrily.

"I'm the tip of the School tail, sir."

The house relieved itself in laughter led by Heriot.

"Have either of you been in yet?"

"I had one ball, sir. It was the last of the innings," said the brazen Sprawson. "The Sixth are just going in, and we expect to have Cave there all the afternoon."

"I'm afraid he can't go in first," said Heriot; "and you'll have to find a substitute to field for you, Sprawson. Or rather I'll see the two captains myself, and explain about you both. That'll save time and you can start at once. You can't do these doughty deeds behind my back and not expect to find them fame, you know."

"But, surely, sir, this is a most high-handed demand of the Major's?"

Charles Cave had never been known to display such heat.

"He's the Chief Constable, and Chief Constables are high-handed people," said Heriot, preparing to sign the orders. "I shouldn't advise either of you to disappoint Major Mangles, much less when he's paying you a compliment as the pair who specially distinguished themselves in the night of battle. He wants you to tell him all about it. There's no reason why that should take long, and if you drive both ways you might be back before any wickets have fallen. But you must see that when a house is entered by common burglars it's a matter for the police and not for us, and as police witnesses you're in their hands and out of ours. To make matters easy for you, however, the Major has very kindly sent his carriage, which I think you'll find waiting for you now outside the quad. If I were you I should go just as you are, and make no more bones about it."

And Heriot sat down to attend to the daily detachment with orders on the tradesmen requiring his signature, while the rest of the house streamed out of the hall in a silence due partly to the eminence of the discomfited ringleaders, and partly to the guilty conscience of the mob as accessories after the fact. Sprawson alone made light of the situation, and that chiefly at the expense of his superfine confederate.

"All aboard the Black Maria!" said Sprawson, taking the other by the arm. "I say, Charles, old cock, I wonder how you'll look with a convict's crop and a quiverful of broad arrows?"

And for once the great Charles made use of the baser language of his inferiors, and tossed his tawny mane in anger as he stalked out of the quad, a Phœbus Apollo setting in a cloud. But it really was the Major's landau that awaited them, a cockaded footman standing at the door. Phœbus gave a dying gleam, and stepped in as though the imposing equipage belonged to him.

And Sprawson shook every hand within reach, and played several kinds of fool with his handkerchief until the landau was out of sight.

Then indeed the quad became a Babel, from which a trained ear might have extracted a consensus of unshaken confidence in Sprawson and Cave major. The house, as a whole entirely trusted them to hoodwink Major Mangles as they had already hoodwinked the Spook and even old Heriot himself. It was the last feat which made all things possible to these arch impostors. And only a severe old sage like Crabtree would have entertained any doubt upon the point, which his trenchant tongue argued against all and sundry till the quad was empty for the afternoon.

Jan happened to be playing in the first game on the Middle, while Chips had a humble place in the second Lower; at the joint call-over for the two grounds (4.30) it was whispered that neither Cave nor Sprawson had returned to the Sixth Form match on the Upper. The whisper had swelled into a Bible Oath, and the indisputable fact into a farrago of pure fiction, before the return of the missing pair made it unsafe even to breathe their names in Heriot's quad. They were not quite the same young men who had made a state departure in the Major's landau. Their flannels were powdered with the drab dust of the wayside, and they limped a little in the fives-shoes for which they had changed their spikes before coming down from the Upper. Cave moreover looked a diabolically dangerous customer, to whom Loder himself shrank from addressing a remark, after crossing the quad with that obvious intention. Sprawson as usual preserved a genial countenance; but the unlucky Bingley, betrayed into a tactless question by a mysterious wink, had his arm nearly twisted out of its socket as he deserved.

"Now I feel better!" says Sprawson, with ferocious glee. "I'm much obliged to you, Toby, and I hope you'll regain the use of your arm in time."

But the house was no wiser until after prayers. At tea Cave major never spoke, and Sprawson only grinned into his plate. But Miss Heriot had scarcely withdrawn after prayers, when Heriot, taking up his nightly position before the fireplace, asked the two swells how they got on. And the entire house stayed in the hall to hear.

"Major Mangles," returned Cave major, with cutting deliberation, "may be Chief Constable of the county, and anything he likes by birth, but he's no gentleman for all that."

"Really, Cave? That's a serious indictment. Why, what has he done?"

"You'd better ask Sprawson," says Charles Cave, with a haughty jerk of his fine fair head. He looked a very stormy Phœbus now, but still every inch that grand young god.

"Well, Sprawson?"

"I'm sure Cave can tell you better than I can, sir," says Sprawson of the wicked humour.

"But Sprawson will make the most of it," says the cricketer with icy sneer.

"It's not a tale that wants much varnish, sir, if that's what he means," said Sprawson, happily. "I'll tell you the facts, sir, and Cave can check them if he'll be so kind. You said we should find the Major's carriage waiting for us outside the quad, and so we did. It was the landau, sir, a very good one nicely hung, and capital cattle tooling us along like lords. The country was looking beautiful. Roads rather dusty, but a smell of hay that turned it into a sort of delicate snuff, sir. It really was a most delightful drive."

"Speak for yourself, Sprawson, if you don't mind."

"I shouldn't dream of speaking for you, Cave. You didn't seem to me to take any interest in the scenery. I may be wrong, but I couldn't help thinking your heart was at the wicket, flogging our poor bowling all over the parish, and I was so thankful to be where I was! But that was only on the way, sir, it was nothing to what we were in for at the other end. The footman said we should find the Major on the lawn. So we did, sir—playing tennis like a three-year-old—and half the county looking on!"

"Not a garden-party?" inquired Heriot incredulously.

"That sort of thing, sir."

"My poor fellows! Pray go on."

"Of course we couldn't interrupt him in the middle of his set, sir, and when he'd finished it he crossed straight over and started another without ever seeming to see that we were there. Nobody else took any notice of us either," continued Sprawson, with a sly glance at the still stately Cave. "We might have been a pair of garden statues, or tennis professionals waiting to play an exhibition match."

"It reminds me of Dr. Johnson and Lord Chesterfield," said Heriot darkly. "Your fame is perhaps more parochial, Sprawson. But is it possible that you, Cave, are personally unknown to Major Mangles?"

"I haven't the least idea," replied Charles Cave magnificently. "I should have said he might have known me by the times I've bowled him."

"And you never thought of coming away again? I shouldn't have blamed you, upon my word."

"Of course we thought of it, sir," said Sprawson. "But the carriage had gone round to the stables, and we couldn't very well order it ourselves."

"I should have walked."

"It's a terrible tramp, sir, on a hot afternoon, and in rubber soles!" Sprawson winced involuntarily at the recollection; but the thought of his companion consoled him yet again. "Especially after bowling all the morning," he added, "and expecting to go in the moment you got back!"

"Well, that wouldn't have been necessary," said Heriot. "It must be some satisfaction to you that the Sixth won so easily, even without your certain century, Cave."

"It doesn't alter the fact that he had to walk back after all," said Sprawson, when the greater man had been given ample time to answer for himself.

"So had you!" he thundered then, not like a great man at all, but in a voice that gave some idea of that homeward tramp and its recriminations, in which Sprawson was suddenly felt to be having the last word now.

"But surely Major Mangles interviewed you first?" inquired Heriot, with becoming gravity.

"Oh, yes; he took us under the trees and asked us questions," said Sprawson, forcing the gay note a little for the first time.

"Questions he'd no earthly right to ask!" cried Cave with confidence.

"You didn't take that tone with Major Mangles, I hope, Cave?"

"I daresay I did, sir."

"Then I can't say I wonder at his letting you both walk back. Of course, if you didn't answer his questions satisfactorily, it might alter his whole view of the matter, at least so far as you two were concerned in it."

"We couldn't tell him more than we knew ourselves, sir," protested Sprawson.

"Not more," said Heriot, pensively. "No—certainly not more!" It was only his tone that added "if as much"—and only the few who heard through it. "I hope, at any rate, that you got your tea?" said Heriot, with a brisk glance at the clock over the row of cups.

Cave major looked blacker than before, but Sprawson brightened at once.

"Oh, yes, sir, thank you! Lady Augusta sent for us on purpose, and it ended in our handing round the cups and things. That was the redeeming feature of the afternoon. But of course I'm only speaking for myself."

Cave's chiselled nostrils spoke for him.

"Well, there seems no more to be said," remarked Heriot, in valedictory voice. The attentive throng parted before his stride. "I must confess," he added, however, turning at the door, "that I myself don't understand the Major's tactics altogether—if you've reported him fully. I can't help thinking that something or other has escaped your memory. Otherwise it sounds to me rather like a practical joke at your expense. But I should be sorry to suspect a real humorist, like Major Mangles, of that very poor form of humour, unless"—a moment's pause, with twinkling glasses—"unless it were as a sort of payment in kind. That's the only excuse for practical joking, in my opinion; and now I think we can let the whole subject drop. I only hope that the next time some knave, or fool, thinks of breaking into my house, he'll have the pluck to come when I'm at home. Good-night all!"

The house filtered out into the quad, drifted over to the studies, and presently back again to bed, with few comments and less laughter; and that night there was little talk but much constraint in both the top and lower dormitories, ruled respectively by Sprawson and Cave major. Only in the little one, overlooking the street, was the topic in everybody's mind on anybody's lips; and there it was monopolised by Crabtree, who reviewed the entire episode in mordant monologue, broken only by the shaking of the bed beneath his fits of helpless mirth.

CHAPTER XVII

THE FUN OF THE FAIR

There were three days in the year when the venerable market-place was out of bounds, all but the draggled ribbon of pavement running round it and the few shops opening thereon. The rest was monopolised and profaned by the vans and booths of a travelling fair, which reached the town usually about the second week in March. The school took little notice of the tawdry encampment and its boorish revels; but the incessant strains of a steam merry-go-round became part of the place for the time being, and made night especially hideous in the town houses nearest the scene.

Nearest of all was Heriot's house, and greatest of all sufferers the four boys in the little top room with the dormer window over the street. Jan was still one of them, and Bingley another. But Joyce had left, and Crabtree had taken charge of one of the long dormitories overlooking the quad. Chips Carpenter and a new boy had succeeded to their partitions; and if in one case the intellectual loss was irreparable, in the other that of an incorrigible vocabulary was perhaps less to be deplored.

But Jan's was still the silent corner; even to Chips he would have little to say before the other two; for in this his fifth term he had fallen on another evil time. It had nothing to do with his work, however, and neither could he curse his luck for a split hand or a maligned heart. He had played football every day of his second winter term—not brilliantly, for he was never quite quick enough on the ball—but with a truculent tenacity which had been rewarded with the black trimmings of the Second Lower Upper. In form he was no longer a laughing-stock; and his form was now the Middle Fifth, where one began to cope with Greek iambics as well as Latin elegiacs. But all three Fifths were beds of roses after the Middle Remove, and Dudley Relton an angel of forbearance after that inhuman old Haigh.

Dudley Relton, however, besides being man enough to take the Middle Fifth on his accession to the staff, was that pioneer of cricket masters who had made a note of Jan's name at the valued instigation of A. G. Swallow. He had also watched Jan bowling in the one game in which he had played on the Upper, thanks to the departed Sprawson, and he had his eye on the young left-hander with the queer individual action. But it was the cool eye of a long-headed cricketer, and Jan never read it for an instant. Chips might have done so if he had been in the form, but he was now in the Upper Fifth, and his sanguine prophecies were neither remembered nor renewed. Jan only wished that Relton would not look at him, sometimes, almost as though he knew all about a fellow; and it rather bothered him to get off lighter than he deserved for a false concord in his prose or a vile copy of verses.

But that was not his trouble on the nights when the steam merry-go-round enlivened the small dormitory with "Over the Garden Wall" and "Lardy-dah," those egregious ditties of their day. It was the first round of the All Ages Mile that kept Jan from sleeping either night until the steam tunes stopped.

On the strength of his performance the year before and of several inches since added to his stature, Jan had found himself seriously fancied for a place in the Mile. The dash of premature notoriety, combined with a superfluity of sage advice, made him sadly self-conscious and over-anxious before the event, which ended in a complete fiasco so far as he was concerned. It was his fate to meet the ultimate winner (down with his eyes the year before) in the very first heat. Jan dogged him as gratuitously advised, instead of making the running as flesh and blood implored. And having no spurt he was not only badly beaten, but failed even to come in third, and was thus out of the running in the first round.

That was bad enough; hardy enemies of the Shockley type took care to make it worse. They became suddenly alive to an alleged "roll" put on by Jan in anticipation of his success; and Jan was sufficiently down on himself to take their remarks for once to heart. He felt still more the silence of many who had believed in him; even the cheery sympathy of a few only aggravated his sense of failure; and as for the loquacious Chips, and his well-meant efforts to keep the dormitory talk to any other topic, they were almost as maddening as the steam merry-go-round, that filled every pause with its infernal "Lardy-dah." That tenacious tune had supplied the accompaniment to his hopes and fears of the night before; it had run in his head throughout the fatal race; and now it made merry over his utterly idiotic and unpardonable failure.

It will be seen that the robust Jan had grown a crop of sensibilities almost worthy of his friend Carpenter, except that Jan's were wholly and grimly inarticulate. But he was now sixteen, and that is the age of surprises in a boy. It took Jan in more ways than one. It made him long to do startling things, and it made him do some foolish ones instead; hence his hard training for the mile, and his actual running when the time came. It made him feel that he had done less than nothing at school so far, that he was less than nobody, and yet that there was more in him than anybody knew; and now he wanted them to know it; and now he didn't care a blow what happened to him, or what was thought, at a school to which he had been sent against his will. There was no forgetting that at a time like this. If he was a failure, if he went on failing, well, at any rate it would be a score off those who had sent him there, and never gave him enough pocket money, or wrote him an unnecessary line.

So Jan came back to a very early position of his, only trailing the accumulated grievances of a year and a half; and by the third and last night of the fair he had the whole collection to brood upon, in gigantic array, in proportion the more colossal and grotesque because he could not and would not speak of them to a soul. And there was that fool Chips, jawing away as usual to anybody who would listen, about anything and everything except the sports.

"I shall be jolly glad when that beastly old fair moves on," quoth Chips after an interval of "Over the Garden Wall."

Jan agreed so heartily that he could scarcely hold his tongue.

"I don't know that I shall," said the new boy in Crabtree's corner. "It sounds rather jolly when you're dropping off."

Jan could have pulled every stitch off the little brute's bed. But the remark was very properly ignored.

"I suppose you know," said Bingley, "that two fellows were once bunked for going to it?"

"Going to what?" asked Chips.

"This very fair."

"They must've been fools!" said Jan, raising his voice at last.

"I thought you were asleep?" cried the new boy, who had no sense.

"You keep your thoughts to yourself," growled Jan, "or I'll come and show you whether I am or not."

"They were fools," assented Bingley, "but they were rather sportsmen too. They got out of one of the hill houses at night, and came down in disguise, in bowlers and false beards! But they were spotted right enough, and they'd got to go."

"And serve them jolly well right!" said Jan, cantankerously.

"I don't call it such a crime, Tiger."

"Who's talking about crimes? You've got 'em on the brain, Bingley."

"I thought you said they deserved to be bunked?"

"So they did—for going and getting cobbed."

"Oh, I see! You'd've looked every master in the face, I suppose, without being recognised?"

"I wouldn't've made them look twice at me, by sticking on a false beard," snorted Jan, stung by the tone he had been the first to employ. Chips understood his mood, and liked him too much to join in the discussion. But Bingley had been longer in the school than either of them, and he was not going to knuckle under in a minute.

"It's a pity you weren't here, Tiger," said he, "to show them how to do it."

"It's a thing any fool could do if he tried," returned Jan. "I'd back myself to get out of this house in five minutes."

"Not you, old chap!" said Chips, making an unfortunate entry into the discussion after all.

"I would so," declared Jan hot-headedly. "I'd do it to-morrow if the fair wasn't going away."

Bingley began to jeer.

"I like that, when you jolly well know it is going!"

"I'll go to-night, if you say much more, you fool!"

Jan's springs twanged and wheezed as he sat bolt upright in his bed.

"You know you won't be such a silly idiot," said Chips, in an earnest voice.

"Of course he does!" jeered Bingley. "Nobody knows it quite so well."

There was an instant's pause, filled by a sounding blast from the market-place, and then the thud of bare feet planted on the floor.

"Surely you're not going to let him dare you—"

"Not he; don't you worry!"

It was Bingley who cut Chips short, and Jan thanked him as he slid into his trousers in the dark. His voice was strange, and not without the tremor of high excitement. There was a jingle of curtain rings across the dormitory. Carpenter was out of his partition in defiance of the rules; he appeared dimly at the foot of Jan's, into which Bingley was already peering over the partition.

"Are you off your chump?" demanded Chips.

"Not he," said Bingley again. "He's only bunging us up!"

Bingley might have been an infant Mephistopheles; but he was really only an incredulous, irritated, and rather excited schoolboy.

"You'll see directly," muttered Jan, slipping his braces over his night-shirt.

"You'll be caught to a certainty, and bunked if you're caught!"

That was Chips, in desperation now.

"And a good job too! I've had about enough of this place."

That was the Jan of their first term together.

"And it's raining like the very dickens!"

This was the child in Crabtree's corner, an insensible little sinner, who seemed to take the imminent enormity as an absolute matter of course.

"So much the better," said Jan. "I'll take a brolly and run all the less risk of being seen, and you see if I don't bring you all something from the fair."

"It's something he's gone and got to-day," whispered Bingley for Chips's consolation. "It's all a swizzle, you'll see."

"You look out of the window in about five minutes," retorted Jan from the door, "and p'r'aps you'll see!"

And out he actually stole, carrying the clean boots that he had brought up to dormitory in readiness for first school, and leaving Chips in muzzled consternation on the threshold.

The rain pelted on the skylight over the stairs. It had been a showery day, but it was a very wet night, and Jan was almost as glad of it as he had just professed himself. He saw a distant complication of wet clothes, but as a mere umbrella among umbrellas he stood a really fair chance of not being seen. It was still only a chance; but that was half the fun. And fun it was, though a terrifying form of fun, and though Jan was already feeling a bit unsound about the knees, he had to go on with it; there was as yet no question in his mind about that, and hardly any looking back at the ridiculous combination of taunt and impulse which had committed him to this mad adventure.

Conversation had ceased in the top long dormitory; in the one below a dropping fire was still maintained; and the intervening flight of lead-lined stairs, taken one at a time, with terrible deliberation, and in his socks, struck a chill to the adventurer's marrow. He began to think he really was a fool; but he would look a bigger one if he went back now. So he gained the foot of the second flight in safety, and paused to consider his next move. The flags were colder than the leaden stairs; so he sat on the slate table while he put on his boots; and the slate table was colder than the flags.

His first idea had been to get out into the quad, as he had got out into it his very first morning in the place, through the hall windows. But the rain rather spoilt that plan; the rain was not an unmixed blessing after all. The umbrellas, now he came to think of it, were kept in the lower study passage; and how was he to break in there? Of course the outer doors would be locked; and he might get wet through in the quad, before effecting an entry into the lower studies, and even then leaving a dripping trail behind him.

No; if he wanted an umbrella he must borrow old Bob Heriot's. That was a paralysing alternative, but it was the only one to returning humiliated to dormitory. After all, the hat-stand was only just on the other side of the green baize door under which Jan could see the thinnest thread of light from Heriot's outer hall. And dear old Bob sat up till all hours; that was notorious; and his study was beyond the dining-room, leading out of it, so that in all probability there would be two shut doors between the intruder and the unsuspecting master of the house.

But the long lean figure of Robert Heriot, smoking his pipe in the inner sanctuary, cocking a quick ear at the furtive footstep on his side of the house, and finally confronting the audacious offender, with bristling beard and flashing spectacles, made all at once the most portentous picture in Jan's mind. Heriot of all men! The one master with whom the boldest boy never dared to take a liberty; the one whose good opinion was best worth having, and perhaps hardest to win; why had he not thought of Heriot before? To think of him now so vividly was to abandon the whole adventure in a panic. Better the scorn of fifty Bingleys, for the rest of the term, than the wrath of one Heriot for a single minute such as he had just gone through in a paroxysm of the imagination.

Jan found himself creeping upstairs more gingerly than ever in his boots, climbing nearer and nearer to the dropping voices in the lower dormitory. That was Shockley's guttural monologue. It was Shockley who had said the hardest thing to Jan about his running, in just that hateful voice. It was Shockley who would have the most and the worst to say if it came to his ears, as no doubt it would, that one of his special butts had made such a feeble fool of himself as Jan knew that he was making now. And then life would be duller even than it had been before, and school a rottener place, and himself a greater nonentity than ever. Nay, all these changes for the worse had already taken place in the last minute of ignominious retreat. But a minute ago, yes, a minute ago there had been some excitement in life, and a fellow had felt somebody for once!

"I'm blowed if I do," said Jan deliberately to himself; and down he went with equal deliberation to the green baize door. It opened with scarcely a sound. A light was burning in the little entrance hall beyond. And the dining-room door was providentially shut.

Here was Heriot's umbrella; and it was wet. Hanging over it was an Irish tweed cape, a characteristic garment, also a bit wet about the hem. Old Bob Heriot had been out, but he had come in again, and it could not be quite eleven. Unless tradition lied he was safe in his den for another hour.

From his fit of cowardice Jan had flown to the opposite extreme of foolhardy audacity. What better disguise than Heriot's coat and even Heriot's hat, the soft felt one that was also rather wet already? Jan had them on in a twinkling, drunk as he was already with the magnitude of his impudence. It would give them something to talk about, whether he was caught or not. That was Jan's way of expressing to himself his intention of contributing to the annals of the school, whatever happened.

The front door had not been locked up for the night, and it never was by day. Heriot had his happy-go-lucky ways, but the town as a rule was as quiet as the sleepiest hollow. Jan managed to shut the door almost noiselessly behind him, never thinking now of his return. Out in the rain the umbrella went up at once; like an extinguisher, he jammed it down about his ears; and the instinct of further concealment drove his left hand deep into a capacious pocket. It came upon one of old Heriot's many pipes. Next instant the pipe was between the madman's teeth, and Jan, on the opposite pavement of a dripping and deserted street, was flourishing the umbrella and pointing out the pipe to three white faces at a window in the shiny roof.

He would not have cared, at that moment, if he had known that he was going to be caught the next. But nobody was abroad just then in that rain to catch him. And not further down the street than Jan could have jerked a fives-ball, the glare of the market-place lit up the stone front and archway of the Mitre. And the blare of the steam merry-go-round waxed fast and furious as he marched under Heriot's umbrella into the zone of light.

"He wears a penny flower in his coat—
Lardy-dah—
And a penny paper collar round his throat—
Lardy-dah—
In his hand a penny stick,
In his tooth a penny pick,
And a penny in his pocket—
Lardy-dah—lardy-dah—
And a penny in his pocket—
Lardy-dah!"

Jan had picked up the words from some fellow who used to render such rubbish to a worse accompaniment on the hall piano; and they ran in his head with the outrageous tune. They reminded him that he had scarcely a penny in his own pocket, thanks to his munificent people in Norfolk, and for once it was just as well. Otherwise he would certainly have had a ride, in Heriot's well-known foul-weather garb, on one of "Collinson's Royal Racing Thoroughbreds, the Greatest and Most Elaborate Machine now Travelling."

Last nights are popular nights, and the fair was crowded in spite of the rain. Round and round went the wooden horses, carrying half the young bloods of the little place, with here and there an apple-cheeked son or daughter of the surrounding soil. Jan tilted his umbrella to have a look at them; their shouts were drowned by the shattering crash of the steam organ, but their flushed faces caught fresh fire from a great naked light as they whirled nearest to where Jan stood. One purple countenance he recognised as the pace slackened; it was Mulberry, the local reprobate of evil memory, swaying in his stirrups and whacking his wooden mount as though they were in the straight.

The deafening blare sank to a dying whine; the flare-light sputtered audibly in the rain, and Jan jerked his umbrella forward as the dizzy riders dismounted within a few yards of him. Jan turned his back on them, and contemplated the cobbles under his nose, and the lighted puddles that ringed them round, like meshes of liquid gold. He watched for the unsteady corduroys of Mulberry, and withdrew at their approach. But there was no certain escape short of immediate departure from the fair, which occupied little more than the area of a full-sized lawn tennis court, and covered half of that with the merry-go-round, and another quarter with stalls and vans.

One of the stalls displayed a legend which seemed to Jan to deserve more custom than it attracted.

Rings Must Lie to Win

Watch-la!

2 Rings 1d.
ALL YOU RING YOU HAVE.

The watches lay in open cardboard boxes on a sloping board. There was a supply of wooden rings that just fitted round the boxes. Jan watched one oaf run through several coppers, his rings always lying between the boxes or on top of one. Jan felt it was a case for a spin, and he longed to have a try with that cunning left hand of his. But he had actually only twopence on him, and the first necessity was two-pennyworth of evidence that he had really been to the fair. Yet what trophy could compare with one of those cheap watches in its cardboard box?

It so happened that Jan had a watch of his own worth everything on sale at this trumpery fair; but he could almost have bartered it for one of these that would show the top dormitory, at any rate, the kind of chap he was. And yet he was not the kind who often saw himself in heroic proportions; but an abnormal mood was at the back and front of this whole adventure; and perhaps no more fitting climax could have inflamed a reeling mind. He produced his pennies with sudden determination, yet with a hand as cool as his brain was hot, and as cool a preliminary survey to make sure that Mulberry was not already dogging him.

"Two rings a penny," said the fur-capped custodian of the watches, handing the rings to Jan. "An' wot you rings you 'aves."

Jan stood alone before the sloping board, kept a few feet off by an intervening table, and he poised his first ring as the steam fiend broke out again with "Over the Garden Wall." A back-handed spin sent it well among the watches, and it went on spinning until it settled at an angle over one of the boxes, as though loth to abandon the attempt to ring it properly.

"Rings must lie flat to win," said the fellow in the fur cap, with a quick squint at Jan. "Try again, mister; you'll do better with less spin."

Jan grinned dryly as he resolved to put on a bit more. He had heard his father drive hard bargains in the Saturday night's marketing aforetime. Old Rutter had known how to take care of himself across any stall or barrow, even when his gait was like Mulberry's on the way home; and Jan had a sense of similar capacity as he poised his second ring against the voluminous folds of Mr. Heriot's cape. Thence it skimmed with graceful trajectory, in palpable gyrations; had circled one of the square boxes before he knew it, and was spinning down it like a nut on a bolt, when the man in the fur cap whipped a finger between the ring and the table.

"That's a near one, mister!" cried he. "But it don't lie flat."

Nor did it. The ring had jammed obliquely on the cardboard box, a finger's breadth from the board.

"It would've done if you'd left it alone!" shouted Jan above the steam fiend's roar.

"That it wouldn't! It's a bit o' bad luck, that's wot it is; never knew it to 'appen afore, I didn't; but it don't lie straight, now do it?"

"It would've done," replied Jan through his teeth. "And the watch is mine, so let's have it."

Whether he said that more than once, or what the fur-capped foe replied, Jan never knew. The merry-go-round robbed him of half that passed between them, and all that was to follow blurred the rest as soon as it had taken place. One or two salient moments were to stand out in his mind like rocks. He was sprawling across the intervening table, he had seized the watch that he had fairly won, and the ruffian in the cap had seized his wrist. That horny grip remained like the memory of a handcuff. The thing developed into a semi-recumbent tug-of-war, in which Jan more than held his own. The watches in their boxes came sliding down the sloping board, the fur-cap followed them, and a head like a fluffy melon hung a-ripening as the blood rushed into it. Jan beheld swelling veins in a stupor of angry satisfaction, and without a thought of his own position until a rap on the back went through him like a stab.

It was only a country policeman in streaming leggings; but he had not arrived alone upon the scene; and Jan felt the flooded cobble-stones heaving under him, as he relinquished his prize at once, and recoiled from the gaze of countless eyes.

Yet the policeman for one was not looking at him. The policeman was levelling an open hand at the melon-headed rogue, and reiterating a demand which only added to Jan's embarrassment.

"You give this young feller what he fairly won. I saw what you did. I've had my eye on you all night. You give him that watch, or you'll hear a bit more about it!"

Jan tried to raise his voice in cowardly repudiation, but his tongue refused the base office. The lights of the fair were going round and round him. The policeman, the rogue, and three or four more, had been joined by the drunken Mulberry, who was staring and pointing and trying to say something which nobody could understand. The policeman sent him about his business with a cuff, and Jan began to breathe. He felt the watch put into his unwilling hand. He heard a good-humoured little cheer. He saw the policeman looking at him strangely, and he wondered if a tip was expected of him. Even at that moment Jan felt a bitter wave of resentment against those who sent him to school, against his will, with half-a-sovereign for a whole term's pocket-money. He could only thank the policeman with a stutter and a gulp, and slink from the scene like the beaten dog he felt.

Luckily his legs were cooler than his head; they carried him down the street in the opposite direction to his house and the school buildings; and he had not taken many strides on the comparatively dark and quite deserted pavement, when his mind began to recover tone rapidly. It recovered more tone than it had lost. He had given himself up, and now he realised that he was not only safe so far, but successful beyond his wildest dreams. Not only had he been to the fair, but thanks to the policeman (whom he wished more than ever to reward substantially) he had come away with a silver watch to show for the adventure. What would they have to say to that in the small dormitory? They would never be able to keep it to themselves; it would get about the school, and make him somebody after all. He would acquire, perhaps, undying fame as the fellow who got out at a moment's notice, and went to the fair in a master's hat and coat, and won a prize at watch-la, and brought it back in triumph to dormitory, at Heriot's of all houses in the school!

He would probably tell Heriot before he left. Old Bob was just the man to laugh over such an escapade, more heartily perhaps if one kept it till one came down as an Old Boy. Jan felt ridiculously brave again under old Bob's umbrella, which he had dropped for a moment during the fracas at the fair. That, of course, was why he had also lost his head. But now he was as bold as any lion, and particularly determined to do something at school after all, so that he might come down as an Old Boy to recount this very adventure.

Not that he had the egotistical temperament, even to the extent that (for instance) poor old Chips had it. But this was that abnormal mood which had only been interrupted by a minute of pure panic at the fair. And now the swimming pavement floated under his feet like air.

Still airier was an overtaking stride which Jan never so much as heard until a strong arm slid through his, and a voice that he heard every day addressed him in every-day tones.

CHAPTER XVIII

DARK HORSES

"Do you mind my coming under your umbrella?"

It was Dudley Relton, and his forearm felt like a steel girder. Yet his tone was preternaturally polite as between master and boy. There was not even the sound of his own surname to assure Jan that he was recognised. But he was far too startled to attempt to take advantage of that.

"Oh, sir!" he sang out as if in pain.

"I shouldn't tell all the town, if I were you," returned Relton, coolly. "You'd better come in here and pull yourself together."

He had thrust his latch-key into the side door of a shuttered shop. Over the shop were lighted windows which Jan suddenly connected with Relton's rooms. He had been up there once or twice with extra work, and now he was made to lead the way.

The sitting room was comfortably furnished, with a soft settee in front of a dying fire, and book-cases on either side of it. Jan awoke from a nightmare of certain consequences, never fully realised until now, to find himself meanwhile ensconced in the settee, and much fascinated with the muddy boots of Dudley Relton, who had poked the fire before standing upright with his back to it.

"Of course you know what is practically bound to happen to you, Rutter. Still, in case there's anything you'd like me to say in reporting the matter, I thought I'd give you the opportunity of speaking to me first. I don't honestly suppose that it can make much difference. But you're in my form, and I'm naturally sorry that you should have made such a fatal fool of yourself."

The young man sounded sorry. That was just like him. He had always been decent to Jan, and he was sorry because he knew that it was necessarily all over with a fellow who was caught getting out at night. Of course it was all over with him, so what was the good of saying anything? Jan kept his eyes on those muddy boots, and answered never a word.

"I suppose you got out for the sake of getting out, and saying you'd been to the fair? I don't suppose there was anything worse behind it. But I'm afraid that's quite bad enough, Rutter."

And Mr. Relton heaved an unmistakable sigh. It had the effect of breaking down the silence which Jan was still only too apt to maintain in any trouble. He mumbled something about "a lark," and the young master took him up quite eagerly.

"I know that! I saw you at the fair—spotted you in a moment as I was passing—but I wasn't going to make a scene for all the town to talk about. I can say what I saw you doing. But I'm afraid it won't make much difference. It's a final offence at any school, to go and get out at night."

Jan thought he heard another sigh; but he had nothing more to say. He was comparing the two pairs of boots under his downcast eyes. His own were the cleanest; they still had the boot-boy's shine on them, amid splashes of mud and dull blots of rain. They took him back to the little dormitory at the top of Heriot's house.

"Why did you want to do it?" cried Relton, with sudden exasperation. "Did you think it was going to make a hero of you in the eyes of the school?"

Sullen silence confessed some such thought.

"You!" continued Relton, with sharp contempt. "You who might really have been a bit of a hero, if only you'd waited till next term!"

Jan looked up at last.

"Next term, sir?"

"Yes, next term, as a left-hand bowler! I saw you bowl the only time you ever played on the Upper last year. It was too late then, but I meant to make something of you this season. You were my dark horse, Rutter. I had my eye on you for the Eleven, and you go and do a rotten thing for which you'll have to go as sure as you're sitting there!"

So that was the meaning of kind words and light penalties. The Eleven itself! Jan had not been so long at school without discovering that the most heroic of all distinctions was to become a member of the school eleven. Once or twice he had dreamt of it as an ultimate possibility in his own case; it was really Chips who had put the idea into his head, but even Chips had regarded it only as a distant goal. And to think it might have been next term—just when there was to be no next term at all!

"Don't make it worse than it is, sir," mumbled Jan, as the firelight played on the two pairs of drying boots. The other pair shifted impatiently on the hearth-rug.

"I couldn't. It's as bad as bad can be; I'm only considering if it's possible to make it the least bit better. If I could get you off with the biggest licking you ever had in your life, I'd do so whether you liked it better or worse. But what can I do except speak to Mr. Heriot? And what can he do except report the matter to the Head Master? And do you think Mr. Thrale's the man to let a fellow off because he happens to be a bit of a left-hand bowler? I don't, I tell you frankly," said Dudley Relton. "I'll say and do all I can for you, Rutter, but it would be folly to pretend that it can make much difference."

Jan never forgot the angry, reproachful, and yet not unsympathetic expression of a face that was only less boyish than his own. He felt he liked Dudley Relton more than ever, and that Dudley Relton really had a sneaking fondness for him, even apart from his promise with the ball. But that only added poignancy to his self-reproaches, the bitterness of satire to his inevitable fate. Here was a friend who would have made all the difference to his school life, getting him into the Eleven next year if not next term, fanning his little spark of talent into a famous flame! It was too tragic only to see it as they marched back together, once more under Heriot's umbrella, to the house and Heriot himself, with his flashing spectacles and his annihilating rage.

The steam merry-go-round was still and dumb at last. In the emptying market-place the work of dismantling the fair was beginning even as the church clock struck twelve. Stalls were being cleared, and half the lights were already out. But Heriot's study windows threw luminous bars across the glistening pavement, and his front-door was still unlocked. Relton opened it softly, and shut it with equal care behind the quaking boy.

"You'd better take those things off and hang them up," he whispered. So he had recognised Heriot's garments, but had deemed that aggravation a detail compared with the cardinal crime!

Jan himself had forgotten it, but he took the hint with trembling hands.

"Now slip up to dormitory and hold your tongue. That's essential. I'll say what I can for you, but the less you talk the better."

Jan would have seen that for himself; even if he had not seen it, he was the last person to confide in anybody if he could help it. But as it was there were three fellows in the secret of his escapade, and all three doubtless lying awake to learn its termination. It would be impossible not to talk to them. Jan could only resolve upon the fewest words, as he groped his way to the lead-lined stairs. In the two dormitories overlooking the quad, the last tongue had long been still, and in the utter silence Heriot's voice sounded in startled greeting on his side of the house. Jan shivered as he sank down on the lowest stair but one, to take off his boots. Was it any good taking them off? Would not the green baize door burst open, and Heriot be upon him before the first lace was undone? He undid it with the heavy deliberation of an entirely absent mind. Still no Heriot appeared, and even Jan could catch no further sound of voices beyond the dividing door. He crept up, dangling his boots.

The small dormitory was as still as the other two. Jan could not believe that his comrades had fallen asleep, at their posts as it almost seemed to him, but for an instant the suspicion piqued him in spite of everything. Then came simultaneous whispers from opposite corners.

"Is it you, Tiger?"

"You old caution, I couldn't have believed it of you!"

"You didn't know him as well as I did."

"I'm proud to know him now, though. Shake hands across the 'tish."

"Thank goodness you're back!"

"But how did you get back?"

"Same way I got out," muttered Jan at last. "Are you all three awake."

"All but young Eaton. Eaton!"

No answer from the new boy's corner.

"He's a pretty cool hand"—from Bingley.

"But he's taken his dying oath not to tell a soul"—from Chips.

"He won't have to keep it long, then." Jan was creeping into bed.

"Why not?"

"I've gone and got cobbed."

"You haven't!"

"I'm afraid so."

"Oh, Tiger!"

"But you're back, man?"

"I was seen first. I'm certain I was. It's no use talking about it now; you'll all know soon enough. I've been a fool. I deserve all I'm bound to get."

"I was worse!" gasped Bingley over the partition. "I dared you to do what I wouldn't've done myself for a hundred pounds. But I never thought you would, either. I thought you were only hustling. I swear I did, Tiger!"

Bingley was in real distress. Chips combined sore anxiety with a curiosity which Jan might have gratified but for Dudley Relton's parting piece of advice. It occurred to Jan that Relton might have been thinking of himself over that injunction; he might not wish it to be generally known that he had taken the delinquent up into his own rooms before haling him back to his house. At all events Jan felt he owed so good a fellow the benefit of any doubt upon the point. And his silence was the measure of his gratitude for the one redeeming feature of the whole miserable affair.

Miserable it was to the last degree, and most humiliating in its utterly unforeseen effect upon himself. His previous expressions of magnificent indifference, as to whether he was expelled or not, had not been altogether the boyish idle boast that they had sounded at the time. He had meant them rather more than less. His whole school life had seemed a failure; his early hatred of it had taken fresh hold of him. The provocation supplied by Bingley had been but a spark to the tinder already in Jan's heart. He had seen no prospect of creditable notoriety, and that of a discreditable kind had suddenly appealed to his aching young ambition. The fact that he had ambition, however crude and egotistical, might have shown him that school meant more to him than to many who accepted a humdrum lot with entire complacency. But Jan was not naturally introspective; the curse of consciousness was in him a recent growth; and like other young healthy minds, forced by circumstance into that alien habit, he misconceived himself on very many points. It had seemed a really fine thing to have got out at night, a fine fate even to be caught and expelled for it. But now that he really had been caught, and the drab reality of expulsion stared him in the face, he saw not only how inglorious it all was, but the glory that might have been his at the school he had affected to despise.

He had never despised it in his heart. He knew that now. He had begun by hating it as a wild creature hates captivity. He had learned to loathe it as the place where an awkward manner and a marked accent exposed one to incessant ridicule. But even in the days of hatred and of loathing, when his chief satisfaction had been to damp the ardour of an old enthusiast like Chips Carpenter, Jan himself had been conscious of a sneaking veneration for the great machine into which he had been thrust. He had meant it to make something of him, though that was not quite the light in which he had seen his own intention. He had meant at any rate to do as well as other fellows, to show them that he was as good as they were, though he might not have their manners or address. That had been the master impulse of his secret heart; he could trace it back to the beginning of his first term, to the football which was stopped, to the paper-chase in which he had run in spite of them, and then to last year's Mile and the cricket which was stopped again. How many things had been against him, and yet how little he had suspected his own strongest point! Only to think that he might have bowled for the school this coming season.

Relton might have kept that to himself. He had talked about making things better, but he had only made them worse to bear. He need not have said that about Jan's cricket. It was enough to drive a fellow mad with the thought of all that he was losing through his criminal folly. Individuals filled the stage of Jan's cruel visions, Evan Devereux in the limelight; what would he have said if Jan had got into the Eleven? Might it not have brought them together again? Evan had got into the Sixth Upper; he had been in the First Lower the term before Jan came; and Jan had been left out of even the lowest eleven on the Middle Ground, which Evan had skipped altogether. It would have been a case of the hare and the tortoise, but in the end they might both have been in the school team together, and then they could scarcely have failed to be friends. So simply did Jan think of the fellow with whom he now seldom exchanged so much as a nod; he was nevertheless the one to whom Jan felt that he owed more than to the whole school put together; for had he not kept Something right loyally to himself?

Then there was old Haigh. He would have seen that there might be something in a fellow who could not write Latin verses, something in even a sulky fellow! And Jan no longer sulked as he used; he was getting out of that; and yet he had done this thing, and would have to go.

Then there was Shockley and all that lot, the rotten element in the house. If he had really got into the Eleven, it would have made all the difference in the world between Jan and them. They never touched him as it was, but their words were often worse than blows, and far more difficult to return. But if Jan had got into the Eleven ... and Relton spoke as if he really would have a chance, but for this thing that he had done!

He lay in his bed and groaned aloud, and then found himself listening for even an answering movement from one of the others. He felt he could have opened out to them now, to any one of them; but they were all three evidently fast asleep. The church clock had struck two some time ago. And Jan was still poignantly awake; he had not lain awake like this since his very first night in the school and that partition; and now it was most probably his last.

To-morrow night he might be back in the rectory attic where he was less at home than here, and back under the blackest cloud of all his boyhood. That was saying something. Term-time was still preferable to the holidays, except when he went to stay with Chips and see some of the sights of London. And now it was the last night of his last term, unless a miracle was wrought to save him.

And now it was the last morning, and Jan felt yet another creature, because he had slept like a top after all, and the wild adventure of the night was no longer the sharp reality which had kept him awake so many hours. It was much more like a dream; it might or might not have happened. If it had happened, and they knew it had, why were Chips and Bingley washing and dressing without a word about it? Jan forgot about young Eaton, similarly employed in the fourth partition; but at the back of his muddled mind he knew well enough that it was no dream, even before his muddy boots afforded final proof. Yet he rushed downstairs as the last bell was ringing, flew along the street without a bite of dog-rock or a drop of milk, and hurled himself through the school-room door as the præpostor of the week was about to shut it in his face. As though it still mattered whether he was late or not!

He thought of that while he recovered his breath during the psalms; throughout the prayers he could only think of the awful voice reading them, and whether it would pronounce his doom before the whole school at ten o'clock, and whether it would not be even more appalling in private. Jan watched the pale old face, forearmed with another day's stock of stern care. And he wondered whether his beggarly case would add a flash to those austere eyes, or a passing furrow to that formidable brow.

Heriot's place at prayers was such that Jan could not see his face, but his shoulders looked inexorable, and from the poise of his head it was certain that his beard was sticking out. There was no catching Heriot's eye after prayers; and yet even Relton, at first school, looked as though nothing had happened overnight. He took his form in Greek history with that rather perfunctory air which marked all his work in school; but so far from ignoring Jan, or showing him any special consideration, Relton was down upon him twice for inattention, and on the second occasion ordered him to stay behind the rest. Jan did so in due course, and was not called up until the last of the others had left.

"I didn't keep you back for inattention," calmly explained young Relton. "I could hardly expect you to attend this morning. I kept you back to tell you of my conversation with Mr. Heriot last night."

"Thank you, sir."

"I began by sounding him on the punishment for getting out at night—even on the venial pretext of a lark—in which I was prepared to corroborate your statement as far as possible."

Dudley Relton was already falling into the schoolmaster's trick of literary language, and here was at least one word of which Jan did not know the meaning. But he expressed his gratitude again. And Relton gathered his books together with some care before proceeding.

"It's perfectly plain from what he says that the one and only punishment is—the sack!"

Jan said nothing. But neither did he wince. He was prepared for the blow, and from Dudley Relton he could bear it like a man.

"That being so," continued the other, stepping down from his desk, "I said nothing about last night, Rutter."

"You said nothing about it?"

This was far harder to hear unmoved. Jan even forgot to say "sir."

"Please don't raise your voice, Rutter."

"But—sir! Do you mean that you never told Mr. Heriot at all?"

"I do. I went in to tell him, but I soon saw it meant the end of you. So I said nothing about you after all. You'll kindly return the compliment, Rutter, or it may mean the end of me."

They faced each other in the empty class-room, the very young man and the well-grown boy. In actual age there were only some seven years between them, but at the moment there might have been much less. The spice of boyish mischief made the man look younger than his years, while a sudden sense of responsibility aged the boy.

It was Jan who first broke into a smothered jumble of thanks, expostulations, and solemn vows. There were only three fellows who knew he had got out at all; but even they did not know that he had actually encountered any master, and now they never should. His gratitude was less coherent, but his anxiety on Mr. Relton's behalf such as that unconventional usher was compelled to laugh to scorn.

"We're in each other's hands," said he, "and perhaps my motives were not so pure as you think. Remember at any rate, that you're my dark horse, Rutter. Run like a good 'un, and you'll soon be even with me. But never you run amuck again as you did last night!"

"I never will, sir, that I'll swear."

"I don't only mean to that extent. I saw a pipe in your mouth before the row. You weren't actually smoking, but I fancy you do."

"I have done, sir," said Jan, without entering into particulars about that pipe.

"Well, give it up. If you want to do something for me, don't go smoking again while you're here. It's bad for your eye and worse for your hand, and a bowler has need of both. Run as straight as a die, Rutter, and let's hope you'll bowl as straight as you run!"

CHAPTER XIX

FAME AND FORTUNE

There was really only one bowler in that year's Eleven, and Chips Carpenter was his prophet. There were others who took turns at the other end, who even captured a few wickets between them in the course of the season; but "the mainstay of our attack was Rutter," as the Mag. found more than one occasion to remark. That organ betrayed a marked belief in the new bowler, from his very first appearance, with the black school cap of previous obscurity pulled down behind his prominent ears. Its rather too pointed praises were widely attributed to the new Editor, none other than Jan's old Crabtree, now a præpostor and captain of Heriot's house. The fact was, however, that Crabtree employed Carpenter as cricket scribe and occasional poetaster, and had to edit him severely both in prose and verse, but especially in those very remarks which found disfavour in other houses.

Old Crabtree, who had suddenly grown into a young man, made by far the best captain the house ever had in Jan's time. But he was a terrible martinet. You had to shut yourself up in your study to breathe the mildest expletive with any safety, and it cost you sixpence to cast the smallest stone in the quad. Crabtree was not precisely popular; but he was respected for his scornful courage and his caustic tongue. It was his distinction to rule by dint of personality unaided by athletic prowess, and during his four terms of authority there can have been few better houses than Heriot's in any school. Shockley likened it to a nunnery without the nuns, and left in disgust for reasons best known to himself and Crabtree. Buggins and the portly Eyre grew into comparatively harmless and even useful members of the community. And the fluent and versatile Chips learnt a lesson or so for the term of his literary life.

"I wish you'd write of people by their names, instead of 'the latter' and 'the former'!" said Crabtree, coming into Chips's study with a proof. "And I say, look here! I'm blowed if I have 'The Promise of May' dragged in because we happen to have lost a match in June! And we won't butter Rutter more than twice in four lines, if you don't mind, Chips."

But Crabtree was not cricketer enough to perceive the quality of the butter apart from the quantity, and some sad samples escaped detection. They still disfigure certain back numbers to be found upon the shelves of the new school library. "Rutter took out his bat for a steadily-played five," for instance; and "the third ball—a beauty—bowled Rutter for a well-earned eight." They were certainly Jan's two longest scores for the team, for he was no batsman, but even on firmer ground the partial historian went much too far. "Better bowling than Rutter's in this match it would be impossible to imagine. His length was only surpassed by his break, and many of his deliveries were simply unplayable." Jan really had taken six wickets on the occasion of this eulogy, but at no inconsiderable cost, and the writer was unable to maintain his own note in the concluding paragraph of the report: "At the end of the first day's play I. T. Rutter received his first XI colours, which it is needless to say, were thoroughly well merited."

Jan's best performance, however, was in the match of the season, against the Old Boys on Founder's Day. Repton and Haileybury it was good to meet, and better to defeat, especially on the home ground with a partisan crowd applauding every stroke. Yet for the maintenance of high excitement the whole of the rival school should have been there as well; on the other hand, it cannot be contended that even the Old Boys' Match was necessarily exciting from a cricket point of view. It had other qualities less dependent on the glorious uncertainty of the game. It was the most popular feature of the prime festival in the school year. It afforded the rising generation an inspiring glimpse of famous forerunners, and it enabled those judges of the game to gauge the prowess of posterity. The Old Boys' Match had proved itself the cradle of many a reputation, and the early grave of one or two.

This year the Old Boys came down in force. There was old Boots Ommaney, the apple of the late professional's eye, who had played for England time and again at both ends of the earth. There was A. G. Swallow, for some seasons the best bowler, and still the finest all-round player, the school had ever turned out. There was the inevitable Swiller Wilman, a younger cricketer of less exalted class who nevertheless compiled an almost annual century in the match, and was the cheeriest creature in either team. In all there were six former captains of the Eleven, and four old University Blues. But Jan had seven of them in the first innings—five clean blowed—on a wicket just less than fast but as true as steel.

"Well bowled again!" said Dudley Relton in the pavilion. "Don't be disappointed if you don't do quite as well next innings, or even next year. But on that wicket you might run through the best side in England—for the first time of asking."

"It's the break that does it," replied Jan, modestly; "and I don't even know how I put it on."

"It's that break when they're expecting the other. Most left-handers break away from you; it's expected of them, and you do the unexpected, therefore you can bowl. Your break is the easier to play, once they're ready for it. If you only had 'em both, with your length and pace of the pitch, there'd be no holding you in any state of life. You're coming to the Conversazione, of course?"

"I don't think so, sir," answered Jan, blushing furiously.

"But you've got your colours, and all the team came last year. It's the school songs from the choir, and ices and things for all hands, you know."

"I know, sir."

"Then why aren't you coming?"

Jan looked right and left to see that no inquisitive ear was cocked above the collar of contiguous blazer. And then for a second he contemplated the characteristic person of Dudley Relton, as dapper and well-groomed and unlike a pedagogue as Jan knew him to be in grain.

"I haven't got a dress-suit; that's why, sir!" he whispered bitterly.

"What infernal luck!" Relton looked as indignant as Jan felt—and then lit up. "I say, though, we're much the same build, aren't we? I suppose you wouldn't let me see if I can fix you up, Jan?"

Had it been possible to strengthen the peculiar bond already existing between man and boy, these words and their successful sequel would have achieved that result. But indeed the last and least of the words counted for more with Jan than anything that came of them. It was the first time that Dudley Relton had called him by his Christian name. True, it was a school tradition that the Eleven went by theirs among their peers. But as yet the Eleven had not treated Jan precisely as one of themselves. He was younger than any of them, and lower in the school than most. In moments of excitement, such as occur in every match, there was still an unfortunate breadth about his vowels; and when he pulled even his Eleven cap tight over his head, making his ears stick out more than ever, and parting his back hair horizontally to the skin, there was sometimes a wink or a grin behind his back, though the little trick was not seldom the prelude to a wicket. It was characteristic, at all events, and as quickly noted by the many on the rugs as by the rest of the side in the field.

"Don't hustle," you would hear some fellow say; "the Tiger's got his cap pulled down, and I want to watch."

The saying was to acquire almost proverbial value. It proclaimed an omen as sinister in its way as the cloth on Table Mountain, or the sticking out of Bob Heriot's beard. But Crabtree censured an allusion to it in his cricket scribe's account of the Old Boys' Match.

That was a halcyon term for Jan, and to crown all he was still in Dudley Relton's form, and treated with cynical indulgence by that uncompromising specialist. Relton was there to uphold a cricketing tradition, to bridge a gap that could not be filled, and he would not have upset his best bowler even if there had been no other tie between them. The other tie never passed the lips of either, but the memory of it sweetened the bowler's triumph, and very likely that of the coach as well.

Heriot, moreover, was delighted to see a colleague obtain precisely that hold over Jan which a rare delicacy had rendered difficult in his own case. There was no flaw of jealousy or narrowness in Robert Heriot. He was a staunch champion of the much younger man, whose methods and temperament scarcely commended themselves to such hardened schoolmasters as Mr. Haigh and the notorious but insensible Spook. But then Heriot himself was having a very good term. His house was indeed in order under the incomparable Crabtree, nor was Rutter the only fellow in it playing for the Eleven. Stratten had got in for wicket-keeping, and Jellicoe was almost certain of his colours. The trio provided a bit of the best of everything for the house eleven; it was already carrying all before it in the All Ages competition; and Haigh had not spoken to Heriot for two whole days after the hill house went down before "the most obstinate blockhead that ever cumbered my hall."

Jan enjoyed that match; but it must be confessed that he showed far less enjoyment of all his triumphs than did Chips Carpenter on his behalf. Chips Carpenter, not content with singing his praises in print, was now prepared to talk about his friend by the hour together, and became so vociferous during the match in question as to have it straight from Mr. Haigh that he was "behaving like a private-school cad." His own house-master, on the other hand, had never thought so much of him; he knew what the mere enthusiast would have given to be a practical exponent of the game he had to talk and write about instead.

And Heriot liked Jan no less for sticking to his first friend as he did, and would have given something to have overheard one of the Sunday evening chats which the pair still had by weekly permission in Chips's study, because it was the only one of the two fit to sit in. Jan had not grown less indifferent to his immediate surroundings; he had still no soul for plush or Oxford frames; not only had the grease-spots multiplied on the green table-cloth foisted upon him by Shockley, but the papers on the floor were transparent with blots of oil from his bat. Carpenter, on the contrary, had made a miniature museum of his tiny den, and his lucubrations were promoted by the wise glass eyes of a moulting owl, purchased as a relic at Charles Cave's auction.

"I hope you're keeping the scores of all your matches," said he one night. "You ought to stick 'em in a book; if you won't I'll do it for you."

"What's the good?" inquired Jan, with the genial indolence of an athlete on his day off.

"Good? Well, for one thing, it'll be jolly interesting for your kids some day."

Chips had not smiled, but Jan grinned from ear to ear.

"Steady on! It's like you to look a hundred years ahead."

"Well, but surely your people would take an interest in them?"

"My people!"

Chips knew it was a sore subject. He knew more about it than he ever intended to betray; but he had committed his blunder, and it would have made bad worse to try to retrieve it by a suspicious silence or an incontinent change of topic. Besides, a part of his knowledge came from Jan's own deliverances on the sort of time he had in Norfolk.

"But surely they're jolly proud of your being in the Eleven?"

"My uncle might be. But he's in India."

"And I suppose the old people don't know what it means?"

"They might. I haven't told them, if you want to know."

Chips looked as though he could hardly believe his ears. Comment was impossible now; he shifted his ground to the sporting personal interest of such records as he would have treasured in Jan's place.

"You'll bowl for the Gentlemen before you've done," said Chips, "and then you'll be sorry you haven't got the first chapter in black and white. You should see the book A. G. Swallow keeps! I saw it once, when he came to stay at my private school. He's even got his Leave to be in the Eleven, signed by Jerry; but upon my Sam if I were you I'd have that in a frame!"

It was a characteristic enactment that nobody could obtain his Eleven or Fifteen colours without a permit signed and countersigned by House Master and Form Master, and finally endorsed by Mr. Thrale himself, whose autograph was seldom added without a cordial word of congratulation.

"I believe I have got that," said Jan, "somewhere or other."

And Chips eventually discovered it among the Greek and Latin litter on the floor.

"What a chap you are!" he cried. "I'm going to keep this for you until one or other of us leaves, Tiger. You're—I won't say you're not fit to be in the Eleven—nobody was ever more so—but I'm blowed if you deserve to own a precious document like this!"

Yet there was another missive, and souvenir of his success, which Jan had already under lock and key, except when he took it out to read once more. Chips never saw or heard of this one; but he would have recognised the fluent writing at a glance, and Jan knew what sort of glance it would have been.

This was the little note, word for word:—

"The Lodge,

"June 1st.

"Dear old Jan,

"I can never tell you how I rejoice at your tremendous success. Heaps of congratulations! I'm proud of you, so will they all be at home.

"School is awful for dividing old friends unless you're in the same house or form. You know that's all it is or ever was! Will you forgive me and come for a walk after second chapel on Sunday? Always your old friend,

"Evan."

Chips knew nothing until the Sunday, when he said he supposed Jan was coming out after second chapel as usual, and Jan answered very off-hand that he was awfully sorry he was engaged. "One of the Eleven, I suppose?" says Chips, not in the least disposed to grudge him to them. Then Jan told the truth aggressively, and Chips made a tactless comment, whereupon Jan told him he could get somebody else to sit in his study that night. It was the first break in an arrangement which had lasted since their first term. Jan was sorry, and not only because it was so open to misconstruction; he was man enough to go in after all as though nothing had happened. And silly old Chips nearly wept with delight. But nothing was said about the afternoon walk and talk, which Jan had enjoyed more than any since the affair of the haunted house.

It was just as well that Carpenter had been left out of it this time. Two is not only company, but to drag in a third is to invite the critics, and Chips would not have found Evan Devereux improved. Indeed he saw quite enough of Devereux in school to have a strong opinion as to that already; but they never fraternised in the least, and it is in his intimate moments that a boy is at his best or worst.

Evan was at once as intimate with Jan as though they had been at different schools for the last year and here was another reunion of which they must make the most. He took Jan's arm outside the chapel, and off they went together like old inseparables. Evan seemed a good deal more than a year older; his voice had settled in a fine rich key; his reddish hair was something crisper and perhaps less red. But he was still short for his age, and by way of acquiring the cock-sparrow strut of some short men. His conversation strutted deliciously. It would have made Carpenter roar—afterwards—but grind his teeth at the time. Of course it was cricket conversation, but Evan soon turned it from Jan's department of the game. Jan followed him in all humility. Evan had been a bit of a batsman all his life. True, in old days the stable lad had usually been able to bowl him out at will, but he had always wished that he could bat as well himself. He said so now, and Evan, who was going to get into the third eleven with luck, was full of sympathy with the best bowler in the school.

"It must be beastly always going in last," said Evan. "I expect you're jolly glad when you don't get a ball. But you don't have to walk back alone—that's one thing!"

"I'm always afraid I may have to go in when a few are wanted to win the match, and some good bat well set at the other end. That's the only thing I should mind," said Jan.

"You remember the Pinchington ground?" said Evan abruptly, as though he had not been listening.

"I do that!" cried Jan, and Evan looked round at him. As small boys they had played at least one match together on the ground in question; and Jan still wondered what he would not have given to be in flannels then like Master Evan, instead of in his Sunday shirt and trousers; but Evan was thinking that the school bowler had spoken exactly like the stable lad.

"I got up a match there," he continued, "at the end of last holidays, and I'm going to get up two or three this August. It's an awful hustle! We play the Pinchington Juniors—awful chaps—but so are some of mine. My best bowler's learning to drive a hearse. We've a new under-gardener who can hit like smoke. I'd have got a lot myself if it had been a decent wicket, but I mean to have one next holiday."

"Does old Crutchy still bowl?" asked Jan, grinning allusively.

"Rather! Hobbles up to the wicket, clumps down his crutch and slings 'em in like a demon. He would be jam on a decent pitch! I was going to say, I got 48 one day last summer holidays. It wasn't against the Juniors—it was a boys' match at Woodyatt Hall—but I did give 'm stick!"

"Well done!" said Jan, quite impressed. "I never made anything like that in my life. You're playing for your house, aren't you?"

"Rather! I should hope so. I got 19 not out the other day against the United—including two fours to leg off Whitfield major."

And so forth with copious details. Whitfield major was the hard hitter of the Eleven, and as bad a fast bowler as ever took an occasional wicket. Jan, who always preferred doing a thing to talking about it, and who wanted to know a lot of things that he did not like to ask, made sundry attempts to change the conversation. He asked after the horses, and was both sorry and embarrassed to gather that the stable had been reduced. He tried Evan's friends, the Miss Christies, as a safer topic; he had always admired them himself, at the tremendous distance of old days; but this time he called them "the Christies," and it was Evan who perhaps inadvertently supplied the "Miss" in answering.

No; cricket was the only talk. And as they wandered back towards the thin church spire with the golden cock atop, looking rather like an inverted note of exclamation on a sheet of pale blue paper, it was made more and more plain to Jan that he was not to regard himself as the only cricketer. But he had no desire to do so, and nothing could have been heartier than his attitude on the point implied.

"You'll get your colours next year, Evan, and then we'll be in the same game every day of our lives!"

"I have my hopes, I must say; but it's not so easy to get in as a bat."

"No; you may get a trial and not come off, but a bowler's bound to if he's any good. Anyhow you're in a jolly strong house, and that's always a help."

"We ought to be in the final this year," said Evan, thoughtfully.

"And so ought we," said Jan.

They were both right; and the last match of the term on the Upper was the decisive tussle between their two houses. It was also Evan's first appearance in the very middle of that august stage, and a few days before the event he told Jan that his people were coming down to see it. Jan could not conceal his nervousness at the prospect. But it left him more than ever determined that Heriot's should have the cup. He had some flannels specially done up at the last moment, and his hair cut the day before the match.

But he pulled his cap down further than ever when he took the ball, and it gashed his back hair the more conspicuously to the scalp. In one word, and in spite of his spotless flannels, he looked dreadfully like the rather palpable "pro." of those days, and his bowling only fostered the suggestion. There was a regularity about the short quick run, an amount of character in the twiddling fore-arm action, a precision of length and a flick off the pitch that set a professional stamp upon his least deadly delivery. Above all there was that naturally unnatural break which Jan only lost when he began to think about it, or when the ground was a great deal harder than he was fortunate enough to find it in the final house-match.

It was just the least bit dead that day—a heart-breaking wicket for most bowlers—but one that might have been specially prepared for Jan. He had the mysterious power of making his own pace off such a pitch, and the fact that the ball only rose stump-high simply enabled him to bowl bailer after bailer, one and all with that uncanny turn from the off. Variety was lacking; a first-class batsman would have taken the measure of the attack in about an over; but there was scarcely the makings of one such in the Lodge team, and great was the fall of that strong house. Statistics would be a shame. Suffice it that Heriot's lost the toss, but won a low-scoring match by an innings in the course of the afternoon. Jan had fifteen wickets in all, including Evan's twice over. The first time he was assisted by a snap-catch in the slips, and Evan's nought might fairly be accounted hard lines. But in the second innings it was a complex moment for Jan when Evan strutted in with all the air of a saviour of situations. Jan did not want him to fail again, and yet he did because Evan's people were looking on! He felt mean and yet exalted as he led off with a trimmer, and the leg-bail hit Stratten in the face.

Then Jan showed want of tact.

"I'm awfully sorry!" he stammered out, but Evan passed him in a flame, without look or sign of having heard.

Mr. Devereux, however, could afford to treat the whole affair differently. And he did.

He was a fine-looking man of the florid type, with a light grey bowler, a flower in his coat, and a boisterous self-confidence, which made him almost too conspicuous on the unequal field. Mr. Devereux was far from grudging Jan his great success; on the contrary, he seemed only too inclined to transfer his paternal pride to his old coachman's son, and in reality was sorely tempted to boast of him in that relationship. Some saving sense of fitness, abetted by an early hint (but nothing more) from Heriot, sealed his itching lips; but in talking to the lad himself, Mr. Devereux naturally saw no necessity for restraint.

"I remember when you used to bowl to my son in front of your father's—ah—in front of those cottages of mine—with a solid india-rubber ball! We never thought of all this then, did we? But I congratulate you, my lad, and very glad I am to have the opportunity."

"Thank you very much, sir," said Jan, in a grateful glow from head to heel.

"I'll tell them all about you down there; and some day you must come and stay with us, as a guest, you know, and play a match of two for Evan and his friends at Pinchington. You'll be one too many for the village lads. Quite a hero, you'll find yourself."

Jan was not so sure what to say to that; and he could only be as fervid as before when Mr. Devereux slipped a sovereign into his hand, though it was the first that he had received all at once in all his schooldays.

CHAPTER XX

THE EVE OF OFFICE

Thenceforward the career of Jan was that of the public-school cricketer who is less readily remembered as anything else. One forgets that he had to rush out to early school like other people, and even work harder than most to keep afloat in form. It takes a dip into bound volumes of the Mag. to assure one that "solid work in the bullies" (of the old hybrid game) eventually landed him into the Fifteen, and that he was placed more than once in the Mile and the Steeplechase without ever winning either. Those were not Jan's strong points, though he took them no less seriously at the time. They kept him fit during the winter, but not through them would his name be alive to-day. Some of his bowling analyses, on the other hand, are as unforgettable as the date of the Conquest; and it is with his Eleven cap pulled down over his eyes, and a grim twinkle under the peak, that the mind's eye sees him first and almost last.

His second year in the Eleven was nearly—not quite—as successful as his first. He took even more Haileyburian and Reptonian wickets, but experienced batsmen who came down with other teams made sometimes almost light of that clockwork break from the off. The cheery Swiller (who of course owed his nickname to a notorious teetotalism) did not again fail to compile his habitual century for the Old Boys. It was a hotter summer, and the wickets just a trifle faster than those after Jan's own heart.

Still he had a fine season, and a marvellously happy one. He was now somebody on the side; not a mere upstart bowler of no previous status, rather out of it with the Eleven off the field. The new captain was a very nice fellow in one of the hill houses; he not only gave Jan his choice of ends on all occasions, and an absolute say in the placing of his field, but took his best bowler's opinion on the others and consulted him on all sorts of points. Jan found himself in a position of high authority without the cares of office, and the day came when he appreciated the distinction.

Stratten and Jellicoe were in the team for their second and last year, and the All Ages cup remained undisturbed on the baize shelf in Heriot's hall. Crabtree, moreover, was still the captain of a house in which his word was martial law. But he also was leaving; all the bigwigs were, except Jan himself. And after the holidays Heriot had to face a younger house than for some years past, with a certain colourless præpostor in command till Christmas, and only old Chips Carpenter to succeed him.

Chips was now a præpostor himself, being actually in the Upper Sixth, thanks to the deliberately modest standard of learning throughout the school. He could write Latin verses against the best of them, however, and he now edited the precious periodical to which he had so long contributed. This gave him his own standing in the school, while a really genial temperament was no longer discounted by the somewhat assertive piety of his earlier youth. And yet it was not only a touch of priggishness that Chips had outgrown; the old enthusiasm was often missing; it was his bad patch of boyhood, and he had struck it rather later than most, and was taking himself to heart under all the jokes and writings of this period.

Chips was still in no eleven at all; he thought he ought to have been in one on the Middle, at any rate, and perhaps he was right. He was a very ardent wicket-keeper, who had incurred a certain flogging in his saintliest days by cutting a detention when engaged to keep wicket on the Lower. In the winter months, with his new Lillywhite usually concealed about his person, he used still to dream of runs from his own unhandy bat; but in his heart he must have known his only place in the game, as student and trumpeter of glories beyond his grasp. Was he not frank about it in his lament for the holiday task he had failed to learn "in the holidays, while there was time?"

"But 'tis no use lamenting. What is done
You couldn't undo if you tried....
O, if only they'd set us some Wisden,
Or Lillywhite's Guide!"

Many fellows liked old Chips nowadays, and more took a charitable view of his writings; but few would have picked him out as a born leader of men, and he certainly had no practice in the little dormitory at the top of the house. It was rather by way of being a cripples' ward, for Carpenter was still debarred from football by his bronchitis, and the small boy Eaton, who was not so young as he looked, but an amusing rogue, had trumped up a heart of the type imputed to Jan Rutter when he fainted in the Spook's mathematical. Eaton was a shameless "sloper," but he had heaps of character, and he saved the prospective captain of the house some embarrassment by leaving at Christmas.

Chips had taken to photography as a winter pursuit; and so rare was the hobby in those days that for some time he was the only photographer in the school. Eaton accompanied him on many a foray, and swung the tripod while Chips changed the case containing the camera from hand to hand. They obtained excellent negatives of some of the delightful old churches in the neighbourhood, including the belfry tower at Burston, seen through its leafless beeches, and the alabaster monument in the chancel at Stoke Overton. But by far the most popular success was the speaking picture of Mr. and Mrs. Maltby, on the doorstep of their famous resort in the market-place; to satisfy the vast demand for that masterpiece, the præpostor was placed in a bit of a quandary, but young Eaton borrowed the negative and did a roaring trade at sixpence a print.

In the meantime Evan Devereux had been elected Captain of Games: a most important officer in the Easter term, the games in question being nothing of the kind, except in an Olympic sense, but just the ordinary athletic sports. The Captain of Games arranged the heats, fixed the times, acted as starter, superintended everything and exercised over all concerned a control that just suited Evan. He proved himself a born master of ceremonies, with a jealous eye for detail, but a little apt to fuss and strut at the last moment on a course cleared of the common herd. He dressed well, and had a pointed way of taking off his hat to the master's ladies. There were those, of course, who crudely described his mannerisms as mere "roll"; but on the whole it would have been hard to find a keener or more capable Captain of Games.

The office was usually held by a member of the Eleven or of the Fifteen. Evan was in neither yet, though on the edge of both. On the other hand, he was very high in the Upper Sixth; for he had lost neither his facility for acquiring knowledge, nor his inveterate horror of laying himself open to rebuke.

It is at first sight a little odd that such a blameless boy should ever have made a friend of one Sandham, a big fellow low down in the school, and in another house. Sandham, however, was a handsome daredevil of strong but questionable character, and it suited him to have a leading præpostor for his friend. One hesitates to add that he was a younger son of a rather prominent peer, lest the statement be taken as in any way accounting for Evan's side of the friendship. It is only the thousandth boy, however, who troubles himself to think twice about another's fellow's people, high or low. Of all beings boys are in this respect the least snobbish, and Evan Devereux was of all schoolboys the last to embody an exception to that or any other general rule. Sandham was not the only fellow whose hereditary quality was denoted by a "Mr." in the list; the others were nobodies in the school, and neither Evan nor anybody else made up to them. But to the aristocracy of athletics he could bow as low as his neighbour, and his friend Sandham was an athlete of the first water. Half-back in the fifteen, as good a bat as there was in the Eleven, and a conjuror at extra cover, the gifted youth must needs signalise his friend's Captaincy of Games by adding the Athletic Championship to his bag of honours. Winner of the Steeplechase, Hurdles, Hundred-yards, Quarter-mile and Wide-jump, not only was Sandham Champion but the rest were nowhere in the table of marks. It must be added that he wore his halo with a rakish indifference which lent some colour to the report that "Mr." Sandham had been removed from Eton before old Thrale gave him another chance.

"He's a marvellous athlete, whatever else he is," said Chips to Jan, on the last Sunday of the Easter term.

"I'm blowed if I know what else he is," replied Jan, "but I should be sorry to see quite so much of him if I were Evan."

"Not you," cried Chips, "if you were Evan! You'd jolly well see all you could of anybody at the top of the tree!"

"Look here, Chips, dry up! Evan's pretty near the top himself."

"Are you going to stick him in the Eleven?"

"If he's good enough, and I hope he will be."

"Of course it's expected of you."

"Who expects it?"

"Sandham for one, and Devereux himself for another. Didn't you see how they stopped to make up to you when they overtook us just now?"

"I don't know what you mean. Evan's a friend of mine, and of course I've seen a lot of Sandham. They only asked if I was going to get any practice in the holidays."

"They took good care to let you know they were going to have some. So Evan's going to stay with Sandham's people, is he?"

"It was Sandham said that."

"And they're going to have a professor down from Lord's!"

"Well, they might be worse employed."

"They might so. I should rather like to know what they're up to at this very minute."

The scene was one of the many undulating country roads that radiated from the little town like tentacles. Chips and Jan were strolling lazily between the jewelled hedge-rows of early April; the other two had overtaken them rather suddenly, walking very fast, and had stopped, as if on second thoughts, to make perfunctory conversation. Evan had turned rather red, as he still would in a manner that must have been a trial to him. There had followed the few words about the holidays to which Chips had alluded, but in which he had not joined. He also had his old faults in various stages of preservation; touchiness was one of them, jealousy another. But his last words had been called forth by nothing more or worse than a fresh sight of Evan and Sandham on the sky-line, climbing a gate into a field.

"I votes we go some other way," said Jan. "I don't like spying on chaps, even when it's only a case of a cigarette."

"No more do I," his friend agreed, thoughtfully. And another way they went. But the conversation languished between them, until rather suddenly Carpenter ran his arm through Jan's.

"Isn't it beastly to be so near the end of our time, Tiger? Only one more term!"

"It is a bit," assented Jan, lukewarmly. "I know you feel it, but I often think I'd have done better to have left a year ago."

Chips looked round at him as they walked.

"And you Captain of Cricket!"

"That's why," said Jan, in the old grim way.

"But, my dear chap, it's by far the biggest honour you can possibly have here!"

"I know all that, Chipsy; but there's a good deal more in it than honour and glory. There's any amount to do. You're responsible for all sorts of things. Bruce used to tell me last year. It isn't only writing out the order, nor yet changing your bowling and altering the field."

"No; you've first got to catch your Eleven."

"And not only that, but all the other elevens on the Upper, and captains for both the other grounds. You're responsible for all the lot, and you've got to make up your mind that you can't please everybody."

Chips said nothing. Some keen præpostor was invariably made Captain of the Middle. Chips would have loved the unexalted post; but as he had never been in any eleven at all, even that distinction would be denied him by a rigid adherence to tradition. And evidently Jan had no intention of favouring his friends, if indeed this particular idea had crossed his mind.

"One ought to know every fellow in the school by sight," he continued. "But I don't know half as many as I did. Do you remember how you were always finding out fellows' names, Chips, our first year or so? You didn't rest till you could put a name to everybody above us in the school; but I doubt we neither of us take much stock of the crowd below."

"I find the house takes me all my time, and you must feel the same way about the Eleven, only much more so. By Jove, but I'd give all I'm ever likely to have on earth to change places with you!"

"And I'm not sure that I wouldn't change places with you. Somehow things always look different when you really get anywhere," sighed Jan, discovering an eternal truth for himself.

"But to captain the Eleven!"

"To make a good captain! That's the thing."

"But you will, Jan; look at your bowling."

"It's not everything. You've got to drive your team; it's no good only putting your own shoulder to the wheel. And they may be a difficult team to drive."

"Sandham may. And if Devereux—"

"Sandham's not the only one," interrupted Jan, who was not talking gloomily, but only frankly as he felt. "There's Goose and Ibbotson—who're in already—and Chilton who's bound to get in. A regular gang of them, and I'm not in it, and never was."

"But you're in another class!" argued Carpenter, forgetting himself entirely in that affectionate concern for a friend which was his finest point. "You're one of the very best bowlers there ever was in the school, Jan."

"I may have been. I'm not now. But I might be again if I could get that leg-break."

"You shall practise it every day on our lawn when you come to us these holidays."

"Thanks, old chap. Everybody says it's what I want. That uncle of mine said so the very first match we played together, when he was home again last year."

"Well, he ought to know."

And the conversation declined to a highly technical discussion in which Chips Carpenter, the rather puny præpostor who could never get into any eleven, held his own and more; for the strange fact was that he still knew more about cricket than the captain of the school team. At heart, indeed, he was the more complete cricketer of the two; for Jan was just a natural left-hand bowler, only too well aware of his limitations, and in some danger of losing his gift through the laborious cultivation of quite another knack which did not happen to be his by nature.

The trouble had begun about the time of the last Old Boys' Match, when Jan had heard more than enough of the break which was not then at his command; egged on by Captain Ambrose in the summer holidays, he had tried it with some success in village cricket, and had thought about it all the winter. Now especially it was the question uppermost in his mind. Was he going to make the ball break both ways this season? The point mattered more than the constitution of the Eleven, Evan's inclusion in it (much as that was to be desired), or the personal relations of the various members. If only Jan himself could bowl better than ever, or even up to his first year's form, then he would carry the whole side to victory on his shoulders.

CHAPTER XXI

OUT OF FORM

There was one great loss which the school and Jan had suffered since the previous summer. Tempted by the prospect of a free hand, unfettered by tradition, and really very lucky in his selection for the post, Dudley Relton had accepted the head-mastership of a Church of England Grammar School in Victoria. Already he was out there, doubtless at work on the raw material of future Australia teams, while Jan was left sighing for the rather masterful support which the last two captains had been apt a little to resent. Relton was not replaced by another of his still rare kind, but by the experienced captain of a purely professional county team—a fine player and a steady man—but not an inspired teacher of the game. To coach anybody in anything, it is obviously better to know a little and to be able to impart it, than to know everything but the art of transmitting your knowledge. George Grimwood had plenty of patience, but expended too much in a vain attempt to inculcate certain strokes of genius which he himself made by light of nature. He flew a bit too high for his young beginners, and he naturally encouraged Jan to persevere with his leg-breaks.

Not a day of that term but the Captain of Cricket sighed for Dudley Relton, with his confident counsels and his uncanny knowledge of the game. Especially was this the case in the early part of May, when trial matches had to be arranged without the assistance of a single outsider who knew anything about anybody's previous form. Jan found that he knew really very little about the new men himself; and Grimwood's idea of a trial match was that it was "matterless" who played for the Eleven and who for the Rest (with Grimwood). The new captain no doubt took his duties too seriously from the first, but he had looked to the new professional for more assistance outside his net. On the other hand, he was under a cross-fire of suggestions from the other fellows already in the team—of whom there were four. Now, five old choices make a fine backbone to any school eleven; but Jan could not always resist the thought that his task would have been lighter with only one or two in a position to offer him advice, especially as house feeling ran rather high in the school.

Thus old Goose, who as Captain of Football deserved his surname but little in public opinion, though very thoroughly in that of the masters, would have filled half the vacant places from his own house; and his friend Ibbotson, a steady bat but an unsteady youth, had other axes to grind. Tom Buckley, a dull good fellow who ought to have been second to Jan in authority, invariably advocated the last view confided to him. But what annoyed Jan most was the way in which Sandham ran Evan as his candidate, from the very first day of the term, pressing his claims as though other people were bent on disregarding them.

"I saw Evan play before you did, Sandham," said Jan, bluntly; "and there's nobody keener than me to see him come off."

"But you didn't see him play in the holidays. The two bowlers we had down from Lord's thought no end of him. I don't think you know what a fine bat Evan is."

"Well, I'm only too ready to learn. He's got the term before him, like all the lot of us."

"Yes, but he's the sort to put in early, Rutter; you take my word for it. He has more nerves in his little finger than you and I in our whole bodies."

"I know him," said Jan, rather tickled at having Evan of all people expounded to him.

"Then you must know that he's not the fellow to do himself justice till he gets his colours."

"Well, I can't give him them till he does, can I?"

"I don't know. You might if you'd seen him playing those professors. And then you're a friend of his, aren't you, Rutter?"

"Well, I can't give him his colours for that!"

"Nobody said you could; but you might give him a chance," returned Sandham, sharply.

"I might," Jan agreed, "even without you telling me, Sandham!"

And they parted company with mutual displeasure; for Jan resented the suggestion that he was not going to give his own friend a fair chance, even more than the strong hint to favour him as such; and

Sandham, who had expected a rough dog like Rutter to be rather flattered by his confidential advice, went about warning the others that they had to deal with a Jack-in-office who wouldn't listen to a word from any of them.

Nevertheless Evan played in the first two matches, made 5, 0 and 1, and was not given a place against the M.C.C. Jan perhaps unwisely sent him a note of very real regret, which Evan acknowledged with a sneer when they met on the Upper.

Jan had even said in his note, in a purple patch of deplorable imprudence, that on his present form he knew he ought not to be playing himself, only as captain he supposed it was his duty to do his best. He could not very well kick himself out, but if he could he would have given Evan his place that day.

Indeed, he had not proved worth his place in either of the first two matches. Scores were not expected of him, though he no longer went in absolutely last; but his bowling had given away any number of runs, while accounting for hardly any wickets at all. Jan had lost his bowling. That was the simple truth of the matter. He had squandered his natural gifts of length and spin in the sedulous cultivation of a ball which Nature had never intended him to bowl. In striving to acquire a new and conscious subtlety, his hand had lost its original and innate cunning. It is a phase in the development of every artist, but it had come upon Jan at a most inopportune stage of his career. Moreover it had come with a gust of unpopularity in itself enough to chill the ardour of a more enthusiastic cricketer than Jan Rutter.

Jan had never professed a really disinterested enthusiasm for the game. He had been a match-winning bowler, who had thoroughly enjoyed winning matches, especially when they looked as bad as lost; he could never have nursed a hopeless passion for the game, like poor old futile Chips Carpenter. But he still had the faculty of meeting his troubles with a glow rather than a shiver; and he bowled like a lonely demon against the M.C.C. It was a performance not to be named in the same breath as his olden deeds, but he did get wickets, and all of them with the old ball that whipped off the pitch with his arm. The new ball betrayed itself by an unconscious change of action—pitched anywhere—and went for four nearly every time. Nevertheless, in the obstinacy of that glowing heart of his, Jan still bowled the new ball once or twice an over. And the school were beaten by the M.C.C.

There was, however, one continual excuse for a bowler of this type that term. It was no summer; the easy wet wicket seldom dried into a really difficult one. When it did, that was not the wicket on which Jan was most dangerous; and for all his erudition in the matter, Chips was quite beside the great mark made aforetime by his friend, when he sang of the game for almost the last time in the Mag.—

"Break, break, break,
On a dead slow pitch, O Ball!
And I would that the field would butter
The catch that's the end of all!"

 "And the beastly balls come in—"

But the trouble was that Jan's came in so slowly on the juicy wickets that a strong back-player had leisure to put them where he liked.

Some matches were abandoned without a ball being bowled; but towards Founder's Day there was some improvement, and to insult the injured cricketer there had been several fine Sundays before that.

On one of these, the last of a few dry days in early June, Chips and Jan were out for another walk together, in the direction of Yardley Wood.

It was the road on which Devereux and Sandham had overhauled them before the Easter holidays; this time they pursued it to a pleasant upland lane where they leant against some posts and rails, and looked down across a couple of great sloping meadows to the famous covert packed into the valley with more fields rising beyond. The nearest meadow was bright emerald after so much rain. The next one had already a glint of gold in the middle distance. But the fields that rose again beyond the dense, dark wood, over a mile away, were neither green nor yellow, but smoky blue.

It was the wood itself, within half that distance, that drew and held the boys' attention. It might have been a patch of dark green lichen in the venerable roof of England, and the further fields its mossy slates.

"It looks about as good a jungle as they make," said Chips. "I should go down and practise finding my way across it, if I was thinking of going out to Australia."

Chips looked round as he spoke. But Jan confined his attention to the wood.

"It'd take you all your time," he answered. "It's more like a bit of overgrown cocoanut matting than anything else."

Chips liked the simile, especially as a sign of liveliness in Jan; but it dodged the subject he was trying to introduce. The fact was that Jan's future was just now a matter of anxiety to himself and his friends. There had long been some talk of his going to Australia, to an uncle who had settled out there, whereas he himself would have given anything to go for a soldier like his other uncle. This was an impracticable dream; but Dudley Relton, consulted on the alternative, had written back to say that in his opinion Australia was the very place for such as Jan. Heriot, on the other hand, had quite other ideas; and Jan was too divided in his own mind, and too sick of the whole question, to wish to discuss it for the hundredth time with such a talker as old Chips.

"Just about room for the foxes," he went on about the covert, "and that's all."

"Is it, though!" cried Carpenter.

"Well, I'm blowed," muttered Jan.

An arresting figure had emerged from one of the sides for which Yardley Wood was celebrated. At least Jan pointed out a white mark in the dense woodland wall, and Chips could believe it was a gate, as he screwed up his eyes to sharpen their vision of the man advancing into the lower meadow. All he could make out was a purple face, a staggering gait, and a pair of wildly waving arms.

"What's up, do you suppose?" asked Chips, excitedly.

"I'm just waiting to see."

The unsteady figure was signalling and gesticulating with increasing vivacity. The dark edge of the wood threw out the faded brown of his corduroys, the incredible plum-colour of his complexion. Signals were never flown against better background.

"Something must have happened!" exclaimed Chips. "Hadn't we better go and see what it is?"

"Not quite. Don't you see who it is?"

Chips screwed his eyes into slits behind his glasses.

"Is it old Mulberry?"

"Did you ever see another face that colour?"

"You're right. But what does he want with us? Look at him beckoning! Can you hear what he's shouting out?"

A hoarse voice had reached them, roaring.

"No, and I don't want to; he's as drunk as a fool, as usual."

"I'm not so sure, Jan. I believe something's up."

"Well, we'll soon see. I'm not sure but what you're right after all."

Mulberry was nearing the nearer meadow, still waving and ranting as he came. Chips said he knew he was right, and it was a shame not to meet the fellow half-way; there might have been some accident in the wood. Chips had actually mounted the lowest of the rails against which they had been leaning, and so far Jan had made no further protest, when the drunkard halted in the golden meadow, snatched off his battered hat, and bowed so low that he nearly fell over on his infamous nose. Then he turned his back on them, and retreated rapidly to the wood, with only an occasional stumble in his hurried stride.

"Come on," said Jan with a swing of the shoulder. "I never could bear the sight of that brute. He's spoilt the view."

In a minute the boys were out of the green lane, and back upon the hilly road, one in the grip of a double memory, the other puzzling over what had just occurred.

"I can't make out what he meant by it, can you, Jan? It was as though he thought he knew us, and then found he didn't."

Jan came back to the present to consider this explanation. He not only agreed with it, but he carried it a step further on his own account.

"You've hit it! He took us for two other fellows in the school."

"In the school? I hadn't thought of that."

"Who else about here wears a topper on Sundays, except you Pollies?[1] Besides, he came near enough to see my school cap."

"But what fellows in the school would have anything to do with a creature like that?"

"I don't know," said Jan. "We're not all nobility and gentry; there's some might get him to do some dirty work or other for them. It might be a bet, or it might be a bit of poaching, for all you know."

"That doesn't sound like a præpostor," said Chips, speaking up for the Upper Sixth like a man after old Thrale's heart.

"You never know," said Jan.

The discussion was not prolonged. It was interrupted, first by a rising duet of invisible steps, and then by the apparition of Evan Devereux and his friend Sandham hurrying up the hill with glistening faces.

"Talk of the nobility and gentry!" said Chips, when the pair had passed with a greeting too curt to invite a stoppage. But Jan's chance phrase was not the only coincidence. The encounter had occurred at the very corner where the same four fellows had met by similar accident on the last Sunday of last term. Moreover Evan, like Chips, was wearing the præpostor's Sunday hat, while Sandham and Jan were in their ordinary school caps.

[1] Præpostors.

CHAPTER XXII

THE OLD BOYS' MATCH

Founder's Day was mercifully fine. A hot sun lit the usual scene outside the colonnade, where the Old Boys assembled before the special service with which the day began, and greeted each other to the merry measure of the chapel bells. Most of the hardy annual faces were early on the spot, with here and there a bronzed one not to be seen every year, but a good sprinkling as smooth as the other day when they left the school. These were the men of fashion, coming down at last in any clothes they liked; among them Bruce, last year's captain, and Stratten his wicket-keeper, who was also a friend of Jan's.

Under the straw hats with the famous ribbons were Swallow and Wilman, who never looked a day older, and the great Charles Cave who did. It was his first appearance as an Old Boy, and perhaps only due to the fact that his young brother was playing for the school. Charles Cave wore a Zingari ribbon and a Quidnunc tie, but there was every hope of seeing the Cambridge sash round his lithe waist later. His tawny hair seemed to have lost a little of its lustre, and he looked down his aristocratic nose at oral reports of the Eleven and of the captain's bowling. But fancy that young Rutter being in at all, let alone captain! Fine bowler his first year? So were lots of them, but how many lasted? It was the old story, and Charles Cave looked the Methusaleh of Cricket as he shook that handsome head of his.

But the captain's bowling was not the worst; they did say his actual captaincy was just as bad, and that he was frightfully "barred" by the team. Of course he never had been quite the man for the job, whatever young Stratten chose to say. Stratten would stick up for anybody, especially of his own house; he would soon see for himself. And what about these measles? A regular outbreak, apparently, within the last week; fresh cases every day; among others, the best bat in the school! That young Sandham, no less. Hard luck? Scarcely worth playing the match, with such a jolly good lot of Old Boys down.... So the heads and tongues wagged together, and with them those happy chapel bells, until one was left ringing more sedately by itself, and the Old Boys filed in and up to their prominent places at the top of the right-hand aisle.

Evan Devereux, always a musical member of a very musical school, sat in the choir in full view of the young men of all ages. But he did not look twice at them; he might not have known that they were there. Yet it was not the obviously assumed indifference of one only too conscious that they were there, and who they all were, and which of them were going to play in the match. Evan might have felt that he ought to have been playing against them, that only a brute with a spite against him would have left him out; but he did not look as though he were thinking of that now. He did not look bitter or contemptuous; he did look worried and distrait. Any one, sufficiently interested in his flushed face and sharp yet sensitive features, might have observed that he seldom turned over a leaf, or remembered to open his compressed mouth; from it alone they might have seen that he was miserable, but they could not possibly have guessed why.

Neither did Jan when he chased Evan to his study immediately after chapel.

"It's all right, Evan! You've got to play, if you don't mind!"

"Who says so?" cried Evan, swinging round.

Of course it was not his old study, but it was just as dark inside, like all the Lodge studies leading straight out into the quad; and Jan very naturally misconstrued the angry tone, missing altogether its note of alarm.

"I do, of course. I was awfully sorry ever to leave you out, but what else was I to do? Thank goodness you've got your chance again, and I only hope you'll make a century!"

Jan was keen to the point of fervour; no ill-will of any sort or kind, not even the reflex resentment of an unpopular character, seemed to survive in his mind. His delight on his friend's behalf seemed almost to have restored his confidence in himself.

"Then I'll see if I can't bowl a bit," he added, "and between us we'll make Charles Cave & Co. sit up!"

"I—I don't think I'm awfully keen on playing, thank you," said Evan, in a wavering voice of would-be stiffness.

"You are!"

"I'm not, really, thanks all the same."

"But you can't refuse to play for the school, just because I simply was obliged—"

"It isn't that!" snapped Evan from his heart. It was too late to recall it. He did not try. He stood for some time without adding a syllable, and then—"I thought I wasn't even twelfth man?" he sneered.

"Well, as a matter of fact—"

Jan had not the heart to state the fact outright.

"I thought Norgate had got Sandham's place?"

"Well, so he had. I couldn't help it, Evan! I really couldn't. But now Norgate has got measles, too, and you've simply got to come in instead. You will, Evan! Of course you will; and I'll bowl twice as well for having you on the side. I simply hated leaving you out. But there's life in the old dog yet, and I'll let 'em know it, and so will you!"

He penetrated deeper into the dusky den; his hand flew out spasmodically. There was not another living being to whom he would have made so demonstrative an advance; but he had just described himself more aptly than he knew. Evan always awakened the faithful old hound in Jan, as Jerry Thrale had stirred the lion in him, Haigh the mule, and sane Bob Heriot the mere man. So we all hit each other in different places. But it was only Evan who had found Jan's softest spot, and therefore only Evan who could hurt him as he did without delay.

"Oh, all right. I'll play. Anything to oblige, I'm sure! But there's nothing to shake hands about, is there?"

So history repeated and exaggerated itself. But it was a long time before Jan thought of that. And then he was not angry with himself, as he had been four years before; he was far too hurt to be angry with anybody at all. And in that old dog, for one, there was very little life that day.

He went through the preliminary forms of office, which generally caused him visible embarrassment, with a casual unconcern even less to be admired; but it was almost the fact that Jan only realised he had lost the toss when he found himself as mechanically leading his men into the field. He had been thinking of Evan all that time, but now he took himself in hand, set his field and opened the bowling himself in a fit of desperation. It was no good; he had lost the art. That fatal new ball of his was an expensive present to such batsmen as Cave and Wilman; and the soft green wicket was still too slow for the one that came with his arm; they could step back to it, and place it for a single every time. After three overs Jan took himself off, and watched the rest of the innings from various positions in the field.

It lasted well into the afternoon, when the pitch became difficult and one of the change bowlers took advantage of it, subsequently receiving his colours for a very creditable performance. It was the younger Cave, and he had secured the last five wickets for under thirty runs, apart from a couple in the morning. His gifted brother had taken just enough trouble to contribute an elegant 29 out of 47 for the first wicket; the celebrated Swallow had batted up to his great reputation for three-quarters of an hour; and Swiller Wilman, who played serious cricket with a misleading chuckle, would certainly have achieved his usual century but for the collapse of the Old Boys' rearguard. He carried his bat through the innings for 83 out of 212, but was good enough to express indebtedness to Jan, to whom he had been delightful all day.

"If you'd gone on again after lunch," said Wilman, "I believe you'd have made much shorter work of us. I know I was jolly glad you didn't—but you shouldn't take a bad streak too seriously, Rutter. It'll all come back before you know where you are."

Jan shook a hopeless head, but he was grateful for the other's friendliness. It had made three or four hours in the field pass quicker than in previous matches; it had even affected the manner of the rest of the Eleven towards him—or Jan thought it had—because the Swiller was undoubtedly the most popular personality, man or boy, upon the ground. Jan was none the less thankful to write out the order of going in and then to retire into a corner of the pavilion for the rest of the afternoon.

That, however, was not ordained by the Fates who had turned a slow wicket into a sticky one, after robbing the school of its best batsman. Two wickets were down before double figures appeared on the board, and four for under 50. Then came something of a stand, in which the younger Cave, who had his share of the family insolence, seized the opportunity of treating his big brother's bowling with ostentatious disrespect. It was not, however, Charles Cave who had been taking the wickets, though his graceful action and his excellent length had been admired as much as ever. It was A. G. Swallow, the finest bowler the school etc.—until he became her most brilliant bat. The wicket was just adapted for a taste of his earlier quality; for over an hour he had the boys at his mercy, and perhaps might have done even greater execution than he did in that time. Then, however, a passing shower made matters easier; and when Jan went in, seventh wicket down, there was just a chance of saving the follow-on, with 91 on the board and half-an-hour to go. Somehow he managed to survive that half-hour, and was not out 20 at close of play, when the score was 128 with one more wicket to fall.

At the Conversazione in the evening, he found that he still had a certain number of friends, who not only made far too much of his little innings, but still more of his election to the Pilgrims during the day. The Pilgrims C.C. was the famous and exclusive Old Boys' club for which few indeed were chosen out of each year's Eleven; this year the honour was reserved for Jan and the absent Sandham; and with his new colours, worn as all good Pilgrims wear them on these occasions, in a transverse band between the evening shirt and waistcoat, the fine awkward fellow was a salient object of congratulations. Wilman was as pointedly nice as he had been to Jan in the field, after hearing in the morning of his unpopularity. Stratten had never been anything else to anybody in his life, but he could not have been nicer about this if he had been a Pilgrim himself instead of feeling rather sore that he was not one. A. G. Swallow affected to see another good bowler degenerating into a batsman in accordance with his own bad example. And the other old choices of the present team very properly disguised their disaffection for the nonce.

Only Evan Devereux, who again had failed to get into double figures, said nothing at all; but he seemed so lost without Sandham, and looked so wretched when he was not laughing rather loud, that Jan was not at first altogether surprised at what the next morning brought forth.

CHAPTER XXIII

INTERLUDE IN A STUDY

It was in Jan's study, now of course one of the large ones up the steps at the end of the passage. Chips was in there, jawing away about the match, and the prospect of a wicket after Jan's own heart at last.

Jan sat under him with the tolerant twinkle which was quite enough to encourage Chips to go on and on. It was tolerance tinged with real affection, especially of late months; and never had captain of a house a more invaluable ally. If Chips raised the voice of command, it was the thews and sinews in the next study that presented themselves to the insubordinate mind as an argument against revolt. And old Chips was man enough not to trade on this, and yet to recognise in his heart the true source of nearly all the power that he contrived to wield. And the house as a whole was in satisfactory case, because the two big fellows were such friends.

Yet Jan seldom dropped into Chips's study, and never dragged him out for walks, but preferred to go alone unless Chips took the initiative. And this was his delicacy, not a cricketer's superiority; he was really afraid of seeming to fall back on old Chips as the second string to Evan that he really was; for, of course, it was just in these days that Evan had taken up with Sandham, after having honoured Jan off and on since his first year in the Eleven. And yet Sandham had only to vanish to the Sanatorium, for Evan to come round to Jan's study directly after breakfast, this second morning of the Old Boys' Match!

Chips retired with speaking spectacles. They flashed out plainly that Evan had no shame; but the funny thing was that Evan did for once look very much ashamed of himself, as he shut the door with a mumbled apology, and so turned awkwardly to Jan. He had reddened characteristically, and his words ran together in a laboured undertone that betrayed both effort and precaution.

"I say, Jan, do you think there's any chance of our getting them out again this morning?"

"This morning!" Jan grinned. "Why, they've got to get us out first, Evan. And they may make us follow on."

"You'll save that, won't you?"

"I hope so, but you never know. We want other five runs. Suppose we get them, it'd be a job to run through a side like that by tea-time, let alone lunch."

"You did it two years ago."

"Well, that's not now. But what's the hurry, Evan, if we can save the match?"

"Oh, nothing much; only I'm afraid I shan't be able to field after lunch."

Evan had floundered to his point over some stiff impediment. He was not even looking at Jan, who jumped out of his chair with one glance at Evan.

"I knew it!"

"What did you know?"

"You're not fit. You weren't yesterday, but now it's as plain as a pikestaff. You're in for these infernal measles!"

It was a fair deduction from a face so flushed and such heavy eyes: again Evan dropped them, and shook a head that looked heavier still.

"Oh, no, I'm not. I rather wish I was!" he muttered bitterly.

"Why? What's happened? What's wrong?"

Evan flung up his hangdog head in sudden desperation.

"I'm in a frightful scrape!"

"Not you, Evan!"

"I am, though."

"What sort of scrape?"

"I don't know how to tell you. I don't know what you'll think."

Jan got him into the arm-chair, and took the other one himself. It was something to feel that Evan cared what he thought.

"Come! I don't suppose it's anything so very bad," said he, encouragingly.

"Bad enough to prevent me from playing to-day, I'm afraid."

"You surely don't mean—that anybody's dead?"

"I know I wish I was!"

"It isn't that, then?"

"No; but I've got to meet somebody at two o'clock. I simply must," declared Evan, with an air of dull determination.

"Some of your people?" asked Jan, and supplied the negative himself before Evan could shake his head. "I thought not. Then do you mind telling me who it is?"

No answer from Evan but averted looks.

"Well, where is it that you've got to meet them?"

"Yardley Wood."

Jan was there in a flash; he was looking over the posts and rails at the besotted figure waving and beckoning in the lower meadow; he was meeting Sandham and Evan, hurrying up the lane, not five minutes afterwards.

"Is it old Mulberry?" asked Jan, with absolute certainty that it was.

"What do you know about him?" cried Evan suspiciously.

Jan forced a conciliatory grin. "I thought everybody knew something about Mulberry," he said.

"But what makes you think of him the moment I mention Yardley Wood?"

"I saw him come out the other Sunday."

"I daresay. He hides there half the summer. But what's that got to do with me?"

"He waved to us by mistake, and the next thing was that we met you and Sandham coming up as we went down."

"So you put two and two together on the spot?"

"Well, more or less between us."

"Oh, Carpenter, of course! He was with you, wasn't he?"

"Yes. But Chips wouldn't let out a word, any more than I would, Evan. Not," added Jan, "that there's anything to let out in what you've told me as yet…. Is there, Evan?" The opportunity afforded by a pointed pause had not been taken. "You may as well tell me now you've got so far—but don't you if you've thought better of it." There again was the studious delicacy that was growing on Jan, that had always been in his blood.

Evan flung up his head once more.

"I'll tell you, of course. I came to tell you. It's nothing awful after all. There's no harm in it, really; only you can do things at home, quite openly, with your people, that become a crime if you do them here."

"That's true enough," said Jan who still smoked his pipe in Norfolk. He felt relieved. Evidently it was some such trifle that law-abiding Evan was magnifying in his constitutional horror of a row.

Jan asked outright if it was smoking, if Mulberry had been getting them cigars, and was at once informed eagerly that he had. But that was not all; the old tell-tale face was scarlet with the rest. And out it all came at last.

"The fact is, Sandham and I have had a bit of a spree now and again in Yardley Wood. Champagne. Not a drop too much, of course, or you'd have heard of it, and so should we. No more harm in it than if you had it in the holidays. I know at one time we used to have champagne every night at home. Heaps of people do; they certainly did at Lord Allenborough's. And yet it's such a frightful crime to touch it here!"

"I suppose Mulberry found out?"

"No—he got it for us."

"I see. And I suppose you paid him through the nose?" continued Jan at length. He would have been the first to take Evan's lenient view of such a peccadillo, if Evan himself had said less in extenuation. But just as Chips Carpenter would dry Jan's genial currents by the overflow of his own, so even Evan had taken the excuses out of his mouth, and left it shut awhile.

"That's just it," replied Evan. "We have paid a wicked price, but we haven't quite squared up, and now it's all falling on me."

"How much do you still owe him?"

"Between four and five pounds."

Jan looked grave; any such sum seemed a great deal to him.

"Can't you raise it from your people?" he suggested.

"No, I can't. They're all abroad, for one thing."

"What about Sandham and his lot?"

"I can't write to him, you see. Anybody might get hold of it; besides, there's no time."

"He's pressing you, is he?"

"I've got to pay up this afternoon."

"The moment Sandham's out of the way!"

Jan's eyes had brightened; but Evan was too miserable to meet them any more; he could speak more freely without facing his confessor. His tone was frankly injured, ingenuously superior, as though the worst of all was having to come with his troubles to the likes of Jan, if he would kindly bear that in mind.

Details came out piecemeal, each with its covering excuse. As some debaters fight every inch in controversy, so Evan went over the humiliating ground planting flags of defiant self-justification. The business had begun last term; and still Sandham had been easy Champion; that showed how harmless the whole thing had been. But when Jan asked how much Mulberry had been paid already, the amount amazed him. Evan had given it without thinking; but when asked whether he and Sandham had got through all that alone, he refused to answer, saying that was their business, and turning again very red. At any rate he was not going to drag in anybody else, he declared as though he were standing up to old Thrale himself, and by way of suffering the extreme penalty for his silence.

Jan saw exactly what had happened. It was Sandham who had led Evan into mischief; but that was the last thing of all that Evan could be expected to admit. Between them these two might have led others; but all that mattered to Jan was the old story of the strong villain and the weak-kneed accomplice. Of course it was the villain who escaped the consequences; and very hard it seemed even to Jan. Sandham was reported to have his own banking account; he could have written a cheque for four or five pounds without feeling it; probably he had refused to do so, probably the whole thing was a dexterous attempt to blackmail Evan while his masterful friend was out of reach.

Jan asked a few questions, and extracted answers which left him nodding to himself with rare self-satisfaction. On Evan they had an opposite effect. Unless he went with the money to the wood, before three o'clock, the villainous Mulberry was "coming in to blab the whole thing out to Jerry." And he would do it, too, a low wretch like that, with nothing to lose by it! And what would that mean but being bunked in one's last term—but breaking one's people's hearts—Jan knew them—as well as one's own?

Evan's voice broke as it was. He laid his forehead on his hand, thus hiding and yet trying to save his face; and Jan could not help a thrill of joy at the sight of Evan, of all people, come to him, of all others, for aid in such a pass. He was ashamed of feeling as he did; and yet it was no ignoble sense of power, much less of poetic justice or revenge, that touched and fired this still very simple heart. It was only the final conviction that here at last was his chance of doing something for Evan, something to win a new place in his regard, and to efface for ever the subtly tenacious memory of the old ignominious footing between them. That was all Jan felt, as he sat and looked, with renewed compassion, yet with just that thrilling human perception of his own great ultimate gain, at the bowed head and abject figure of him whom he had loved and envied all his days.

"He doesn't happen to have put his threat into black and white, I suppose?"

Jan felt that he was asking a stupid question. Of course he would have heard of anything of the kind before this. He did not realise the break that Evan's vanity was still putting on Evan's tongue. But when a dirty little document was produced, even now reluctantly, and found to contain that very word "blab," with the time, place, and exact amount stipulated, Jan soon saw why it had not been put in before. It referred to a broken appointment on the day of writing. That was another thing Evan had not mentioned. It accounted for his strange unreadiness to play in the match, as well as for the threats accompanying the impudently definite demand.

"This is what he asks, eh? So this would settle him?"

"There's no saying," replied Evan, doubtfully. "I thought we had settled, more or less."

"More or less is no good. Have you nothing to show by way of a receipt?"

"Sandham may have. I know he stumped up a lot that very Sunday you saw us."

"Then what did you think of doing, if you did get out to see him after dinner?"

"Stave him off till the holidays, I suppose."

"You didn't mean to stump up any more?"

"No, I'm hard up, that's the point."

"And you'd have stayed him off by promising him a good bit more if he'd wait?"

"By hook or crook!" cried Evan, desperately. "But unless I can get away from the match, I'm done."

Jan put on an air of sombre mystery, lightened only by the crafty twinkle in his eyes. Chips would have read it as Jan's first step to the rescue. But Evan missed the twinkle, and everything else except the explicit statement:

"You can't get away, Evan."

"Then it's all up with me!"

"Not yet a bit."

"But the fellow means it!"

"Let him mean it."

"If I'm not there—"

"Somebody else may take your place."

"In the field? My dear fellow—"

"No, not in the field, Evan, nor yet at the crease. In Yardley Wood!"

Jan allowed himself a smile at last. And Chips could not have been quicker than Evan to see his meaning now.

"Who will you get to go, Jan," he was asking eagerly without more ado.

"You must leave that to me, Evan."

"One of the Old Boys?"

"If I'm to help you, Evan, you must leave it all to me."

"Of course you know so many more of them than I do. It's your third year...."

Evan was unconsciously accounting for an enviable influence among the young men with the famous colours. To be sure, Jan was now a Pilgrim himself; he was already one of them. Jan Rutter! But it was certainly decent of him, very decent indeed, especially when they had seen so little of each other all the year. Evan was not unaware that he had treated Jan rather badly, that Jan was therefore treating him really very well. It enabled him to overlook the rather triumphant air of secrecy which it pleased Jan to adopt. After all, it was perhaps better that he should not know beforehand who was actually going to step into the breach. The chances were that almost any Old Boy, remembering that blackguard Mulberry, would be only too glad to give him a fright, if not to lend the money to pay him off.

But even Evan was not blinded, by these lightening considerations, to his immediate obligations to Jan.

"I never expected you to help me like this," he said frankly. "I only came to ask you about this afternoon. I—I was thinking of shamming seedy!"

Jan seemed struck with the idea; he said, more than once, that it was a jolly good idea; but there would have been a great risk of his being seen, and now thank goodness all that was unnecessary. If only they could first save the follow, and then get those Old Boys out quickly before lunch! That would be worth doing still, Jan hastened to add, as though aware of some inconsistency in his remarks. His eyes were alight. He looked capable of all his old feats, as he stood up in the litter from which a fag could not cleanse the Augean study.

But Evan fell into a shamefaced mood; he was getting a sad insight into himself as compared with Jan; his self-conceit was suffering even on the surface. Jan would never have fallen into Mulberry's clutches; he would have kept him in his place, as indeed Sandham had done; either of those two were capable of coping with fifty Mulberrys, whereas Evan had to own to himself that he was no match for one. He may even have realised, even at that early stage of his career, that in all the desperate passes of life he was a natural follower and a ready leaner on others. If he was not so very ready to lean on Jan, there were reasons for his reluctance.... And at least one reason did him credit.

"I don't know why you should want to do all this for me," he murmured on their way down to the ground. "It isn't as if I'd ever done anything for you!"

"Haven't you!" said Jan. They were arm-in-arm once more, to his huge inward joy.

"I'll do anything in the world after this. I'll never forget it in all my days."

"You've done quite enough as it is."

"I wish I knew what!" sighed Evan, honestly.

And he seemed quite startled when Jan reminded him.

CHAPTER XXIV

THE SECOND MORNING'S PLAY

"By Jove!" exclaimed Carpenter in the scoring tent. "I haven't seen Jan do that for years. It used to mean that he was on the spot."

"He did it when he went in just now," replied the præpostor who was scoring. "It only meant five more runs to him then."

"But those five saved the follow! I don't believe he meant to get any more."

"You don't suggest that he got out on purpose, Chips?"

"I shouldn't wonder. I know he told me the wicket would be just right for him when the heavy roller had been over it. By Jove, he's doing it again!"

What Jan had done, and was doing again, was something which had been chaffed out of him his first year in the Eleven. He was pulling the white cap, with the honourably faded blue ribbon, tight down over his head, so that his ears became unduly prominent, and his back hair gaped transversely to the scalp.

The scorer remarked that he had better sharpen his pencil, and Jan retorted that he had better watch the over first. It was the first over of the Old Boys' second innings, and the redoubtable Swiller had already taken guard. Jan ran up to the wicket, with all his old clumsy precision, but more buoyancy and verve than he put into his run now as a rule. And the Swiller's shaven face broke into a good-humoured grin as the ball went thud into the wicket-keeper's gloves; it had beaten him completely; the next one he played; off the third he scored a brisk single; and this brought Charles Cave to the striker's crease, with the air of the player who need never have got out in the first innings, and had half a mind not to do it again.

Curious to find that even in those comparatively recent days there were only four balls to the over in an ordinary two-day match; but such was the case, according to the bound volume consulted on the point; and the fourth and last ball of Jan's first over in a memorable innings has a long line to itself in the report. It appears to have been his own old patent, irreproachable in length, but pitching well outside the off-stump, and whipping in like lightning. It sent Charles Cave's leg-bail flying over thirty yards, if we are to believe contemporary measurements. But the reporter refrains from stating that Jan had given the peak of his cap a special tweak, though the fact was not lost upon him at the time.

"Bowled, sir, bowled indeed!" roared Chips from the tent. "I knew it'd be a trimmer; didn't you fellows see how he pulled down his cap?"

And the now really great Charles Cave stalked back to the pavilion with the nonchalant dignity of a Greek statue put into flannels and animated with the best old English blood. But at the pavilion chains he had a word to say to the next batsman, already emerging with indecent haste.

The next batsman was one of the bronzed brigade who could not grace the old ground every season. This one had been in the Eleven two years in his time, and had since made prodigious scores in regimental cricket in India. In the first innings, nevertheless, he had shown want of practice and failed to score; hence this bustle to avoid the dreaded pair. He was rewarded by watching Swiller Wilman play an over from young Cave with ease, scoring three off the last ball, and then playing a maiden from Jan with more pains than confidence. The gallant soldier did indeed draw blood, with a sweeping swipe in the following over from the younger Cave. But the first ball he had from Jan was also his last; and the very next one was too much for ex-captain Bruce.

"I told you it'd all come back, Rutter," said Wilman with wry laughter at the bowler's end. "I'm sorry I commenced prophet quite so soon."

"It's the wicket," Jan explained, genuinely enough. "I always liked a wicket like this—the least bit less than fast—but you've got its pace to a nicety."

"I wish I had yours. You're making them come as quick off the pitch as you did two years ago. I wish old Boots Ommaney was here again."

"I'd rather have him to bowl to than the next man in. Ommaney always plays like a book, but Swallow's the man to knock you off your length in the first over!"

Swallow looked that man as he came in grinning but square-jawed, with a kind of sunny storm-light in his keen, skilled eyes. It was capital fun to find this boy suddenly at his best again; good for the boy, better for the Eleven, and by no means bad for an old man of thirty-eight who was actually on the point of turning out once more for the Gentlemen at Lord's. Practice and the bowler apart, however, it would never do for the Old Boys to go to pieces after leading a rather weak school Eleven as it was only proper that they should. It was time for a stand, and certainly a stand was made.

But A. G. Swallow did not knock Jan off his length; he played him with flattering care, and was content to make his runs off Cave. Jan made a change at the other end, but went on pegging away himself. Wilman began to treat him with less respect than the cricketer of highest class; in club cricket, to be sure, there were few sounder or more consistent players than the Swiller. He watched the ball on to the very middle of a perpendicular bat, and played the one that came with Jan's arm so near to his left leg that there was no room for it between bat and pad. And he played it so hard that with luck it went to the boundary without really being hit at all.

Twenty, thirty, forty, fifty, went up in sedate yet slightly accelerated succession. Jan was trying all he knew, and now he had Cave back at the other end. Another ten or so, and he felt that he himself must take a rest, especially as A. G. Swallow was beginning to hit ruthlessly all round the wicket. Yet Wilman's was the wicket he most wanted, and it was on Wilman that he was trying all his wiles—but one. That fatal leg-break was not in his repertoire for the day; he had forsworn it to himself before taking the field, and he kept his vow like a man.

What he was trying to do was to pitch the other ball a little straighter, a fraction slower, and just about three inches shorter than all the rest; at last he did it to perfection. Wilman played forward pretty hard, the ball came skimming between the bowler and mid-off, and Jan shot out his left hand before recovering his balance. The ball hit it in the right place, his fingers closed automatically, and he had made a very clever catch off his own bowling.

"Well caught, old fellow!" cried Evan from mid-off before any of them. "I was afraid I'd baulked you."

The others were as loud in their congratulations, and the field rang with cheers. But Evan kept Jan buttonholed at mid-off, and they had a whisper together while the new batsman was on his way out.

"What about bowling them all out by lunch? You might almost do it after all!"

"I mean to, now."

"Six wickets in three quarters of an hour?"

"But there's not another Wilman or Swallow."

"We shan't get him in a hurry."

"Even if we don't I believe I can run through the rest."

"You're a wonder!" exclaimed Evan, then drew still nearer and dropped his voice. "I say, Jan!"

"What is it? There's a man in."

"If you did get them I might still go by myself this afternoon."

"Rot!"

"I'd have time if you put me in as late as I deserve. I can fight my own battle. I really—"

"Shut up, will you? Man in!"

Two overs later the new batsman had succumbed to Jan after a lofty couple through the slips; but A. G. Swallow had begun to force the game in a manner more delightful to watch from the ring than at close quarters. He did not say it was his only chance. He was too old a hand to discuss casualties with the enemy. He kept his own counsel in the now frequent intervals, but his keen eyes sparkled with appreciation of the attack (from one end) and with zest in the exercise of his own higher powers. Enterprise and defense had not been demanded of him in such equal measure for some past time; and yet with all his preoccupation he had a fatherly eye upon the young bowler who was making this tax upon his tried resources. Really, on his day, the boy was good enough to bowl for almost any side; and he seemed quite a nice boy, too, to A. G. Swallow, though perhaps a little rough. As to unpopularity, there was no sign of that now; that good-looking little chap at mid-off seemed fond enough of him; and he was not the only one. At the fall of each wicket a bigger and more enthusiastic band surrounded the heroic bowler; the cheers were louder from every quarter. If an unpopular fellow could achieve this popular success, well, it said all the more for his pluck and personality.

Eight wickets were down for 95, and Jan had taken every one of them, before Stratten stayed with Swallow and there was another stand. Stratten was only a moderate bats, but he had been two years in the team with Jan, and three years in the same house, and he knew how to throw his left leg across to the ball that looked as though it wanted cutting. He had never made 30 runs off Jan in a game, and he did not make 10 to-day, but he stayed while the score rose to 130 and the clock crept round to 1.15; then he spoilt Jan's chance of all ten wickets by being caught in the country off a half-volley from Goose—last hope at the other end.

Swallow had crossed before the catch was made, and he trotted straight up to Jan in the slips.

"Hard luck, Rutter! I hoped you were going to set up a new school record."

"I don't care as long as we get you all out before lunch."

Jan was wiping the cluster of beads from his forehead, and dashing more from the peak of his cap before pulling it down once more over his nose. He only saw his mistake when A. G. Swallow looked at him with a smile.

"Why before lunch, with the afternoon before us?"

"Because I feel dead!" exclaimed Jan with abnormal presence of mind. "I could go on now till I drop, but I feel more like lying up than lunch."

"Not measles, I hope?" said Swallow; and certainly Jan looked very red.

"Had 'em," said he laconically.

"Then it's either cause or effect," remarked Swallow, turning to George Grimwood, who had long looked as inflated as though he had taught Jan all he knew. "I've often noticed that one does one's best things when one isn't absolutely fighting fit, and I've heard lots of fellows say the same."

Now George Grimwood, as already stated, was a professional cricketer of high standing and achievement; but by this time he was also a school umpire of the keenest type, and his original humanity had not shown itself altogether proof against the foibles of that subtly demoralising office. Not only did he take to himself entirely undue credit for Mr. Rutter's remarkable performance, but he grudged Mr. Goose that last wicket far more than Jan did. One hope, however, the professional had cherished all the morning, and it was not yet dead in his breast. He longed to see Mr. Swallow, his own old opponent on many a first-class field, succumb to his young colt in the end; and now there was not much chance of it, with only one more over before lunch, especially if Mr. Rutter was really going to lie up afterwards.

So this was what happened—it may have been the very soundest verdict—but as the climax of a great performance it was not altogether satisfactory. Whitfield major, the last batsman, who really might have gone in earlier, clubbed the first ball of Jan's last over for three. The next ball may or may not have been on the off-stump. It appeared to come from a tired arm, to lack the sting of previous deliveries, to be rather a slower ball and as such just short of a really good length. But A. G. Swallow, still notoriously nimble on his feet, came out to hit across a straight half-volley on the strength of the usual break. He missed the ball, and it hit his pad; but there was no appeal from the bowler. That was the great point against George Grimwood. Jan was giving his cap another tug over his nose, when consequential Evan appealed for him from mid-off.

"Out!" roared the redoubtable George without an instant's hesitation. The Old Boys' second innings had closed for 133. Jan had taken 9 wickets for 41 runs. And A. G. Swallow was last out for 57—if out at all— and his eagle eye was clouded with his own opinion on the point.

The school was already streaming off the ground on its way back to dinner in the houses; but many remained, and some turned back, to give batsmen and bowler the reception they deserved. More articulate praises pursued them to the dressing-room. These ran like water off Jan's back as he sat stolidly changing his shoes; for in those days the players dispersed to luncheon in the houses also. He explained his apparent ungraciousness by some further mention of "a splitting head." But as a matter of fact he had every one of his wits about him, and his most immediate anxiety was to avoid Evan, whom he saw obviously waiting to waylay him. He made a point of writing out the order of going in before leaving the pavilion. It was the same order as before, except that Jan promoted the last two men and wrote his own name last of all.

"I'll turn up if I can," he announced as he tacked himself on to Charles Cave, of all people, to Evan's final discomfiture. "But let's hope I shan't be wanted; unless it's a case of watching the other fellow make the winning hit, I shall be as much use in my study as on the pitch."

Evan heard this as he walked as near them as he very well could. The narrow street was a running river of men and boys with glistening foreheads, who hugged the shadows and shrank ungratefully from the first hot sunshine of the term. Charles Cave, stalking indolently next the wall, said he hoped Jan was going up to the 'Varsity, as they wanted bowlers there, and a man who could bowl like that would stand a good chance of his Blue at either Oxford or Cambridge. Jan replied that he was afraid he was not going to either, but to the Colonies, a scheme which the other seemed to consider so deplorable that Evan dropped out of earshot from a feeling that the conversation was beginning to take a private turn. And sure enough, after a pause, it took one that surprised Jan himself almost as much as it did Charles Cave.

"Beggars can't be choosers," said Jan with apparent deliberation, but in reality on as sudden an impulse as ever dictated spoken words. "You see, you don't know what it is to be a beggar, Cave!"

"I don't, I'm glad to say."

"Well, I do, and it's rather awkward when you're captain of the Eleven."

"It must be."

"It is, Cave, and if you could lend me a fiver I'd promise to pay you back before the end of the term."

The calm speech was so extraordinarily calm, the tone so matter-of-fact and every-day, that after a second's amazement the Old Boy could only assume that Jan's splitting head had already affected the mind within. That charitable construction did not prevent Charles Cave from refusing the monstrous request with equal coolness and promptitude; and an utterly unabashed reception of the rebuff only confirmed his conclusion.

"After all, why should you?" asked Jan, with a strange chuckle. "But I shall have to raise it somewhere, and I daresay you won't tell anybody that I tried you first."

And before there could be any answer to that, Jan had turned without ceremony into Heath's, the saddler's shop, where the boys bespoke flies to take them to their trains at the end of the term. As a rule these orders were booked weeks beforehand, but the fly that Jan now ordered was to be outside Mr. Heriot's quad at 2.45 that afternoon.

"Is it to go to Molton, sir?"

"That's it."

"But there's no train before the 4.10, Mr. Rutter."

"I can't help that. I was asked to order it for some people who're down for the match. They may be going to see some of the sights of the country first."

Outside the shop, he found Evan waiting for him.

"I say, Jan, what's all this about your being seedy?"

"That's my business. Do you think I'm shamming?"

Evan missed the twinkle again. There was some excuse for him. It was unintentional now.

"I don't know, but if I thought you were going yourself—"

"Shut up, Evan! That's all settled. You go in fourth wicket down again, and mind you make some."

"But if you're seen—"

"What on earth makes you think I'm going? I've fixed up the whole thing. That should be good enough. I thought you left it to me?"

At Heriot's corner, old Bob himself was standing in conversation with Mr. Haigh, the two of them mechanically returning the no less perfunctory salutes of the passing stream. Charles Cave had paused a moment before going on into the house.

"I'm afraid the hero of the morning's a bit off-colour, Mr. Heriot."

"Not Rutter?"

Cave nodded.

"He says his head's bad. I think it must be. It looks to me like a touch of the sun."

"I hope not," said Heriot, as Cave passed on. "He really is a fine fellow, Haigh, as well as the fine bowler you've just seen once more. I sometimes think you might forget what he was, after all these years."

"Oh, I've nothing against the fellow," said Haigh, rather grandly. "But I take a boy as I find him, and I found Rutter the most infernal nuisance I ever had in my form."

"Years ago!"

"Well, at all events, there's no question of a grudge on my side. I wouldn't condescend to bear a grudge against a boy."

Haigh spoke as though he really wished to mean what he said. His general principles were as sound as his heart could be kind, but both were influenced by a temper never meant for schoolmastering. At this moment Jan and Evan hove into sight, and Heriot detained the cricketer of his house, questioned him about his head, reassured himself as to a former authentic attack of measles, and finally agreed with Jan's suggestion that he should stay quietly in his study until he felt fit to go back to the ground. He did not want any lunch.

Meanwhile, Haigh had not gone off up the hill, but had stayed to put in a difficult word or two of his own, as though to prove the truth of his assertion to Heriot. He went further as Jan was about to turn down to the quad.

"By the way, Rutter, I've a very good prescription for that kind of thing, now I think of it. I'll send it up to you if you like."

"Oh, thank you, sir," said Jan politely.

"You shall have it as soon as they can make it up. They've probably kept a copy at the chemist's. I'll go in and see."

Jan could only thank his old enemy again, and so retreat from the embarrassment of further tributes to his successful malingering. It was a loathsome part to play, especially for a blunt creature who had very seldom played a part in his life. But there were worse things in front of him, if he was to carry out his resolve, and do the deed which he never seriously dreamt of deputing to another. It was more than risky. But it could be done; nor was the risk the greatest obstacle. Money was at once the crux and the touchstone of the situation. No use tackling Cerberus without a decent sop up one's sleeve! And Jan had only just eight shillings left.

He sat in his bleak, untidy study, listening to the sound of knives and forks and voices in the hall, and eyeing those few possessions of his which conceivably might be turned into substantial coin of the realm. There were the four or five second and third prizes that he had won in the sports, and there was his mother's gold watch. It he had worn throughout his schooldays; and it had struck him very much in the beginning that nobody had ever asked him why he wore a lady's watch; but there were some things about which even a new boy's feelings were respected, now he came to think of it.... He came to think of too many things that had nothing to do with the pressing question; of the other watch that he had won at the fair, and sold at the time for the very few shillings it would bring; of the mad way in which he had thrown himself into that adventure, just as he was throwing himself into this one now. But it was no good raking up the past and comparing it with the present. Besides, there had been no sense in the risk he ran then; and now there was not only sense but necessity.

So absolute was the necessity in Jan's view that he would not have hesitated to part with his precious watch for the time being, if only there had been a pawnbroker's shop within reach; but, perhaps by arrangement with the school authorities, there was no such establishment in the little town; and there was no time to try the ordinary tradesmen, even if there was one of them likely to comply and to hold his tongue. Jan thought of Lloyd, the authorised jeweller, thought of George Grimwood and old Maltby, and was still only thinking when the quad filled under his window, the study passage creaked and clattered with boots, and Chips Carpenter was heard demanding less noise in a far more authoritative voice than usual.

It was almost too much to hear poor old Chips steal into his own study next door like any mouse to hear what he was about, and how quietly, and then to see the solicitous face he poked into Jan's study before going back to the Upper. Chips left him his Saturday allowance of a shilling—that made nine—but it was no good consulting or trying to borrow from a chap who hated Evan. Jan got rid of him with a twitch of preposterous excruciation, and in a very few minutes had the studies to himself.

CHAPTER XXV

INTERLUDE IN THE WOOD

Morgan, the man-servant, and his myrmidon of the boots and knives, were busy and out of sight in the pantry near the hall, as Jan knew they would be by this time. Yet he was flushed and flurried as he ran down into the empty quad, and dived into the closed fly which had just pulled up outside. He leant as far back as possible. The road broadened, the town came to an end. The driver drove on phlegmatically, without troubling his head as to why one of the cricketing young gentlemen should be faring forth alone, in his flannels, too, and without any luggage either. He would be going to meet his friends at Molton, likely, and bring them back to see the cricket. So thought the seedy handler of shabby ribbons, so far as he may be said to have thought at all, until a bare head stuck out behind him at Burston Corner, and he was told to pull up.

"Jump down a minute, will you? I want to speak to you."

The fly stopped in one of the great dappled shadows that trembled across the wooded road. A bucolic countenance peered over a huge horse-shoe pin into the recesses of the vehicle.

"See here, my man; here's nine bob for you. I'm sorry it isn't ten, but I'll make it up to a pound at the end of the term."

"I'm very much obliged to you, sir, I'm sure!"

"Wait a bit. That's only on condition you keep your mouth shut; there may be a bit more in it when you've kept it jolly well shut till then."

"You're not going to get me into any trouble, sir?"

"Not if I can help it and you hold your tongue. We're only going round by Yardley Wood instead of to Molton, and I shan't keep you waiting there above half an hour. It's—it's only a bit of a lark!"

A sinful smile grew into the crab-apple face at the fly-window.

"I been a-watching you over them palings at bottom end o' ground all the morning, Mr. Rutter, but I didn't see it was you just now, not at first. Lord, how you did bool 'em down! I'll take an' chance it for you, sir, jiggered if I don't!"

The fly rolled to the left of Burston church, now buried belfry-deep in the fretful foliage of its noble avenue. It threaded the road in which Chips had encountered Evan on their first Sunday walk; there was the stile where Jan had waited in the background, against the hedge. Strange to think of Evan's attitude then and long afterwards, and of Jan's errand now; but lots of things were strange if you were fool enough to stop to think about them. That was not Jan's form of folly when once committed to a definite course of action; and any such tendency was extremely quickly quelled on this occasion. He had more than enough to think about in the interview now before him. It was almost his first opportunity of considering seriously what he was to say, how he had better begin, what line exactly it would be wisest to take, and what tone at the start. It was annoying not to be able to decide absolutely beforehand; it was disconcerting, too, because in his first glow the very words had come to him together with his plan. He had made short work of the noxious Mulberry almost as soon as the creature had taken shape in his mind. But on second thoughts it appeared possible to make too short work of a scoundrel with tales to tell, money or no money. And by the time the horse was walking up the last hill, with the green lane on top, Jan had thought of the monstrous Cacus in the Aventine woods, without feeling in the least like the superhuman hero of the legend.

There lay the celebrated covert, in its hollow in the great grass country. In the heavy sunlight of a rainy summer, the smear of woodland, dense and compressed, was like a forest herded in a lane. So smoky was the tint of it, from the green heights above, that one would have said any moment it might burst into flames, like a damp bonfire. But Jan only thought of the monster in its depths, as he marched down through the lush meadows, with something jingling on him at every other stride.

Yardley Wood was bounded by a dyke and a fence, and presented such a formidable tangle of trees and undergrowth within, that Jan, though anxious for immediate cover, steered a bold course for the made opening. The white wicket looked positively painted on the dark edge of the wood. It led into a broad green ride, spattered with buttercups as thick as freckles on a country face.

Jan entered the ride, and peered into the tangled thicket on either hand. Its sombre depths, unplumbed by a ray of sun, reminded him of a striking description in one of the many novels that Chips had made him read: it was twilight there already, it must be "dark as midnight at dusk, and black as the ninth plague of Egypt at midnight." And there was another plague of Egypt that Jan recalled before he had penetrated a yard into the fringe of tangle-wood. He became at once the sport and target of a myriad flies. The creatures buzzed aggressively in the sudden stillness of the natural catacomb; and yet above their hum the tree-tops made Æolian music from the first moment that he stood beneath them, while last year's leaves, dry enough there even in that wet summer, rustled at every jingling step he took.

And now his steps followed the wavering line of least resistance, and so turned and twisted continually; but he would not have taken very many in this haphazard, tentative fashion, and was beginning in fact to bend them back towards the ride, when the bulbous nose of Mulberry appeared under his very own.

It was making music worthy of its painful size, as he lay like a log on the broad of his back, in a small open space. His battered hat lay beside him, along with a stout green cudgel newly cut, Jan had half a mind to remove this ugly weapon as a first preliminary; but it was not the half which had learnt to give points rather than receive them, and the impulse was no sooner felt than it was scorned. Yet the drunkard was a man of no light build. Neither did he lie like one just then particularly drunk, or even very sound asleep. The flies were not allowed to batten on his bloated visage; every now and then the snoring stopped as he shook them off; and presently a pair of bloodshot eyes rested on Jan's person.

"So you've come, have you?" grunted Mulberry; and the red eyes shut again ostentatiously, without troubling to climb to Jan's face.

"I have," said he, with dry emphasis. It was either too dry or else not emphatic enough for Mulberry.

"You're late, then, hear that? Like your cheek to be late. Now you can wait for me."

"Not another second!" cried Jan, all his premeditated niceties forgotten in that molecule of time. Mulberry sat up, blinking.

"I thought it was Mr. Devereux!"

"I know you did."

"Have you come instead of him?"

"Looks like it, doesn't it?"

"I don't know you! I won't have anything to do with you," exclaimed Mulberry, with a drunken dignity rendered the more grotesque by his difficulty in getting to his feet.

"Well, you certainly won't have anything more to do with Mr. Devereux," retorted Jan, only to add: "So I'm afraid you'll have to put up with me," in a much more conciliatory voice. He had just remembered his second thoughts on the way.

"Why? What's happened him?" asked Mulberry, suspiciously.

"Never you mind. He can't come; that's good enough. But I've come instead—to settle up with you."

"You have, have you?"

"On the spot. Once for all."

Jan slapped one of the pockets that could not be abolished in cricket trousers. It rang like a money-bag flung upon a counter. The reprobate looked impressed, but still suspicious about Evan.

"He was to come here yesterday, and he never did."

"It wasn't his fault; that's why I've come to-day."

"I said I'd go in and report him to Mr. Thrale, if he slipped me up twice."

"'Blab' was your word, Mulberry!"

"Have you seen what I wrote?"

"I happen to have got it in my pocket."

Mulberry lurched a little nearer. Jan shook his head with a grin.

"It may come in useful, Mulberry, if you ever get drunk enough to do as you threaten."

"Useful, may it?"

If the red eyes fixed on Jan had been capable of flashing, they would have done so now. They merely watered as though with blood. Till this moment man and boy had been only less preoccupied with the flies than with each other. Mulberry with the battered hat had vied with Jan and his handkerchief in keeping the little brutes at bay. But at this point the swollen sot allowed the flies to cover his hideousness like a spotted veil. It was only for seconds, yet to Jan it was almost proof that the scamp had something to fear, that his pressure on Evan was rather more than extortionate. His expressionless stare had turned suddenly expressive. That could not be the flies. Nor was it only what Jan thought it was.

"I've seen you before, young feller!" exclaimed Mulberry.

"You've had chances enough of seeing me these four years."

"I don't mean at school. I don't mean at school," repeated Mulberry, racking his muddled wits for whatever it might be that he did mean. Jan was under no such necessity; already he was back at the fair, that wet and fateful night in March—but he did not intend Mulberry to join him there again.

"It's no good you trying to change the subject, Mulberry! I've got your letter to Mr. Devereux, and you'll hear more about it if you go making trouble at the school. If you want trouble, Mulberry, you shall have all the trouble you want, and p'r'aps we'll give the police a bit more to make 'em happy. See? But I came to square up with you, and the sooner we get it done the better for all the lot of us."

Jan was at home. Something contracted ages ago, nay, something that he had brought with him into the world, something of his father, was breaking through the layer of the last five years. It had broken through before. It had helped him to fight his earliest battles. But it had never had free play in all these terms, or in the holidays between terms. This was neither home nor school; this was a bite of life as Jan would have had to swallow it if his old life had never altered. And all at once it was a strapping lad from the stables, an Alcides of his own kidney and no young gentleman, with whom the local Cacus had to reckon.

"Come on!" said he sullenly. "Let's see the colour o' yer coin, an' done with it."

Jan gave a conquerer's grin; yet knew in his heart that the tussle was still to come; and if he had brought a cap with him, instead of driving out bare-headed this was the moment at which he would have given the peak a tug. He plunged his hand into the jingling pocket. He brought out a fistful of silver of all sizes, and one or two half-sovereigns. In the act he shifted his position, and happened to tread—but left his foot firmly planted—upon that ugly cudgel just as its owner stooped to pick it up and almost overbalanced in the attempt.

"Look out, mister! That's my little stick. I'd forgotten it was there."

"Had you? I hadn't," said Jan, one eye on his money and the other on his man. "You don't want it now, do you, Mulberry?"

"Not partic'ly."

"Then attend to me. There's your money. Not so fast!"

His fist closed. Mulberry withdrew a horrid paw.

"I thought you said it was mine, mister?"

"It will be, in good time. Have a look at it first."

"Lot o' little silver, ain't it?"

"One or two bits of gold as well."

"It may be more than it looks; better let me count it, mister."

"It's been counted. That's the amount; you sign that, and it's yours."

With his other hand Jan had taken from another pocket an envelope, stamped and inscribed, but not as for the post, and a stylographic pen. The stamp was just under the middle of the envelope; above was written, in Jan's hand and in ink:

Received in final payment for everything supplied in Yardley Wood to end of June—£2 18s. 6d.

"Sign across the stamp." said Jan briskly. Underneath was the date.

The envelope fluttered in the drunkard's fingers.

"Two p'un' eighteen—look here—this won't do!" he cried less thickly than he had spoken yet. "What the devil d'you take me for? It's close on five golden sovereigns that I'm owed. This is under three."

"It's all you'll get, Mulberry, and it's a darned sight more than you deserve for swindling and blackmailing. If you don't take this you won't get anything, except what you don't reckon on!"

The man understood; but he was almost foaming at the mouth.

"I tell you it's a dozen and a half this summer! Half a dozen bottles and a dozen—"

"I don't care what it is. I know what there's been, what you've charged for it, and what you've been paid already." Jan thought it time for a bit of bluff. "This is all you'll get; but you don't touch a penny of it till you've signed the receipt."

"Don't I!" snarled Mulberry. Without lowering his flaming eyes, or giving Jan time to lower his, he slapped the back of the upturned hand and sent the money flying in all directions. Neither looked where it fell. Mulberry was ready for a blow. Jan never moved an eye, scarcely a muscle. And over them rose and fell such sylvan music as had been rising and falling all the time; only now their silence brought it home.

"You'll simply have to pick it all up again," said Jan quietly. "But if you don't sign this, Mulberry, I'm going to break every bone in your beastly body with your own infernal stick."

He finished as quietly as he had begun; it must have been his face that said still more, or his long and lissom body, or his cricketer's wrists. Whatever the medium, the message was understood, and twitching hands held out in token of submission. Jan put the pen in one, the prepared receipt in the other, and Mulberry turned a back bowed with defeat. Close behind him grew a stunted old oak, forked like a catapult, with ivy winding up the twin stems. Down sat Mulberry in the fork, and with such careless precision that Jan might have seen it was a favourite seat, and the whole little open space, with its rustling carpet and its whispering roof, its acorns and its cigar ends, a tried old haunt of others besides Mulberry. But Jan kept so close an eye on his man that the receipt was being signed, on one corduroy knee, before he looked up to see the broad bust of a third party enclosed in the same oak frame.

It was Mr. Haigh, and in an instant Jan saw him redder than Mulberry himself. It was Haigh with a limp collar and a streaming face. So he had smelt a rat, set a watch, and followed the fly on foot like the old athlete that he was! But how much more like him all the rest. Jan not only came tumbling back into school life, as from that other which was to have been his, but back with a thud into the Middle Remove and all its old miseries and animosities.

"I might have known what to expect!" he cried with futile passion. "It's about your form, doing the spy!"

Haigh took less notice of this insult than Jan had known him to take of a false quantity in school. His only comment was to transfer his attention to Mulberry, who by now had scrambled to his legs. Leaning through the forked tree, the master held out his hand for the stamped envelope, obtained possession of it without a word, and read it as he came round into the open.

"This looks like your writing, Rutter?"

"It is mine."

Jan was still more indignant than abashed.

"May I ask what it refers to?"

"You may ask what you please, Mr. Haigh."

"Come, Rutter! I might have put worse posers, I should have thought. Still, as it won't be for me to deal with you for being here, instead of wherever you're supposed to be, I won't press inquiries into the nature of your dealings with this man."

It was Mulberry's turn to burst into the breach; he did so as though it were the ring, dashing his battered hat to the ground with ominous exultation.

"Do you want to know what he's had off me?" he demanded of Haigh. "If he won't tell you, I will!"

Jan's heart sank as he met a leer of vindictive triumph. "Who's going to believe your lies?" he was rash enough to cry out, in a horror that increased with every moment he had for thought.

"I'm not going to listen to him," remarked Haigh, unexpectedly. "Or to you either!" he snapped at Jan.

"Oh, ain't you?" crowed Mulberry. "Well, you can shut your ears, and you needn't believe anything but your own eyes. I'll show you! I'll show you!"

He dived into a bramble bush alongside the old forked tree. It was a literal dive. His head disappeared in the dense green tangle. He almost lost his legs. Then a hand came out behind him, and flung something at their feet. It was an empty champagne bottle. Another followed, then another and another till the open space was strewn with them. Neither Haigh nor Jan said a word; but from the bush there came a gust of ribaldry or rancour with every bottle, and last of all the man himself, waving one about him like an Indian club.

"A live 'un among the deaders!" he roared deliriously. "Now I can drink your blessed healths before I go!"

Master and boy looked on like waxworks, without raising a hand to stop him, or a finger between them to brush away a fly. Jan for his part neither realised nor cared what was happening; it was the end of all things, for him or Evan, if not for them both. Evan would hear of it—and then—and then! But would he hear? Would he, necessarily? Jan glanced at Haigh, and saw something that he almost liked in him at last; something human, after all these years; but only until Haigh saw him, and promptly fell upon the flies.

Mulberry meanwhile had knocked the neck off the unopened bottle with a dexterous blow from one of the empties. A fountain of foam leapt up like a plume of smoke; the pothouse expert blew it to the winds, and drank till the jagged bottle stood on end upon his upturned visage. His blood ran with the overflowing wine—scarlet on purple—and for a space the draught had the curiously clarifying effect of liquor on the chronic inebriate. It made him sublimely sober for about a minute. The sparkle passed from the wine into those dim red eyes. They fixed themselves on Jan's set face. They burst into a flame of sudden recognition.

"Now I remember! Now I remember! I told him I'd seen him—"

He stopped himself with a gleam of inspired cunning. He had nearly defeated his immediate ends. He looked Jan deliberately up and down, did the same by Haigh, and only then snatched up his ugly bludgeon.

"You'd better be careful with that," snapped Haigh, with the face which had terrorised generations of young boys. "And the sooner you clear out altogether, let me tell you, the safer it'll be for you!"

"No indecent haste," replied Mulberry, leaning at ease upon his weapon. The sparkle of the wine even reached that treacherous tongue of his, reviving its humour and the smatterings of other days. "Festina Whats-'er-name—meaning don't you be in such a blooming hurry! That nice young man o' yours and me, we're old partic'lars, though you mightn't think it; don't you run away with the idea that he's emptied all them bottles by his little self! It wouldn't be just. I've had my share; but he don't like paying his, and that's where there's trouble. Now we don't keep company no more, and I'm going to tell you where that nice young man an' me first took up with each other. Strictly 'tween ourselves."

"I've no wish to hear," cried Haigh. He looked as Jan had seen him look before running some fellow out of his hall. "Are you going of your own accord—"

"Let him finish," said Jan, with a grim impersonal interest in the point. In any case it was all over with him now.

"Very kind o' nice young man—always was nice young man!" said Mulberry. "Stric'ly 'tween shelves it was in your market-place, one blooming fair, when all good boys should ha' been tucked up in bed an' 'sleep. Nasty night, too! But that's where I see 'im, havin' barney about watch, I recollec'. That's where we first got old partic'lars. Arcade Sambo—birds of eather—as we used say when I was at school. I seen better days, remember, an' that nice young man'll see worse, an' serve him right for the way he's tret his ol' p'rtic'lar, that took such care of him at the fair! Put that in your little pipes an' smoke it at the school. Farewell, a long farewell! Gobleshyer ... Gobleshyer ..."

They heard his reiterated blessings for some time after he was out of sight. It was not only distance that rendered them less and less distinct. The champagne was his master—but it had been a good servant first.

"At any rate there was no truth in that, Rutter?" Haigh seemed almost to hope that there was none.

"It's perfectly true, sir, that about the fair."

"Yet you had the coolness to suggest that he was lying about the wine!"

"I don't suggest anything now."

Jan kicked an empty bottle out of the way. The man's second tone had cut him as deep as in old odious days in form.

"Is that your money he's left behind him?"

Jan's answer was to go down on his knees and begin carefully picking up the forgotten coins from the carpet of last year's leaves. Haigh watched him under arched eyebrows; and once more the flies were allowed to settle on the master's limp collar and wet wry face. Then he moved a bottle or so with furtive foot, and kicked a coin or two into greater prominence, behind Jan's bent back.

"When you're quite ready, Rutter!" said Haigh at length.

CHAPTER XXVI

CLOSE OF PLAY

It is remarked of many people, that though they go through life fretting and fuming over trifles, and making scenes out of nothing at all, yet in a real emergency their calmness is quite amazing. It need not amaze anybody who gives the matter a little thought; for a crisis brings its own armour, but a man is naked to the insect enemies of the passing moment, and he may have a tender moral and intellectual skin. This was the trouble with Mr. Haigh—a naturally irritable man, who in long years of chartered tyranny had gradually ceased to control his temper in the absence of some special reason why he should. But fellows in his house used to say that in the worst type of row they could trust Haigh to sort out the sinned against from the sinning, and not to lose his head, though he might still smack theirs for whistling in his quad.

Thus it is scarcely to be doubted that already Mr. Haigh had more sympathy with the serious offender whom he had caught red-handed with little clods who ended pentameters with adjectives or showed a depraved disregard for the cæsura. But for once he did not wear his heart upon his sleeve, or in his austere eyes and distended nostrils; his very shoulders, as Jan followed them through the wood, looked laden with fate inexorable. A composure so alien and abnormal is at least as terrible as the wrath that is slow to rise; it chilled Jan's blood, but it also gave him time to see things, and to make up his mind.

In the wood and in the ride Haigh did not even turn his head to see that he was being duly followed; but in the lower meadow he stopped short, and waited sombrely for Jan.

"There's nothing to be said, Rutter, as between you and me, except on one small point that doesn't matter to anybody else. I gathered just now that you were not particularly surprised at being caught by me—that it's what you would have expected of me—playing the spy! Well, I have played it during the last hour; but I never should have dreamt of doing so if your own rashness had not thrust the part upon me."

"I suppose you saw me get into the fly?" said Jan, with a certain curiosity in the incidence of his frustration.

"I couldn't help seeing you. I had called for this myself, and was in the act of bringing it to you for your—splitting head!"

Haigh had produced an obvious medicine bottle sealed up in white paper. Jan could not resent his sneer.

"I'm sorry you had the trouble, sir. There was nothing the matter with my head."

"And you can stand there—"

Haigh did not finish his sentence, except by dashing the medicine bottle to the ground in his disgust, so that it broke even in that rank grass, and its contents soaked the smooth white paper. This was the old Adam, but only for a moment. Jan could almost have done with more of him.

"I know what you must think of me, sir," he said. "I had to meet a blackmailer at his own time and place. But that's no excuse for me."

"I'm glad you don't make it one, I must say! I was going on to tell you that I followed the fly, only naturally, as I think you'll agree. But it wasn't my fault you didn't hear me in the wood before you saw me, Rutter. I made noise enough, but you were so taken up with your—boon companion!"

Jan resented that; but he had made up his mind not even to start the dangerous game of self-defence.

"He exaggerated that part of it," was all that Jan said, dryly.

"So I should hope. It's not my business to ask for explanations—"

"And I've none to give, sir."

"It's only for me to report the whole matter, Rutter, as of course I must at once."

Jan looked alarmed.

"Do you mean before the match is over? Must the Eleven and all those Old Boys—"

"Hear all about it? Not necessarily, I should say, but it won't be in my hands. The facts are usually kept quiet in—in the worst cases—as you know. But I shan't have anything to say to that."

"You would if it were a fellow in your house!" Jan could not help rejoining. "You'd take jolly good care to have as little known as possible—if you don't mind my saying so!"

Haigh did mind; he was a man to mind the slightest word, and yet he took this from Jan without a word in reply. The fact was that, much to his annoyance and embarrassment, he was beginning to respect the youth more in his downfall than at the height of his cricketing fame. Indeed, while he had grudged a great and unforeseen school success to as surly a young numskull as ever impeded the work of the Middle Remove (and the only one who ever, ever scored off Mr. Haigh), he could not but recognise the manhood of the same boy's bearing in adversity—and such adversity at such a stage in his career! There had been nothing abject about it for a moment, and now there was neither impertinence nor bravado, but rather an unsuspected sensibility, rather a redeeming spirit altogether. Yet it was an aggravated case, if ever there had been one in the whole history of schools; a more deliberate and daring piece of trickery could not be imagined. In that respect it was typical of the drinking row of Haigh's experience. And yet he found himself making jaunty remarks to Jan about the weather, and even bringing off his raucous laugh about nothing, for the fly-man's benefit, as they came up to where that vehicle was waiting in the lane.

Haigh, of all masters, and Jan Rutter of all the boys who had ever been through his hands!

That was the feeling that preyed upon the man, the weight he tried to get off his chest when they had dismissed the fly outside the town, and had walked in together as far as Heriot's quad.

"Well, Rutter, there never was much love lost between us, was there? And yet—I don't mind telling you—I wish any other man in the place had the job you've given me!"

The quad was still deserted, but Jan had scarcely reached his study when a hurried but uncertain step sounded in the passage, and a small fag from another house appeared at his open door.

"Oh, please, Rutter, I was sent to fetch you if you're well enough to bat."

"Who sent you?"

"Goose."

"How many of them are out?"

"Seven when I left."

"How many runs?"

"Hundred and sixty just gone up."

"It hadn't! Who's been getting them?"

"Devereux, principally."

The fag from another house always said that Rutter lit up at this as though the runs were already made, and then that he gave the most extraordinary laugh, but suddenly asked if Devereux was out.

"And when I told him he wasn't," said the fag, "he simply sent me flying out of his way, and by the time I got into the street he was almost out of sight at the other end!"

Certainly they were the only two creatures connected with the school who were to be seen about the town at half-past four that Saturday afternoon; and half the town itself seemed glued to those palings affected by Jan's fly-man; and on the ground every available boy in the school, every master except Haigh, and every single master's lady, watched the game without a word about any other topic under the sun. Even the tea-tent, a great feature of the festival, under the auspices of Miss Heriot and other ladies, was deserted alike by all parties to its usually popular entertainment.

Evan was still in, said to have made over 70, and to be playing the innings of his life, the innings of the season for the school. But another wicket must have fallen soon after the small fag fled for Jan, and Chilton who had gone in was not shaping with conspicuous confidence. Evan looked, however, as though he had enough for two, from the one glimpse Jan had of his heated but collected face, and the one stroke he saw him make, before diving into the dressing-room to clap on his pads. To think that Evan was still in, and on the high road to a century if anybody could stop with him! To think he should have chosen this very afternoon!

It was at this point that the hard Fates softened, for a time only, yet a time worth the worst they could do to Jan now. They might not have given him pause to put his pads on properly; they might not have suffered him to get his breath. When he had done both, and even had a wash, and pulled his cap well over his wet hair, they might have kept him waiting till the full flavour of their late misdeeds turned his heart sick and faint within him. Instead of all or any of this, they propped up Chilton for another 15 runs, and then sent Jan in with 33 to get and Evan not out 84.

But they might have spared the doomed wretch the tremendous cheering that greeted his supposed resurrection from the sick-room to which—obviously—his heroic efforts of the morning had brought him. It took Evan to counteract the irony of that reception with a little dose on his own account.

"Keep your end up," whispered Evan, coming out to meet the captain a few yards from the pitch, "and I can get them. Swallow's off the spot and the rest are pifflers. Keep up your end and leave the runs to me."

It was the tone of pure injunction, from the one who might have been captain to his last hope. But that refinement was lost on Jan; he could only stare at the cool yet heated face, all eagerness and confidence, as though nothing whatever had been happening off the ground. And his stare did draw a change of look—a swift unspoken question—the least little cloud, that vanished at Jan's reply.

"It's all right," said Jan, oracularly. "You won't be bothered any more!"

"Good man!" said Evan. "Then only keep your end up, and we'll have the fun of a lifetime between us!"

Jan nodded as he went to the crease; really the fellow had done him good. And in yet another little thing the Fates were kind; he had not to take the next ball, and Evan took care to make a single off the last one of the over, which gave the newcomer a good look at both bowlers before being called upon to play a ball.

But then it was A. G. Swallow whom he had to face; and, in spite of Evan's expert testimony to the contrary, that great cricketer certainly looked as full of wisdom, wiles, and genial malice as an egg is full of meat.

A. G. Swallow took his rhythmical little ball-room amble of a run, threw his left shoulder down, heaved his right arm up, and flicked finger and thumb together as though the departing ball were a pinch of snuff. I. T. Rutter—one of the many left-hand bowlers who bat right, it is now worth while to state— watched its high trajectory with terror tempered by a bowler's knowledge of the kind of break put on. He thought it was never going to pitch, but when it did—well to the off—he scrambled in front of his wicket and played the thing somehow with bat and pads combined. But A. G. Swallow awaited the ball's return with a smile of settled sweetness, and E. Devereux had frowned.

The next ball flew higher, with even more spin, but broke so much from leg as to beat everything except Stratten's hands behind the sticks. But Jan had not moved out of his ground; he had simply stood there and been shot at, yet already he was beginning to perspire. Two balls and two such escapes were enough to upset anybody's nerve; and now, of course, Jan knew enough about batting to know what a bad bat he was, and the knowledge often made him worse still. He had just one point: as a bowler he would put himself in the bowler's place and consider what he himself would try next if he were bowling.

Now perhaps the finest feature of Swallow's slow bowling was the fast one that he could send down, when he liked, without perceptible change of action; but the other good bowler rightly guessed that this fast ball was coming now, was more than ready for it, let go early and with all his might, and happened to time it to perfection. It went off his bat like a lawn-tennis ball from a tight racket, flew high and square (though really intended for an on drive), and came down on the pavilion roof with a heavenly crash.

The school made music, too; but Evan Devereux looked distinctly disturbed, and indeed it was a good thing there was not another ball in the over. A. G. Swallow did not like being hit; it was his only foible; but to hit him half by accident was to expose one's wicket to all the knavish tricks that could possibly be combined and concentrated in the very next delivery.

Now, however, Evan had his turn again, and picked five more runs off three very moderate balls from the vigorous Whitfield; the fourth did not defeat Jan, and Evan had Swallow's next over. He played it like a professional, but ran rather a sharp single off the last ball, and in short proceeded to "nurse" the bowling as though his partner had not made 25 not out in the first innings and already hit a sixer in his second.

Jan did not resent this in the least. The height of his own momentary ambition was simply to stay there until the runs were made; the next essential was for Evan to achieve his century, but the larger hope involved that consummation, and at this rate he would not be very long about it. To Jan his performance was a composite revelation of character and capacity. Surely it was not Evan Devereux batting at all, but a higher order of cricketer in Evan's image, an altogether stronger soul in his skin! Even that looked different, so fiery red and yet so free from the nervous perspiration welling from Jan's pores; surely some sheer enchantment had quickened hand and foot, and sharpened an eye that looked abnormally bright at twenty yards!

So thought Jan at the other end; and he wondered if the original stimulus could have been the very weight of an anxiety greater than any connected with the game; but he entertained these searching speculations almost unawares, and alongside all manner of impressions, visions and reminiscences, of a still more intimate character. The truth was that Jan himself was in a rarefied atmosphere, out there on the pitch, seeing and doing things for the last time, and somehow more vividly and with greater zest than he had ever seen or done such things before.

Though he had played upon it literally hundreds of times, never until to-day had he seen what a beautiful ground the Upper really was. On three sides a smiling land fell away in fine slopes from the very boundary, as though a hill-top had been sliced off to make the field; on those three sides you could see for miles, and they were miles of grazing country checkered with hedges, and of blue distance blotted with trees. But even as a cricket-field Jan felt that he had never before appreciated his dear Upper as he ought. It lay so high that at one end the batsman stood in position against the sky from the pads upwards, and the empyrean was the screen behind the bowler's arm.

Of course these fresh features of a familiar scene were due more to mental exaltation than to the first perfect day of the term; but they owed little or nothing to the conscientious sentimentality of a farewell appearance. Jan was a great deal too excited to think of anything but the ball while the ball was in play. But between the overs the spectres of the early afternoon were at his elbow, and in one such pause he espied Haigh in the flesh watching from the ring.

Yes! There was Haigh freshly groomed, in a clean collar and another suit of clothes, the grey hair brushed back from his pink temples, but his mouth inexorably shut on the tidings it was soon to utter. Decent of Haigh to wait until the match was lost or won; but then Haigh resembled the Upper inasmuch as Jan already liked everything about him better than he had ever done before. In front of the pavilion, in tall hat, frock-coat and white cravat, sat splendid little old Jerry himself, that flogging judge of other days, soon to assume the black cap at last, but still ignorant of the capital offence committed, still beaming with delight and pride in a glorious finish. Elsewhere a triangle of familiar faces made themselves seen and heard; its apex was gaunt old Heriot, who in his innocence had bawled a salvo for the sixer; and the gay old dog on his right was his friend Major Mangles, while Oxford had already turned the austere Crabtree into the gay young dog on his left.

Jan wondered what Crabtree would think—and then what the Major was saying as he poked Bob Heriot in the ribs. He soon saw what they were saying; all that Cambridge and Lord's had left of the original Charles Cave was going on to bowl instead of Swallow, and those three tense faces on the boundary had relaxed in esoteric laughter. But it was Jan who had to play Cave's over, and it was almost worthy of the Cantab's youth three years ago. Jan, however, was almost at home by this time; all four balls found the middle of his bat; and then the public-spirited policy of A. G. Swallow dictated an audacious move.

Of course he must know what he was doing, for he had led a first-class county in his day, and had never been the captain to take himself off without reason. No doubt he understood the value of a double change; but was it really wise to put on Swiller Wilman at Whitfield's end with lobs when only 15 runs were wanted to win the match? Pavilion critics had their oracular doubts about it; old judges on the rugs had none at all, but gave Devereux a couple of covers for the winning hit; and only Evan himself betrayed a certain apprehension as he crossed beckoning to Jan before the lobs began.

"Have you any idea how many I've got?" he asked below his breath. The second hundred had just gone up to loud applause.

"I can tell you to a run if you want to know."

"I'm asking you."

"You've made 94."

"Rot!"

"You have. You'd made 84 when I came in. I've counted your runs since then."

"I'd no idea it was nearly so many!"

"And I didn't mean to tell you."

There Jan had been quite right, but it was not so tactful to remind the batsman of every batsman's anxiety on nearing the century. Evan, to be sure, repudiated the faint suggestion with some asperity; but his very lips looked redder than before.

"Well, don't you get out off him," said Evan, consequentially.

"I'll try not to. Let's both follow the rule, eh?"

"What rule?"

"Dudley Relton's for lobs: a single off every ball, never more and never less, and nothing whatever on the half-volley."

"Oh, be blowed!" said Evan. "We've been going far too slow these last few overs as it is."

Accordingly he hit the first lob just over mid-on's head for three, and Jan got his single off the next, but off both of the next two balls Evan was very nearly out for 97 and the match lost by 10 runs.

On the second occasion even George Grimwood gratuitously conceded that off a lob a fraction faster Mr. Devereux would indeed have been stumped; as it was he had only just got back in time. This explanation was not acknowledged by Mr. Stratten, whose vain appeal had been echoed by half the field. The nice fellow seemed to have lost all his looks as he crossed to the other end.

The next incident was a full-pitch to leg from Charles Cave and a fourer to Jan Rutter. That made 6 to tie and 7 to win, but only about another hit to Jan if Evan was to get his century. Jan thought of that as he played hard forward to the next ball but one, and felt it leap and heard it hiss through the covers; for even his old bat was driving as it had never done before; but a delightful deep-field sprinter just saved the boundary, and Jan would not risk the more than possible third run.

At this stage only 5 runs were wanted to win the match. And Evan Devereux, within 3 of every cricketer's ambition, again faced the merry underhand bowler against whom he had shaped so precariously the over before last.

George Grimwood might have been seen shifting from foot to foot, and jingling pence in his accomplished palm. Another of those near things was not wanted this over, with the whole match hanging to it, and Mr. Stratten still looking like that....

A bit better, was that! A nice two for Mr. Devereux to the unprotected off—no!—blessed if they aren't running again. They must be daft; one of them'll be out, one of 'em must be! No—a bad return—but Mr. Cave has it now. How beautifully this gentleman always throws! You wouldn't think it of him, to see him crossing over, or even batting or bowling; he's got a return like a young cannon, and here it comes!

No umpire will be able to give this in; there's Mr. Rutter a good two yards down the pitch, legging it for dear life; and here comes the ball like a bullet. He's out if it doesn't miss the wicket after all; but it does miss it, by a coat of varnish, and ricochets to the boundary for other four, that win the match for the school, the ultimate honour of three figures, for Evan Devereux, and peace beyond this racket for George Grimwood.

Over the ground swarm the whole school like a small Surrey crowd, but Evan and Jan have been too quick for them; they break through the swift outer fringe; and it is not Lord's or the Oval after all. Nobody cares so much who wins this match, it's the magnificent finish that matters and will matter while the school exists.

So the dense mass before the pavilion parts in two, and the smiling Old Boys march through the lane; but it does not close up again until Rutter has come out and given Devereux his colours in the dear old way, by taking the blue sash from his own waist and tying it round that of his friend.

Did somebody say that Devereux was blubbing from excitement? It was not the case; but nobody was watching Jan.

CHAPTER XXVII

THE EXTREME PENALTY

It is not to be pretended that a cloud of live young eye-witnesses make quite so much of these excitements as the historian old or young; they may yell themselves hoarse in front of the pavilion, but the beads are not wiped from their heroes' brows before the question is, "What shall we do till lock-up?" It is only the Eleven who want to talk it all over in that sanctum of swelldom, the back room at Maltby's, and only its latest member who has a tremendous telegram to send to his people first. And then it so happens that he does not join them; neither does the Captain of Cricket, though for once in his captaincy he would be really welcome.

Evan had retired to his house, and not a bit as though the school belonged to him, but with curiously little of the habitual strut (now that he had something to strut about) in his almost unsteady gait. Jan, too, was ensconced in Heriot's, and quite unnecessarily prepared to dodge Evan at any moment, or to protect himself with a third person if run to ground. The third person was naturally Chips Carpenter, who had gone mad on the ground, and was now working off the fit in a parody of "The Battle of Blenheim" in place of an ordinary prose report of the latest and most famous of all victories.

Though there was no sign of Evan, and after an hour or so little likelihood of his appearance, still Jan kept dodging in and out of the Editor's study, like an uneasy spirit. And once he remarked that there was an awful row in the lower passage, apparently suggesting that Chips ought to go down and quell it. But Chips had never been a Crabtree in the house, and at present he was too deep in his rhyming dictionary to hear either the row or Jan.

Lock-up at last. The little block of ivy-mantled studies became a manufactory of proses and verses, all Latin but Chips's, and the Greek iambics of others high up in the school, and all but the English effort to be signed by Mr. Heriot after prayers that night or first thing in the morning, to show that the Sabbath had not been broken by secular composition. Nine o'clock and prayers were actually approaching; and yet Jan still sat, or stood about, unmolested in his disorderly study; and yet the heavens had not fallen, or earth trembled with the wrath of Heriot or anybody else. Could it be that for the second time Jan was to be let off by the soft-heartedness of a master who knew enough to hang him?

Hardly! Haigh, of all men! Yet he had been most awfully decent about it all; it was a revelation to Jan that there was so much common decency after all in his oldest enemy....

Now he would soon know. Hark at the old harsh bell, rung by Morgan outside the hall, across the quad!

Prayers.

Jan had scarcely expected to go in to prayers again, and as he went he remembered his first impressions of the function at the beginning of his first term. He remembered the small boy standing sentinel in the flagged passage leading to the green-baize door, and all the fellows armed with hymn-books and chatting merrily in their places at table. That small boy was a big fellow at the Sixth Form table now, and the chat was more animated but less merry than it had seemed to Jan then. Something was in the air already. Could it have leaked out before the sword descended? No; it must be something else. Everybody was eager to tell him about it, as he repeated ancient history by coming in almost last.

"Have you heard about Devereux?"

"Have you heard, Rutter?"

"Haven't you heard?"

His heart missed a beat.

"No. What?"

"He's down with measles!"

"That all?" exclaimed Jan, tingling with returning animation.

If his own downfall had been in vain!

"It's bad enough," said the big fellow who had stood sentinel four years ago. "They say he must have had them on him when he was in, and the whole thing may make him jolly bad."

"Who says so?"

"Morgan; he's just heard it."

Poverty of detail was eked out by fertile speculation. Jan was hardly listening; he could not help considering how far this new catastrophe would affect himself. Evan was as strong as a horse, and that moreover with the strength which had never been outgrown; besides, he would have his magnificent century to look back upon from his pillow. That was enough to see anybody through anything. And now there would be no fear of mental complication, no question of his coming forward and owning up: for who was going to carry a school scandal into the Sanatorium, even if the school ever learnt the rights?

And yet somehow Jan felt as though a loophole had been stopped at the back of his brain; and an inquiry within made him ashamed to discover what the loophole had been. Evan would have found out, and never have let him bear the brunt; in the end Evan's honesty would have saved them both, because nothing paid like honesty with dear old Thrale. That was what Jan saw, now that seeing it could only make him feel a beast! It was almost a relief to realise that Evan would still be ruined if the truth leaked out through other lips, and that a friend's were thus sealed closer than before.

The Heriots were very late in coming in. Why was that? But at last the sentinel showed an important face, fulminating "Hush!" And sister and brother entered in the usual silence.

Miss Heriot took her place at the piano under the shelf bearing the now solitary cup of which Jan might almost be described as the solitary winner; at any rate the present house eleven consisted, like the historic Harrow eleven, of Rutter "and ten others." The ten, nay, the thirty others then present could not have guessed a tenth or a thirtieth part of all that was in their bowler's mind that night.

Mr. or Miss Heriot always chose a good hymn; to-night it was No. 22, Ancient and Modern; a simple thing, and only appropriate to the time of year, but still rather a favourite of Jan's. He found himself braying out the air from the top of the Sixth Form table, as though nothing could happen to him, while Chips Carpenter lorded it like every captain of that house, with his back to the empty grate, and fondly imagined that he was singing bass. Neither friend and contemporary would ever have done much credit to the most musical school in England, and now only one of them would be able to go about saying that he had ever been there!

Unless ... and there was no telling from Heriot's voice.

It was the same unaffected, manly voice which had appealed to Jan on his very first night in hall; the prayers were the same, a characteristic selection only used in that house; but whereas a few phrases had struck Jan even on that occasion, now he knew them all off by heart, but listened with no less care in order to remember them if possible at the ends of the earth.

"O Lord, Who knowest our peculiar temptations here, help us by Thy Holy Spirit to struggle against them. Save us from being ashamed of Thee and of our duty. Save us from the base and degrading fear of one another...." Jan hoped he had stood up sufficiently to the other old choices in the Eleven; he could not help an ungodly feeling that he had; but he had been very down on his luck earlier in the term.

"Grant, O Lord, that we may always remember that our bodies are the temple of the living God, and that we may not pollute them by evil thoughts or evil words.... Give us grace never to approve or by consent to sanction in others what our consciences tell us is wrong, but to reprove it either by word or by silence. Let us never ourselves act the part of tempter to others, never place a stumbling-block in our brother's way, or offend any of our companions, for Jesus Christ's sake. Amen."

Well, he had never played the tempter or placed stumbling-blocks, whatever else he had done; it was not for that that he would have to go; but he was not so sure about evil words. He had said some things, sometimes, which might have earned him his now imminent fate, if they had reached some ears; so perhaps he had little to complain about after all. Not that foul language had ever been his habit; but he had never been so particular as Chips, for example, now so devout in the Lord's Prayer at the other end of the Sixth Form table. Old Chips in his early days had gone to the foolhardy and (in him) futile length of reproof by word; even now he was rising from his knees as though he had been really praying; but Jan had only been thinking his own thoughts, though kneeling there without doubt for the last time.

And yet a second moment's doubt did thrill him as Heriot took up his usual stand in front of the grate, and some of the fellows made a dash for milk and dog-rocks at the bottom of the long table, but more clustered round the fireplace to hear Heriot and Jan discuss the match. They actually did discuss it for a minute or two; but Heriot was dry as tinder in spite of his intentions; and when he suddenly announced that he would sign all verses in the morning, but would just like to speak to Rutter for a minute, Jan followed him through into the private part with a stabbing conviction that all was over with him.

"I've heard Mr. Haigh's story," said Heriot very coldly in his study. "Do you wish me to hear yours?"

"No, sir."

Jan did not wince at Heriot's tone, but Heriot did at his. The one was to be expected, the other almost brazen in its unblushing alacrity.

"You have nothing whatever to say for yourself, after all these years, after—"

Heriot pulled himself up—as on his haunches—with a jerk of the grizzled head and a fierce flash of the glasses.

"But from all I hear I'm not surprised," he added with bitter significance. "I find I've been mistaken in you all along."

Yet Jan did not see his meaning at the time, and the bitterness only enabled him to preserve apparent insensibility.

"There's nothing to say, sir. I was shamming right enough, and I suppose Mr. Haigh has told you why."

"He has, indeed! The matter has also been reported to the Head Master, and he wishes to see you at once. I need hardly warn you what to expect, I should think."

"No, sir. I expect to go."

"Evidently you won't be sorry, so I shan't waste any sympathy upon you. But I must say I think you might have thought of the house!"

The matter had not presented itself in that light to Jan; now that it did, he felt with Heriot on the spot, and did not perceive an unworthy although most human element in the man's outlook. The house would not be ruined for life. On the other hand, in his determination to put a stiff lip on every phase of his downfall, and beyond all things not to betray himself by ever breaking down, Jan had over-acted like most unskilled histrions, and had already created an impression of coarse bravado on a mind prepared to stretch any possible point in his favour.

But it was no time to think about the accomplished interview with Bob Heriot, with truly terrific retribution even now awaiting him at the hands of the redoubtable old Jerry. About a hundred yards of the soft summer night, and he would stand in that awful presence for the last time. And it was all very well for Jan to call him "old Jerry" in his heart up to the last, and to ask himself what there was, after all, to fear so acutely from a man of nearly seventy who could not eat him; his heart quaked none the less, and if he had been obliged to answer himself it would have been with a trembling lip.

He dared to dawdle on the way, rehearsing his scanty past relations with the great little old man. There was the time when he was nearly flogged, after the Abinger affair. Well, the old man might have been far more severe than he really was on that occasion. There was that other early scene when Jan was told that another time he would not sit down so comfortably, and Chips's story about his friend Olympus. It was all grim humour that appealed to this delinquent; but it was a humour that became terrible when the whole school were arraigned and held responsible for some individual vileness, pronounced inconceivable in a really sound community; for then they were all dogs and curs together, and, that demonstrated, it was "Dogs, go to your kennels!" And go they would, feeling beaten mongrels every one; never laughing at the odd old man, never even reviling him; often loving but always fearing him.

Jan feared him now the more because of late especially he had been learning to love Mr. Thrale. Though still only in the Lower Sixth, as Captain of Cricket he had come in for sundry ex officio honours, in the shape of invitations to breakfast and audiences formal and informal. On all such occasions Jan had been embarrassed and yet braced, puzzled by parables but enlightened in flashes, stimulated in soul and sinew but awed from skin to core; and now the awe was undiluted, crude, and overwhelming. He felt that every word from that trenchant tongue would leave a scar for life, and the scorn in those old eyes haunt him to his grave.

Sub-consciously he was still thinking of the judge and executioner in his gown of office, on his carved judgment seat, as the day's crop of petty offenders found and faced him after twelve. In his library Jan had seldom before set foot, never with the seeing eye that he brought to-night; and the smallness and simplicity of it struck him through all his tremors when the servant had shown him in. It was not so very much larger than the large studies at Heriot's. Only a gangway of floor surrounded a great desk in a litter after Jan's own heart; garden smells came through an open lattice, and with them a maze of midges to dance round the one lamp set amid the litter; and in the light of that lamp, a pale face framed in silvery hair, wide eyes filled with heart-broken disgust, and a mouth that might have been closed for ever.

At last it came to mobile life, and Jan heard in strangely dispassionate tones a brief recital of all that had been heard and seen of his proceedings in the fatal hour when pretended illness kept him from the match. Again he was asked if he had anything to challenge or to add; for it was Heriot's question in other words, and Jan had no new answer; but this time he could only shake a bowed head humbly, as he had bent it in acknowledgment of his own writing on the envelope. Jerry was far less fierce than he had expected, but a hundredfold more terrible in his pale grief and scorn. Jan felt an even sorrier and meaner figure than on coming up for judgment after the Abinger affair; so far from the support of secret heroics, it was impossible to stand in the white light of that nobly reproachful countenance, and even to remember that he was not altogether the vile thing he seemed.

"If there is one form of treachery worse than another," said Mr. Thrale, "it is treachery in high places. The office that you have occupied, Rutter, is rightly or wrongly a high one in this school; but you have dragged it in the dust, and our honour stands above our cricket. On the eve of our school matches, when we had a right to look to you to keep our flag flying, you have betrayed your trust and forfeited your post and your existence here; but if it were the end of cricket in this school, I would not keep you another day."

Jan looked up suddenly.

"Am I to go on a Sunday, sir?"

The thought of his return to the Norfolk rectory, in this dire disgrace, had taken sudden and most poignant shape. On a Sunday it would be too awful, with the somnolent yet captious household in a state of either complacent indolence or sanctified fuss, assimilating sirloin or starting for church, according to the hour of his arrival.

Mr. Thrale seemed already to have taken this into humane consideration, for he promptly replied: "You will remain till Monday; meanwhile you are to consider yourself a prisoner on parole, and mix no more in the society for which you have shown yourself unfit. So far as this school goes you are condemned to death for lying betrayal, and mock-manly meanness. Murder will out, Rutter, but you are not condemned for any undiscovered crime of the past. Yet if it is true that you ever got out of your house at night—"

Jan could not meet the awful mien with which Mr. Thrale here made dramatic pause; but he filled it by mumbling that it was quite true, he had got out once, over two years ago.

"Once," said Mr. Thrale, "is enough to deprive you of the previous good character that might otherwise have been taken into consideration. I do not say it could have saved you; but nothing can save the traitor guilty of repeated acts of treason. A certain consideration you will receive at Mr. Heriot's hands, by his special request, until you go on Monday morning. And that, Rutter, is all I have to say to you as Head Master of this school."

Even so is the convicted murderer handed over to the High Sheriff for destruction; but just as other judges soften the dread language of the law with more human utterances on their own account, so before he was done did Mr. Thrale address himself to Jan as man to man, merely reversing the legal order. He asked the boy what he was going to do in life, and besought him not to look upon his whole life as necessarily ruined. The greater the fall, the greater the merit of rising again; he had almost said, and he would say, the greater the sport of rising! Jan had pulled matches out of the fire; let him take life as a game, bowl out the Devil that was in him, and pull his own soul out of Hell! Here he enlarged upon the lust of drink, bluntly but with a tender breadth of understanding, as a snare set alike for the just and the unjust, a curse most accursed in its destruction of the moral fibre, as in this very case; and Jan could not have listened more humbly if his own whole body and soul had been already undermined. He thought he saw tears in the old man's eyes; he knew he had them in his own. These last words of earnest exhortation, beginning as they did between man and man, went on and finished almost as between father and son, with a handshake and "God guide you!" There was even the offer of a letter which, while not glozing the worst, would yet say those other things that could still be said, and might stand Jan in good stead if he were man enough to show it in Australia.

But meanwhile he had been expelled from school, expelled in his last term, when Captain of Cricket, and on top of his one triumph in that capacity. And on his way back to his house, Jan stopped in the starlit street, and what do you think he did?

He laughed aloud as he suddenly remembered the actual facts of the case.

CHAPTER XXVIII

"LIKE LUCIFER"

Mr. Heriot himself showed Jan to his room, the spare bedroom on the private side of the house, where he was to remain until he went. All his belongings had been brought down from dormitory, and some few already from his study. The bed was made and turned down, with clean sheets as if for a guest; and there was an adjoining dressing-room at his disposal, with the gas lit and hot water placed in readiness by some unenlightened maid.

This led Heriot to explain, gruffly enough, the special consideration to which Mr. Thrale had referred.

"The whole thing's a secret from the house so far, and of course the servants don't know anything about it. They probably think you're suspected of measles, not strongly enough for the Sanatorium but too strongly for the sick-room in the boys' part. I shall allow that impression to prevail until—as long as you remain."

"Thank you, sir."

"I remember better days, Rutter; we had seen a good many together before you came to anything like this, I'm quite sure." His glasses flashed. "Yet all the time—"

He stopped himself as before, turned on his heel and shut a window which he had opened on entering the room. And now Jan grasped what it was that his house-master kept remembering, but could not trust himself to mention. And the mutual constraint made the prisoner thankful when he was bidden an abrupt good-night, and left alone at last.

Alone in the condemned cell, or rather a luxurious suite of cells! The luxury was an irony not lost on Jan; he was as much alive to every detail of his environment as he had been towards the end of the match. And the grim humours of the situation, which had only come home to him since his interview with the Head Master, were still a relief after the deceptive solemnity of that ordeal. He must never again forget that he was guiltless. That made all the difference in the world. Would he have been able to think of condemned cells if he had deserved to be in one, or of the portmanteau he now discovered in the dressing-room, lying ready to be packed, as the open coffin of his school life?

And yet it was, it was!

But the waking night was a long succession of obstacles to oblivion. Forgotten circumstances came back with new and dolorous significance; this began when he emptied his pockets before undressing, and missed his watch. It was the first night in all his schooldays that he had been without the small gold watch which had been his mother's when she ran away from home. Again he remembered wondering if the boys would laugh at him for having a lady's watch; but they were marvellously decent about some things; not one of them had ever made a single remark about it. The little gold watch had timed him through all these years, and the first time he left it behind him he came to grief. It was only in the studies; but it would never bring his luck back now.

Then there was that pocketful of small silver and stray gold. Two pounds eighteen and sixpence, he ought to make it; and he did. The amount was not the only point about the money that he recalled in lurid flashes as he counted it all out upon the dressing-table. He took an envelope from the stationery case on another table, swept all the coins in and stuck it up with care. He even wrote the amount outside, then dropped the jingling packet into a drawer. Soon after this he got to bed in the superfine sheets dedicated to guests; of course his own sheets would not have stretched across this great bedstead; and yet these reminded every inch of him where he was, every hour of the night.

He heard them all struck by the old blue monkey of a church clock. It was the first time he had heard it like this since his removal from the little front dormitory, his first year in the Eleven. It was strange to be sleeping over the street again, listening to all its old noises ... listening ... listening again ... at last listening to the old harsh bell!

That was the worst noise of all; for he must have been asleep, in spite of everything; he only really woke up standing on the soft, spacious, unfamiliar floor. The spare bedroom was full of summer sunshine. The fine weather had come to stay. They would get a fast wicket over at Repton, and Goose would have to win the toss.

Goose!

Meanwhile it was only Sunday, and Jan knew the habits of his house on Sunday morning; now was his chance of the bath. Bathrooms were not as plentiful then as now; there was only one between both sides of the house, of course not counting the shower off the lavatory. That, however, was now out of bounds; the bathroom was not, and Jan got to it first, bolted both doors and looked out into the quad while the bath was filling.

O cursed memories! Here was another, of his very first sight of the quad, his very first morning in the school.... Well, he had lived to be cock of that walk, at any rate; on those fives-courts, moreover, with their unorthodox back wall, he was certainly leaving no superior. But how pleasant it all looked in the cool morning sun! There is a peculiar quality about Sunday sunshine, a restfulness at once real and imaginary; it was very real to Jan as he took leave of the quiet study windows down the further side, and down this one the empty garden seats shaded by the laburnum with its shrivelled blossoms, the little acacia, and the plane-tree which had been blown down once and ever since held in leash by a chain. Closer at hand, hardly out of reach, the dormitory windows stood wide open; but nobody got up in dormitory till the last five minutes on a Sunday morning, and so Jan gloated unobserved on the set-scene of so much that had happened to the house and him—of the burglar-hunt led by the egregious Spook—of Sprawson's open pranks and Shockley's wary brutalities. It was down there that Mulberry first showed his fatal nose, and Jan was christened Tiger, and it was there they all lit up a slide with candles at the end of his first winter term. Now it was the end of all terms for Jan, and in a night the old quad had changed into a place of the past.

It was better in the cells at the front of the house; it might have been quite bearable there, but for the bells. But on a Sunday the cracked bell rung by Morgan was nothing to the bells you heard on the other side of the house, if you came to listen to them as Jan did. Apparently there was early celebration in the parish church as well as in chapel; but that was the only time the rival bells rang an actual duet of sedate discords. They followed each other with due propriety all the rest of the day.

The chapel bells led off with their incorrigibly merry measure. Worse hearing was the accompanying tramp of boys in twos and threes, in Sunday tails or Eton jackets; looking heartlessly content with life; taking off præpostorial hats, or touching those hot school caps, to gowned and hooded masters; for Jan was obliged to peep through the casement blinds, not deliberately to make things worse, but for the sake or on the chance of a single moment's distraction. That was all he got. It was quite true that there were heaps of fellows now to whom he could not put a name. There could not have been more in his second or third term; mere mortal boys do not excite the curiosity of gods; but once or twice poor Lucifer espied some still unfallen angel in the ribbon of shade across the street. One was Ibbotson, a god with clay feet, if ever there was one; but there he went, looking all he should be, to the happy jingle of those callous bells. Ibbotson would come down as an Old Boy, and never think twice of what he had really been. Why should he? Jan, at all events, was not his judge; and yet he would be one of Jan's.

The church bells came as a relief, richer in tone, poorer in association, with townspeople on the pavement and not a sound in the house. Jan fell to and packed. All his wardrobe had been brought in now; his study possessions would be sent after him; so Mr. Heriot had looked in to say, and at the same time to extract an explicit pledge that Jan would not again set foot on the boys' side of the house. He wondered if the bath had been judged a step in that direction, and what it was feared that he might do when all their backs were turned. But he gave his word without complaining; never, to be sure, had condemned man less cause for complaint. His dietary was on the traditional scale; excellent meals were brought to the spare room. There was the usual sound fare for dinner, including the inevitable cold apple-pie with cloves in it, and a long glass of beer because Jan's exalted place in the house entitled him (in those unregenerate days) to two ordinary glasses. Morgan, at any rate, could not know what he was there for! Jan was wondering whether it was enough to make him sleepy after his wretched night, and so kill an hour of this more wretched day, when the door burst open, without preliminary knock, and Carpenter stood wheezing on the other side of the bed.

His high shoulders heaved. His rather unhealthy face looked grotesquely intense and agonised. It was plain at a glance that Old Chips knew something.

"Oh, Jan!" he cried. "What did you do it for?"

"That's my business. Who sent you here?"

"I got leave from Heriot."

"Very good of you, I'm sure!"

"That wasn't why I came," said Chips, braced though stung by this reception. He had shut the door behind him. He walked round the bed with the extremely determined air of one in whom determination was not a habit.

"Well, why did you come?" inquired Jan, though he was beginning to guess.

"You did a thing I couldn't have believed you'd do!"

"Many things, it seems."

"I'm only thinking of one. The others don't concern me. You went into my locker and—and broke into the house money-box!"

"I left you something worth five times as much, and I owned what I'd done in black and white."

"I know that. Here's your watch and your I.O.U. I found them after chapel this morning."

Jan took his treasure eagerly, laid it on the dressing-table, and produced his packet of coins from one of the small side drawers.

"And here's your money," said he. "You'd better count it; you won't find a sixpence missing."

Chips stared at him with round eyes.

"But what on earth did you borrow it for?"

"That's my business," said Jan, in the same tone as before, though Chips had changed his.

"I don't know how you knew I had all this money. It isn't usual late in the term like this, when all the subs. have been banked long ago."

Jan showed no disposition to explain the deed.

"This is my business, you know," persisted Chips.

"Oh! is it? Then I don't mind telling you I heard you filling your precious coffers after dinner."

It was Chips's own term for the money-box in which as captain of the house he placed the various house subscriptions as he received them. He looked distressed.

"I was afraid you must have heard me."

"Then why did you ask?"

"I hoped you hadn't."

"What difference does it make?"

"You heard me with the money, and yet you couldn't come in and ask me to lend it to you."

"I should like to have seen you do it!"

"The money was for something special, Jan."

"I thought it was."

"Half the house had just been giving me their allowances, but some had got more from home expressly."

"Yet you pretend you'd have let me touch it!"

Chips bore this taunt without heat, yet with a treacherous lip.

"I would, Jan, every penny of it."

"Why should you?"

"Because it was yours already! It was only for something we were all going to give you because of—because of those cups we got through you—and—and everything else you've done for the house, Jan!"

An emotional dog, this Chips, he still had the sense to see that it was not for him to show emotion then, and the self-control to act up to his lights. But he could not help thrusting the packet back towards Jan, as much as to say that it was still his and he must really take it with the good wishes he now needed more than ever. Not a word of the kind from his lips, and yet every syllable in his eyes and gestures. But Jan only shook his head, wheeled round, and stood looking down into the street.

CHAPTER XXIX

CHIPS AND JAN

Anybody entering the room just then would have smelt bad blood between the fellow looking out of the window and the other fellow sitting on the edge of the bed. Jan's whole attitude was one of injury, and Chips looked thoroughly guilty of a grave offence against the laws of friendship. Even when Jan turned round it was with the glare which is the first skin over an Englishman's wound; only a hoarse solicitude of tone confessed the wound self-inflicted, and the visitor a bringer of balm hardly to be borne.

"I suppose you know what's happened, Chips?"

"I don't know much."

"Not that I'm—going?"

"That's about all."

"Isn't it enough, Chips?"

"No. I want to know why."

Jan's look grew searching.

"If Heriot told you so much—"

"He didn't till I pressed him."

"Why should you have pressed him, Chips? What had you heard?"

"Only something they were saying in the Sixth Form Room; there's nothing really got about yet."

"You might tell me what they're saying! I—I don't want to be made out ever so much worse than I am."

That was not quite the case. He wanted to know whether there was any movement, or even any strong feeling, in his favour; but it was a sudden want, and he could not bring himself to clothe it in words. It was his prototype's hope of a reprieve, entertained with as little reason, more as a passing irresistible thought.

"They say there was nothing the matter with you yesterday afternoon."

"No more there was. I was shamming."

Chips experienced something of Heriot's revulsion at this avowal.

"They say you went off—to—meet somebody."

"How did they get hold of that, I should like to know?"

Of course the masters had been talking; why should they not? But then why had Heriot pretended that nobody was to know just yet? Why had Haigh talked about the worst cases being kept quiet? Chips allayed rising resentment by saying he believed it had come through a fly-man, whereupon Jan admitted that it was perfectly true.

"They say you drove out to Yardley Wood."

"So I did."

"It was madness!"

Jan shrugged his powerful shoulders.

"I took my risks, and I was bowled out, that's all."

Chips looked at him; the cynically glib admissions were ceasing to grate on him, were beginning to excite the incredulity with which he had first heard of the suicidal escapade. This shameless front was not a bit like Jan, whatever he had done, and Chips who knew him best was the first to perceive it.

"I wish I knew why you'd done it!" he exclaimed ingenuously.

"What do they say about that?" inquired Jan.

"Well, there was some talk about—about a bit of a—romance!"

Jan's grin made him look quite himself.

"Nicely put, Chips! But you can contradict that on the best authority."

"Now it's got about that it's a drinking row."

"That's more like it."

"It's what most fellows believe," said Chips, with questionable tact.

"Oh, is it? Think I look the part, do they?"

"Not you, Jan—"

"What then?"

Chips did not like going on, but was obliged to now.

"Well, some fellows seem to think that—except yesterday, of course—your bowling—"

"Has suffered from it, eh? Go on, Chips! I like this. I like it awfully!"

And this time Jan laughed outright, but did not look himself.

"It's not what I say, Jan! I wouldn't hear of it."

"Very kind of you, I'm sure; but I shouldn't wonder if you thought it all the same."

"I don't, I tell you!"

"I wouldn't blame you if you did. How things fit in! Any other circumstantial evidence against me?"

Chips hesitated again.

"Out with it, man. I may as well know."

"Well, some say—but only some—that's why you've been going about so much by yourself!"

"To go off on the spree alone?"

Chips nodded. "You see, you often refused to go out even with me," he said reproachfully; not as though he believed the worst himself, but in a tone of excuse for those who did.

Jan could only stare. His unsociability had been due of course to his unpopularity with his Eleven, his estrangement from Evan, and his delicacy about falling back on Chips. And even Chips could not see that for himself, but saw if anything with the other idiots! This was too much for Jan; it made him look more embittered than was wise if he still wished to be taken as the only villain of the piece. But the fact was that for the moment he was forgetting to act.

"Solitary drinking!" he ejaculated. "Bad case, isn't it?"

"It isn't a case at all," returned Chips, looking him in the face. "I don't believe a word of the whole thing! Even if it's true that you went out to Yardley to meet Mulberry—"

"Who say's that?"

"Oh, it's one of the things that's got about. But I can jolly well see that if you did go to meet him it wasn't on your own account!"

Confound old Chips! He was looking as if he could fairly see into a fellow's skull, and very likely making a fellow look in turn as big a fool as he felt!

"Of course you know more about it than I do!" sneered Jan, desperately. "But do you suppose I'd do a thing like that for anybody but myself?"

"I believe you'd do a jolly sight more," replied Chips, "for Evan Devereux!"

Jan made no reply beyond an unconvincing little laugh; of plain denial he looked as incapable as he actually was, in his surprise at so shrewd a thrust.

"The whole thing was for Devereux!" pursued Carpenter with explosive conviction. "What about him and Sandham out at Yardley the other Sunday, when old Mulberry beckoned to us by mistake? Obviously he mistook us for them; I thought so at the time, but you wouldn't have it, just because it was Devereux! What about his coming to you yesterday morning, in such a stew about something? Oh, I didn't listen, but anybody could spot that something was up. What a fool I was not to see the whole thing from the first! Why, of course you'd never have touched that money for yourself, let alone planting out the thing I know you value more than anything else you've got!"

Still Jan said nothing, even when explicitly challenged to deny it if he could. He only stood still and looked mysterious, while he racked his brain for something to explain his look along with those other appearances which Chips had interpreted so unerringly. He felt in a great rage with Chips, and yet somehow in nothing like such a rage as he had been in before. It had taken old Chips to see that he was not such a blackguard as he had made himself out; that was something to remember in the silly fool's favour; he was the only one, when all was said and done, to believe the best of a fellow in spite of everything, even in spite of the fellow himself.

Condemned men cannot afford to send their only friends to blazes. But Chips soon went the way to get himself that happy dispatch.

"Why should you do all this for Evan Devereux?" he demanded.

"All what, Chips? I never said I'd done anything."

"Oh, all right, you haven't! But what's he ever done for you?"

"Plenty."

"Name something—anything—he's ever done except when you were in a position to do more for him!"

And then Jan did tell him where to go. But Chips only laughed in his face, with the spendthrift courage of a fellow who did not as a rule show enough, though he had it all the same when his blood was up. And now he was in as great a passion as Jan, and just for a moment it was as fine a passion too.

"You start cursing me because you haven't any answer. Curse away, and come to blows if you like; you shan't shift me out of this until I've said what I've got to say, not if I have to hang on to this bedstead and bring the place about our ears!"

"Don't be a fool, Chips," said Jan, perceiving that he required self-control for two. "You know you've always had a down on Evan."

"Well, perhaps I have. Doesn't he deserve it? What did he ever do for you your first term—though he'd known you at home?"

"That was no reason why he should do anything. What could he do? We were in different houses and different forms; besides, I was higher up in the school, as it happened, as well as a bit older."

"That's nothing; still I rather agree with you, though he was here first, remember. But what about your second term or my third? He overtook us each in turn, but did he ever go out of his way to say a civil word to either of us, though he'd known us both before?"

"Yes; he did."

"Yes, he did! When you'd made a little bit of a name for yourself over the Mile he was out for a walk with you in a minute. That's the fellow all over, and has been all the time. I remember how it was when you got in the Eleven, if you don't!"

But Jan did remember, and it made him think. Like most boys who are good at games, he had acquired in their practice great fairness of mind. He thought Chips was unfair to Evan, and yet he wanted to be fair to Chips, whom he recognised in his heart as by far the sounder fellow of the two. Chips was the loyal, unswerving, faithful friend who not only bore a friend's infirmities but blew his trumpet as few would blow their own. But he had without doubt some of the usual defects of such qualities; he was touchy, he could be jealous, though Jan was not the one to tell him that; but on the touchiness he dwelt with a tact made tender by his own trouble.

"The fact is, Chips, you're such a good old chap yourself that you want everybody else to be the same as you. You wouldn't hurt a fellow's feelings, so you can't forgive the chaps who do it without thinking. Not one in a hundred makes as much of things as you do, or takes things so to heart. But that's because you're what you are, Chips; you oughtn't to be down on everybody who doesn't happen to be built as straight and true."

"Don't be too sure that I'm either!" exclaimed Carpenter, flinching unaccountably.

"You're only about the straightest chap in the whole school, Chips. Everybody knows that, I should think."

"I've a good mind to set everybody right!" cried Carpenter, worked up to more than he had dreamed of saying, a wild impulse burning in his eyes. "I can't see you bunked for nothing, when others including me have done all sorts of things to deserve it. Yes, Jan, including me! You think I've been so straight! So I was in the beginning; so I am now, if you like, but I've not been all the time. Don't stop me. I won't be stopped; but that's about all I've got to say. I've always wanted you to know. You're the only fellow in the place I care much for, who cares much for me, though not so much—"

"Yes I do, Chips, yes I do! I never thought so much of you as I do this minute.... I don't say it never crossed my mind.... But don't you make yourself out worse than you ever were, even to me!"

"I don't want to.... It didn't go on so long, and it's all over now.... But I shall get the præpostor's medal when I leave—unless I'm man enough to refuse it—and you've been bunked for standing by a fellow who never would have stood by you!"

"That's where you're wrong, Chips," said Jan, gently.

"No, I'm not. It's the other way about."

"You don't know how Evan's stood by me all these years."

Carpenter maintained a strange silence—very strange in him, just then especially—a silence that made him ashamed and yet exultant.

"Do you know, Chips?"

"It depends what you think he's done."

"I'll tell you," said Jan with sudden yet quiet resolution, and a lift of his head as though the peak of a cap had been pulled down too far. "I had a secret when I came here, and Evan knew it but nobody else. It was a big secret—about my people and me too—and if it had come out then I'd have bolted like a rabbit. I know now that it wouldn't have mattered as much as I thought it would; things about your people, or anything that ever happened anywhere else, don't hurt or help much in a place like this. It's what you can do and how you take things that matters here. But I didn't know that then and I don't suppose Evan did either. Yet he kept a quiet tongue in his head about everything he did know. And that's what I owe him—all it meant to me then, and does still in a way—his holding his tongue like that!"

Still Chips held his; and now Jan was the prey of doubts which his own voice had silenced. All that the familiar debt had gained by clear statement was counteracted by the stony demeanour of its first auditor.

"Did he ever tell you, Chips?"

"The very first time I saw him, our very first term!"

"Not—not about my father and—the stables—and all that?"

"Everything!"

Jan threw himself back four years.

"Yet when I sounded you at the time—"

"I told you the lie of my life!" said Chips. "I couldn't help myself. But this is the truth!"

And Jan took it with the enviable composure which had only deserted him when Evan was being traduced; it was several seconds before he made a sound, still standing there with his back to the bedroom window; and then the sound was very like a chuckle.

"Well, at any rate he can't have told many!"

"I don't suppose he did."

"Then he picked the right one, Chipsey, and I still owe him almost as much as I do you."

"You owe old Heriot more than either of us."

"Heriot! Why? Does he know?"

"He knew all along, but he never meant you to know that he knew. He guessed how you'd feel it if you did; he guesses everything! Why, that very first Saturday, if you remember, when Devereux turned up for call-over and began telling me the minute afterwards, it was as though Bob Heriot simply saw what he was saying! He pounced upon us both that instant, dropped a pretty plain hint on the spot, but asked us to breakfast next morning and then absolutely bound us over never to let out a single word about you in all our days here!"

"So Evan'd been talking before he told me he never would," mused Jan. "Well, I can't blame him so much for that. I'm not sure, Chips, that I should have done so differently now even if I'd known. I liked him even in the old days when we were kids. Must you go?"

The question was asked in a very wistful tone. Chips felt, rather uneasily, that in these few minutes he had ousted Evan and taken his old place. He could not help it if he had. It had not been his intention on coming into the room. It was no use regretting it now.

"I told Heriot I wouldn't stay very long," he answered. "I'll get him to let me come up again."

"And you won't tell him anything about Evan?"

"How do you mean?"

"You won't tell him a single word about our having seen him and Sandham that day?"

Chips was silent.

"Surely you wouldn't go getting them bunked as well as me?"

"Well—no—not exactly."

"I should think not! It wouldn't do any good, you see, even if you did," said Jan, suddenly discovering why he had looked so mysterious some minutes back. "You forget that Evan and I used to go about together quite as much as he and Sandham have been doing all this year. What if it was me that first started playing the fool in Yardley Wood? What if old Mulberry knows more against me than anybody else? It wouldn't do me much good to put them in the same boat, would it?"

"But does he, Jan, honestly?"

"Honestly, I'm sorry to say."

"It's too awful!"

"But you will hold your tongue about the other two, won't you, Chips?"

"If you like."

"You promise?"

"Very well. I promise."

But Chips Carpenter was reckoning without Mr. Heriot, a magnificent schoolmaster, but a Grand Inquisitor at getting things out of fellows when he liked. To his credit, he never did like a task which some schoolmasters seem to enjoy; but he was not the man to shirk a distasteful duty. Carpenter had long outstayed his leave upstairs and the spare room was directly over Heriot's study. Voices had been raised at one time to an angry pitch, and this had set the man below thinking, but certainly not listening more than he could help. Nor had he caught a single word; but he had to remember that Carpenter's pretext for the visit was a private money matter, and other circumstances connected with Jan's finances.

He waylaid Chips on his way down.

"Well, Carpenter, you've been a long time?"

"I'm afraid I have, sir."

"I gave you ten minutes and you took five-and-twenty. However, I hope you got your money?"

Chips started.

"What money, sir?"

"Didn't you go to collect a private debt?"

"I don't know how you knew, sir."

"I happen to know that Rutter had a good deal of money on Saturday, and that he never as a rule has half enough."

"Yes, sir; he paid me back every penny," said Chips, without attempting to escape.

He was in fact extremely interested in this question of the money, which had been driven out of his mind by other matters, only to return now with evident and yet puzzling significance. He was wondering whether this was not a point on which he could confide honourably in Heriot, since Jan had laid no embargo on the subject. He might only have forgotten to do so—Chips had a high conception of honour in such matters—but anything to throw light on the mystery before it was too late!

"Now, you and Rutter have been great friends, haven't you, Carpenter?"

It was the skilful questioner proceeding on his own repugnant lines.

"Yes, sir, I think we have, on the whole."

"Has he ever borrowed money from you before?"

"Never a penny, sir."

"Had he rather strong principles on the point?"

"I used to think he had, sir."

"Do you think he'd break them for his own sake, Carpenter?"

"No, sir, I don't! I—I practically told him so," replied Chips, after considering whether he was free to say as much.

"I've only one other question to ask you, Carpenter. You told me, before I let you go up, that several of the leading fellows know something about what's happened."

"They do, sir."

"Can you think of anybody who doesn't know, and perhaps ought to know, while there's time?"

Chips felt his heart leap within him, only to sink under the weight of his last promise to Jan; he shrank from the very mention of Evan's name after such a solemn undertaking as that. And yet Jan came first.

"Well, sir, I—could."

"Then won't you?"

"If you wouldn't ask me for my reasons, sir."

Heriot smiled in incipient inquisitorial triumph. It was a wry smile over a wry job, but he had come to his feet, and his spectacles were flashing formidably. The poor lad's honest reservation was more eloquent than unconditional indiscretion in ears attuned to puerile nuances.

"I may ask you anything I like, Carpenter, but I can't make you answer anything you don't like! I can only suggest to you that there's probably some fellow who might help us if he were not in the dark. Will you give me the name that occurred to you?"

CHAPTER XXX

HIS LAST FLING

Jan turned back to the bedroom window, and stood looking out with eyes that saw less than ever. The window was open at the bottom; he kept a discreet distance from the sill, but might have seen a strip of the pavement opposite, now dappled by a sudden shower. He was as the blind, however, until a slight crash below made him pop his head out without thinking. Then he saw that it was raining, because Mr. Heriot had emerged from the house, and broken into a run instead of returning for his umbrella.

The only thought Jan gave him was a twinge of wonder that he could go his ways so briskly with the virtual head of his house lying under sentence of expulsion in the spare room. Heriot was mighty keen on his house, keenly critical and appreciative of every fellow in it, but keener yet on a corporate entity, mysteriously independent of the individuals that made it up, which expressed itself in Jan's mind as "the house itself." He too had felt like that about the house cricket and the school Eleven; the best bat got measles, and it was no good giving him another thought. And yet somehow it made Jan himself feel bitterly small to see Heriot gadding about his business like that in the rain.

Otherwise the sight did him good, in liberating his mind from the overload of new ideas that weighed it down. Always a great talker, that poor old Chips had told him so much in such quick time that it was impossible to keep his outpourings distinct and apart from each other; they were like the blots of rain on the pavement, spreading, joining, overlapping into a featureless whole. But the shower ceased even as Jan looked down; the pavement began to dry before all semblance of design was obliterated; and the fusion of fresh impressions suffered an analogous arrest.

Evan dried by himself....

Jan brought a cane chair to the window, and sat down to think about Evan, to be fair to old Evan at all costs. It was easy to be down on him, to feel he had been guilty of unpardonable perfidy; but had he? Was there any great reason why he should not have told Chips—Chips whom he knew of old, and whom he had seen with Jan? Surely it was the most natural confidence in the world; and then it was the only one, even Chips thought that, though Jan was not so sure when he recalled the bold scorn of Sandham and some others in the Eleven—their indistinguishable whispers and their unmistakable looks. But, even so! Had he ever asked Evan to keep his secret? Had not Evan, on the other hand, kept it on the whole unasked? Was it not due to him first and last that the whole school had not got hold of it? Chips might say what he liked about Heriot, but no master could impose secrecy upon a boy against the boy's will. Evan's will towards Jan must always have been of the best. It was Jan's own fault if he had imagined himself under an inconceivable obligation; it only showed what a simpleton he had always been about Evan Devereux. That was it! He was far too simple altogether; even now he could not shake off all his unreasonable disappointment because Evan had been a trifle less loyal to him, in the very beginning, than he had chosen to flatter himself all these years.

It was a comfort to turn to the other side of the account. Thank goodness he had been able to do something for Evan in the end! He did owe it to him, whatever Chips chose to say or think. Chips was a jealous old fool; there was no getting away from that. Jan only hoped he had not given Chips an inkling of the real facts of the case. He did not think he had. It had been a happy thought to pretend that Evan's connection with his downfall was that of the feeble accomplice whom he and not Sandham had led astray; it really made expulsion too good for him, so Chips would be under no temptation to let it out or to drag in Evan's name at all. In any case he had promised. He was a man of his word. He was the soul of honour and integrity, old Chips ... so at least Jan had always thought him down to this very afternoon. Simpleton again!

Chips, of all people, not always any better than he should have been.... Jan could not get that out of his head; it was another disappointment to his simplicity. He had thought he knew the worst of Chips, his touchiness, his jealousy, taking too much notice of himself and sometimes thinking that other people did not take enough. A bit weak-minded and excitable, Jan would have called him, thinking of the morbid and emotional side of his friend's character which had certainly shown itself that day. But what enthusiasm, what a heart, and what a head too in its way! It only showed that you knew very little, really, about anybody else, even your intimate house-mate; but it might also have shown Jan that he was slow to think evil, slow to perceive the worst side of the life around him, and not only simple but pure in heart in spite of all those years about the stables.

He supposed he had not the same temptations as other fellows. Here were his two friends, as opposite to each other as they were to him, the three of them as far apart as the points of an equilateral triangle. Each of the other two had gone wrong in his way. And yet perhaps neither of them would have touched money that did not belong to him, on any pretext or in any circumstances whatsoever!

The money took Jan back to the wood; the wood led him straight to Mulberry; and suddenly he wondered whether Evan had really heard the last of that vagabond. The very thought of a doubt about it made Jan uneasy. Had he frightened the blackmailer sufficiently as such? He had gone away without his money; that might or might not be mere drunken forgetfulness. Jan, however, would have felt rather more certain of his man if he had put himself more in the wrong by actually taking every penny he could get; that and the very drastic form of receipt—never signed—had been the pivot of his scheme for scotching Mulberry. If it were to miscarry after all, in its prime object of saving Evan from persecution and disgrace; if appearances should still be doubted and Mulberry be bribed or frightened into telling the truth; why, then—good Lord!—then he himself might yet be reinstated—at Evan's expense!

Once more Jan despised himself for harbouring any such thought for a single moment; he kicked it out like a very Mulberry of the mind, and saw it in the mental gutter as a most unlikely contingency. He considered his own handling of the creature, the motive given him for revenge, the dexterous promptitude with which revenge had been taken. No; such an enemy, so made, would never willingly avow a very inspiration of low cunning....

The mossy, wrinkled roofs of the old tiled houses opposite Heriot's stood out once more against a cloudless sky; the pavement underneath was dry as a bone; the little town was basking in the sleepy sunshine of the Sunday afternoon. Suddenly those irrepressible chapel bells broke out with their boyish clangour.

Boyish they are and always will be while there are boys to hear them; they ring in the veins after thirty years, and make old blood pelt like young. Surely there is no such hearty, happy peal elsewhere on earth! It got into Jan's blood though he was only leaving next morning, and would never, never be able to come down as an authorised Old Boy. So he would never be allowed in chapel again, unless he stole in when nobody was about, some day, a bearded bushman "home for a spell." It seemed hard. There went the bells again! They might have let him obey their kindling call for the last time; it might have made some difference to his life.

How could they stop him? Could they stop him? Would they if they could? The questions followed each other almost as quickly as the three bright bells; they got into his blood as well. And it was blood always susceptible to a sudden impulse; that was a thing Jan did not see in himself, though all his escapades came of that hereditary drop of pure recklessness. It did not often come to a bubble, but when it did the precipitate was some rash act.

Already the street was "alive with boys and masters," like another more famous but not more dear; masters in silken hoods, masters in humble rabbit-skins, and boys in cut-away coats, boys in Eton jackets. Jan had put on his Sunday tails as usual; it had never occurred to him not to dress that morning as a member of the school still subject to the rules. His school cap was already packed, a sad memento filled with collars. He had it out in an instant, and the collars strewed the floor, for he was going to chapel whether they liked it or not. They would never make a scandal by turning him out, but he must slip in at the last moment after everybody else, and the last bell had not begun yet. Jan was waiting for it in great excitement, touching up his hair in the dressing-room, when the landing shook to a familiar stride and the bedroom door opened unceremoniously for the second time that afternoon.

"Rutter! Where are you, Rutter?"

Heriot, of course, when he was least wanted! Jan slipped behind the dressing-room door, and saw him through the crack as he looked in hastily. Luckily there was no time for an exhaustive search. Heriot gave it up, the door below drowned the opening strokes of the last bell, and Jan had shut it softly in his turn before they stopped.

The fellows went into chapel there in droves under gowned and hooded shepherds. Jan so timed matters as to enter in the wake of the last lot, but well before the appearance of Mr. Thrale and his chaplain. Not being in the choir, his place in chapel, where the seats were allotted on a principle unknown to the boys, was mercifully unexalted, and he reached it with no worse sign or portent than the raised eyebrows and whispered welcome of his immediate neighbours. A congregation of four hundred persons absorbs even a Captain of Cricket more effectually than he thinks. And a voluntary, bright and exhilarating as all the music in that chapel, gave him heart and hope until the arrival of the officiating pair afforded an ineffable sense of security and relief.

Jan stood up with the rest, not quite at his full height, yet with his eyes turned in sheer fascination towards the little old Head Master. He looked very pale and stern, but his eyes could not have been fixed more steadfastly in front of him if he himself had been marching to his doom. In his left hand he held something that Jan was glad to see; it was dear old Jerry's purple and embroidered sermon-case, a gift no doubt, and yet almost an incongruous vanity in that uncompromising hand.

Jan sank down and breathed his thanks for the last mercy of this service, for his perhaps undeserved escape from open humiliation and public shame. It was not to be seen through his forcible composure, but the glow of momentary victory filled every cell of a heart which the bells had first expanded. And he had never joined in the quick and swinging psalms with a zest more grateful to himself or so distressing to one or two of his hypercritical neighbours; there could not have been much wrong with Rutter, either physically or morally, these opined; or else he had been let off, and was already wallowing in an indecent odour of sanctity.

Wallowing he was, but for once only in the present, without dwelling on old days or on the wrath already come. This was not the house of wrath, but of brightness and light; he was not going to darken it for the last time with cheap memories and easy phantoms. Any fool could think of his first Sunday, and recall his first impressions of chapel; it was rather Jan's desire so to receive his last impression as to have something really worth recalling all the days of his life; but even that was a vague and secondary consideration, whereas the present recompense was certain, vivid, and acute.

One wonders whether any fellow ever loved a public-school chapel as much as Jan loved his that afternoon, and not from the conscious promptings of reverence and piety, but purely as a familiar place of peace and comfort which he might never see again. The circumstances were probably unique, and they gave him that new eye for an old haunt which had been opened on the pitch the day before. But then he had been as a dying man, and now he was as the dead come sneaking back to life for an hour or less; the defiant enjoyment of forbidden fruit was among the springs of his infinite exaltation.

The great east window made the first impress on his sensitised film of vision; he had not been at the school four years, on a cricketer's easy footing with so many of the masters, without hearing that window frankly depreciated; but it was light and bright, and good enough for Jan. Then there were the huge brass candelabra in the chancel, pyramids of light on winter evenings, trees of gold this golden afternoon; for the summer sun came slanting in over everybody's right shoulder, as all sat in rows facing the altar, and not in the long opposing lines of other school chapels. Tablets to Old Boys who had lived great lives or died gallant deaths brought a sigh of envy for the first time. They were the only sight that reminded Jan sorely of himself, until he looked up and saw dear old Jerry standing in his marble pulpit for the last time. The hymn ceased. The organ purred like a cat until the last stop had been driven in. Jan supposed it must have done it always. A sparrow chirped outside, and Mr. Thrale pronounced the invocation in that voice which knew no lip-service, but prayed and preached as it taught and thundered, from the heart.

"He that findeth his life shall lose it: and he that loseth his life for my sake shall find it."

That was his text; and many there were present, boys and Old Boys, masters and masters' wives, who reverenced the preacher before all living men, yet knew what was coming and faced it with something akin to resignation. Life was the first word in his language, if not his last. It meant so much to him. He never used it in the narrow sense. True Life was his simple watchword; where the noun was, the adjective was never far away, and together the two rolled out like noble thunder. The corporate life, the life of a nation, the life of that school, it was into those great streams that he sought to pour the truth that was in him—sometimes at the expense of the individual ripple. Boys do not listen to abstractions; abstract truths are better read than heard by boy or man. Mr. Thrale was too elusive, perhaps too deep, for ordinary ears; in his daily teaching he was direct, concrete, and dramatic, but from his pulpit he soared above heads of all ages. Yet that earnest voice and noble mien, which had so impressed Jan on his very first Sunday in the school, were as the voice from Sinai and the face of God to him to-day.

He began by drinking in every syllable; but again it was too soon the look and tone rather than the words that thrilled him. He began listening with eyes glued to that noble countenance in its setting of silver hair; but soon they drooped to the edge and corners of the purple sermon-case, to the leaves that rose and fell, at regular intervals, under that strong, unrelenting, and yet most tender hand. Jan could feel its farewell grip again; he was back in the study full of garden smells and midges in the lamplight.... Goodness! He really had been back there for an instant; it was the old trouble of keeping awake at this time of the afternoon. It had struck him painfully in others, on his very first Sunday in the school; but almost ever since he had felt it himself, say after a long walk; and he simply could not help feeling it after an almost sleepless night and that condemned man's allowance of beer....

I say! It was incredible, it was contemptible, unpardonable in Jan of all the congregation that sunny afternoon. But it would not happen again; something had awakened him once and for all.

It was something in the old man's voice. His voice had changed, his manner had changed, he was no longer reading from the purple case, but speaking directly and dramatically as was his wont elsewhere. His hands were clasped upon his manuscript. He was looking steadfastly before him—just a trifle downward—looking indeed Jan's way, in clear-sighted criticism, in gentle and yet strong rebuke.

"... There is the life of the individual too. 'He that findeth his life shall lose it: and he that loseth his life for my sake shall find it.' But let him be sure for whose sake he would lose his life; let him not take his own life, on any provocation or under temptation whatsoever—not even to save his dearest friend—for Christ did not make and cannot countenance such a sacrifice. No soldier of Christ can die by his own hand, even to save his comrade; he must think of the army, think of those to whom his own life is valuable and dear, before he throws it away from a mistaken or unbalanced sense of sacrifice. I will have no false or showy standards of self-sacrifice in this school; I will have no moral suicides. Suicide is a crime, no matter the motive; evil is evil, good cannot come of it, and to step in between a friend and his folly is to stand accessory after the fact. And yet—humanum est errare! And he who errs only to save an erring brother has the divine spark somewhere in his humanity: may it light his brain as well as fire his heart, give him judgment as well as courage, and burn out of him the Upas growth of wrong-headed self-sacrifice. You cannot rob Peter to pay Paul, just because you happen to be Peter yourself. Has Paul the first or only claim upon you? Yet my heart goes out to the boy or man who can pick his own pocket, ay, or shed his own blood for his friend! Blame him I do, but I honour him, and I forgive him."

In such parables spake their Master to those who sat daily at his feet; not often so to the school in chapel, nor was it to them that he was speaking now. Yet few indeed knew that he was addressing Jan Rutter, who sat spellbound in his place, chidden and yet shriven, head and heart throbbing in a flood of light and warmth.

CHAPTER XXXI

VALE

The only two fellows who were leaving out of Heriot's house had been dining with the Heriots on the last night of the term. One of them, after holding forth to Miss Heriot like a man and a brother, had gone on to the Sanatorium to take leave of a convalescent; the other accompanied Mr. Heriot into the jumble of books and papers, old oak and the insignia of many hobbies, which made his study such an uncomfortable yet stimulating little room. It appeared smaller and more crowded than ever when invaded by two tall ungainly men; for the young fellow, though never likely to be as lanky as the other, but already sturdier in build, stood about six feet from his rather flat soles to the unruly crest of his straight light hair. A fine figure of a man he made, and still under nineteen; yet his good and regular features were perhaps only redeemed from dulness by a delightfully stubborn mouth, and by the dark eyes that followed Heriot affectionately about the room.

"There's one thing we've had in common from the start," said Heriot, "and that's our infernally untidy studies! I remember Loder speaking to me once about yours. I brought him in here to discuss the point, and he went out agreeing that indifference to your surroundings doesn't necessarily spell the complete scoundrel. But it isn't a merit either, Rutter, and I expect Carpenter to embellish life more than either of us."

"I wonder what he'll do, sir?"

"Get things into the Granta for a start. Not all his things; his style wants purging. Smoke, Rutter?"

Heriot was filling his own pipe; but it was one thing for a master to consider himself free to smoke before a leaving boy, on the last night of the term, in defiance of Mr. Thrale's despotic attitude on the point, and quite another thing for him to offer the boy a cigarette. Jan declined the abrupt invitation with an almost shocked embarrassment.

"I thought a cigarette was no use to you," said Heriot, laughing. "And yet you've never gone back to your pipe, I believe?"

"Sir!"

Heriot was smiling the beatified smile that always broke through his first cloud.

"You don't suppose I didn't know, Rutter, that you used to smoke when you first came here?"

"You never let me see that you knew it, sir."

"You never let me catch you! I 'smelt it off you,' as they say, all the same; but I shouldn't have done so if I hadn't known all those things I was not supposed to know."

"It was magnificent of you to hush them up as you did!"

"It was a duty. But it wouldn't have been quite fair to trade on one's knowledge at the same time."

"Every master wouldn't look at it like that."

"Perhaps I had a sneaking sympathy as well," laughed Heriot, when he had blown a fresh cloud. "Still, I should have caught you if you hadn't given it up; and I've often wondered why you ever did."

"It was all Mr. Relton," said Jan after a pause. "I promised him I wouldn't smoke if I got into the Eleven."

"Relton, eh?" Jan found himself gazing into still spectacles. "I've been wondering lately, Rutter, whether you're the fellow he thought he saw at the fair?"

Jan was more taken aback than he had been about the smoking. This was the first time Heriot had ever mentioned the ancient escapade which had come to light with so much else a month ago. It was the one thing they had not threshed out since the Sunday after Founder's Day, and yet on that awful Saturday night Jan felt that Heriot had been twice on the edge of the subject, and twice stopped short because he could not trust himself to discuss it calmly. Getting out of the best house in the school was an offence not to be condoned or belittled by the best house-master, even after two long years and a quarter. So Jan had felt till this minute; even now he had to face a lingering austerity behind the fixed glasses.

"Did he tell you he saw somebody, sir?"

"Not in so many words. He came in and asked what I thought would happen to a fellow who got out and went to the fair. I told him what I knew would happen. Then he began to hedge a bit, and I smelt a rat before he went. But I little dreamt it was a rat from my own wainscot! However, I'm not going to ask any questions now."

Cunning old Heriot! Jan made a clean breast on the spot, conceiving that the whole truth said more for Dudley Relton than Bob Heriot was the man to gainsay when he heard it. But Jan added a good deal on his own account, ascribing even more than was justly due to that old night's work, and yet extracting an ultimate admission that meant much from Mr. Heriot.

"I'm glad he took the law into his own hands, Jan; it would be an affectation to pretend I'm not, at this time of day. But I'm thankful I never knew about it when he was here! What beats me most is your own audacity in marching out, as you say, without the least premeditation, and therefore presumably without any sort or shape of disguise?"

Jan took his courage between his teeth.

"I not only walked out of your own door, sir, but I went and walked out in your own coat and hat!"

Heriot flushed and flashed. He could not have been the martinet he was without seeing himself as such, and for the moment in a light injurious to that essential quality. Then he laughed heartily, but not very long, and his laughter left him grave.

"You were an awful young fool, you know! It would have been the end of you, without the option of a præpostors' licking, if not with one from me thrown in! But you may tell Dudley Relton, when you see him out there, that I'm glad to know what a debt I've owed him these last three years. I won't write to him, in case I might say something else while I was about it. But Lord! I do envy you both the crack you'll have in those forsaken wilds!"

Mr. Heriot perhaps pictured the flourishing port of Geelong as a bush township, only celebrated for Dudley Relton and his young barbarians. Colonial geography, unlike that of Ancient Greece, was not then a recognised item in the public-school curriculum. It may be now; but on the whole it is more probable that Mr. Heriot was having a little dig at the land to which he grudged Jan Rutter even more than Dudley Relton. And Jan really was going to the wilderness, or a lodge therein where one of the uncles on his mother's side ran sheep by the hundred thousand. It was said to be a good opening. Jan liked the letters he had read and the photographs he had seen; and if that uncle proved a patch on the one in the Indian Army, he was certain to fall on his feet; but his house-master held that after a more or less stormy schooling the peace (with cricket) of the University would have replenished the man without impairing the eventual squatter. The immediate man was Mr. Heriot's chief concern; but when the thing had been decided against him, after a brief correspondence with the Revd. Canon Ambrose, he saw the best side of a settled future, and took an extra interest from his own point of view.

"What are your sheep going to get out of your Public School?" said Heriot. "Will you herd them any better for having floundered through the verbs in μι? Don't you think a lot that you have learnt here will be wasted?"

"I hope not, sir," replied Jan, with the solemn face due to the occasion, though there was an independent twinkle behind Heriot's glasses.

"So do I, indeed," said he. "But I shall be interested; you're a bit of a test case—you see—and you may help us all."

"I only know I'm jolly glad I came here," said Jan devoutly. "I wasn't once, but I am now, and have been long enough."

"But what have you gained?" asked Heriot. "That's what I always want to know—for certain. A bit of Latin and a lot of cricket, no doubt; but how far are they coming in? If you get up a match at the back of beyond, you'll spoil it with your bowling. On the other hand, of course, you'll be able to measure your paddocks in parasangs and call your buggy-horses Dactyl and Spondee—or Hex and Pen if you like it better!"

Jan guffawed, but there was an unsatisfied sound about Heriot's chuckle.

"I want a fellow like you, Rutter, to get as nearly as possible 100 per cent. out of himself in life; and I should like to think that—what?—say 10 or 20 per cent. of the best of you came from this place. Yet you might have learnt to bowl as well on any local ground. And I wonder if we've taught you a single concrete thing that will come in useful in the bush."

"I might have been a pro. by this time," said Jan, set thinking of his prospects in his father's life-time. "I certainly was more used to horses when I came here than I am now."

"It isn't as if we'd taught you book-keeping, for instance," continued Heriot, pursuing his own line of thought. "That, I believe, is an important job on the most remote stations; but I doubt if we've even fitted you to audit books that have been kept for you. The only books we have rubbed into you are the very ones you'll never open again. And what have you got out of them?"

"I can think of one thing," said Jan—"and I got it from Mr. Haigh, too! Possunt quia posse videntur—you can because you think you can. I've often said that to myself when there was a good man in—and sometimes I've got him!"

"That's good!" exclaimed Heriot. "That's fine, Jan; you must let me tell Haigh that. Can you think of anything else?"

"I don't know, sir. I never was much good at work. But sometimes I've thought it teaches you your place, a school like this."

"It does—if you want teaching. But you—"

"I'd learnt it somewhere else, but I had it to learn all over again here."

"You always have—each time you get your step—that's one of the chief points about promotion! You may have been schoolmastering for fifteen years, but you've got to learn your place even in your own house when you get one."

That touch put Jan more at his ease.

"And you may have been in the Eleven two or three years," said he, "but you've got a new job to tackle when you're captain. They say there's room at the top, but there isn't room to sit down!"

"That was worth learning!" cried Heriot, eagerly. "I'm not sure it wasn't worth coming here to pick up that alone. And you'll manage your men all right, though I daresay they're not any easier out there than here. That's all to the good, Rutter."

"But suppose I hadn't been a left-hand bowler?"

Jan grinned; it had struck him as a poser.

"Well, you'd have come to the front in something else. You did, you know, in other things besides cricket. It's a case of character, and that was never wanting."

But if he had not been an athlete at all! That was the real poser. Heriot was glad it was not put to him. It would have been unanswerable in the case of perhaps half the athletes in the school. What would Goose have been?

"Then there's manners," said Jan, who could warm up to a discussion if he was given time. "But I doubt I'm no judge of them."

"They're the very worst criterion in the world, Jan. The only way to use your judgment, there, is not to judge anybody on earth by his manners."

That was not quite what Jan meant, but he felt vaguely comforted and Heriot breathed again. He was not a man who could say what he did not mean to people whom he did care about. He knew that Jan could still be uncouth, that it might tell against him here and there in life, and yet that what he meant was no more than flotsam on the surface of a noble stream—strong, transparent, deep—and in its depths still undefiled. Indeed, there were no lees in Jan. And Heriot loved him; and they fell to talking for the last time (and almost the first) of old Thrale's sermon on the Sunday after the Old Boys' Match, and the curious fact that he meant Jan to be there, that Heriot himself had come to fetch him; that was when Jan hid behind the door, little dreaming that Evan had owned up everything on learning what had happened.

"I might have known he would!" said Jan fondly. "It was only a question of time; but you say he didn't hesitate an instant? He wouldn't! But thank goodness he didn't go and make bad worse like I did for him. It would have killed him to get expelled; he says it was the bare thought that very nearly did, as it was."

Jan did not see that was a confession he could not have made, or have had to make, about himself; and Heriot did not point it out to him. Presently Chips came in from the Sanatorium. He reported Evan as convalescent in body and mind, and so appreciative of the verses on the Old Boys' Match in the July Mag. that he was getting them framed with the score.

"We've been talking about what you fellows get out of a school like this," said Heriot. "If you ever take to your pen, I think you may owe us more than most, Carpenter; but there was one man once who said what we're all three probably thinking to-night. Here's his little book of verses. I've had a copy bound for each of you. Here they are."

The little books were bound in the almost royal blue of the Eleven sash and cap-trimming. Carpenter had scarcely opened his when he exclaimed, "Here's an old friend!" and read out:

"They told me, Heraclitus, they told me you were dead,
They brought me bitter news to hear and bitter tears to shed.
I wept, as I remembered, how often you and I
Had tired the sun with talking and sent him down the sky."
"Rather an old enemy, that," said Jan, grinning.

"Then, my good fellow, you're incapable of appreciating four of the most classically perfect lines in a modern language!"

Heriot had quite turned on Jan. It took Chips to explain their former acquaintance with the lines, which he did with much gusto. And then they all three laughed heartily over his misconstruction of "Still are thy quiet voices, thy nightingales, awake," in the second stanza, and roared at Jan's nostro loquendo in the first.

"But that's not the poem I mean," said Heriot, borrowing Jan's copy. "It's this 'Retrospect of School Life.' Can you stand it?"

"Rather, sir!"

And Heriot read a verse that made them hold their breath; then this one, with his head turned towards Jan, and a rich tremor in his virile voice:

"There courteous strivings with my peers,
And duties not bound up in books,

And courage fanned by stormy cheers,
And wisdom writ in pleasant looks,
And hardship buoyed with hope, and pain
Encountered for the common weal,
And glories void of vulgar gain,
Were mine to take, were mine to feel."

"Isn't that rather what we were driving at?" he asked of Jan.

Jan nodded. Chips begged for more, with a break in his voice. Heriot wagged his spectacles and went on....

"Much lost I; something stayed behind,
A snatch, maybe, of ancient song;
Some breathings of a deathless mind,
Some love of truth, some hate of wrong."
"And to myself in games I said,
'What mean the books? Can I win fame?
I would be like the faithful dead
A fearless man, and pure of blame.
I may have failed, my School may fail;
I tremble, but thus much I dare;
I love her. Let the critics rail,
My brethren and my home are there.'"

Chips had laid an emotional hand on Jan's arm after the last line but four; and Heriot went almost as far after the last one of all; but Jan had himself well in hand.

"That's what you and I were forgetting, and we mustn't," Heriot said to him. "Your name isn't only up in the pavilion. It's in some of our hearts as well. Your brethren and your home are here!"

Still Jan looked rather stolid.

"There's just one line I should like to alter," said he with hardihood. "Do you mind reading the first verse over again, sir?"

And Heriot read:

"I go, and men who know me not,
When I am reckoned man, will ask,
'What is it then that thou hast got
By drudging through that five-year task?
What knowledge or what art is thine?
Set out thy stock, thy craft declare.'
Then this child-answer shall be mine,
'I only know they loved me there.'"

"It's just that last line," said Jan. "It should be the other way about."

Ernest William Hornung was born on 7th June 1866 at Cleveland Villas, Marton, Middlesbrough. He was the third son, and youngest of eight children, to John Peter Hornung and his wife Harriet née Armstrong.

By the age of 13 Hornung had joined St Ninian's Preparatory School in Moffat, Dumfriesshire before enrolling at the exclusive Uppingham School, in Rutland, in 1880.

Hornung suffered from a general state of bad health, including asthma and poor eyesight but managed to be well-liked at school and to develop a life-long passion of cricket. He loved to play despite the obvious fact that his talents were rather limited.

At 17 his health worsened, and he left Uppingham to travel to Australia, where a sunnier climate was deemed to be better for his various ailments.

Upon arriving he worked as a tutor to the Parsons family in Mossgiel, in New South Wales. As well as teaching he spent time working in remote sheep stations in the outback and began to contribute materials to the weekly magazine; The Bulletin. It was also at this time that he began work on his first novel.

After two years of very valuable life experiences Hornung returned to England in February 1886, a few months before the death of his father, in November, whose deteriorating business interests had become a constant worry.

Hornung found work in London as a journalist and story writer. In 1887 he published his first story under his own name, 'Stroke of Five', which appeared in Belgravia magazine. His work as a journalist coincided with the reign of terror brought about by Jack the Ripper's grisly murders. From this Hornung developed an interest in criminal behaviour.

He had completed the manuscript of the novel he brought back from Australia and, between July and November 1890, the story, 'A Bride from the Bush', was published in five parts in the respected Cornhill Magazine. It was released later that year in book form. This, his first novel, was well received by critics.

Hoping to further his talents in cricket Hornung, in 1891, became a member of two cricket clubs: the Idlers, whose members included Arthur Conan Doyle and Jerome K. Jerome, and the Strand club.

Hornung knew Doyle's sister, Constance ('Connie') from when he had visited Portugal. Connie was described as attractive, "with pre-Raphaelite looks ... the most sought-after of the Doyle daughters".

They were married on 27th September 1893, although Doyle was not at the wedding and relations between the two writers were occasionally difficult. The Hornung's had their only child, a son, Arthur Oscar (but always called just Oscar), in 1895.

In 1894 Doyle and Hornung began work on a play for Henry Irving, on the subject of boxing; Doyle was, at first, eager to begin and paid Hornung a £50 advance but then withdrew before the first act had been completed: the play was never finished.

Like Hornung's first novel, 'Tiny Luttrell' had Australia as a backdrop and the device of an Australian woman in a culturally alien environment. This theme ran through his next four novels: 'The Boss of Taroomba' (1894), 'The Unbidden Guest' (1894), 'Irralie's Bushranger' (1896), in this Hornung introduced the character of Stingaree, an Oxford-educated, Australian gentleman thief. In 'The Rogue's March' (1896) Hornung began to show a growing fascination with the motivation behind criminal behaviour and was sympathetic to the criminal hero as a victim of events. It was different thinking but caused some consternation for others.

In 1898 Hornung's mother died and he dedicated his next book, a series of short stories; Some Persons Unknown, to her memory.

Later that year Hornung and Connie spent six months in Posillipo, Italy. An account of this trip was published in the May 1899 issue of the Cornhill Magazine.

The fictional character Stingaree was re-written to become his most famous creation; A. J. Raffles; the gentleman thief, first used in six short stories published in 1898 in Cassell's Magazine. Modelled on George Cecil Ives, a Cambridge-educated criminologist and talented cricketer who, like Raffles, lived in the Albany, a gentlemen's only residence in Mayfair. The first tale of the series 'In the Chains of Crime' was published in June that year, titled 'The Ides of March'.

Another account adds to the richness by asserting that Raffles and his sidekick, Bunny Manders, were based not only on Doyle's Holmes and Watson but also on his friends Oscar Wilde and his lover, Lord Alfred Douglas. Whatever the exact amalgam the characters were warmly embraced by the reading public who turned it into both a popular and financial success, although some critics echoed Doyle's own fears of the dubious nature of a criminal being used as a hero.

In early 1899, the Hornung's returned to London, and resided in Pitt Street, West Kensington, for the next six years.

After publishing two novels, 'Dead Men Tell No Tales' (1899) and 'Peccavi' (1900), Hornung published a second collection of Raffles stories, 'The Black Mask', in 1901. The critics again complained about the criminal aspect. The public who bought them had no such qualms.

In 1903 Hornung collaborated with Eugène Presbrey to write a four-act play, 'Raffles, The Amateur Cracksman', which was based on two previously published short stories, 'Gentlemen and Players' and 'The Return Match'. The play was first performed at the Princess Theatre, New York, on 27th October 1903 and ran for 168 performances.

In 1905, after publishing four other books in the interim, Hornung brought back the character Stingaree. Later that year, in response to public demand he published a third collection of Raffles stories in 'A Thief in the Night', in which Manders relates some of the earlier adventures he had had with Raffles.

In 1909 the final Raffles story was published, the full-length novel 'Mr. Justice Raffles'. It was poorly received. The Observer reviewer asking if "Hornung is perhaps a little tired of Raffles".

It seems not. That same year he partnered with Charles Sansom for the play 'A Visit From Raffles', which was performed in November that year at the Brixton Empress Theatre, London.

Hornung turned away from Raffles thereafter, and in February 1911 published 'The Camera Fiend', a thriller whose narrator is an asthmatic cricket enthusiast and his attempts to photograph the soul as it leaves the body. This was followed by 'Fathers of Men' (1912) and 'The Thousandth Woman' (1913) before 'Witching Hill' (1913), a collection of eight short stories in which he introduced the characters Uvo Delavoye and the narrator Gillon. In 1914 his fictional works ceased with 'The Crime Doctor'.

His son, Oscar, left Eton College in 1914, and was due to proceed to King's College, Cambridge later that year. However, the terrors of WWI were about to unleash themselves all over Europe. Oscar volunteered, and was commissioned into the Essex Regiment. He was killed, aged a mere 20, at the Second Battle of Ypres on 6th July 1915.

Although heartbroken Hornung edited and issued privately a collection of Oscar's letters home under the title 'Trusty and Well Beloved', in 1916.

Around this time Hornung himself joined an anti-aircraft unit. He also joined the YMCA and did volunteer work in England for soldiers on leave. In March 1917 he visited France, writing a poem about his experience afterwards—something he had been doing more frequently since Oscar's death—and a collection of his war poetry, 'Ballad of Ensign Joy', was published later that year.

In July 1917 Hornung's poem, 'Wooden Crosses', was published in The Times, and in September, 'Bond and Free' appeared. A few months later he was accepted as a volunteer in a YMCA canteen and library just a few miles behind the Front Line.

Hornung was concerned about support for pacifism among troops and wrote to Connie about it. She spoke to Doyle and, rather than discussing it with Hornung, he informed the military authorities. Hornung was naturally angered by Doyle's action and relations between the two men were further strained as a result. He continued to work at the library until a German offensive overran the British positions and he was forced to retreat, firstly to Amiens and then, in April, back to England. He stayed in England until November 1918, when he again took up his YMCA duties, establishing a rest hut and library in Cologne.

In 1919 Hornung's account of his time spent in France, 'Notes of a Camp-Follower on the Western Front', was published. Doyle later wrote of the book that "there are parts of it which are brilliant in their vivid portrayal". That year Hornung also published his third and final volume of poetry, 'The Young Guard'.

Hornung finished his YMCA work and returned to England in early 1919. He worked on a new novel but was hampered by poor health. But Connie's was of greater concern. In February 1921 they took a holiday in the south of France to recuperate. Whilst travelling there on the train Hornung fell ill with a chill that progressed to influenza and finally pneumonia.

Ernest William Hornung died on 22nd March 1921, aged 54.

He was buried in Saint-Jean-de-Luz, in the south of France, in a grave adjacent to that of George Gissing.

E. W. Hornung – A Concise Bibliography

Periodicals
Stroke of Five (1887, Belgravia)
Spoilt Negative (1887, Belgravia)
Nettleship's Score (January 1890, Cornhill Magazine)
A Bride From the Bush (5 Parts. July-Nov, Cornhill Magazine, 1890)
Thunderbolt's Mate (4 Parts. March 1892, Chambers's Journal)
Kenyon's Innings (April 1892, Longman's Magazine)
The Burrawurra Brand (November 1893, The Idler)
The Unbidden Guest (6 Parts. May-Oct 1894, Longman's Magazine)
The Governess at Greenbush (4 parts. February 1895, Chambers's Journal)
After the Fact (3 Parts. January 1896, Chambers's Journal)
The Ides of March (June 1898, Cassell's Magazine)
A Villa in a Vineyard (May 1899, Cornhill Magazine)
No Sinicure: More Adventures of the Amateur Cracksman (January 1901, Scribner's Magazine)
A Jubilee Present: More Adventures of the Amateur Cracksman (February 1901, Scribner's Magazine)
The Fate of Faustina: More Adventures of the Amateur Cracksman (March 1901, Scribner's Magazine)
The Last Laugh: More Adventures of the Amateur Cracksman (April 1901, Scribner's Magazine)
To Catch a Thief: More Adventures of the Amateur Cracksman (May 1901, Scribner's Magazine)
An Old Flame: More Adventures of the Amateur Cracksman (June 1901, Scribner's Magazine)
The Wrong House: More Adventures of the Amateur Cracksman (Sept 1901, Scribner's Magazine)
Chrystal's Century (June 1903, Atlantic Monthly)
Charles Reade (June 1921, London Mercury)

Novels and Short Story Collection
A Bride from the Bush (1890) Novel
Under Two Skies (1892) Short story collection
Tiny Luttrell (1893) Novel; two volumes
The Boss of Taroomba (1894) Novel
The Unbidden Guest (1894) Novel
Irralie's Bushranger (1896) Novel
The Rogue's March: A Romance (1896) Novel
My Lord Duke (1897) Novel
Some Persons Unknown (1898) Short story collection
Young Blood (1898) Novel
The Amateur Cracksman (1899) Short story collection
Dead Men Tell No Tales (1899) Novel
The Belle of Toorak (1900) Novel; published in the US as The Shadow of a Man
Peccavi (1900) Novel
The Black Mask (1901) Short story collection; republished as Raffles: Further Adventures of the Amateur Cracksman
At Large (1902) Novel
The Shadow of the Rope (1902) Novel

Denis Dent: A Novel (1903) Novel
No Hero (1903) Novel
Stingaree (1905) Novel
A Thief in the Night (1905) Short story collection; republished as A Thief in the Night: Further Adventures of A. J. Raffles, Cricketer and Cracksman
Raffles: The Amateur Cracksman (1906) Short story collection; stories taken from The Amateur Cracksman and The Black Mask
Mr. Justice Raffles (1909) Novel
The Camera Fiend (1911) Novel
Fathers of Men (1912) Novel
The Thousandth Woman (1913) Novel
Witching Hill (1913) Short story collection
The Crime Doctor (1914) Short story collection
Old Offenders and a Few Old Scores (Published posthumously) Short story collection

Plays

Raffles, The Amateur Cracksman (27th October 1903) By Hornung and Eugéne Presbrey; first performed at the Princess Theatre, New York
Stingaree, the Bushranger (1st February 1908) First performed at the Queen's Theatre, London
A Visit From Raffles (1st November 1909) By Hornung and Charles Sansom; first performed at the Brixton Empress Theatre, London

Non-Fiction

'Trusty and Well Beloved', The Little Record of Arthur Oscar Hornung (1915) Privately published
Notes of a Camp-Follower on the Western Front (1919)

Poetry
Ballad of Ensign Joy (1917)
Wooden Cross (1918)
The Young Guard (1919)

www.ingramcontent.com/pod-product-compliance
Lightning Source LLC
Chambersburg PA
CBHW070505260626
47161CB00004B/1464